HOLIDAY CHRISTMAS COZIES

COZY MYSTERIES FROM THE PACIFIC NORTHWEST

AMBER CREWES

PEN-N-A-PAD PUBLISHING

First published in November 2020

For questions and comments about this book, please contact info@ambercrewes.com

ISBN: 9798776459573
Imprint: Independently Published

PERSONAL NOTE FROM THE AUTHOR

I don't know about you but I love the holiday season! It's a time for spending quality time with loved ones, giving and being thankful for the big and little blessings in our lives over the past year.

I also love writing cozy mysteries and three stories I've written, occur over the holiday season.

The first two books; ***Jingle Bells and Deadly Smells*** and ***Queen Tarts and a Christmas Nightmare***, are from the Sandy Bay Cozy Mystery series.

The third book, ***Mistletoe and Deadly Kisses***, is from the Fern Grove series and is written under my pen name, Abby Reede.

The fourth book, **Red Roses and Bloody Noses**, is also from the Fern Grove series.

If you love clean cozies with no swearing or graphic scenes, then you'll love the stories you're about to read.

Happy Holidays!

JINGLE BELLS AND DEADLY SMELLS

1

It was going to be a white Christmas in Sandy Bay, and Meghan Truman could hardly contain her excitement as the glittering white snowflakes tumbled from the sky. Meghan shivered as she adjusted the pink tartan scarf around her neck, thankful for its comfort as she stepped outside into the chilly evening. Meghan set off down the street toward Spark, a new boutique in town. She was ten minutes late for her shopping date with Jackie, her close friend, and Meghan trudged through the snow in her knee-length brown boots.

"Can you spare a dime, Miss?"

Meghan bit her bottom lip as a homeless man on the corner beckoned her toward him. She nervously ran a hand through her long, dark hair, shaking her head as she passed.

"I'm sorry," Meghan muttered as she looked down at her boots. "I don't have any cash."

Her heart sank as she walked away from the homeless man, and her cheeks burned with shame. She truly did not have any cash on her, but her chest tightened with guilt as she considered the man's plight. "Perhaps I could have given him my gloves," she thought to herself. "Or I could have dashed home and fetched some treats for him from the bakery."

She was the sole owner of Truly Sweet, a wildly successful bakery in Sandy Bay. She had opened the bakery after moving to Sandy Bay from Los Angeles less than a year ago, and now, after months of persistence and perseverance, Truly Sweet was one of the most popular bakeries in the Pacific Northwest. Meghan's orders had more than quadrupled in the last three months, and she was thankful for the help of Trudy, her assistant, and Pamela, the high-school girl she had hired to help with the heavy workload.

"I have so much stale bread and old pastries sitting in my pantry," she murmured, still distraught by her interaction with the homeless man. "It is so cold tonight, and he needs to eat. I will just have to be a few more minutes late to my shopping date."

Meghan turned around, treading back through the heavy snow. She unlocked the front door of the bakery, smiling as the familiar sound of the little silver bells attached to the door jingled merrily. She heard her little twin dogs barking upstairs in her apartment, but she ignored them, sprinting into the kitchen of the bakery and removing a bag of old pastries and breads from the closet.

"Perfect," Meghan said, satisfied as she filled a cloth sack with the food. "I can drop these off with that man, and hopefully, he will go to bed with a full belly tonight."

She raced out of the bakery and back onto the slippery streets. She nearly fell as her feet slipped beneath her, but she regained her composure and marched off toward the corner where she had encountered the homeless man.

"Oh no," Meghan sighed as she arrived to find the man had vanished. "He's gone. I was too late."

She hung her head, wishing she had had something to give the man when she first met him. "Maybe I'll see him again someday," Meghan considered as she rested the bag of food down on the side of the street. "Maybe he'll come back. I'll leave this food here for now. I hope he finds it."

Jackie chastised Meghan as she entered the shop. "Where have you been? You are too late, girlfriend. This is the second time this week you've been late to a hangout."

Meghan's cheeks burned, and she sheepishly apologized to Jackie, explaining why she was late.

"Oh, Meghan," Jackie said kindly as she saw the tears in her dark eyes. "You were full of the holiday spirit. I'm proud of you. What a good person you are."

Meghan shrugged. "I just think everyone deserves a full belly and a warm bed, don't you?"

Jackie smiled. "Your heart is truly sweet, Meghan. Hey, speaking of Truly Sweet, are you doing the desserts for Jack's holiday party?"

Meghan grinned at the mention of Jack Irvin, her handsome detective boyfriend. "No," she explained to Jackie. "Chief Nunan reached out and asked me to do the desserts, but I decided to pass the chance up; I want to go to the party as a guest, and I think dealing with the desserts would be a lot of stress."

Jackie nodded. "That makes sense," she told Meghan. "Well, the Sandy Bay Police Department Christmas Party is always a huge event in town. Everyone dresses up, and there is mistletoe, and it's just magical."

Meghan smiled. "I need to find the perfect dress; do you think I would look nice in red velvet?"

Jackie squinted her eyes at Meghan, looking up and down at her curvy frame. "Yes," she finally replied. "I think with your dark hair and olive skin, you would glow in red velvet. Come on! Let's see what this shop has to offer."

"Ladies!"

Meghan and Jackie turned to find Kirsty Fisher beaming at them, her blonde bob sitting elegantly just above her shoulders, and a strand of tiny pearls wrapped around her thin neck. Kirsty was a dedicated philanthropist and organizer in the community; if there was an event or party, it was likely that Kirsty had planned and put on the event, and she was always looking for favors as she dreamed up new functions for the town.

"So good to see you girls," Kirsty cooed as she gave Meghan and Jackie air-kisses on both cheeks. "In fact, I was just thinking of you, Meghan. What are you doing next weekend?"

Meghan grimaced. "Why do you ask, Kirsty?"

Kirsty adjusted her red and green sweater set and smiled warmly. "I'm organizing a celebration of Christmas carols, and I would love if you could help me."

Meghan paused. She had intentionally slowed her schedule over the last week, and she was looking forward to some much-needed rest and recuperation after such a busy, eventful year in Sandy Bay.

"Kirsty," Meghan began. "I'm not really taking on new orders right now; I'm not even doing the desserts for Jack's holiday party. It's been a hectic year, and I am trying to give myself, along with Trudy and Pamela, some time to catch our breath."

Kirsty shook her head. "I don't want your treats," she informed her. "I need your voice. I am trying to recruit anyone and everyone to participate, and for a small donation, you can join in the fun."

Meghan raised an eyebrow. "I have a terrible voice," she told Kirsty. "It's horrendous; I was actually cut from my middle-school choir because I am tone deaf."

Kirsty waved her hands dismissively. "You can just lip-sync, then. Jackie, I'm sure you can sing on pitch. Would you join us?"

Jackie wrinkled her nose. "My voice isn't good..."

Kirsty huffed in frustration. "This is for a good cause, girls," she informed Meghan and Jackie. "The donations are being given to the local homeless agency, and with the holidays just around the corner, it is important to think of others."

The image of the homeless man on the corner from earlier flashed through Meghan's mind, and she nodded emphatically. "Yes, you are right," she said to Kirsty. "We'll both be there."

Kirsty tossed her blonde hair behind her shoulder and smiled haughtily. "That's what I wanted to hear," she told both ladies. "Wonderful. Just bring something for the homeless folks who attend. You can even bring something store-bought, Meghan. Just make sure you have something for them, as well as your donation. Toodles, girls! See you at the Christmas carol."

Jackie rolled her eyes as Kirsty sashayed out of the boutique. "How did we just get roped into that?"

Meghan shrugged. "Kirsty is right," she told Jackie. "It's the season of love and giving. I can whip up a batch of cookies to take with me, and we'll both go. Besides, it's only for a few hours, and it's for a great cause. What could go wrong?"

On the evening of the event, Jack picked Meghan up from the bakery. His blonde hair was smoothed down with gel, and Meghan thought he looked handsome in his green Christmas sweater.

"Thanks for going with me tonight," Meghan said to Jack as she leaned up on her tiptoes to kiss him softly on the lips.

"Of course," he replied. "It's a good cause, and I'm proud of you."

Meghan smiled. "It will be fun. It's always good to give back."

Jack and Meghan drove to the Sandy Bay Community Center, and as he helped Meghan out of the car, her eyes sparkled with joy. "Look at the decorations," she cried, pointing to a ten-foot high Christmas tree positioned outside of the main entry. "It's beautiful."

Jack playfully swatted Meghan on the arm. "Don't you know by now that Sandy Bay knows how to celebrate?"

Jack took Meghan's hand as they entered the massive main room. Meghan saw Kirsty assembling carolers onto bleachers, and she waved at Jackie from across the room. "I'm going to go get settled. Can you put my cookies on that dessert table over there?"

Jack nodded, taking the bag from Meghan's hands. "Of course. You go have fun!"

Meghan scurried over to where the singers were corralled, but as she ascended the stairs to her row on the bleachers, she heard a shout. Meghan turned to see four men shoving each other next to the dessert table.

"I want all of those cookies. You ate too much cake."

"Don't be selfish. My kids need some food too."

"This stupid party was the only way to get some good food, and I'm going to take what I want."

Meghan saw one of the men reach into the bag and take out her cookies. From his tattered clothes and greasy hair, she presumed he was homeless. She watched in horror as he threw her cookies onto the floor.

"I'll be right back," Meghan whispered to Jackie as she took off across the room. "Hey, sir? Sir? I only made enough so that each person could have two cookies."

The man scowled, but he nodded at Meghan. "Sorry. I was just excited."

Meghan felt a hard tap on her shoulder. She heard Jack's deep voice coming toward her. "Don't you touch her!"

Meghan's heart beat faster as she turned around. Jack ran to her side, but as she made eye contact with the man who touched her shoulder, she gasped.

"What do you think you are doing?" Jack demanded as he stepped between Meghan and the man. "Keep your hands off of my girlfriend."

The man chuckled, winking at Meghan. "Who do I think I am? Meghan, honey? Wanna tell em?"

Meghan's jaw-dropped. "Daddy," she whispered. "Daddy, I can't believe you are here."

2

"This is your father?" Jack asked Meghan in a panicked voice.

Meghan nodded. "Jack, this is my father. Daddy, this is my boyfriend, Jack."

Jack reached out his right hand, and it shook as he extended it. "It's an honor to meet you, Mr. Truman," Jack breathed anxiously as Meghan's father peered down at him.

"Call me Henry," Meghan's father ordered.

"Henry," Jack repeated obediently. "It's a pleasure to meet you."

Jack was a tall man, but Henry Truman was even taller; Meghan's father towered over Jack, making Jack look like a little boy. Henry was also brawnier than Jack; Mr. Truman's muscles protruded from his expensive-looking shirt, and Meghan could not believe how intimidated Jack appeared beside her father.

"I'm so sorry to have stood in your way," Jack apologized as Henry stared at his outstretched hand. "I didn't know...."

"Put your hand down," Henry commanded as he planted a paternal kiss on Meghan's forehead. "I'll shake your hand when I've been properly introduced by my daughter. Meggie, sugar, who is this fellow? Is this the boy you've been speaking to your Mama about when you phone us in Texas?"

Meghan nodded. "Yes," she admitted. "Daddy, this is Jack Irvin of the Sandy Bay Police Department. Jack, this is my father, Henry Truman, CEO and founder of The Truman Oil Company."

Henry winked at his daughter. "That was a proper introduction. Okay Jack, now I can shake your hand."

Henry grabbed Jack's hand and pumped it vigorously, and Meghan watched as her boyfriend's face turned beet-red. "Daddy, you're hurting him," she softly protested. "Where's Mama?"

Henry let go of Jack's hand, but he did not break eye contact with Meghan's boyfriend as he answered her question. "She's resting at our hotel," Henry said as he smiled down at his daughter, his own dark eyes sparkling. "She's very excited to see you; it was her idea to surprise you here in Sandy Bay during the holidays, and by the look on your face, I can tell that you had no idea we were coming up this way."

Meghan grinned at her father and wrapped her arms around his neck. She breathed in the familiar, musky scent of Brut, his favorite cologne, and she laughed as she recalled the frightened look on Jack's face. "Daddy, you pulled one on me. I can't believe you and Mama came up here."

Henry's face fell. "We feel terrible that we didn't visit you when you lived in Los Angeles," Henry told her quietly. "With so many children, and my business, it was just too much. Your Mama and I want to make it up to you now; we're staying for an entire week!"

Meghan clapped her hands in excitement. "Who is home watching the children?" she asked, thinking of her many younger siblings back in Texas.

Henry smiled coyly. "We hired a nanny," he informed her. "His name is Garrett, and he is quite helpful; he cooks, he cleans, and he makes sure all things run smoothly at home. Your Mama is an angel for electing to stay home with all of her children and having another pair of hands has been so good for her nerves."

Meghan beamed and took her father's hands. "I'm just so happy the pair of you are here. Sandy Bay is adorable, and I cannot wait to show you the bakery."

Henry hugged his daughter. "I cannot wait to see what your hard work has resulted in," he whispered into her ear. "You've always been my good girl, Meghan. Your mother and I are so proud of you."

Jack stepped into the conversation. "Can I suggest dinner? We could all go out and get to know each other. My treat."

Henry shook his head. "Shhh, John, can't you see I'm having a conversation with my daughter?"

Meghan giggled. "It's Jack, Daddy."

"Jack, John, same thing," Henry sighed. "Dinner is out of the question tonight; your mother is fast asleep in the hotel room, and I am about to drop dead of exhaustion myself. We will plan on being at your bakery bright and early, Meghan, for a grand tour. What do you say?"

Meghan blushed. "It's a small bakery, so it is not quite grand, but yes, please come!"

Jack cleared his throat. "It's a great bakery," he protested. "You should be proud."

Henry raised an eyebrow at Jack. "Let my daughter speak for herself. Anyway, we will see you tomorrow, Meghan. We love you."

Meghan's heart warmed as her father kissed her head, and she squeezed his hand. "Thank you for coming, Daddy. I'll see you tomorrow."

As Jack and Meghan drove home from the event, Meghan could see that Jack was flustered; his cheeks were red, his eyes were narrowed, and his hands were white as he gripped the steering wheel. Meghan knew that her father had not been particularly warm to Jack, but she was unfazed; Henry Truman was notorious for being cold and aloof with his daughters' boyfriends, and Meghan thought that their introduction had gone well.

"I think he really liked you," she assured him as he turned onto her street.

"Oh? What gave you that impression? When he wouldn't shake my hand at first, or when he corrected me for speaking up for you?" he responded angrily. "Why didn't you tell me they were in town? Some notice would have been nice, Meghan."

Meghan shifted awkwardly in her seat. "I didn't know they were coming," she insisted as she tucked a stray dark hair behind her ear. "You heard the conversation, babe. I had no idea. They never visited me when I lived in Los Angeles, so I never expected to see them here without even a word."

Jack sighed. "I know," he whispered. "I heard. I'm just annoyed with myself for not making a better impression on your father. You are important to me, Meghan. I love you. You are so special to me, and someday, who knows? Maybe your father and I will be family. I just want him to respect me as someone who cares deeply for his daughter and treats her well."

"He will," she pleaded. "Just give him some time. He will come around to you, Jack. I promise: by tomorrow, the two of you will be the best of friends!"

* * *

"I DON'T LIKE HIM," Henry whispered into Meghan's ear as they walked into Luciano's, Meghan and Jack's favorite Italian restaurant in Sandy Bay. "He just seems too nervous."

"He is nervous, Daddy," she told her father as the tuxedo-clad waiter guided the group to their table. "Just give him a break. I really like this one."

At nine that morning, Henry and his wife, Rebecca, had shown up at Truly Sweet. "Darling," Meghan's mother had cooed as she embraced her. "It is so nice to see you. Daddy told me you were so surprised."

"I was," Meghan affirmed as she brushed a small piece of lint from her freshly ironed collared shirt. She had carefully chosen her outfit with her mother's fine, Southern taste in mind, and Meghan was proud of the ensemble she had selected. Her collared shirt was carefully tucked into a maroon and tan skirt, and a matching maroon sweater was carefully draped across her shoulders. A string of bulbous white pearls graced Meghan's collarbone, and the buttons on her shirt matched the tiny buttons on her brown leather boots.

"Are those your house clothes?" Rebecca asked her daughter, eyeing Meghan's outfit. "Surely you don't often wear those things around guests. Run upstairs and change, Sugar."

Meghan said nothing, but she turned on her heel and dashed upstairs to change. "My mother has never approved of the way I look, or the way I dress," she grumbled to her dogs who were resting peacefully on her bed. She wrestled with the buttons of her blouse. "With her little waist and long, glossy blonde hair, my mother has always looked like a doll. My sisters look just like her. I'm the only one in the family with dark hair, dark eyes, and curves. I just wish she would think about something else for a change instead of the way I look."

"Meghan? What is taking so long?" she heard her mother call as she threw a pale pink sweater over her head.

"Be right down," she replied, thinking back to how similar this encounter felt to her days in Texas as a teenager.

As Meghan descended the steps, she saw her parents admiring a display case filled with holiday-themed pastries. "Those were made fresh this morning," she announced. "I tried to incorporate all of the winter holidays with my designs."

"They are simply fabulous," Rebecca murmured as she gingerly picked up a cookie in the shape of a dreidel. "You are so creative, Meghan. I'm so happy you decided to give up on being an actress. Your creativity is better suited here in the bakery."

Meghan smiled. "Thanks," she said to her Mum. "I'm happy here, and my business is thriving; I've been written about in five magazines this year, and I'm excited to see what next year brings."

Henry patted his daughter on the head. "Your entrepreneurial spirit is impressive," he declared to her. "You've really made this a special thing. Your mother and I are so proud of you."

Before Meghan could thank her parents for their compliment, Jack burst into the bakery. "Hey, everyone," he said as he clumsily reached for Rebecca's hand. "You must be Meghan's mother. It's nice to meet you, Mrs. Truman."

Rebecca eyed Jack up and down. "It's Rebecca," she said dismissively. "You must be John."

Jack bit his lip, but Meghan shushed him before he could correct her mother. "It's Jack," she murmured. "Jack Irvin. He is a detective. Isn't that exciting?"

Rebecca said nothing, but walked to stand next to her husband, threading her arm through his.

"Meghan? The hotel we're staying at really serves great food, but I'd like something different today. Is there somewhere you could recommend?"

Jack began to nod, his overexcitement making Meghan uncomfortable. "Luciano's!" he shouted. "It's our favorite Italian restaurant. Let's take them there, Meghan."

Meghan shook her head. "My mother doesn't like Italian. She doesn't eat carbs."

Henry waved his hand. "It's fine, Sugar," he told Meghan. "If Johnny here wants to take us out for Italian, then we'll go eat Italian. Let's see what kind of taste Johnny here has."

3

As the Trumans and Jack walked towards Luciano's, Meghan's heart crumbled as she spotted a group of homeless people begging for change. They looked exhausted, and Meghan felt guilty as her parents shepherded her toward the expensive Italian restaurant.

"Can I sing to you folks for a dollar?"

The group turned to see a middle-aged man in a tattered trench coat smiling at them. He was wearing a scraggly white beard and a Santa hat, and his disheveled appearance, as well as the stench emitting from his clothing, was impossible to ignore. He had an enormous pair of headphones atop his head, and he bobbed and swayed to the soft strains of music that came out of the speakers.

"Daddy, let's listen to him," Meghan pleaded as her father tugged on her arm. "He wants to work for our money. Let's give him a listen."

Henry shook his head. "It's not in good taste to appease those kinds of people," he whispered to Meghan as Mrs. Truman ducked inside the restaurant. "You should know better than that."

"Meghan! Ciao, Bella."

Roberto Luciano, the Italian-born founder and owner of Luciano's, bustled outside. "Is this man bothering you? It's been bad for my business to have this group hanging out around here. Come, let me usher you inside. Dessert is on the house tonight."

Meghan smiled kindly at Roberto. "It's good to see you, Roberto. This is my father. He and my mother are visiting from Texas."

Roberto's face glowed. He leaned over and kissed Henry on both cheeks. "I can only say grazie to you for choosing Luciano's," Roberto cooed. "This is the best Italian restaurant in the Pacific Northwest, if I do say so myself, and Meghan and Jack come here often."

Meghan saw Jack shiver as a gust of ocean air stung his cheeks. "Come," Roberto said as he saw Jack's shoulders shake. "It's a cold night. Let's get you all inside and warm you up with some fettuccine. Again, my apologies for this...sight....outside of my restaurant."

Meghan waved apologetically at the group of homeless people, feeling guilty that she was about to go enjoy food and fun with her family when these folks were stuck in the cold.

"Don't think about them," Jack said, seeing the sad look on Meghan's face as they walked into the restaurant. "let's just enjoy our dinner, Meghan. There's nothing you can do to help them."

Meghan nodded and followed Jack inside of the restaurant. The dining room was painted in deep reds, smoldering oranges, and soft yellows, and Meghan felt as though she had been whisked away to Tuscany. Italian songs played softly on the radio, and the room was aglow with flickering candlelight that made the large space feel intimate.

"I reserved their best table," Jack boasted to Mr. and Mrs. Truman. "That one over there in the corner is the very nicest."

Rebecca frowned. "It looks a little cramped, and it's a booth," she said in disgust. "Booths are for people who eat in diners, or for small children. Henry? I would prefer a real table."

Henry nodded. He beckoned over Angela, Roberto's oldest daughter. Angela was the manager of the restaurant, and with her waist-length black hair and sparkling dark eyes, she was arguably the most beautiful woman in Sandy Bay.

"Ciao, Bella," Henry said to Angela with a wink. "Tell me, are there any tables left besides that little cramped booth? My gorgeous wife and I would prefer something a bit more... elegant."

Angela smiled graciously. "Si, sir," she breathed, her heavy accent clearly charming Henry. "Let me show you to our private dining space. I believe that will best accommodate you."

When Angela ensured the group was settled in a quiet private dining room, Henry smirked at Jack. "I thought you said that booth was the best table in the house," he announced. "Seems like a private dining room is a little more refined, Johnny."

"It's Jack," Jack muttered under his breath as Meghan squeezed his knee beneath the table.

"Now, I wonder what this place has to offer. I hope they have that dish you love Henry. Remember when we had it on our vacation last summer? We stayed in the most beautiful little villa in the Italian countryside, Meghan."

Meghan's smile was strained, but she nodded politely. "That sounds nice, Mama."

Angela returned to the table with four menus, as well as a glass pitcher filled with ice water. "Let me tell you about our special tonight," Angela said. "The lamb is divine; the red sauce atop the platter was made by my father this morning, and I have never tasted anything finer. The fettuccine is the perfect choice for our pasta-enthusiasts, and of course, we have a safer dish for the less adventurous. Our chicken dish is delicious, of course, but for those looking for an experience, I would recommend the lamb or the pasta."

Meghan grinned. "I would love the lamb," she told Angela.

"Excellent. And for your lovely parents?"

Henry handed the menu back to Angela. "We'll take the pasta dish and the lamb; we are going to split both."

Angela beamed. "Fantastico," she said, and then, turning to Jack, "and for you?"

Jack awkwardly gave his menu to Angela. "I'll take the chicken," he murmured as Rebecca's blue eyes grew wide.

"The chicken?" Henry questioned. "We're at a nice place, Johnny. Why don't you try something a little less...bland?"

Jack's cheeks turned red, and Meghan took his hand, bringing it atop the table for all to see. She squeezed it lovingly, but Jack's eyes remained distraught. "He wants chicken, Daddy. It isn't a big deal."

Angela retreated from the dining room, and Rebecca addressed Jack, "I've just never heard of someone ordering chicken at a fine dining establishment."

Jack shrugged. "It's my favorite," he muttered.

Rebecca pursed her lips. "Interesting," she offered.

Meghan quickly changed the subject. "Mama, I have some exciting news."

Rebecca's eyes shined. "You've finally joined weight watchers?"

Meghan's face darkened. "No," she whispered.

Henry put his hands up. "Rebecca, you stop that. Our Meghan is perfect. She is the spitting image of my mother, and my mother was a beautiful woman, inside and out."

Rebecca rolled her eyes. "I know you think your mother was perfect," she sighed to her husband. "Meghan? What was your news?"

Meghan sat tall in her seat. "I am going to expand the bakery next year; Truly Sweet has been a massive success, and after some careful thinking, I have decided to add three light lunch options to our menu."

Rebecca clapped her hands in excitement. "That's delightful, dear," she said. "Just make sure you don't indulge too much; I know it can be easy for you to snack when food is around."

Jack put his arm around Meghan. "I'm proud of Meghan for going after her dreams," he declared to the table.

"Jack, just relax," Meghan said to Jack under her breath.

"As are we," Henry countered, placing his arm around his own wife's shoulder. "As Meghan's parents, we only want the best for our daughter."

Meghan watched as her father stared into Jack's blue eyes. "I feel like I have the best of everything in my life right now," she assured her parents. "The best boyfriend, the best job, the best friends, and of course, the best family."

Rebecca smiled. "Family truly is the most important thing this time of year. I love spending time with family and listening to Christmas carols. It's all so magical."

Henry's ears perked up. "Rebecca, do you hear the song playing? It sounds like Bing Crosby's White Christmas. Your favorite!"

Rebecca beamed. "Wonderful food, wonderful company, and my favorite carol? This is a truly sweet holiday trip."

An hour and a half later, after Jack and Henry awkwardly fought for the check, the group was escorted out of the restaurant by Roberto Luciano. "Thank you all so much," Roberto gushed as he smiled at

Henry, who had left Angela a two-hundred dollar tip. "Your kindness is so appreciated this holiday season."

"The food was just superb," Rebecca declared. "It was to die for. Your restaurant is one of the best I have had the pleasure of visiting."

"It was my idea to come here," Jack chirped as Meghan shot him a dirty look.

"Jack, enough," Meghan whispered. "Just act natural."

"Natural?" Jack asked. "How can I do that when your parents hate me?"

Roberto opened the front door for the Trumans. "Thank you again. Oh, no. The homeless people."

Meghan saw the group of homeless people sitting on the curb outside of the restaurant. "We can just walk around them," she told Roberto. "It's no big deal."

Roberto shook his head. "I have worked so hard to build the restaurant, and I cannot have these people milling about when I have fine customers dining. You! You there! Shoo."

The man with the Santa beard and headphones lumbered over to Roberto. "Shoo? We ain't dogs, man."

Roberto frowned. "You are worse. Dogs can be taken away and disposed of, but you people never leave."

The homeless man's jaw dropped. "Man, that was uncalled for," he said to Roberto. "We ain't hurting anyone. We're just minding our business."

Roberto clenched his fists. "Mind your business elsewhere!"

The homeless man hung his head. "Man, you ain't got a clue about the reason for this holiday season, do you? Being good to others is what Christmas is about. Would it kill you to let us hang here? No. It wouldn't."

Roberto furrowed his brow. "It will kill my business. Now, go on. Get. Get out of here before you kill my business. Go on! Get out of here, all of you!"

4

"And just sprinkle the sugar on top. Perfect, Meghan. You are such a fast learner."

The morning after having dinner at Luciano's, Rebecca had appeared at Meghan's front door with a sack of groceries. "We need to have some mother-daughter time," she announced to Meghan as she bustled through the door. "I brought some things over, and I am going to teach you how to make your grandmother's famous ginger snap recipe."

"How wonderful," Meghan agreed as she fastened her favorite monogrammed apron around her neckline. "Trudy and Pamela are both off today, so we will have the place all to ourselves."

The two women got to work, with Rebecca mixing the ingredients together, and Meghan preparing the utensils. "So, now that it's just us girls, let's have a little chat," Rebecca suggested as Meghan smiled.

"What do you want to chat about, Mama?" she asked, tying her long, wavy dark hair into a braid.

Rebecca looked slyly at Meghan. "Jacob Brilander has become a successful businessman."

Meghan gasped. "Mama, Jacob and I broke up ten years ago. Why are you bringing him up?"

Rebecca's eyes twinkled. "I always loved Jacob," she said wistfully. "He was a nice boy from a good family--an old money family. I just spoke with his mother last week, and she mentioned that he is planning to go into politics! Isn't that exciting?"

Meghan gritted her teeth as she thought of her high school boyfriend. Jacob had been right for her at the time, but when she left Texas for college, they had gone their separate ways. "Mama, I heard Jacob was engaged to a girl he met at school. Morgan something?"

"Didn't last," Rebecca informed her daughter. "That Morgan was too dull, I heard, and Jacob and she broke up before they even walked down the aisle."

Meghan shuddered. "Mama, this is none of my business. I haven't thought of him in years. Why are you telling me this?"

Rebecca gently put the ingredients to the side and looked Meghan in the eyes. "Meghan, you aren't getting any younger," she began. "And this John fellow doesn't seem to be serious about you."

Meghan's dark eyes filled with tears at her mother's nagging. "It's Jack, Mama," she said. "Jack. And he is serious about me. He loves me."

Rebecca shrugged. "I don't see a ring on your finger..."

Meghan placed her hands on her hips. "We've only been boyfriend and girlfriend for months, Mama!"

Rebecca shook her head. "Your Daddy and I only dated for two months before we were engaged, Meghan. When you know, you know, and I just don't see the sparks between the two of you."

Meghan felt the heat rising to her face, but she did not want to argue with her mother. She quietly wiped her hands on her apron and returned to work on the ginger snaps.

"Meghan?"

Meghan felt her mother's hand on her shoulder. "Meghan, when are you coming home to Texas? You've been away too long. You told me that you would move home if things in Hollywood didn't work out, and yet, here you are, frittering away in a bakery."

Meghan's stomach sank. "Mama," she quietly protested. "I work hard here. I am the owner. Sure, it isn't glitzy or glamorous, but I'm happy in Sandy Bay. I'm happy with Jack."

Rebecca closed her eyes and leaned against the wall, dramatically fanning her face. "I just don't understand," she told her daughter. "You were a debutante, Meghan. You are from a good family, you have an education, and you could easily come home with Daddy and me to Texas. Your brothers and sisters would love to see you, and I could arrange tea with Jacob and his mother..."

Meghan threw the wooden spoon she had been using on the floor. She was shocked at her own outburst; Meghan was usually a gentle, sweet woman, but now, with her own mother dismissing her successes, she felt a flutter of anger move from her belly to her head.

"What has gotten into you?" Rebecca asked her daughter as she stared at the spoon in horror. "Meghan, that is not how you behave."

Meghan clenched her jaw. "Mama, I like my life here. I love my boyfriend. I am not going back to Texas. You have to let me live my life, Mama. You have to let me make my own choices and chase my own dreams."

Rebecca removed the apron from her neck and folded it, placing it neatly on the counter. She walked to Meghan and planted a long, motherly kiss on her forehead. "I'll just let you work," she murmured as she collected her purse and moved to the door. "You seem… tired. I think it's best if you collected yourself, and then we can spend time together later."

Meghan said nothing as Rebecca turned to blow her a kiss. "Just think about it, Sugar," she insisted as she waved goodbye. "Just think about coming home."

Later that evening, Meghan and Jack were relaxing at Eight Ball, the pool bar frequented by the local police officers. Meghan was fantastic at pool, and she and Jack had made plans earlier in the week to play a few games.

"I'm so glad we get to hang out tonight," she told Jack as she reared back her arm and then shot the ball forward. "Eight Ball is such a fun place to relax, and it doesn't hurt that I've been schooling you in pool!"

Jack did not laugh, and Meghan nervously bit her bottom lip. "Are you having fun?" she asked him as she shot another ball. "Your friends are over there. Should we go say hi?"

Jack shook his head. "Honestly, Meghan, I'm not in the mood to stay here anymore. What you said when we walked in really bugged me, and I think we should call it a night."

Meghan wracked her brain, frantically trying to think of what she and Jack had spoken about when they first arrived at the bar. "Are you talking about the conversation I had with my mother today?" she asked him worriedly. "I thought it was kind of annoying, but kind of funny. I just wanted to fill you in."

Jack looked down at his pool stick.

"Jack?" she asked. "What's wrong?"

Jack grimaced. "It really irks me that your Mom brought up your ex," he admitted to her.

"Jack, I dated Jacob in high school," she protested, placing a hand on Jack's heart. "I love you."

He softly pushed her hand away. "It just doesn't feel great that despite my efforts, your parents want you to leave me, and to leave Sandy Bay."

Meghan pursed her lips, unsure of how to respond to her beloved boyfriend. He was right; he had tried his best to win over the Trumans, but Meghan's parents were hardly giving Jack the time of day. Meghan did not know what to do; she wanted her family to adore her loyal, loving boyfriend as much as she did, but with their eyes on Jacob Brilander, the Trumans would never see Jack for the amazing man he was.

"Look, they just need time to warm up to you," she pleaded. "I'm sorry I mentioned the conversation with my Mom to you. I didn't mean to upset you, Jack. I would never want to upset you."

Jack placed the pool stick beneath the table. "I think we should just go, Meghan. I don't feel like hanging out anymore."

Meghan followed Jack's lead, placing her pool stick in a rack beneath the table. She walked behind him as he left the bar, and they walked toward the bakery in silence. When they reached the front door, Jack leaned in and kissed Meghan on her cheek.

"Not a real kiss?" Meghan asked as she stared up at her boyfriend.

Jack hesitated. "I just don't feel great," he told her. "I think we should just say goodnight. I'll call you tomorrow."

Meghan stared as Jack turned around and began walking away from her. "Jack? Please? Come back."

Jack did not turn around, and as he trudged through the snow that covered the sidewalk, Meghan felt as though her heart had turned to ice.

5

The next morning, Meghan's spirits were lifted when Karen Denton, her dear friend, walked into the bakery. Karen had been Meghan's neighbor when they both lived in Los Angeles, and Karen had been the one to convince Meghan to move to Sandy Bay. Despite being in her early seventies, Karen was the most adventurous, active person Meghan knew, and she always managed to put a smile on Meghan's face.

"How fabulous to see you," Karen greeted her. "I just left my spin class, and I wanted to stop by and see if your folks were around. It's not every day that your dear friend's family is in town."

Meghan smiled and said, "They are upstairs in my apartment visiting with the dogs. I'll go get them."

She returned with her parents in tow, each holding one of Meghan's dogs. "Karen, these are my parents," she announced as Rebecca and Henry smiled at Karen.

"Oh, it is a pleasure to meet you at last," Karen shouted joyfully as she gathered Rebecca into her arms. "Meghan is a doll, and I try to look after her here. She is such a good girl; she really has a good head on her shoulders! But you both know that, of course."

Rebecca gently pulled away from Karen and smiled. "The pleasure is ours. Meghan says you watch out for her here in town. Thank you for being somewhat of a surrogate mother to our girl."

Karen turned to Henry. "And you! Meghan's father? What a thrill."

Henry grinned. "We are pleased to meet you, Karen. It's been so nice meeting Meghan's friends in Sandy Bay."

Karen turned to Meghan and winked. "And what did your folks think of sweet Jack? What a catch he is."

Henry and Rebecca raised their eyebrows, and Karen caught the looks on their faces. "You two have met Jack?"

Rebecca nodded. "We have," she confirmed. "He's... nice."

Karen placed her hands on her hips. "He is more than nice," she countered. "Jack Irvin is one of the most darling boys in this town. He was just promoted to detective, which is a huge deal. He also volunteers with the youth club in town, and he once saved the Minister's dog that was caught on the railway tracks!"

Henry looked at Meghan, his own dark eyes wide. "We've probably been giving him too hard of a time," he muttered as Meghan nodded emphatically. "Rebecca and I just want the best for our little girl."

"Jack is the best," Karen explained to Meghan's parents. "If I had a daughter living in Sandy Bay, I would give my right arm to have her dating such a good boy."

Rebecca frowned. "Maybe we've been too hard on him," she told her husband. "Karen here says that he is wonderful, and if Meghan really likes him...."

Henry nodded vigorously. "We'll make things right with him. Meghan, I'm sorry; I've been missing my dogs at home, and that's put me in a foul mood. I'll make things right with your man, and I'll get back to being myself."

Meghan beamed. "Thanks, Daddy. I didn't realize you were missing your dogs so much. Why don't we go take my dogs out for a walk together? Fiesta and Siesta would love a little walk with their Grandpa."

Henry smiled. "That sounds perfect, Sugar."

Meghan strapped the dogs into their harnesses. She gave one leash to her father, and as they walked out the front door, she asked her mother, "Are you and Karen okay to visit with each other for a bit?"

Rebecca's eyes twinkled. "Karen and I are getting on quite well," she informed her daughter. "We will be chatting away. You two have fun."

Meghan and Henry stepped outside into the cold winter air. Fiesta and Siesta shivered; their hair was short, and Meghan wished that they had coats as warm as hers for the chilly Pacific Northwest winter.

"This is just like when we took walks together when you were a little girl," Henry shared as he and Meghan walked the dogs along the snowy sidewalk. "Of course, we didn't have snow in Texas, but you and I would always go for long walks together with the dogs. Do you remember the dogs we had when you were little? You just loved Dave, the Great Dane we had. He used to sleep with you every night! Your brothers and sisters were always so jealous that he loved you best."

Meghan smiled. "I remember Dave," she told her father as they turned a corner, a flurry of snowflakes came sprinkling down. "I loved our walks together, Daddy. With such a big family, it was special to have alone time with you and Mama."

Henry's eyes filled with tears. "You are just growing up so fast, Meghan," he lamented to his daughter. "I can't believe my little girl is old enough to live so far from home, or own her own business, or even have a boyfriend."

"Hey!"

Meghan and Henry turned to see Jack walking toward them, in his arms, a bouquet of red roses.

"Speak of the devil," Henry muttered as Jack approached them.

"Meghan," Jack began as he stared into Meghan's dark eyes. "I'm sorry I was upset. I'm sorry, and I was coming over to apologize and to bring you these flowers."

Before Meghan could speak, she heard her father clear his throat. Henry looked into Jack's eyes and reached out for his hand. "Jack," he began. "I want to apologize for not being the kindest while my wife and I have been here. Meghan is our little girl, and we want only the best for her. It's clear that you make her happy, and that you've helped her settle here in Sandy Bay. That said, I want to thank you for taking care of my girl."

Jack's eyes widened. "Thank you, sir," he said to Henry. "That means a lot to me."

Henry shook Jack's hand. "Let me make it all up to you. I want to take you two to dinner tonight at Luciano's; their food was just incredible, and I want to start fresh. Can we do that?"

Jack grinned. "Of course," he told Henry. "Well, only if Meghan is up for it. Meghan? Can you forgive me? Can we all start fresh?"

Meghan blushed, aware that her father was watching. "Yes," she whispered to Jack as she leaned up on her tiptoes to kiss him gently on the lips. "Let's start fresh."

That evening, as Henry, Rebecca, Jack, and Meghan stepped out of Henry's rental car and onto the snowy streets, Meghan gasped as she caught sight of a commotion outside of the restaurant.

"What is going on?"

Jack gently tucked Meghan behind him and turned to Henry. "Mr. Truman, I am going to see what's going on," he said as he surveyed the scene. "It looks like a crowd of homeless folks is rioting. Meghan, stay with your father. I will be right back."

Jack returned moments later with a weary look in his blue eyes. "What happened?" Meghan asked her boyfriend as he shook his head. "Jack?"

Jack sighed. "One of the homeless fellows is dead. That guy we saw last time with the Santa beard? I just cleared the area, and he was lying on the ground. I took his pulse, but he's gone. I called for backup and an ambulance, so it's about to get pretty busy here. I have to stay on the scene, for a few minutes, but then I can drive you all back. Henry? Will you please keep an eye on Meghan? I don't want anything to happen to her."

Henry nodded. "Of course I will keep my baby girl safe," he declared. "Come on, Meghan. Stay close to me. This place is brimming with trouble."

6

"I'm so upset, I can hardly think straight," Rebecca lamented as Jack silently wound through the snowy streets to take the Trumans back to their hotel. "First a riot, and now, a man is dead? Meghan, what kind of town is this?"

Meghan said nothing. She stared at the window and shivered as she saw two homeless men outside of Spark. She wondered how they were staying warm in the frigid evening, and she pulled her coat tightly around her.

"Well, here we are," Jack announced as he turned onto the circular driveway outside of the hotel. "I'll walk you in."

"I'll wait in the car," Meghan told her parents as they unbuckled their seatbelts.

"Not a chance," Henry said. "There was a riot and a death tonight... you are coming inside with us."

Meghan frowned, but obeyed her father. She stepped out of the car and sidled up to Jack, looping her elbow through his.

"I am just flabbergasted," Rebecca complained as they entered the luxurious hotel lobby. "Meghan, I do not feel comfortable with you living in such a place."

"Let's discuss this later, Mama," Meghan grumbled as Lewis Templeton, the hotel manager, hurried over to the Trumans. In his fitted white suit and pointed leather shoes, Lewis was the epitome of elegance; he was known in town for having fine taste, and while Meghan didn't know him well, she sensed there was more to him than met the eye.

"Good evening," Lewis cooed. "You must be the Trumans, my newest guests? It is a pleasure to serve you at our finest establishment. I'm Lewis Templeton, the manager of this hotel."

Henry nodded brusquely. "Thanks," he told Lewis.

Lewis leaned in and took Rebecca's hands. "Mrs. Truman? You look upset, and we never want our dear guests to feel upset in our hotel. Is there something I can bring for you? A coffee? A vitamin water? A scone?"

Rebecca shook her head. "Forgive me," she said to Lewis. "I've had the most upsetting evening."

Lewis wrinkled his forehead. "Oh? May I ask why?"

Rebecca scowled. "Those homeless men....they were camped outside of Luciano's, and..."

Lewis' face darkened. "Were they causing trouble again? I had a group of them with the nerve to stay outside of this hotel. You can bet your bottom dollar I had them sent away. I am so sorry you were disturbed, Mrs. Truman. I've told the mayor a million times that we must take care of our homeless problem in Sandy Bay!"

Rebecca smiled weakly. "I appreciate your concern," she breathed. "Mr. Templeton, it was a pleasure to meet you. Henry, take me upstairs. I need a stiff drink, and I need it now."

* * *

THE NEXT DAY, Meghan met her mother at Crumpet, a tea shop on the west side of town.

"I just think you should consider your safety, Meghan," Rebecca lectured as the mother and daughter sipped tea together. "You are a young woman living on your own in a town filled with trouble."

Meghan disagreed. "Sandy Bay isn't filled with trouble," she told her mother. "It's filled with kind, caring people who are passionate about making our little town the best it can be. Look! Over there. It's Kirsty Fisher. She is one of Sandy Bay's biggest philanthropists and organizers. You should meet her, Mama. Kirsty!"

Kirsty smiled her perfectly white teeth at Rebecca and Meghan and flitted over, an organic green tea in her hand. "Meghan, what a pleasure. I was just going over plans for that poor homeless man's funeral with the junior leader of the City Committee. There's no one else to plan it, and we feel everyone in Sandy Bay deserves to be honored when they pass."

Meghan gritted her teeth. She did not want to discuss the death with Kirsty and her mother; she had hoped Kirsty's enthusiasm for Sandy Bay could sway her mother, and she tried to change the subject.

"That's nice, Kirsty, but tell me, what other projects are you working on for the city these days?"

Kirsty bit her lip. "Well, my charity is partnering with the local department store," she told Meghan and Rebecca. "We scout out people to play Santa during the holiday season."

"How lovely," Rebecca cooed. "That sounds like great fun."

"It is," Kirsty agreed. "But it's a bit sad this year; we work with the homeless population to find the perfect Santa; the department store offers one lucky person employment as Santa for the season, and then they receive a twenty-five thousand dollar prize to help them get back on their feet after the holidays are over."

"Twenty-five thousand dollars?" Meghan exclaimed.

Kirsty nodded. "It's such a sweet opportunity for someone to turn their life around. It's just tinged with sadness this year; that man who was killed? He was one of our finalists this year. He came to the audition with a Santa beard and such a wonderful spirit. He received a standing ovation, and he was down to the top three in the competition. The selection committee was very pleased with him, and rumor was that they were going to announce his selection this week. Now, we'll never see him rise up; I'm planning his funeral instead of his congratulatory tea."

Rebecca cocked her head to the side. "I don't believe we've met," she informed Kirsty. "I'm Meghan's mother. And, you are?"

Kirsty flashed her perfect smile at Rebecca and tossed her blonde hair. "I'm Kirsty Fisher," she said to Rebecca. "I live for Sandy Bay events; I adore this town with all of my heart, and Meghan has been such a doll in helping with several of my affairs."

Rebecca studied Kirsty, and then she smiled at her. "I enjoy your passion," she told Kirsty. "Now, sit down. Let's chat. Tell me more about the man who died?"

Meghan cringed. She knew her mother was prying in order to persuade Meghan to leave Sandy Bay, and she wished Kirsty would stop discussing the deceased homeless man.

"It's terribly sad," Kirsty lamented as Rebecca listened with raised eyebrows. "His name was Roger Williams, and he used to be quite the successful Sandy Bay resident. He was a business owner, and from what I hear, an avid volunteer in the community."

Rebecca ran a hand through her blonde hair. "How did his life spiral out of control?"

Meghan gasped. "Mother! That's so rude."

"What?" Rebecca asked. "I'm just asking. Obviously something had to have gone wrong to have a successful businessman lose everything and end up on the streets."

Kirsty bobbed her head up and down. "From what I've been told, Roger's life took a tumble; he went through a nasty divorce, and that just sent him barreling downhill. Roger became paranoid and crazy, and he went in and out of mental hospitals for years. His poor ex-wife finally took his children and left town. Roger then ran out of money, and a few years ago, he was in jail for robbing a grocery store. The authorities determined he was only stealing food, and they let him out after a few nights. From what I've been told, he went back to the mental hospital, was given the proper medication, and then, he had a good few years."

"Then what happened?" Meghan asked, caught up in the story.

"He was given a free apartment to live in, as well as a part-time job," Kirsty explained. "But then, it all went downhill again, and he spiraled out of control. Word on the street is that he finally got help a few months ago, which is the only reason why we could have considered him for the part of Santa. He had a social worker, a therapist, and a case manager, and he was finally doing well."

"And now, he's dead," Meghan whispered sadly.

"He's gone, and we'll have to use our second-choice Santa," Kirsty said in disgust. "Oh, I didn't mean it like that," she said, seeing Meghan's look of horror. "It's just that Roger was so wonderful, and I thought he would do a great job."

"I've been auditioning for forty-seven years, and I've never been selected."

The three women turned to see Mrs. Sally Sheridan hobbling toward them on her cane. Mrs. Sheridan was an elderly woman who had previously loathed Meghan, but after she had come to Mrs.

Sheridan's side during a town protest, the pair had become friendly. Mrs. Sheridan was still known for being fussy and hard to please, but Meghan's heart was softening toward the old woman.

"Mrs. Sheridan," Kirsty greeted her as she maneuvered her way to the table. "It's lovely to see you."

"Yeah, yeah," she grumbled. "I heard you three talking about the Santa auditions. I've been auditioning for years, and I feel like I've never been given a fair shot."

Kirsty pursed her lips. "The role is for Santa Claus," she explained patiently to Mrs. Sheridan. "Santa Claus is a man, Mrs. Sheridan, and you are not a man."

Mrs. Sheridan glared at Kirsty. "That just doesn't seem very progressive of you," she argued. "I'm sure my Santa voice is better than any man's, and I sure have a big belly for the kids to sit on. Just look at it."

Rebecca gasped as Mrs. Sheridan stroked her large, overweight belly. Meghan and Kirsty were used to Mrs. Sheridan's occasional crass remarks, but prim, proper Rebecca Truman did not know how to handle Sally Sheridan.

"Look," Kirsty said to Mrs. Sheridan. "I'm sorry you haven't been selected. I truly appreciate your eagerness to participate and make the children happy as Santa."

Mrs. Sheridan rolled her eyes. "I don't care about the children," she explained to Kirsty. "I care about the money, as well as gaining exposure as an actress. I was born for the stage, Kirsty."

Kirsty sighed. "You are the most dramatic woman in town," she muttered.

"What?" Mrs. Sheridan roared. "Do I need to turn up my hearing aid?"

Kirsty slapped a smile back on her face. "No," she breathed. "Just keep trying out each year, Mrs. Sheridan! You never know what can happen."

Mrs. Sheridan grumbled as she hobbled out of the tea shop. Kirsty looked to Rebecca. "She is an odd duck," Kirsty said apologetically to Rebecca. "But it isn't just her; others have gotten bent out of shape because of the silly Santa competition."

Meghan raised an eyebrow. "What do you mean?"

Kirsty shook her head. "We get so many complaints during the round where we make cuts," she explained to Meghan and Rebecca. "When we send out the notices to tell people that they didn't make it to the next round, they get so angry. We've gotten threats before! It's wild. People would kill for the role of Santa."

Meghan bit her bottom lip. "Kill for the role of Santa, huh? I'm sure it's fun to play Santa, but I'm sure that twenty-five thousand dollar prize attached is something people would be a little more inclined to kill for. I wonder if that had anything to do with Roger's death. You said that he was known to be a top finalist?"

Kirsty nodded. "I hadn't even thought that the contest could be connected to his death," she said to Meghan. "Oh my. How terrible to think of."

Rebecca narrowed her eyes at her daughter. "This charming little town seems a little darker after hearing this, Meghan. I'm just not quite sure how I feel about you staying in Sandy Bay, especially after this information. I think it's time you come home to Texas, and I don't want to hear another peep of an argument about it!"

7

The next morning, Meghan was pleasantly surprised to find Jack at her doorstep before the bakery opened. She wasn't expecting him, and as she peered out the window to see him smiling back at her, she hoped that her messy hair and sleepy eyes wouldn't dissuade him from giving her a good morning kiss.

"Hey there, handsome," she cheerfully greeted her boyfriend as she unlocked the doors. "This is a surprise."

Jack leaned down to kiss Meghan softly on the lips. Meghan felt a shiver run up her spine; she and Jack had been dating for several months now, but it still felt magical when he kissed her.

"To what do I owe this pleasure?" she playfully asked as Jack pulled away. "Would you like some breakfast? It's well before our opening time, but you know I would happily whip something up for you."

Jack shook his head. "I just got off my night shift," he told Meghan as she noticed the dark bags under his eyes. "There's been a break in the case; we have a few suspects, but a new addition to the suspect list has me shaken."

Meghan's dark eyes widened. "Who is it?"

Jack sighed. "Mr. Luciano is on the list," he informed her. "The police think that maybe he was just tired of all the homeless folks outside of the restaurant. You heard how upset he was that day we had dinner with your folks."

Meghan gasped. Mr. Luciano had always been kind to her, and she could hardly believe that he was an official suspect. "Are you sure? Do they know how Roger died, yet?"

Jack frowned. "That was the other disturbing news of my night shift," he muttered. "Roger died from something he ate; how easy it would have been for Roberto to throw out some food for those people to gobble up, and now... someone is dead."

Meghan bit her lip. She recalled the conversation she and her mother had had with Kirsty the day before, and she wagged her finger in protest. "I don't know, Jack," Meghan said. "It just seems too crazy. Mr. Luciano didn't want his restaurant to be plagued with crowds of homeless people out front, but I don't see him killing someone. What about one of Roger's friends? The group of people there looked pretty rough; what if another homeless person killed him?"

Jack shrugged. "I brought that up to Chief Nunan," he murmured. "You said yourself when we spoke last night on the phone that Roger was set to win that department store gig; perhaps someone was angry about it and killed him."

Meghan nodded. "That's what I think. I think rumor was that Roger was going to win the role as Santa, as well as the money, and some sore loser decided to take away the opportunity permanently."

"I floated that idea to the Chief," Jack breathed. "But she wouldn't hear it; she is fixated on Roberto right now. Anyway, I wanted to let you know the news. I need to head home and get some sleep."

Meghan turned on her heel and dashed to the kitchen, returning with a large disposable cup filled with steaming coffee. "For you," she announced as she presented the coffee to Jack. "A large caramel macchiato made with my special homemade whipped cream."

Jack accepted the cup and bent down to kiss Meghan on the forehead. "You are an angel," he told his girlfriend. "Thank you for taking such good care of me."

Meghan reached out to give Jack a playful swat on the bottom. "Now get out of here," she ordered him with a smile on her face. "You need some sleep, Mister!"

* * *

"THAT ISN'T YOUR COLOR, Meghan. Didn't you listen earlier when I told you that?" Rebecca chided as Meghan stepped out of the dressing room at Spark.

Jackie nodded in agreement. "I think she's right," she told Meghan. "That bright orange just doesn't work with your hair."

Meghan politely smiled at her mother and friend, but as she retreated to the dressing room, she scowled. She had been convinced by her mother to go shopping for the afternoon, and while she had at first thought that bringing Jackie along would soften her mother's harsh comments, she was incorrect; Rebecca and Jackie had bonded instantly, and they were constantly teaming up against Meghan.

"I can't believe she chose that sweater," Meghan heard her mother murmur to Jackie. "She and I are just built so differently, and she doesn't seem to understand that with those...womanly looks, she needs to gravitate toward the neutrals."

"I agree," Jackie told Rebecca, and Meghan's stomach churned. "Meghan has such a pretty face, but you cannot wear orange with those curves. I wish she would hit the gym with me every once in awhile. I ask her, Rebecca, but she usually turns me down."

Meghan marched out of the dressing room in her black camisole, her arms crossed across her chest. "I can hear every word you two are saying," she told her mother and Jackie as she shivered, the hair on her arms sticking straight up. "Mama, I wish I were itty bitty like you, but I am not. I know I'm not the most stylish, but I try."

Rebecca rolled her eyes. "Don't do a pity party," she said dismissively to Meghan. "Why don't you just pack up your things and move home to Texas? I can help you open a bakery there, and I can hire a stylist for you. You'll be the talk of the town, Meghan! You could blow every little cafe and bakery out of the water. Your father and I could help you turn Truly Sweet into a franchise!"

Meghan balled her hands into fists. "I don't want to go home to Texas," she declared as Jackie walked away to browse a rack of sweaters on the other side of the store. "Mama, I've told you repeatedly that I am happy here. Why isn't that enough for you?"

Rebecca sighed. "Someday you will understand," she said as Meghan stared at her. "When you have a daughter, you will only want the best for her."

"The best for her is Sandy Bay, you silly goose."

Meghan and Rebecca turned to find Sally Sheridan hobbling toward them, her cane scraping the trendy chestnut-colored wooden floor of the boutique as she wandered closer. "Meghan belongs in Sandy Bay. She lives here. She loves it here. We love her here. She turned that bakery of hers into a success, she's dating the best boy in town, and she makes everyone here happy with her big smile and good spirits."

Tears welled in Meghan's eyes. She and Mrs. Sheridan had grown closer over the last few months, but she never dreamed that Mrs. Sheridan would have such lovely things to say about her. She wiped a tear from her cheeks and walked to Mrs. Sheridan with outstretched arms, eager to embrace the old woman.

"What are you doing?" Mrs. Sheridan asked in alarm as Meghan drew closer. She waved her cane at Meghan's head. "Back up, missy."

"I just want to give you a little hug," she laughed as Mrs. Sheridan stared at her. "Your words touched my heart, and I wanted to give you a squeeze to thank you."

Mrs. Sheridan shook her head. "No, no, no," she said, firmly planting her cane in front of her. "I'm not in a sappy mood today. I'm just telling the truth. The truth is that you belong here, and your mother needs to get off of her high horse and let you be about it. You hear me?"

Rebecca looked startled to be addressed in such a brusque manner, but before she could respond, Mrs. Sheridan began to hobble away. Before she walked outside, she turned back around to shout, "even though Meghan's treats gave me diarrhea once, they are still the best in the Pacific Northwest."

Meghan's face burned with shame; she knew that her treats had never made anyone sick, and she was embarrassed that Mrs. Sheridan had shouted that across the fashionable boutique. Meghan watched as Mrs. Sheridan exited the store and then leaned down to settle into an overstuffed purple armchair. "That was a lot," she sighed to her mother. "I'm sorry she was a bit rude."

Rebecca looked down at her high heels and then looked back at Meghan, a look of shame on her face. "I'm sorry," she whispered to Meghan. "You and I have always been so different, and I have always pushed you too hard. I'm sorry I've been pushing for you to come home. To be honest, Meghan, your Daddy and I miss you. We would like you to be nearby. You're missing so much, Meghan; your brothers and sisters are getting older, and we just want you to be a bigger part of our lives."

Meghan pursed her lips. “I have to live my own life, Mama,” she said softly as a black tear of mascara raced down Rebecca’s cheek.

“I know,” Rebecca replied. “And it seems like you live a good life here. Everyone has such lovely things to say about you. You’ve really made an impression here.”

Meghan smiled. “I love it here.”

“I can see why,” she said. “The people are kind, the shops and restaurants are adorable, and the sight of the ocean nearby is just good for the soul.”

Meghan sighed. “I wish you and Daddy could just live here part of the time,” she lamented.

Rebecca stared into her eyes. “What if we could?”

Meghan raised an eyebrow. “What do you mean? Texas is so far away.”

Rebecca laughed. “In this age, nothing is far away; we have endless airline miles from Daddy’s business, and we have been thinking about investing in some property. What if we added a place in Sandy Bay to our list?”

Meghan jumped up and down in excitement. “Really? That would be wonderful. I love you two so much and would love to see more of you. I know just the person who could help you out! My friend, Kayley, is the best real estate agent around. If you are serious about a place here, she will go all out to help.”

Rebecca leaned forward and kissed her daughter on the forehead, leaving a smudge of pale pink lipstick on Meghan’s skin. “I am serious,” she whispered as she hugged her daughter. “I am serious about moving to Sandy Bay.”

8

"This is a cute office," Rebecca gushed as Meghan led her inside of the local real estate company. "I just love that waterfall in the corner; the aesthetics here are fantastic."

"Thank you, I designed the place myself," said Kayley Kane, one of Sandy Bay's best agents.

She effortlessly strutted across the room, her tall high heels making her legs look like skyscrapers. Kayley and Meghan were friendly; they had been thrown together for various events in town, and today, as Meghan imagined her mother and father buying a second house in Sandy Bay, Meghan was elated to see her real estate agent friend.

"Kayley, good to see you," Meghan said as she gestured her mother to sit beside her in the expensive chairs facing Kayley's desk. "This is my mother, Rebecca Truman. Mama and my Daddy are looking to maybe find a second home in Sandy Bay."

Meghan watched as Kayley's eyes scanned Rebecca's outfit and purse; Kayley was known for having expensive taste, and Meghan was sure she would recognize Rebecca's designer sweater and matching handbag. Kayley leaned forward in her chair and clasped her red-finger nailed hands in front of her nose. "I would be honored to help Mr. and Mrs. Truman in their search. Mrs. Truman, what exactly is your budget for a second home in Sandy Bay?"

Rebecca laughed. "Surely it isn't proper to first discuss finances," she lightheartedly chastised Kayley. "Let's just say Meghan's Daddy and I have enough to be comfortable here."

Kayley's eyes widened. "Of course," she said, twirling a strand of freshly dyed auburn hair around her finger. "Forgive me. Let's talk about your lifestyle. How will you and your family be using a new property?"

Rebecca pursed her lips. "Well, Meghan's Daddy won't be around often; his work keeps him very busy. It would mostly be me here. I would like to have things to do while I am in town; I love throwing charity events and parties, but I wouldn't mind having a shop to duck into, either."

Kayley's eyes sparkled. "We have a lot of properties that offer space for hosting events," she told Rebecca. "And we even have some commercial properties for purchase. You could easily scoop up one of the buildings or lots downtown and run a little shop. What about a flower shop? You could open a flower shop and check in on it while you are here."

Rebecca smiled warmly. "That's a sweet little idea," she said. "I'm not sure how I feel about getting my hands dirty, though. Let's just talk about residential options."

Kayley nodded and rose from her seat behind the desk. "Of course. Excuse me for one moment, and I will go find some pamphlets detailing your options."

As Kayley marched away, Meghan glanced over her shoulder to see a crowd of people sitting angrily in the lobby. "What's going on out there?" Meghan asked as she fidgeted in her seat.

"Ugh, that dead man just ruined so many of our deals," Kayley chirped as she walked back into her office. "I was just about to sell the property next to Luciano's, but because that guy dropped dead there, no one wants it. All of those people out there are trying to cancel deals and property purchases we had signed on. It's madness."

Meghan's eyes widened. "All of those people want to give up on their property deals because that fellow died?"

Kayley rolled her eyes. "I know, it's ridiculous. I'm going to lose out on so much money because of this. I wish that man would have had the courtesy to drop dead elsewhere. My son's tuition bill is coming up soon, and I need the cash to pay for the private school. My ex-husband isn't helping with anything anymore, so this whole debacle makes my life more difficult."

Meghan tried to empathize, but she was disheartened by Kayley's disdain for Roger Williams.

"Kayley," she said softly. "I'm sorry it's stressful, but what about public school? I hear the schools here are great. Couldn't your son go to one of the public schools? You could save so much money."

Kayley narrowed her eyes at Meghan and gestured at a framed photograph of her son. "My little boy deserves the best," she hissed. "Maybe you'll understand when you are a mother someday."

Rebecca uncrossed her legs and picked up her leather handbag. She rose to her feet and beckoned to Meghan to follow suit. "I think it's time we go," she said to Kayley as she tucked her blonde hair behind her ears. "Ms. Kane, we can schedule a showing for next week. It seems best if we get out of your hair; this place looks crowded, and we don't want to take up too much of your time."

Kayley's face was panicked as Rebecca and Meghan walked to the door. "Wait!" she exclaimed. "I apologize for my outburst; I just care deeply about my son, and I don't want to miss an opportunity to help you find your dream home in Sandy Bay, Mrs. Truman."

Rebecca nodded politely. "We'll surely find time to work together later in the week," she told Kayley. "For now, we'll leave you be. Have a nice day, Ms. Kane."

As Meghan and Rebecca left the office, Rebecca sighed. "That woman was impossibly rude," she huffed to Meghan. "Didn't you say you are friendly with her? Really, Meghan, you need to surround yourself with good company if you want to become your best self."

Meghan shrugged. "Kayley and I are friendly, but she isn't my best friend, Mama," she explained. "Besides, she's the best agent in town; she'll do a great job helping you and Daddy find a place. Just give her a chance."

Meghan and Rebecca rounded the corner and found Angela Luciano outside walking a small Italian greyhound. "Angela, so good to see you," Meghan exclaimed. "Is that your dog? He is so cute. We should get together for a doggie playdate sometime."

Angela flashed her bright smile at Meghan and Rebecca before bending down to stroke the mottled gray greyhound behind the ears. "Yes," she breathed in her thick Italian accent. "This is Sarzana. He's my precious bambino. He loves other dogs, and I'm sure he would love your little loves."

Rebecca beamed at Angela. "It's so nice to see you out and about," she gushed as Angela stood beside her dog. "Meghan and I were just out visiting Kayley Kane. I'm looking for a second home here."

"That's wonderful," Angela cooed. "Sandy Bay is a darling town. When my family moved here from Italy when I was a teenager, we were welcomed with open arms. You will make many happy memories in Sandy Bay."

Rebecca tossed her hair behind her shoulder. "I'm just hoping to find the perfect house and the perfect set of activities," she explained to Angela. "It's very important to get connected with the right people and events, and I hope to contribute to Sandy Bay since my daughter loves it so much."

Angela's face brightened. "Are you interested in charities? Our restaurant is connected with many of the local organizations. I could give you some contacts if you are interested."

"I would adore that," Rebecca gushed. "You are just so beautiful and lovely, Angela. Thank you so much."

"Of course," she replied. "In fact, tomorrow, our restaurant is partnering with a charity that gives meals to the homeless. I joke with my father that we give the homeless enough meals, as they dig through our dumpster each night. But all jokes aside, this charity is a good one, and we are pleased to partake. Would you two like to join us tomorrow? Give back this holiday season?"

Meghan shook her head. "Sorry, Angela," she said as Rebecca glared at her. "I have a busy schedule tomorrow, and I put off some of my baking to go out with my mother today. Maybe next time?"

Rebecca gave Meghan a stern look. "That is not in the spirit, Meghan," she whispered to her daughter. "If you want me to be part of this town so badly, then we are going to go volunteer with beautiful Angela. Understood?"

Meghan bit her lip, upset that her mother had spoken to her like a child. "Understood," she muttered as Rebecca's frown turned into a glamorous smile. "Understood, Mama."

9

That evening, Meghan invited Pamela and Trudy to the bakery to meet her mother. Concerned by Kayley's rudeness, Rebecca had insisted on meeting some of Meghan's other Sandy Bay friends.

"I want to make sure that my daughter is spending time with the right people," she told her daughter as they prepared for the girls' night at Truly Sweet. "This will be fun, Meghan. I'm going to teach you all one of my favorite recipes. They will all love it, and we can spend even more time together."

"That's just what we need," Meghan groaned as Rebecca fastened an apron around her neck to protect her vintage Chanel sweater. "More time together."

Rebecca turned to smile at her daughter. "What did you say?"

Meghan shook her head. "Nothing, Mama. Oh, look. Trudy and Pamela are here."

Rebecca smiled graciously as Meghan's two employees walked into the bakery. "Hello! I am Meghan's mother, Rebecca. It's a pleasure to meet you ladies."

Pamela, Meghan's high school-aged employee, was brimming with excitement. "Nice to meet you. Meghan didn't tell us you were so glamorous!"

Rebecca waved a hand to dismiss Pamela's compliment, but Meghan knew her mother was pleased by the teenager's words. "And Mom, this is Trudy," Meghan said as she introduced her middle-aged employee to her mother. Trudy looked frumpy compared to Rebecca; both women were approximately the same age, but with her lumpy holiday sweater, frizzy hair, and knee-length wool skirt, Trudy looked ages older than the refined Rebecca.

"Let's get started with our baking," Rebecca instructed the group as she gestured to the ingredients and utensils she had laid out. "I've done a little prep, and I'm excited to teach you girls."

"Girls?" Trudy murmured. "I'm fifty-five years old, and I've been in the kitchen before."

"I'm just being silly," Rebecca laughed. "Come on, Trudy, get in the spirit!"

The four women got to work. Meghan turned on a holiday radio station, and the sounds of classical Christmas music filled the room. Everyone was in a pleasant mood, and Trudy lit one of the peppermint candles in the kitchen, giving the space a warm, festive glow and smell.

After nearly two hours of holiday fun, out of nowhere, the atmosphere shifted. "No, no, no!" Rebecca screeched as Pamela twisted a thick piece of yellow dough. "That is not the correct shape."

Meghan's dark eyes widened as she looked at the dough. Pamela had spun the pieces into an intricate braid, and Meghan was impressed with the shape and texture of the dough. "Mama," Meghan protested. "Pamela's braid is so pretty. What is the matter?"

"It's not the right size," Rebecca argued. "She made it too thick; it needs to be thinner on the side for it to look right."

Meghan cocked her head to the side. "I disagree," she said to her mother. Meghan saw Pamela's upset face, and she put a shoulder around the girl. "Pamela, you are doing a great job. Keep it up."

Rebecca frowned. "No, Pamela," she insisted. "You aren't doing it correctly."

Meghan stepped in front of her mother and shook her head. "That's enough, Mama," she told Rebecca. "We may be doing your recipe, but this is my bakery. We do things a certain way here, and if I say Pamela's braid looks nice, then that's the way it is."

Rebecca's jaw dropped, but she quickly regained composure and straightened her posture. "Fine," she huffed to Meghan. "I'll just be quiet and go work on the icing."

After a while, Rebecca's mood softened, and she and Trudy chatted about their favorite treats to bake. "My favorite holiday treats are egg-nog eclairs," Trudy told Rebecca. "They have such a unique, festive flavor."

"Those sound delightful," Rebecca affirmed as she dropped four drops of red food coloring into the bowl of frothy icing. "My favorite treat to bake is a coconut custard tart topped with roasted pineapple."

Meghan gasped. "That sounds incredible, Mama," she gushed as Rebecca's eyes sparkled.

"It's your father's favorite," Rebecca declared. "Many Christmases ago, my family attended a party at your father's parents' house. I whipped up one of my coconut tarts, but as I tasted it, I felt it needed more flavor. I looked around my Mama's kitchen, and when

I saw a fresh pineapple, I knew it would be the perfect touch for my treat. I roasted the pineapple and cut the pieces into little stars in honor of the holiday."

Meghan's heart warmed at the dreamy look on her mother's face. "Then what happened?"

"I took the dessert to the party, and when your father tried it, he demanded to be introduced to the baker. I was the baker! We were introduced, and it was love at first bite, as we like to say."

Meghan's face glowed as she imagined her parents as young people in Texas. "That's the best story, Mama. I've never heard it before!"

Rebecca nodded. "It just goes to show that food is a way to a man's heart. In fact, we should finish up these treats and take some to Jack at the station. Didn't you tell me he worked a double shift?"

Meghan bit her lip. "He did," she confirmed. "He's been working day and night to find out just how Roger died."

"Then it's settled," Rebecca announced. "We will finish these treats and then take some to Jack. I have an idea! How about we recreate some of the holiday magic I shared with your father years ago?"

Meghan nervously raised an eyebrow. "What do you mean?"

Rebecca gave her daughter a sly look. "We have all the ingredients we need here," she said. "What if we made coconut tarts with roasted pineapples on top? That was the key to your father's heart, and I'm sure Jack would be delighted to share in some of our family fun! Come on, Meghan! Say yes. It did wonders for your father and me; those tarts are the whole reason you are here."

Meghan giggled. "Well, I don't think the tarts are the only reason I'm here, Mama..."

"Oh, you silly girl. Come on, my dear. Indulge me. Roll up your sleeves and let's make some tarts for your man. It'll make magic happen for you two, I guarantee it!"

Thirty minutes later, Meghan bid farewell to Pamela and Trudy as they left the bakery. She and Rebecca packed up the warm tarts, and they bundled up in their heavy coats to brave the cold night air. It was a windy night, and the breeze stung Meghan's cheeks. "Are you sure you don't want to buy a second home in the Bahamas?" Meghan joked to Rebecca as she navigated through a snow bank.

"Don't tempt me," her Mum countered.

The two arrived at the Sandy Bay Police Station and were directed to Jack's office. As they walked down the hallway, they heard the booming voice of Roberto Luciano. "I had nothing to do with that man's demise," Roberto insisted as he stormed down the hallway past Meghan and Rebecca, Chief Nunan trailing behind him with a notebook in her hands. "This incident is ruining my business. We had ten cancelations last night for our dinner hours, and today, fifteen people have canceled! I am going to have to close my restaurant if something doesn't change. This is preposterous!"

Meghan cringed as Roberto began shouting in Italian. "He is so angry," she whispered to her mother as they watched him stalk down the hallway.

"He has a right to be," Rebecca said. "That man dropping dead in front of his restaurant isn't good for business, just as he said. It's quite sad that such a fine restaurant is losing patrons."

Meghan shrugged. "I think it's quite sad that a man passed away, and all anyone seems to care about is business. Between Roberto and Kayley, it seems like people don't care that a poor man who was down on his luck is now gone. Where is the holiday spirit?"

"I see plenty of the holiday spirit right here."

Meghan looked up to see Jack grinning down at her. He looked tired; with the deep, heavy bags beneath his eyes, his disheveled clothes, and his matted hair, it was evident that he had been working nonstop.

"How are the two most beautiful ladies in Sandy Bay?" Jack asked Meghan and Rebecca.

"We're just fine, Jack," Rebecca answered. "We brought something to you. Meghan says you've been working around the clock, and we thought you needed a treat. Now, I'm sure you wouldn't have to work such long hours if you had a nice, proper business job, but we'll let that be."

Jack gritted his teeth and pasted a smile on his face. "Thank you for thinking of me," he said to Rebecca. "What kind of treat?"

Meghan held up a white wicker basket. "It's filled with coconut tarts topped with roasted pineapple," she said to Jack. "We baked them fresh this afternoon. I was telling Meghan that these were the first treats I ever made for her father, and that you would adore the surprise as well. We're keeping a dear family tradition alive!"

Jack beamed. "You are too good to me," he murmured to Meghan as he lifted a tart out of the basket and took a bite. "This is delicious. Meghan, you are such a sweetheart. I'm going to get you anything you want for Christmas. Anything!"

Rebecca glanced up at Meghan and winked. "See?" she whispered to Meghan. "Food is the key to a man's heart. Maybe by next Christmas, there will be something special on your finger, Meghan. You heard the guy; he's going to get you anything you want for Christmas."

10

The Sandy Bay Food Bank was held each morning at the Sandy Bay Community Gymnasium. Meghan was shocked by how many people were present; by her count, nearly two-hundred homeless people were in line for food and services, and she smiled as she watched groups of people happily eat their meals.

"This is quite the production," Rebecca remarked to Angela as she led them through the gym. "What an efficient process."

"It's great, isn't it?" Angela replied as she walked in front of Rebecca and Meghan. "One of my dear friends from college runs a major food bank on the East Coast, and every year, she comes out here to help us improve our system. Here, come around to the serving side. I'll show you how it's done."

Meghan watched in awe as Angela joined a group of servers giving food to a line of homeless men. The process was efficient; every server gave exactly the same amount of food to each guest, and the portions were very generous. The meals consisted of chicken, spinach salad, an orange, and a roasted red pepper, and Meghan was impressed by the quality of the food.

"The servers all give out food in unison," she said in amazement. "How do they do it?"

Angela stepped forward and joined the line, grabbing a serving spoon and smiling at the guest in front of her while still speaking to Meghan. "We offer a half-day training for everyone who wants to help," she told Meghan as she scooped up a serving of chicken and placed it on a tray. "We train our volunteers to serve quickly and fairly; everyone gets a large, healthy meal, and everyone can leave here with full bellies and good service."

Meghan watched as Angela served three guests in a row in under ten seconds. "You are so fast."

"It's the training," Angela told her. "We practice serving and use timers, and we bring in treats and prizes to make it more like a competition. It's all great fun, and we have a steady group here. I've been volunteering here for years, so I know our guests pretty well."

"It's sweet that you call them guests," Rebecca said as she eyed a man in a tattered pair of overalls.

Angela shrugged. "Here, these folks are our guests. Homeless people matter. They have feelings and needs. We don't believe that if someone is down on their luck, that their life loses value. Sure, it gets frustrating when these people gather in front of our restaurant and scare away customers, but at the end of the day, they are just people."

Meghan looked around the crowded gym. "What can we do to help?" she asked Angela.

"You haven't been trained in the serving process, but you could go chat with some of our guests," Angela told Meghan. "There's a spot at that table over there. Rebecca? Why don't you go visit the nursery? We offer childcare during meal times, and you might enjoy visiting with the little kids."

Meghan and Rebecca set off in their different directions. Meghan took a seat at a table of middle-aged men. "Hi," she said to the man beside her. "I'm Meghan. What's your name?"

The man was dressed in a ratty sock cap and a dirty turtleneck. He had a thick beard that curled around his collarbone, and Meghan could smell his greasy hair. "Why are you talking to me?"

Meghan smiled. "I'm visiting today," she said to the man. "I might start volunteering here."

The man laughed. "Oh, a little spoiled princess working with the poor? That's rich."

A woman beside him elbowed the man in the side. "Alan, be nice to her. She's just being friendly."

Alan frowned. "It's embarrassing that rich folks come in here and talk with us poor people," he replied briskly to the woman. "Look at this girl. She looks like she ain't ever done a lick of hard work in her life."

Meghan pursed her lips and nervously played with her hands beneath the table. "I have worked before," she insisted. "I work at a bakery in town. I own it, actually."

Alan narrowed his eyes and stared into Meghan's face. "Oh? How much of your food do you donate to us homeless? Judging from the look on your face, I would guess that you don't give anything away. I hate that. I hate when rich little girls march in here to volunteer for the day, but in reality, they don't really care. If you really care, little rich girl, you would donate food from your bakery to feed the poor."

"You are right," Meghan agreed. "I should do that. I don't know why I never thought of it, but that is something I need to start doing."

Alan rolled his eyes. "Don't talk down to me, rich girl," he growled as he balled his hands into fists. "You need to get out of my face."

Meghan shook her head. "I just wanted to come over and say hi," she pleaded with the man as his face darkened. "I'm sorry if I offended you."

Alan glared at Meghan and rose to his feet. "Little rich girl here is sorry she offended me, huh? You don't want to know what happened to the last fellow who offended me, rich girl."

Meghan's eyes widened as Alan stormed away. "Just ignore him," the woman begged Meghan. "He doesn't mean to be bad, and we are truly grateful for the chance to get meals here."

Meghan nodded. "It's okay," she said to the woman as she pulled her dark hair back into a ponytail. "I feel bad that I offended him."

Alan circled back around to the table and resumed sitting by Meghan. "Sorry," he muttered as Meghan leaned away from him. "I get angry sometimes. Sorry I was nasty."

Meghan forced herself to smile. "It's fine," she said. "I just want to visit with everyone and spread some holiday cheer."

"I had enough holiday cheer this year," Alan laughed as Meghan raised an eyebrow. "That loser Roger Williams died. That brought enough cheer to my heart for the year."

Meghan's mouth dropped open. "Did you know him?"

Alan smirked. "Oh, I knew him. That idiot didn't deserve to become the store Santa, and I'm glad he...dropped dead before he could."

Alan turned around and grabbed a loaf of bread from the table behind him. "I'm extra hungry today," he said as he stuffed the bread into his mouth.

The table behind him yelled. "That's ours," they shouted. "You jerk."

Alan rose to his feet and grimaced as a portly man from the other table walked over and shoved him. Alan kicked the man's knees, and the man fell to the ground. Alan chuckled to himself as everyone stared at him.

"You all had better let me do what I want," he yelled to the crowd of shocked bystanders. "I wanted more bread, so I took it. I wanted to be the Santa at the store, so....just listen up, people. You mess with me, and I'll mess with you. You should see the last guy I messed with. He was dying to get away from me."

A collective gasped filled the room, and Alan's eyes bulged out from his head. "I didn't kill Roger, or did I? I know what you all are thinking. I'm out of here."

Meghan stared as Alan turned on his heel and bolted out of the gym. She reached into her red purse and retrieved her cell phone, quickly dialing Jack's number. "Babe," she breathed into the phone as Jack answered. "I think I know who did it. I think I know who murdered Roger."

11

"I'm just not sure, Meghan," Jack said as the pair talked on the phone later in the evening. "The officers brought him in and talked with him, but I'm just not sure if this is our guy."

Meghan snuggled deeper into her bed and pulled the comforter up to her neck. She could see the snow falling out the window, and she felt cozy and comfortable amidst the three chai-scented candles burning in her bedroom. Fiesta and Siesta were asleep at her feet, and Meghan wiggled her toes beneath their warm little bodies.

"You did say that Alan had a checkered past," Meghan replied to her boyfriend. "You told me that Chief Nunan pulled some records of his. I even read online that there's even an arrest warrant out for him right now. He stole some cans of tomatoes from the store last week!"

Jack sighed into the phone, and Meghan could hear the angst as he replied. "He kept saying he was innocent, Meghan. You should have heard him; he sounded so earnest as he pleaded with Chief Nunan."

Meghan remembered how intimidated she had been when Alan taunted her at the food bank. He had scared her, and Meghan sensed that Alan was not just an ordinary homeless man. He struck her as a killer, and Meghan's gut was telling her that something was amiss.

"I know he scared you," Jack said. "Don't worry, he's being held in jail pending further investigation into the murder case. Chief Nunan mentioned that there was a similar case to this one out in Maine, and perhaps we have a serial killer on our hands. She wants us to be thoroughly cautious, so she's confined Alan to an isolated cell until we can learn more."

Meghan sighed in relief. "That's good to hear," she told him. "He was so frightening, Jack. He had a scary look in his eyes."

Jack's voice broke. "I just don't want to mess this case up," he choked as Meghan's heart began to race.

"Jack?" Meghan asked in concern. "What's wrong? What's the matter?"

Jack cleared his throat. "It's nothing. I just have some things on my mind."

Meghan bit her lip. "I'm here if you need me, Jack," she said. "I love you."

"I love you too, Meghan," Jack replied, and Meghan's heart soared with those three special words. "I just don't think he did it. My gut is telling me that he didn't. What does Alan have to gain?"

Meghan raised her eyebrows. "The prize money," she argued. "He could have wanted to be the Santa at the store, and Roger was going to be given the part. What if Alan wanted the prize money?"

"That's what Chief Nunan said," Jack admitted. "But I don't know. My gut is telling me something else. Listen, I'm going to get off the phone and go for a walk. I need to clear my head."

"Okay, bye, love," Meghan said as she hung up the phone.

Meghan's cell phone immediately buzzed. Thinking it was Jack, she answered without pausing. She was surprised to hear her father's voice.

"Meghan, what are you up to?"

She looked around her bedroom. "I'm all snuggled up for the night," she said to her father. "Why, Daddy?"

"The snow is falling like crazy, and the moon is so bright. I'm dying to get out of this hotel room. Let's go for a nighttime walk. What do you say?"

Meghan groaned, but she knew that she needed to spend as much time as possible with her parents before they left. "Of course, Daddy," she answered. "Let's meet at the beach in twenty minutes. I'll bring the dogs; they look so precious in their winter coats, and they can't wait to see their Grandpa."

It was nine in the evening by the time Meghan and Henry made it to the beach, but the light of the moon lit up the sand and the sky. "It's just beautiful," Henry gushed as he guided Fiesta along the shore. "The snow looks like diamonds! Your mother would sure like it."

Meghan giggled. "Mama loves diamonds, but she hates getting cold," she replied. "I think she's in the perfect spot in her hotel room, that's for sure."

Henry chuckled good-naturedly, and then he pointed to a lone figure in the distance. "Hey, isn't that your man, Meghan? That's Jack. Look! He has a dog with him."

Meghan whistled, and Dash, Jack's dog, sprinted toward her. Jack ran after the dog, and he smiled when he realized it was Meghan who had called for Dash. "Meghan. Henry. What a surprise."

Meghan leaped into Jack's arms. "I didn't know you would come here to walk. I'm so happy to see you. Are you doing better, babe?"

Jack looked down at his boots, and Henry playfully nudged Jack on the shoulder. "What's wrong, son? Rough day at the office?"

Jack hesitated. "I shouldn't say…"

"Oh, come on, sport," Henry argued. "Tell us what's the matter. My little girl shouldn't have to worry about her man. What's the issue?"

Jack sighed. "It's about the man we arrested. Alan? The homeless man? I just don't think he did it, and I feel terrible."

Meghan placed a hand on Jack's shoulder. "I've never seen you so upset about a case before," she murmured. "Is there something standing out to you about this man?"

Jack's shoulders shook, and Meghan could see that he was trying not to cry. "I just feel like my gut is telling me he is innocent, and I would hate to keep an innocent man locked up. I kept an innocent man locked up for two whole weeks during my rookie year, and man, I never forgot the look on his daughter's face when he was released. I was just doing my job, but she looked at me as if I had hurt someone."

Henry placed a hand on Jack's shoulder and squeezed. "Sport, you can't be too hard on yourself," he said. "If you are following the rules and the law, you are doing what society expects of you. You can't give up, Jack. I'm sure it's difficult, but you have to do your job."

Jack frowned. "It's just hard to ignore my gut."

Henry shrugged. "In life, we have to do hard things," he told him. "In my business, I've had to fire people, and to make hard decisions. The beauty of it is that from hard choices come better outcomes, and I know that if you work hard and do your job, things will work out."

Jack smiled weakly. "Thanks, Mr. Truman," he said.

Henry furrowed his brow. "Really, call me Henry," he insisted.

Meghan's eyes sparkled as she watched the two most important men in her life share a moment together. Her heart warmed, and she felt a sense of relief as Henry embraced her boyfriend.

"Mama is warming to Jack," she thought to herself. "And Daddy is warming to him. Maybe this whole thing... Sandy Bay, the bakery, and Jack... will work out after all."

12

"I'm so glad we could get together and do this," Kayley Kane schmoozed as she led Rebecca and Meghan down the street toward a potential property. "You two have been such good sports with this snow and cold weather. Don't worry, though; this is our last place for the day."

Kayley held out her arms to show Rebecca and Meghan a four-story vacant building right beside Luciano's. "It's been empty for awhile, but it could be the perfect place for a shop, or a restaurant, or even a combination."

Rebecca raised an eyebrow. "It looks a little... rough, Ms. Kane."

Kayley sighed. "It was previously used to house some of the homeless," she admitted to Rebecca. "The owner of the building is moving to the East Coast and wants to sell it quickly, but he wants to sell it to someone with the right priorities."

"What do you mean by that?" Meghan asked as Kayley tapped her heeled shoes against the sidewalk.

Kayley chewed on her bottom lip before responding. "Well, Roberto Luciano tried to buy this place," she explained to the Trumans. "It is just next door to his place. But the owner didn't think Luciano had the right priorities. The owner of the property wants someone with empathy toward the homeless to purchase it, and he didn't feel like Roberto showed that. Roberto's been known for screaming and shouting at the homeless people, and the owner didn't feel right about leaving the property with him."

Rebecca frowned. "If that is the standard... empathy toward the homeless... I don't know if I would make the cut," she told Kayley. "I feel for them, I do, but I would not use this property to better them. I would likely turn it into something fabulous... this town needs a designer handbag shop... and I wouldn't prioritize the homeless' needs while arranging my next business endeavor."

Kayley smiled weakly at Rebecca. "Are you sure? You didn't warm to any of the other properties. Are you sure you couldn't just donate some money to the homeless, or perhaps work with a local agency to employ a homeless person in the store?"

Rebecca frowned. "I believe I made myself clear," she told Kayley. "None of the properties you have shown me have blown me away, Ms. Kane. Until something marvelous comes along, I'm afraid I cannot make a sale with you."

Meghan saw the look of concern in Kayley's eyes. "Mama, why don't you think about some of the places from earlier? That first little building was cute; you could turn that into a little salon or boutique."

Rebecca sighed. "You are so soft, Meghan," she hissed. "I want the best, and Kayley hasn't shown me the best."

Kayley sputtered, knowing that she had possibly blown the sale. "I will make a list of alternative properties," she announced to the Trumans. "Just you wait, ladies. I will come up with the finest places in Sandy Bay, and Mrs. Truman, I can assure you that you will be pleasantly surprised."

"I sure hope so," Rebecca sniffed. "Kayley, I think that's enough for us today. Meghan? Let's go."

Meghan and Rebecca said goodbye to Kayley and walked away. "I just don't know what she was thinking," Rebecca complained. "The properties were fine, but that last one? The stipulations on it were too much. I'm happy to spend a day at a food bank, and Daddy and I write a personal check each year to the shelter in town. I just don't believe in mixing business and handouts. It seems wrong to me."

Meghan pursed her lips. "I don't think it's too much to ask for, Mama," she told Rebecca. "It sounds like the only requirement is simply to respect the homeless and to provide some sort of opportunity for them. Is that too much?"

Rebecca rolled her eyes. "Meghan, if I am going to buy a second home here and open a little business for fun, it's going to be on my terms. Besides, Daddy would never approve of hiring a homeless person to work in a store of ours, and his opinion matters, too."

Meghan walked silently beside her mother, aghast at how privileged and selfish her mother could be. Meghan knew that Rebecca lived in a world of wealth and finery, but she wished that her mother could step outside of herself and see the needs of those around her. From Kayley's desire and need to make a sale with the Trumans, to the homeless, Rebecca seemed oblivious to the plights of those less fortunate than herself.

"Why are you making that sour face?" Rebecca asked her daughter. "Really, you should watch the way you hold your face, Meghan; it could freeze like that if you are not careful, or you could get wrinkles."

Meghan gritted her teeth. "Mama, I think there are more important matters at stake than my face," she huffed. "Kayley really needs to make a sale with you and Daddy. She is a single mom, and her ex-husband hardly helps with anything."

Rebecca narrowed her eyes. "Her finances are not my concern," she explained to her daughter. "Nor are they yours. She should not have mentioned her ex-husband, or her son's schooling. That was very unprofessional, and if she worked anywhere other than this tiny town, she would be fired for that kind of rude behavior."

Meghan sighed. "Mama, Sandy Bay is different than the South," she argued. "All of the prim and proper rules don't matter here. In Sandy Bay, people are candid. They speak their minds here, and they say what they mean. Kayley is worried about making ends meet, and I know how much it would help her to receive a large commission from a sale with you and Daddy."

Rebecca shook her head. "Really, Meghan, you should hear yourself. It's disgraceful. Talking about a stranger's finances is unacceptable."

Meghan crossed her arms in front of her chest. "No, Mama," she responded. "Not caring is unacceptable. We have so much, Mama, and we should be happy to share with others. We've been so blessed and comfortable, and our family should be honored to help others get by."

Rebecca glared at her daughter. "I don't know what's gotten into you," she said to Meghan. "But this behavior is unseemly. This is not a conversation I care to have anymore, so I must excuse myself. I am going back to the hotel and going to the gym."

"The gym?" Meghan asked.

"Yes," Rebecca answered. "I've been indulging during this trip. I typically only eat greens and tofu, but being around the bakery has awoken my sweet tooth. I need to work off some of this nastiness on the elliptical as soon as possible."

Meghan smiled. "I have an idea," she told her mother, eager to salvage their day together. "Remember my friend, Karen Denton?

She is the queen of exercise. She always knows the hippest, trendiest places to squeeze in a sweat. How about I give her a call? We can work out together?"

Rebecca's face brightened. "You are suggesting we work out? How wonderful! I never thought those words would come out of your mouth, but I am so thrilled they did. Give Karen a call. Tell her we will meet her in an hour, and beforehand, I'll take you to Spark to buy a cute workout outfit. How do you feel about spandex?"

13

Meghan stared at her reflection in the mirror of Karen's guest bathroom. She hardly recognized herself in the workout outfit her mother had purchased for her; the tight, clingy leggings and the matching pale pink sweatshirt were not items she would have chosen for herself, but as she studied her appearance, Meghan was pleasantly surprised at how the bottoms accentuated her curves. The leggings were snug in the bottom, and Meghan turned around to admire her backside. "I don't look half bad in nice workout clothes," Meghan admitted as she adjusted the crew neck sweatshirt. "Maybe with the right outfit, I'll enjoy working out more."

Meghan was wrong; despite her expensive new clothes, she detested exercise, and as she ran alongside her mother and Karen, she struggled to catch her breath.

"Try to keep up, Meghan," Rebecca chided her daughter as the women jogged along the main street of Sandy Bay. "We're going at a pace that is ridiculously slow for Karen and me. Surely you can move your legs faster?"

Meghan frowned, but she did her best to pick up her legs at a faster speed. "I'm coming," she called out.

"You're doing a fabulous job, Sweetie," Karen complimented as Meghan caught up to her. "I'm so proud of you."

Meghan smiled, thankful that someone was recognizing her hard work. "I'm doing my best," she grunted.

Rebecca quickened the pace, moving gracefully in a pair of soft periwinkle leggings and a matching knee-length workout sweater. "Come on, ladies, let's step it up," Rebecca ordered. "My trainer back home is going to kick my booty if he finds out I ate my weight in holiday treats here in Sandy Bay. Let's burn some el-bees, girls!"

Rebecca took off at a sprint. Karen followed, and Meghan attempted to keep up. "What are they doing?" Meghan wondered to herself as Rebecca and Karen quickly decreased their speed.

"We're doing intervals," Karen informed Meghan with a grin. "We run fast for thirty seconds, and then, we slow our pace. It's so good for your heart, and it's the best way to burn fat."

Rebecca nodded as she jogged beside her daughter. "Come on, Meghan. Burn some fat with us. It'll be the best gift you give yourself this Christmas."

Before Meghan could respond, Rebecca and Karen took off in a sprint again. "Come on, Meghan," Karen yelled. "It's only thirty seconds of hard work! You can do it."

Meghan took a deep breath. She picked up her knees and pumped her arms vigorously, but just as she reached her fastest pace, her mother and Karen slowed down. Meghan could feel the frustration fill her heart, and she struggled to stay positive as her athletic mother and friend raced down the street. The three women sprinted and jogged for a half hour, and finally, it was time for them to cool down.

"We'll just do a little two-mile run to cool down," Karen said as she high-fived Rebecca. "Feeling good, Meghan?"

Meghan nodded. "I'm… feeling something," she responded breathlessly.

Karen smiled at Meghan. "So, how is Jack doing, Sweetie? I haven't seen much of him in town, lately."

Meghan sighed. "He's been so busy with the case," she told Karen. "I've barely seen him myself."

Karen nodded. "Who do you think did it, Meghan? Does Jack know of any leads?"

Rebecca interjected. "My husband told me that Jack doesn't think that other homeless man, Alan, killed Roger," she said to Karen. "He says that Jack told him that he believes Alan is innocent. I have to disagree. I saw the way that terrible Alan upset my daughter at the food bank, and I think he had something to do with it."

Meghan agreed. "I didn't feel safe around him," she confirmed. "He was a big man, and he had a terrifying look in his eyes. He even told the crowd that he had messed with people before, and I think he meant that he killed Roger."

Karen slowed the pace. "We're going too fast for a cool down, ladies," she warned Rebecca and Meghan. "Anyway, that's terrible that Alan scared you, Meghan. Any other thoughts? They don't have any other suspects, do they?"

Meghan bobbed her head. "Actually, they do have another official suspect," she told Karen. "Roberto Luciano?"

Karen gasped. "Robbie? They think Robbie Luciano killed that man? There's no way he did that."

Meghan shivered as a gust of cold air hit her face. "From what I heard, they think he could have killed Roger because of his disdain for the homeless. A group of homeless guys hangs out outside of Roberto's restaurant nearly every night, and Roberto feels like he loses business because of it."

Karen shook her head. "I just cannot imagine Robbie Luciano hurting a fly," she insisted. "He and his family are such wonderful additions to the community. His wife, Maria, volunteers at the library each morning. His son, Francisco, donated a kidney to a little boy in town who needed a donor. His daughter, Angela, is one of the main coordinators for the local food bank. I just don't believe anyone in that family could have anything to do with the death; the Lucianos just don't have a mean bone in their bodies."

Meghan agreed. "That's how I feel as well," she told Karen. "Roberto gets frustrated with the homeless, but I don't think he is a killer."

Rebecca frowned. "If I were in his situation, though, I would sure be angry," she told the women. "If I owned a fine restaurant in the middle of town, and a group of rowdy homeless men were constantly around, I would be furious. I'm already furious that my own daughter has to deal with such scoundrels in her own town. I hope Roberto didn't kill that man, but if he did, I would understand. What a nuisance."

Meghan's jaw dropped at her mother's callous words. "Mother, how can you say something like that?"

Rebecca maintained her pace. "Obviously I don't condone murder, Meghan; don't be daft. I'm just saying that it's frustrating to see so many people like Roger in one town."

"What do you mean, like Roger?" Meghan asked her mother. "You mean, homeless? Poor? Down on their luck?"

"Precisely," Rebecca answered. "It's terrible to see so many of those people in the place where my daughter lives. I don't think a nice man like Roberto Luciano would kill a homeless man, but if he did, I would surely empathize with his frustrations."

Meghan tugged at the sweatshirt; it was tight around her neck, and her mother's brash words shocked her, making her throat feel tight and her chest swollen in disappointment. "Mama, do you know what holiday is coming up?"

Rebecca smirked. "Of course. It's almost Christmas."

Meghan nodded. "Exactly. And Christmas is all about love, the birth of Jesus in a manger and taking care of those less fortunate than us. I can hardly believe a loving, good woman such as yourself could empathize with someone for killing, but not with the homeless and downtrodden. It shocks me, Mama."

Rebecca came to an abrupt halt. "That is not what I meant, Meghan Truman," she insisted. "You know that. Don't make me out to be some kind of cruel monster."

Karen stepped between the mother and daughter. "Let's change the subject," she said. "What if there is someone we haven't thought of who could be the killer? Wouldn't it be funny if Sally Sheridan had killed him?"

Meghan's eyes widened. "Karen! That's a terrible thing to say."

Karen giggled. "I'm only joking," she said. "But seriously, if Sally Sheridan killed that man, she'd probably get caught trying to get a refund on his body! She would take it back to the coroner to see if she could get some money back."

Meghan erupted into laughter. It had been a tense afternoon with her mother, and despite the macabre nature of Karen's joke, Meghan was thankful for her dear friend for clearing the air. "You are too much, Karen Denton," Meghan said. "You are too much."

Rebecca huffed, reaching down to loosen the string on her pants. "I think I need to go shopping," she said as she let out a sigh of relief. "This run was nice, but I don't think it solved my problems. Meghan, your father and I have a party to attend just hours after we arrive home in Texas, and I am in need of some new dress pants.

How about we take a little jog over to the department store in town? Karen, would you like to join us?"

Karen clapped her hands. "I'm always up for a little jog," she told Rebecca. "Even if it is to a department store."

14

As Meghan, Karen, and Rebecca walked into Sandy Bay Station, the biggest department store in town, Meghan's stomach churned as she realized the racks were nearly bare. "Mama is not going to be happy," she thought to herself. "And I'm sure she'll let us all know that."

Rebecca darted from one section to the next, picking up articles of clothing, wrinkling her nose, and dismissing her finds. "I don't understand," she declared. "How can this department store have enough money to fund a $25,000 prize for an amateur actor to play Santa Claus, but this is the state of the store?"

Karen nodded. "I haven't been in here in a few months," she admitted. "But the inventory is just sad. I wonder what happened here."

Meghan perused a shabby holiday display, cringing at the static playing over the in-store radio. "I don't know if we're going to find what you're looking for, Mama," she whispered to Rebecca. "It seems like slim-pickings here. Why don't we try Spark? They have some cute things, and I'm sure we could find something for you. Or we could drive up to Portland. I'm sure they have some designer stores there."

Rebecca shook her head. "Let's just keep looking," she told her daughter. "Why don't you ask an associate if there is more merchandise upstairs? Maybe they've hidden some things away."

Meghan scurried away to the Help Desk and found a sales associate. He was tall and thin, with pasty skin and thick glasses. Meghan flashed her brightest smile and waved. "Hi! I'm Meghan. I'm looking for outfits for women in their mid-fifties. Do you have other sections with things like that?"

The boy shuffled awkwardly behind the desk. "This is all we have, Ma'am."

Meghan cocked her head to the side. "Really? This is the largest store in town. You guys sponsor that major Christmas competition each year for the homeless. What kind of major store has almost no inventory?"

The boy shrugged. "This is just between us," he whispered, leaning in toward Meghan. "The store is under some major pressure from Corporate, and from what my manager told me, we might be going under."

Meghan's eyes widened. "Seriously?"

"Yeah," the boy nodded. "It's awful; I've worked here for two years, and when you make it to your third year, you get a big bonus. If we close before next October, I won't get my bonus, and I'll have no job."

"That's terrible," she said. "Do you think things will get better?"

The boy shook his head. "Rumor around the staff lounge is that cuts are going to be made soon. Those at the bottom of the seniority list will be let go, and then, they'll start working down from the top. It's a mess."

Meghan gave him a sympathetic look. "I'm sorry to hear that. Business can be so complicated."

The boy raised an eyebrow. "You know, you look familiar. I've seen you before. Aren't you Meghan Truman, the owner of that little bakery?"

Meghan smiled. "Guilty as charged."

"Are you hiring by any chance?" whispered the boy as Meghan bit her lip. "A few buddies from the store and I could really use something more stable. Any way you would take on some extra hands in the New Year?"

Meghan pursed her lips. "I'm not sure about that," she admitted. "Things are very stable at my bakery, and I don't know how I could budget for additional staff. I'll keep you in my thoughts, though. I'm sorry things are tense here at the store."

The boy gave Meghan a weak smile. "Thanks," he said. "And by the way, there's rack of nice clothes for women upstairs. It's the last of our women's inventory, and we just set it out today. You had better make your way up there before someone else gets to it."

"Thanks," Meghan said. "And happy holidays."

An hour later, the three ladies were sipping on coffee at Bean, the coffee shop around the corner from the bakery. Meghan was friendly with the owner, and he always gave her a discount on her lattes.

"I think it's cute," Karen argued with Rebecca over the outfit she had chosen. "It's not designer, and it's not fancy, but I think the lilac will be such a pretty color on you."

"Yes, it will," Meghan agreed. "Mama, everything doesn't always have to be fancy, and I think it's good you made a purchase. The sales associate told me the store is struggling, and I'm glad we could help."

Rebecca rolled her eyes. "Meghan, what have I told you? You cannot get invested in the business of salespeople. If the store is struggling, that isn't our problem. I just hope this lilac suit will be worth the thirty dollars I paid for it."

"At least it was a bargain," Meghan offered as Rebecca scoffed.

"Hey, what's that on the news?" Karen asked, pointing at the little television in the corner of the coffee shop. "That looks like the department store."

"Let me go turn it up," Meghan replied. She walked to the television and turned up the volume. A gaggle of employees from the store were being featured, and Meghan spotted the sales associate who had helped her. The screen then flashed back to a red-haired reporter holding a green microphone.

"Breaking news from our local department store," the reporter stated as she grimly read from the offscreen teleprompter. "Christian Evans, the managing director of the store, is under investigation for fraudulent activities. He is also reported to have embezzled over a quarter of a million dollars from the store's employee compensation account."

"Mama, did you hear that?" Meghan asked as she stared at the screen. "That explains why the racks were so bare."

"In a statement from the Corporate office in Indianapolis, Indiana, it appears that if the allegations are true, the Sandy Bay location will be shut down immediately."

The shot flashed to a suited woman with glasses shaking her head at the camera. "I'm Miranda Mullins, the CEO, and it is a shame that this is happening in one of our stores," she lamented. "This has jeopardized the health of our company. From my records, it appears we wouldn't have even been able to sponsor the $25,000

Santa Claus competition in Sandy Bay given our finances. What a shame."

Meghan's jaw dropped. She turned the volume back down on the television and returned to her seat. "Can you believe that?" she asked her mother and Karen. "That Christian Evans stole all of that money, and now, his people will be out of jobs."

Karen shook her head. "Christian has always been a greedy scoundrel," she informed the group. "I grew up with him; he's a Sandy Bay local, but he doesn't have a Sandy Bay heart. He used to steal money from our school charities when we were children, and I heard that when he divorced his wife, he left her with nothing. No, I can't say I'm surprised he's behind something like this."

Rebecca clucked. "He is innocent until proven guilty," she haughtily told Karen. "We shouldn't jump to conclusions."

Meghan frowned. "I think it's a pretty clear conclusion," she said slowly. "The man who was set to win the $25,000 prize dies out of the blue, and then it comes out that there was going to be no prize and the department store is going under? It sounds fishy to me."

Karen's lips turned downward into a frown. "Meghan, do you think Jack knows anything about this? I think Christian Evans is the perfect suspect; he has the motive and the means, and I wouldn't be shocked if he killed that fellow with his own two greedy hands."

Meghan whipped out her cell phone and began dialing. "I think you're right," she agreed. "I'm giving Jack a call right now."

Jack picked up on the first ring. "Sweetheart?"

"Jack, have you seen the news?" Meghan asked. "That Christian Evans guy? The manager at the department store? I think he has a serious reason to have done away with the man who died."

Jack groaned. "Ugh, I was hoping that news wouldn't be broken so quickly," he admitted. "I didn't want it to turn into a field day at the department store. Don't worry, babe; we have our team investigating Mr. Evans. We've been watching him for weeks."

Meghan smiled, relieved that Jack knew of her concerns. "You're always on the case, Jack," she gushed. "You're always on top of things."

15

It was a truly festive evening at the bakery. Meghan had ordered three boxes of holiday decorations from Spark, and as Jack and Pamela helped her dress up Truly Sweet, Christmas music played in the background. Meghan had made a plate of fresh, steaming cinnamon rolls for the occasion, and as she hung ornaments and strung lights, her heart was filled with joy.

"This is my favorite time of the year," Pamela exclaimed as she wound a strand of garland around the front counter. "It's just magical!"

"I agree," Jack replied as he took a sip of the coffee Meghan had made for him. He was still working double shifts, and she was thrilled that he was able to steal away for a few hours to help her decorate.

Meghan smiled as she reached into the last of the three boxes from Spark. "Oooh, look at these," she said to Pamela and Jack. "A set of jingle bells! They are so shiny and beautiful. The designs on each bell are just spectacular."

Pamela dropped the strand of garland and ran to Meghan's side. "Wow," she murmured in appreciation as she examined the jingle bells. "They are gorgeous, Meghan. Can I hang them up somewhere special?"

"Of course," she answered. "Jingle bells bring good luck! Why don't you hang them on the register, Pamela? Maybe they'll bring good luck to my business."

Pamela laughed at Meghan's joke. "This place looks so pretty. Thanks for inviting me to help you deck the halls."

Suddenly, Meghan heard the familiar tone of Jack's work phone. She groaned, disappointed that her beloved boyfriend would likely be called to the station sooner than later.

"This is Detective Irvin," Jack answered in a business-like tone. "Yes, Chief, I am available."

Meghan's heart sank. She had been having such an enjoyable evening, and now, Jack would have to leave. He had been so busy with work lately, and she felt as though they had hardly gotten to do any fun, festive holiday activities. She tried to keep a pleasant look on her face as Jack hung up the phone and walked to her, but Meghan felt the frown creep across her lips.

"What's wrong?" Jack asked.

"Nothing," Meghan responded. "I'm just sad that you have to leave. That was Chief Nunan, I heard. Do you have to go?"

Jack nodded. "I'm sorry," he said. "It's for work. Surely you understand."

Meghan bit her lip. "I've just had to understand a lot, lately," she said sharply. "You've been working so much."

Jack thought for a moment. "I have an idea," he said. "Chief Nunan said they'll only need me for an hour or so. How about you send

Pamela home, and then you can ride with me to the station? We can go out for a drink or a treat after. What do you say?"

Meghan paused, but seeing the hopeful look in Jack's eyes, she smiled. "That sounds fine," she told him.

When Jack and Meghan arrived at the station twenty minutes later, Chief Nunan met them at the door. "It's a big break, Jack," she told him as they walked down the hall toward the interrogation room. "He told us he is ready to confess, but for some reason, he wanted you in attendance."

Meghan's eyes widened. "Should I go to your office?"

Jack nodded. "Yes," he agreed. "Wait for me. This shouldn't take long."

When Jack returned to his office, his face was shell-shocked. "You won't believe what's happened," he whispered to Meghan.

"What's going on?" Meghan asked.

Jack took a long, deep breath. "Well, he didn't quite confess to murder," Jack informed Meghan as she leaned forward in her chair. "He told me he and Roger had been sharing a bottle of vodka together on the night Roger died. They drank too much, and when Alan regained consciousness, he was lying in front of the toy store downtown. Roger was gone."

Meghan raised an eyebrow. "I don't understand," she murmured.

"There's more," Jack said. "Alan confessed that he and Roger were close friends. They had a falling out awhile back, but they were buddies. They told each other everything."

Meghan shook her head. "I don't understand."

Jack closed his eyes. "I think Alan knows more than he is letting on," he told Meghan. "It just doesn't make sense that these two old pals could spend the evening together, and then, Roger ended up dead. Alan has too much to lose in this case. I'm ordering him thrown back in jail, and I'm going to find out just how he killed Roger. Maybe he worked with Christian Evans, or maybe he worked alone, but either way, I have a feeling that he had something to do with it."

16

"Mama? Mama, you forgot your sweater at the bakery. I came by to return it, like you asked me to."

Meghan stood outside of her parents' hotel room, hoping they were available. She had been just about to close her eyes for a quick nap when her phone had rung; Rebecca insisted that she come to the hotel to return the sweater immediately, and Meghan had dutifully agreed. Now, as she stood in the hallway, she wished she had let her phone go to voicemail and taken her nap.

"Henry, I want to move here full time," she heard her mother shout through the thick oak door. "It isn't fair that I can't make the decision myself, and I think you are being a bully about this!"

Meghan heard the anger in her mother's voice, and she pressed her ear against the door. "Moving to Sandy Bay full-time is impossible, Rebecca," Henry announced. "I have business to attend to in Texas! You have your groups and social activities. Why would you want to give all of that up for this dinky little town?"

Meghan heard her mother sniffle. "I miss our Meghan," Rebecca cried. "She's been away for so long. We are practically strangers! She doesn't understand my sense of humor, or style, and I don't understand hers. I want to change that, Henry."

"Then why don't we stick with the original plan and buy a second home here?" Henry asked.

"It isn't enough," Rebecca pleaded. "I can tell that Meghan is in love with Jack, and before we know it, she will be getting married and having babies. I want some time to get to know my daughter as an adult, and I want that time before she is consumed with being a wife and a mother. I don't think that is too much to ask."

There was a long pause, and Meghan decided to let herself into the hotel room. She opened the door, and her parents stared at her. "Meghan," Rebecca exclaimed. "What are you doing here?"

Meghan held the mint green designer sweater up for her mother to see. "You asked me to bring this to you, remember?"

Rebecca nodded and smiled through her tears. "Of course, dear. I sure hope you didn't hear your Daddy and I quarreling in here. It's rude to let others hear your private matters, you know."

Henry nodded. "Your mother and I were just discussing the holiday," he lied to his daughter as Meghan politely nodded.

"Yes," Rebecca confirmed. "The holiday. Anyway, my phone is ringing; let me take this, and Henry? Can you offer Meghan some refreshments?"

Henry ushered Meghan further into the hotel suite. It was a magnificent set of rooms complete with an opulent master bedroom, a spare bedroom, three bathrooms, an in-suite study, and a personal butler to meet guests' every need. "This is a nice place, Daddy," Meghan said in awe as she examined the art on the wall. "This is nicer than my apartment."

"You know how your mother likes nice things," Henry told his daughter as he gestured at a leather armchair. "Sit down, Meghan. It's nearly happy hour. What can I make you to drink?"

Meghan thought for a moment. "A Tom Collins?"

"Coming right up," Henry informed her, walking to the yellow telephone on the wall and giving it a ring. "Hello? This is Henry Truman, and I would like to order a Tom Collins, a gin on the rocks, and a whiskey sour. Yes, we would also like some appetizers. Let's get an order of the spinach dip, the crab legs, eighteen oysters... no, make that twenty-four, and a spread of cheese and pate. Yes, charge it to the room. Thank you."

Meghan smiled. "You have quite the appetite, Daddy," she said as Henry settled in the chair next to hers.

Henry shrugged. "Your mother likes to have options," he explained. "And frankly, I am worn out from arguing with her. I need some food in my belly if I'm going to go around with her about it again."

"About what, Daddy?" Meghan pried.

Henry gave his daughter a knowing look. "I'm sure you heard us from the hallway," he stated. "Your mother wants to move here permanently, and much as I would love to be near you full time, my dear, it just won't work for our businesses. This is one of your mother's flights of fancy, and she just needs to accept that we are not moving here."

Suddenly, Rebecca burst into the sitting room, a joyful look on her face. "That was Kayley Kane on the phone," she exclaimed. "She has a new property that has everything I want, Henry! Everything. She assures me that it will meet all of my needs, and that it will be to my liking."

Henry shifted in his chair. "Rebecca, we just spoke about this," he told his wife. "Why don't you sit down? It's almost happy hour, and I've ordered snacks and drinks for all of us. I ordered you a whiskey sour, just the way you like it. Sit down, my dear, and let's just enjoy this time together. I don't want to spend another minute of our visit with Meghan fighting about properties or second homes."

Rebecca glared at her husband. "Henry, this is important to me," she hissed. "I want to see this property, and I want you to go with me. You are my husband, and I can't finalize anything without you. Come with me, fall in love with the place, and let's pursue it together. Please?"

Meghan stifled a giggle as her mother pouted dramatically, extending her bottom lip out and making sad eyes at Henry.

"Fine," Henry said. "Fine. But I hope you remember this in two weeks when we vacation in Greece. You will inevitably do this same song and dance and beg for a home there, and my answer will be…"

"Your answer will be whatever makes me happy," Rebecca informed her husband as she winked at him. "Meghan, this is a great lesson for you for someday: happy wife, happy life. Isn't that right, Henry, my love?"

The Trumans bundled up and walked the two blocks to Kayley's office. As Henry held the door for his wife and daughter, Lewis Templeton, the manager of the fine hotel where they were staying, marched outside with a grin on his face. He stopped to greet the Trumans, and Meghan was surprised with how familiar Lewis was with her parents; he kissed Rebecca on both cheeks and gave Henry a firm handshake.

"The Trumans," Lewis gushed. "Such lovely people. It's been such a delight hosting you in my hotel."

Rebecca blushed. Lewis was very handsome, and Meghan could see her mother's cheeks burning as she reveled in Lewis' compliments.

"You are a doll," Rebecca told Lewis. "You truly know good service, unlike other businesses around here. We went into that department store, and they had next to nothing on their racks. Unacceptable, yes?"

"Oh, yes," Lewis cooed as he dusted lint from his perfectly tailored trousers. "To be honest, I am happy they might be going out of business."

"Oh?" Meghan asked. "Why is that?"

Lewis shrugged. "I feel torn regarding that department store's dealings with the homeless. On one hand, I think it's amazing that they gave away so much money to help someone get back on their feet. I do, however, think that we have a homeless problem here in Sandy Bay. The economic impact of the homeless population is undeniable; when they loiter, businesses typically see a decrease in their revenue, and as someone invested in this town's prosperity, I find it alarming that we encourage them through the department store contest."

Meghan raised an eyebrow at Lewis, who stared into her dark eyes. He adjusted his popped collar and cleared his throat. "Look," he said to Meghan. "I love this town, just like you, Meghan, and I want it to grow. I have brought in so much business with the hotel, and I want to attract the right crowds. Like your parents. Rebecca and Henry are our ideal clients, and I want to see more fine people exploring what our sleepy little town has to offer. Sandy Bay is so beautiful, and with its proximity to the sea, well, I think we should be seeing more tourism than we are."

Meghan bit her lip. "I don't get it," she said to Lewis. "What does that have to do with our homeless population?"

Lewis sighed. "We have such a large homeless population," he said. "And "I think they drive away the right kind of people. Your mother told me that the group of homeless people outside of Luciano's was disturbing to her, and I can only imagine it would be disturbing to others."

"But there are homeless people everywhere," Meghan countered.

"Not so," Lewis argued. "Plenty of finer communities have rules that make it impossible for them to simply camp out in the towns. It's time we adopted those rules. I just met with Kayley about purchasing that lot next to Luciano's for a boutique inn, but I told her that if we can't eradicate the problem outside of Luciano's, I will have to pass on the property."

Meghan's eyes widened. "You mean eradicate the homeless?"

Lewis nodded. "Precisely. They simply must go if this town is going to thrive, Meghan, and I'm not going to let a gang of hooligans prevent my boutique inn from being the next best business in Sandy Bay. Thankfully, she has another perfect little bungalow ready for me to buy that isn't teeming with scoundrels. Anyway, I have to run; I'm due for some shopping and tea soon, and I'm already late. Toodles, Trumans!"

Meghan's heart pounded as her parents led her into Kayley's office. "Lewis seemed awfully eager to do away with the homeless people. Could he have anything to do with…"

"Trumans!" Kayley screeched as they walked into her office, interrupting Meghan's train of thought. "What a pleasure. Sit down, all of you."

"Nice to see you again, Ms. Kane," Rebecca said politely. "Tell me what you called us in for. We want all the details."

Kayley glowed. "It's been such a great day," she chirped. "Lewis wanted to buy the property next to Luciano's, but another buyer came through last minute, so I was able to make quite the commission. Now, I have found the perfect property for you."

Meghan gasped. "So does the new owner care about the homeless people out front? Isn't that what Lewis was concerned about?"

Kayley winked. "I will take care of that little issue, no problem. Besides, it was the Luciano family who purchased the lot. They decided to get it and expand their business! Now, Trumans, let's get down to business. I have the ideal location for you. This property is on the coast, just outside of town. The main house has ten bedrooms, a workout facility, and an infinity pool on the second-story terrace. There is also a guest house with its own bedroom, bathroom, and kitchen, a pool house, and a private dock."

Henry grinned. "Private dock, huh? Okay, Rebecca, Ms. Kane has my attention now."

Kayley beamed. "With its marble fireplaces, original wood floors, and elegant interior, this property is one of the hottest on the entire west coast right now. There's even a little building on the property that could be turned into a shop for you to run in your spare time, Mrs. Truman."

Rebecca's eyes shined. "I think it sounds marvelous," she breathed as Kayley's face lit up like a star on a Christmas tree. "Kayley, I think you need to tell me every little detail."

Meghan raised her eyebrows, still thinking about their encounter with Lewis earlier. She was dismayed by his attitude toward the homeless, and his comment about eradicating them had startled her. "Kayley?"

Kayley looked up from the photographs of the beach property. "Yes, Meghan?"

Meghan took a deep breath. "Kayley, can you tell me more about the property next to Luciano's? I'm just confused as to why they would choose to expand at this kind of time. What is Roberto thinking?"

Kayley shrugged. "It isn't my business," she said. "But to be honest, Roberto wasn't really the one driving the purchase..."

"Maria wants to expand?" Meghan asked. "His wife?"

Kayley shook her head. "No, it was Angela. She came in here with a business plan and some ideas, and after she and Lewis went around and around on bids, it appeared that Angela's offer was the best. It works out well for all involved, as I was able to sell another property to Lewis at a great price."

Suddenly, there was a knock on the door of Kayley's office. The Trumans' heads turned, and everyone smiled as Angela Luciano walked into the room.

"Speak of the devil," Henry said as he rose to his feet and shook Angela's hand. "Sounds like congratulations are in order, little lady. Ms. Kane here just told us that you purchased the lot next to your father's business and are hoping to expand."

Angela grinned. "Yes," she confirmed. "My father is letting me handle the expansion deal; we are going to put in a little Italian dessert alcove that connects to our restaurant. It will feature some of Italy's finest sweet treats, and I could not be more excited to handle this responsibility. I am honored my father and mother trust me so!"

Rebecca kissed Angela on both cheeks. "How lovely for you," she cooed. "We will certainly have to try your new place when it opens."

Angela nodded, her face bright with excitement. "That would be fantasticio," she declared. "We love having Jack and Meghan in for dinner, and we have certainly loved getting to know Meghan's lovely family."

Kayley interjected. "Speaking of Meghan's lovely family, I was just in a meeting with them to discuss a new property," Kayley matter-of-factly told Angela. "Was I expecting you, Angela?"

"Oh, no," Angela told Kayley. "My father wanted me to stop by and see if you had the papers drawn up yet, and I was in the neighborhood and wanted to check."

Kayley shook her head. "No, they will be ready tomorrow," she told Angela. "But let me finish my meeting with the Trumans, and I'll be right with you."

"You found a property?" Angela asked Rebecca. "How exciting. I suppose congratulations are in order for you as well. Sandy Bay is a world class town, and I am so happy to see it blossom."

Rebecca smiled. "We haven't decided yet," she told Angela as she glanced at her husband. "But I think we will make it work."

"That's wonderful," Angela exclaimed. "What a wonderful day for Sandy Bay to have the Trumans being part of our community."

At that moment, Meghan was hit with the realization that she was supposed to meet Jack for a movie at six. She glanced at her watch and realized it was six-fifteen. She frantically pulled out her cell phone and dialed Jack's number.

"Meghan, what are you doing?" Rebecca asked her daughter. "We're having a conversation with Angela and Kayley. Put your phone down right now."

"Sorry, Mama," she apologized. "I can't. I didn't expect to be at your hotel today, and I completely forgot about my plans to meet Jack for a movie. I need to call him quickly. Excuse me."

Meghan stepped out of Kayley's office. As she closed the door, Jack picked up the phone call.

"Meghan? Where are you? Are you okay?"

She felt a knot in her stomach as she heard the concern in Jack's voice. "I'm fine," she told him. "Totally fine. I ended up running over to my parents' hotel room, and they coerced me into visiting Kayley Kane's office."

"What?" Jack asked in confusion.

"Kayley is looking for properties for my parents, remember? She found something Mama is interested in, and Mama dragged us all here tonight."

Jack sighed. "Well, I'm glad you are fine. I was worried about you."

"So sorry, Jack," she said. "I got caught here talking with my parents, Kayley, and Angela."

"Angela? Angela Luciano?"

"Yes, Angela Luciano," Meghan said. "What other Angelas do we know?"

"What is she doing at Kayley's office with you and your family?"

"I guess she purchased that lot next to her family business," she told him. "She's going to turn it into an Italian dessert place and attach it to her restaurant. Obviously, I don't love having her as competition; Angela is basically perfect in every regard. Like today, for example, I show up to this office in my sweats, and Angela is wearing this gorgeous red poncho that brings out her eyes. I feel like some unsightly potato, haha. I am, however, excited to try some of her authentic Italian treats. Maybe she and I can collaborate on something in the future."

Jack took a long breath. "Meghan? Is Angela sitting next to you right now?"

"No," she replied.

"Where is she?"

"She's in Kayley's office chatting with my folks. I stepped out to give you a call."

The phone went dead, and Meghan tried to redial Jack's number. It went straight to his voicemail, and Meghan pursed her lips. She walked back into the office and resumed her place in the chair beside her parents.

"How is Jack? Was he fussy that you forgot about your plans? Really, Meghan, I didn't raise you like this; you should have a proper day planner and write down your engagements so that you don't miss anything."

Meghan gritted her teeth as her mother chided her. "Jack is fine," she told Rebecca. "He didn't seem mad.

"I would have been downright annoyed," Henry announced as Rebecca nodded. "It's not nice to miss dates."

Meghan pasted a smile on her lips. "Well, he said it is fine," she reiterated. "The only weird part of our conversation was the end. He hung up the phone abruptly, or his phone died. It was weird. I tried dialing it back, and I can't get through to him."

"Maybe missing your date wasn't as "okay" as you thought," Rebecca smirked.

The color drained from Angela's face. "I really should be going," she said as she rose to her feet and pushed in her chair. "Kayley, it was a pleasure, as always. Trumans, I hope to see you all before you leave. Ciao for now, to all of you."

"Stop right there."

Meghan gasped as Jack appeared in the doorway, a gun in his hand. Behind him were three other Sandy Bay police officers, all holding weapons of their own.

"Jack? What's going on here?" Meghan whimpered.

"That's a nice gun," Henry chuckled. "The boy will fit right in in Texas, won't he, Rebecca?"

Jack shook his head. "This is no time for jokes," he declared. "Angela Luciano, you are under arrest for the murder of Roger Williams!"

17

"What?" Angela sputtered as everyone stared at her. "What are you talking about, Jack?"

"It's Detective Irvin to you," he told Angela as he fastened a pair of handcuffs around her slim wrists. "Angela, we have hard evidence of your crimes. It's time you come with us to the station."

Angela squirmed as a female deputy helped her to her feet. "Get off of me," she cried. "I had nothing to do with Roger's death. I wouldn't kill a fly."

"You may not kill flies," Jack announced. "But you certainly made your mark on the homeless population here by killing five homeless people in the last two weeks, starting with Roger."

Meghan gasped. "Jack, this can't be true. Angela is a devoted volunteer for the homeless. She is a champion for their plight. You should see her at the food bank; she has such a passion for helping them."

Jack scoffed. "More like a passion for murdering them," he corrected his girlfriend. "We have proof that Angela Luciano killed several homeless people in cold blood."

"Jack, this is terribly frightening," Rebecca whimpered. "Put those guns down."

"Seriously," Kayley snapped. "You're gonna break something in my office. Either get Angela out of here, or you get out of here, Jack."

Jack motioned to the female deputy to take Angela away, but Henry stepped between her and Angela. "Now, Jack," Henry argued. "This little lady and her family have been nothing but good to my family. It would be a shame to further distress her. Look how scared she is."

"Yes," Angela sobbed. "I am so scared. Please, Jack, let me go."

"It's Detective Irvin," Jack replied coldly. "And Henry? I need you to sit down; I'm doing my job here, and you are in the way. Have a seat."

Henry frowned, but obeyed Jack's order. Jack turned to stare at Angela.

"Angela, I have no choice here; there is evidence that you are to blame for these deaths, and I am under orders to take you in."

The female officer led Angela out of the office, and Jack nodded at Kayley and the Trumans. "I apologize that you had to see that," he said as he put his hands in his pockets.

Meghan frowned. "What is the evidence, Jack?" she asked. "Everyone in town knows that Christian Evans killed Roger. What about Lewis from the hotel? Maybe he had something to do with it. I talked to him today, and he said some nasty things about the homeless people."

Jack pursed his lips. "Saying nasty things and doing nasty things are two different stories," he explained to his girlfriend. "We have investigated Christian's misdeeds, and he is guilty of a lot, but he has not killed anyone. Lewis is just full of hot air, Meghan. It's Angela who killed Roger, along with several others, and it's Angela who is on her way to jail."

Rebecca frowned. "It just seems scandalous to take a pretty young lady like Angela off to jail," she admonished.

Jack shook his head. We have proof. One of the busboys at Luciano's took his dog into the vet; he thought the dog had been poisoned by a mean neighbor, and he filed a complaint with the police."

Henry wrinkled his nose. "What does a sick dog have to do with any of this?"

"A lot, actually," Jack continued. "We looked into the complaint, and after speaking with the busboy, we learned that Angela had stayed late at the restaurant the night the dog became ill. We went through the sick dog's stool, and after testing, it was determined that the only thing in his stomach was food from Luciano's. Just for curiosity's sake, I decided to review the security footage from outside of Luciano's that night. Well, who was outside at 1am?"

Henry shook his head. "I don't understand this, Jack."

Jack shrugged. "Angela was outside, and the footage caught her feeding sandwiches to the little dog right before she took a bag of sandwiches to the homeless fellows outside. We have footage that shows her giving them food. Most of them were asleep, and the fellow who died, Roger, gobbled up all the sandwiches by himself."

Meghan's eyes widened. "So Angela gave poisoned food to the dog and the homeless guys?"

"Exactly." Jack confirmed.

"Are you sure about this, Jack?"

Jack smiled. "I wasn't sure until ten minutes ago when Meghan and I spoke," he said. "The security footage was grainy enough that we couldn't quite make out the face of the killer, but we could see them in a red poncho. Well, remember what Angela was wearing?"

Meghan gasped. "She was wearing her red poncho," she whispered. "The same one Jack had described from the film."

Jack nodded. "It's terrible," he admitted. "But think about it: she has a clear motive. Angela wanted to get rid of the homeless population one by one so that she could continue to grow her business. It makes sense. I can't believe I didn't think of it sooner."

Rebecca slumped back in her chair. "Well, that was a shock," she uttered as she dramatically fanned her face. "I cannot believe that Angela was the killer. What a terrible crime from such a lovely girl."

Henry shook his head. "That's what happens when ambition turns to poison," he declared. He pointed a finger at Meghan. "Don't you ever let your business stand in the way of you doing the right thing and treating people well. Business and ambition can turn even the purest hearts to stone, and that's what happened to Angela Luciano."

"Oh, Daddy," Meghan said as she reached to hug her father. "I love my work, and I love serving the people of Sandy Bay, but my business is just a business to me. I'm passionate about my shop, but I would never, ever harm anyone in pursuit of my own success."

"Good girl," Henry said as he hugged his daughter. "And Ms. Kane, I hope you follow the same principles. I know you are a successful gal, but I hope tonight's events teach you a good lesson, too."

Kayley stared at Mr. Truman. She yawned, looking bored, and examined her nails.

"Kayley?" Mr. Truman pressed.

Kayley sighed. "I'll never let my business or ambitions stand in the way of someone else's health or well-being," she said robotically as Henry and Rebecca nodded and smiled. "But that doesn't mean I won't do everything in my power to get to the top every other way."

Meghan laughed. "We know, Kayley," she said. "We know."

That night, Meghan shared a quiet dinner with her parents back at the hotel. The news of Angela's arrest was all over Sandy Bay, and Meghan wanted a reprieve from the heinous story of the beautiful, remorseless killer. She ordered a variety of tacos and three types of queso from her favorite street taco vendor and asked her father to order margaritas from the hotel bar.

"That's a lot of fattening food," Rebecca said as Meghan walked in with the bags of tacos.

"Daddy said you like options, so I brought options," Meghan replied. "Besides, we had a long night, and I need some good food to help me relax. Come on, Mama, try the pork tacos. Or try the fish tacos. I think you will love the lime sauce."

Rebecca sighed, but took a seat next to Meghan on the velvet couch. She unwrapped a chicken taco and took a bite. "This is quite good," she admitted. "Thank you for bringing dinner to us."

"No problem," Meghan said. "It's the least I could do. I know you are upset now that the beach house deal is off."

Rebecca shrugged. "Given tonight's events, your father and I just don't feel as though it's the right time or place to make such an investment," she told her daughter. "We do want to see you more, Meghan, and we are going to make every effort to be bigger parts of your life. We love you, and we miss you, and we want to watch you grow into the wonderful woman you are becoming."

Meghan's eyes filled with tears at her mother's compliments. Rebecca was certainly hard to please, and Meghan was thrilled that her mother acknowledged her hard work and growth. "Thank you, Mama," Meghan whispered as she returned her taco to its plate and hugged her mother.

"Careful, this dress is Dior," Rebecca warned Meghan as she leaned away.

"Your mother and I have talked, and we want you and Jack to visit us in Texas in the New Year," Henry announced as he strode into the sitting area carrying a tray of margaritas. "Jack is a good man, and he will take care of you. I trust him, and I think we need to get to know him better."

Meghan smiled. "I would like that, Daddy," she told him.

"Perfect," he said. "We'll purchase some tickets for you two for Christmas. How does first-class sound? That will be our gift to the pair of you, a trip to Texas on us."

"That sounds amazing," Meghan squealed, jumping up to hug her father. "What a sweet gift. Thank you both!"

18

One week later, on Christmas Eve, Meghan and Jack were hosting the Trumans for a farewell brunch at Truly Sweet. Meghan had gone above and beyond to cook a feast her parents would love; she had made gourmet omelettes, chicken sausage, fresh caramel strudel, and a hot plate of turkey bacon. Jack had helped set the table with Meghan's nicest dishes, and as they ate, Meghan's parents clucked over the meal she had prepared.

Meghan was quite proud of herself. Dressed in her favorite maroon dress, her dark hair tumbled down her back, and from the look on Jack's face when she answered the door, she knew she looked beautiful. Her mother had even complimented her on the outfit, and as she served brunch to her parents, Meghan felt as though she were finally being treated as the adult business owner she was.

"It's perfect, Meghan," Henry told his daughter as he stuffed a third piece of bacon in his mouth.

"Truly sweet, Sugar," Rebecca agreed. "You are quite the hostess. I am so impressed by the little soiree you have thrown together for us. You have been quite the hostess this holiday season!"

Meghan smiled. Her mother was referring to the event she had held at the bakery the previous day. Given the events of the season, Meghan's heart hurt for the homeless population in Sandy Bay. She, Pamela, Trudy, and Rebecca had spent an entire day preparing an abundance of treats, and Meghan had hosted a holiday celebration for the homeless folks in town. She had hired a group of carolers to sing festive songs, made pretty decorations, and even organized a variety of games and activities for her guests. The event had made the local news, and Meghan was pleased to learn that the publicity had drawn attention to the homeless population, and donations had been flooding in for the food bank.

"This is a great thing you're doing for the folks who are down on their luck," Jack had told Meghan at the event. "You are a truly sweet woman, Meghan."

"It's my pleasure to do it for them," Meghan told her boyfriend. "These people have so little and we have so much. Why not take time to give back? This is the way businesses should be run--to not only make profits, but to give back to the community."

The event drew over ninety people into the bakery, and Meghan was pleased that every last treat had been taken by the end of the night. As she showered and prepared for bed after she had bid the last guest farewell, she was certain that she had done the right thing by opening her business to those in need. She loved serving others, and she made a vow to keep the homeless in mind as she moved forward.

Now, on Christmas Eve, Meghan was glowing as she basked in the attention of her parents.

Meghan leaned back in her chair, pleased by their compliments. "Thank you both," she told them. "And thank you for visiting. I am so sad that you are leaving today, and I am so disappointed that you won't be buying a second home here."

Rebecca shrugged. "It was going to be an impulse buy," she admitted. "Now that I know that you are safe here with Jack, I don't think we need to buy another home. I do, however, think that we need to invest in a better airline credit card, don't you, Henry? We will be missing our girl terribly, and I want to visit Sandy Bay more than once a year! We can't wait for you two to visit Texas, but I don't want to wait until the summer to see you again. I plan to visit next month, and Henry, I hope you will help me make the arrangements."

Henry nodded. "Yes, we will certainly do that," he told his wife. "I'm just glad to know that the homeless population here is not dangerous. It was a shock to hear that Angela killed that man, but the entire situation has just touched my heart. Meghan, your mother and I have agreed to donate ten thousand dollars to the food bank this Christmas, and we want you to deliver the check to the organization."

Meghan's eyes filled with tears. "Thank you, Daddy," she murmured as she rose from her chair and moved to hug her father. "Thank you, Mama. This means so much to me."

Henry nodded. "We were just so impressed with your kindness," he told his daughter. "You gave away so many of your treats to the homeless, not to mention your attention and time. That spirit of philanthropy inspired me, Meghan, and I plan to incorporate that into my own business ventures. You have certainly made us proud."

Jack also rose to his feet and gently tapped Henry on the shoulder. "Henry? Can we talk privately for a moment?"

Henry nodded and followed Jack into the kitchen. "Henry," Jack began as he shifted nervously. "I love your daughter. I would do anything for her. She is an amazing woman, and I have something I need to ask you."

Henry smiled. "I think I know where this is going. What do you need to ask me, Jack?"

Jack grinned. "I want you to know that I am saving for a ring for Meghan. With your blessing, I want to ask her to marry me in the year to come. I will have enough money put away to buy a ring in a few months, and by next Christmas, I would like for Meghan to be my wife."

Henry beamed. He pulled Jack into a tight hug. "You have my blessing, sport," he told Jack. "Now, just make sure you run that ring by Rebecca before you buy it; Meghan's mother has an affinity for nice things, and surely she'll want you to have her opinion. Meghan is easy to please; surely she will love whatever you find for her, but you know my wife..."

Jack laughed. "I'm sure that will be an interesting conversation when the time comes. Anyway, thank you for your support, Henry. It truly means the world. I cannot wait to ask Meghan to marry me. Now, I just need to keep saving for the ring, and I need to plan the proposal."

Henry shook Jack's hand. "My pleasure, son. I'm happy for the pair of you. Meghan sparkles when she is with you, and I see from the look in your eyes right now that you are excited at this next step in your life. I remember feeling this way the night I met Rebecca. I was at a party, and I took a bite of this amazing coconut tart. It was topped with roasted pineapple, and it was to die for. Anyway, I asked to meet the cook, and sure enough, Rebecca had made the treat."

Jack smiled. "That's a great story."

Henry nodded. "It gets better. Rebecca's tarts brought us together, and on the night we were engaged, little did I know that she had spent all morning making my favorite tarts for me. Everytime I think about those tarts, and the woman behind them, I get that look in my eye...the same one you have now."

Jack chuckled. "I'm lucky to have found a Truman woman."

Henry winked. "Yes, you are, Jack Irvin. Hmmm. Meghan Irvin. That sounds nice, I think. Now! Let's get back to brunch. I am going to pour some champagne into our orange juices... I believe we have something to celebrate, even if my little girl doesn't know it yet."

Jack followed Henry back into the dining room and grinned as Henry poured the bubbly into everyone's glass.

"Daddy?" Meghan asked. "What is this for? You two are traveling today! Are you sure you want to dive into the champagne?"

Henry winked at his daughter and then shot a look at Jack. Jack blushed, and Henry laughed. "I'm sure, Meghan," Henry said. "Absolutely sure."

"Henry, you know what champagne does to my stomach," Rebecca protested. Henry reached over and whispered Jack's news into Rebecca's ear, and she squealed.

"What, Mama?" Meghan asked. "What is this fuss about?"

Rebecca quickly regained her composure. "Oh, it's nothing, dear," she told her daughter. "Nothing. Let's just have a nice little breakfast drink and a toast."

"A toast," Henry announced. "To our little girl and her big heart, her big business, her big dreams, and her big, bright future. I believe Meghan will have a lot of joy in the year ahead. Merry Christmas to you, my girl, and happy holidays to all of you. Cheers!"

"Cheers!" everyone called out.

As everyone lifted their glasses, Meghan felt a happy tear trail from her eyes. She looked at her father, who was merrily raising a glass in her honor, and to her mother, whose time in Sandy Bay had been precious to her. Meghan lastly looked at Jack, her handsome boyfriend. She loved Jack with all of her heart, and as she sat next to him on Christmas Eve, she hoped that she would spend every Christmas with Jack.

"Cheers," Meghan exclaimed as she lifted her own glass. "Cheers to the sweetest days ahead."

The End

QUEEN TARTS AND A CHRISTMAS NIGHTMARE

1

It was a chilly winter morning in Sandy Bay, a small town on the Pacific Coast. The holidays were just around the corner, and the town was abuzz with merriment as lights were being strung, parties were being held, and the snow began to regularly pour from the sky.

Meghan Truman was elated to be home in Sandy Bay; she had just returned from an impromptu trip to visit her fiancé's parents, and after being cooped up at their home for nearly three weeks, she was ready to be back in her normal routine. Jack, her darling fiancé, had whisked her away practically the moment after he had asked her to marry him; he begged for her to run away to Eagan, his hometown, to spend the Thanksgiving holiday with his family. Filled with the excitement of the engagement, she had obliged, but now, as she walked downstairs to Truly Sweet, the bakery she owned and managed, she was happier than ever to be back in her element.

She opened the door, and Pamela, her sweet teenage employee, rushed at her. "Meghan! You are back! Finally!"

Meghan hugged her. "It's so good to see you."

"I would say it's good to see you too, but the only thing I want to see is the rock!"

Pamela pawed at Meghan's left hand. "It's HUGE!"

"Jack did well," Trudy, her other employee, complimented as she peered at Meghan's ring finger. "That boy has taste."

"It is exactly what I always dreamed of," Meghan gushed, extending her left hand in the air so they could better admire the ring. "I had no idea he was going to propose! We had been bickering, as you remember, but then, before I knew it, he was down on one knee."

"I can't believe he didn't tell me he was going to do it," Pamela pouted, her bangs in her face. "He proposed, and then he kidnapped you to Eagan. How unfair! We wanted to celebrate with you."

"I know," she shrugged. "I didn't expect any of that to happen. Thank you both for holding down the fort here at the bakery. I'm sure you were busy with the Thanksgiving rush. I was just in such shock when he asked me to marry him, and I said yes to going home to celebrate with his parents."

"You mean, your future in-laws," Trudy winked, her eyes sparkling. "They will be your family sooner than later, Meghan. You had better get used to running off to Eagan at a moment's notice."

Meghan laughed. "Oh, come on," she said as she tossed her dark wavy hair behind her shoulders. "I'm twenty-nine years old, not a child, and Jack is into his thirties. The spur-of-the-moment trip was just a chance to celebrate with his family, nothing more. Not a regular thing."

Trudy chuckled. "That's what they all say," she informed Meghan. "It's hard for a grown man to refuse his mama when she asks to see him, just you wait."

"Oh, don't spoil this, Trudy," Pamela chastised. "Meghan, we are both happy for you, and we were happy to help while you were gone. It sounds like you had a good time."

She nodded. "His parents were very sweet," she told them. "His mother gave me a bracelet from Jack's grandmother; she said she wanted to keep it in the family."

"More jewelry?" Pamela screeched as her eyes bugged out of her head. "Let's see it!"

Meghan pulled up the sleeve of her navy blue sweater. "Oh," Pamela sighed. "It's... pretty?"

Meghan giggled. "I don't like it either," she admitted. "It's too chunky for me, and I'm not really a fan of gold. I prefer rose gold or silver. I have to pretend to like it though, so keep it between us. This is our secret."

"Just between us," Pamela agreed as Meghan rolled her sleeve down.

They all heard the familiar chiming of the little silver bells attached to the front door of the bakery. "A customer already?" Trudy wondered aloud. "It's a bit early, isn't it?"

"Where is my gorgeous fiancé?"

Meghan grinned as she heard Jack's voice in the dining room. "Back in the kitchen, babe."

Jack entered the room, and Pamela ran to him, throwing her arms around his middle. "You proposed!" she cried with joy. "You proposed to our Meghan at last! Congratulations, Jack. I am so happy for you. Can I be the flower girl?"

Trudy raised an eyebrow. "You are too old to be a flower girl," she admonished. "You would have to be a bridesmaid or a junior bridesmaid, and that is still only if Meghan asks you. Hinting is rude, so stop it at once."

Jack laughed, his blue eyes dancing as he patted Pamela on the shoulder. "She is just excited," he told the older woman. "And she should be. I know I am. I am marrying the most beautiful girl in the world."

Meghan stuck out her tongue. "Oh yeah? You're marrying some beautiful girl? Who is she?"

He dashed across the kitchen and picked her up, spinning her around and planting a kiss on her lips. "You! It's you, my dear. We are getting married, and I am just so overjoyed. I had to visit the bakery and say hello. I missed you so much."

"We've only been apart an hour!"

"It's an hour too long."

"You two are adorable," Pamela cooed as Meghan kissed Jack's cheek.

"Easy there," Trudy ordered as she slipped her hands over Pamela's eyes. "Keep the public displays of affection on the lowdown, kiddos. Pamela here is just a young one, and we don't want to give her any wrong ideas..."

Pamela pushed Trudy's hands away as Jack placed Meghan back on the ground. "Love isn't a wrong idea!" she declared, reaching for Meghan and Jack's hands. "Love is the best thing in the world, isn't it, guys?"

Meghan turned to gaze into Jack's eyes. She ran a hand through his icy blonde locks. "It is," she agreed. "It is."

After bidding Jack farewell, she and the other women got to work in the bakery. They had a few large orders to fill before the end of the week, and Meghan worked through her lunch break to see the work through. Finally, when her shift was over, she left the building and headed down the block to see Jackie, her friend, and business partner. Jackie owned a salon in town, and together with Meghan, owned and managed a local event space at a barn just outside of town. Meghan hadn't gotten to celebrate her engagement with Jackie yet, and she couldn't wait to see her friend.

"Are you ready to see it?" she teased as she walked into the salon and hugged Jackie.

"Of course I am ready," Jackie told her. "I can't believe you got engaged, ran off out-of-town to Jack's parents, and didn't even send me a photo of your ring. What kind of friend are you?"

"A good one who wanted to share the surprise in person," Meghan said defensively as she slowly pulled her green glove off of her right hand. "Now, do you want to see it or not?"

Jackie reached for Meghan's left hand, tearing off her glove. "Wow! It's gorgeous!"

The light hit the ring perfectly as they both admired it. "The center stone is my favorite," Meghan told her as they stared at the glittering jewel. "But the side stones are from his great-grandmother's art deco ring from the twenties."

"It's exactly what I want someday," Jackie breathed enviously, sliding the ring off Meghan's fingers and placing it onto her hand. "I think my hands were meant to hold fine jewelry, don't you think?"

Meghan felt her phone vibrate in her pocket, but she ignored it; it was probably just Jack trying to see her again. He had been calling and texting nonstop throughout the day, and while she missed him, she needed some time with her friend.

"Sure," Meghan agreed as she reached out her hand, indicating she wanted her ring back. "Sure thing, Jackie."

Jackie pouted as Meghan placed the ring back on her finger. "I just wish I could find someone to be engaged to," she murmured. "Your ring is so pretty, and your wedding will be even prettier."

Meghan shook her head. "It isn't about the ring or even the wedding day," she told Jackie. "It's about being with someone who brings out your best, challenges you, and makes you happy. It's about choosing to be partners with someone, not just during the magic and glitter of an engagement or wedding day, but during the hardships of everyday life. Jack and I have had our difficulties, but I know he loves me, and I know that together, we can be our best. I am so excited to marry him."

Jackie cocked her head to the side. Her newly dyed magenta hair fell in her face, and she frustratedly pushed it out of the way. "I want what you two have," she whispered, hanging her head. "No one has ever loved me the way Jack loves you. My ex-husband certainly didn't think of marriage as you described it. If he did, we'd still be married. I just want someone to love me for me, someone to put a shiny ring on my hand, and someone to do both of those things soon. I'm close to just asking the homeless guy on the corner downtown to marry me. I'm sure he'd be a sweetie…"

Meghan put a hand on Jackie's shoulder. "Hey," she said kindly. "Chin up, my friend. You are a smart, business-minded, funny person. Mr. Right is out there for you. I always thought I would meet the love of my life when I lived in Hollywood, and when I moved to Sandy Bay as a single woman, I had given up hope. The right guy always comes along when you least expect it, when you aren't waiting on him. Just dive into your own life, Jackie. Make yourself the best you can be and do it for you. The man of your dreams will walk into your life when you least expect it, and he'll come sooner than you think. I promise."

Jackie wiped a tear from her eye and nodded. "You're right," she agreed. "I've been spending so much time thinking about how alone I am, and I should concentrate on myself!"

Meghan stifled the urge to roll her eyes. She adored Jackie, but Jackie didn't neglect a single opportunity to concentrate on herself;

she was a sweet but selfish person, but Meghan knew that did not need to be said.

Her phone vibrated again. "Hey, do you mind if I check my phone?" she asked. "It's been going off like crazy. It's probably Jack. I don't mean to be rude, but..."

"Go ahead," Jackie advised. "I don't care."

She realized the calls and messages were not from Jack, but rather from her mother. She opened her messages and saw nearly twenty. "What's going on?" she wondered aloud as she opened the most recent one.

Meghan, I don't know if you are getting your messages or not, but when you do, please call. Your dad is very sick. Please come home as soon as you can. It's urgent.

2

Back at her apartment, Meghan began frantically packing. She had called her mother immediately, and Mrs. Truman informed her that her father was very sick. "You need to come home at once, my sweetheart," she had cried to Meghan. "I'll book you a ticket on the late flight tonight. Just come home!"

She had called Jack, and he rushed over as she began to pull her things together.

"Do you have to go?" Jack asked as Meghan threw a pile of sweaters into her floral Vera Bradley duffle bag. "Babe, you said we would spend the holidays together this year, just the two of us."

Meghan frowned. "Honey," she said through gritted teeth. "I don't think you understand... my mom said he is sick, and that I need to come home. I don't know what's going to happen, but this doesn't sound like great news."

He nodded. "I'm sorry," he told her. "I wish I could help."

"Can you come?" she asked. "I have enough points on my credit card to book a flight for you. I can do it right now."

He shook his head. "I can't," he frowned as she moved on to her underwear drawer and began to dump socks into the bag. "Chief Nunan won't let me take the time; she says if your dad.... well... I have enough bereavement time left for the year...just not personal time."

She folded her arms across her chest. "So if my dad dies, you can come, but otherwise, you're tied up at work?"

Jack came over and wrapped his arms around her. "You know I wish it were different," he murmured into her ear. "I wish I could come. I am going to fly down this weekend if things are still bad; I can switch some shifts with another detective and make it. Is that okay?"

"It will have to be okay," she said coldly.

"I love you," he whispered as he kissed her forehead. "I am so sorry this is happening. What can I do for you?"

She jerked her chin at Fiesta and Siesta, her two twin dogs. "Can you watch the babies? I don't have enough time to pull their carrier out of the attic, and I think they'll just be underfoot if they come to my parents' house in Texas with me..."

"Of course," he said without a pause. "And I'll take you to the airport. Are you ready?"

"Ready."

"Let's go."

They walked downstairs, and Jack helped load Meghan's bag into his squad car. She climbed in, and as she fastened her seatbelt, Jack turned on the sirens. "Are you allowed to do that?"

He winked. "I'm a detective," he told her. "I can do what I want with my car."

They raced toward the airport. Jack reached for Meghan's hand, and he squeezed it. She pulled out her phone and checked her messages.

"They haven't returned my calls in an hour," she fretted. "Why aren't they returning my calls?"

"I'm sure everything is okay," he assured her. "They must be busy, I'm sure. Or perhaps their phones died."

Meghan wriggled anxiously in her seat. "Distract me?" she asked, her dark eyes wide. "Can we talk about something happy?"

He nodded. "Let's talk about.... our engagement," Jack suggested. "What did your parents say when you told them? Were they as happy as my parents?"

Meghan's stomach churned. "Yeah," she told him. "They were happy."

The Truman's had not been happy; Meghan and Jack had broken up a few weeks before he had proposed, and in that time, they had reached out to Fred James, Meghan's high school boyfriend. They had liked Jack enough, but the Truman's had always hoped that Meghan would end up with someone with southern roots and an impressive inheritance. Fred had both things, and Jack did not, and the Truman's, who were from old southern money themselves, were less than thrilled when Meghan had called them to tell them the news of their engagement.

"They weren't happy, were they?" Jack asked as he read Meghan's face.

"No, they were!" she lied. "I think they just wish they could have been here to see our engagement."

"Oh," he said. "Well, I can't wait to see them both soon and celebrate with them. Your dad will be fine, honey. I'm sure it's all under control."

Six hours later, Meghan awoke from a troubled slumber as her plane touched down in Texas. She was not a great flier, nor did she ever sleep well on an airplane, and she rubbed her swollen eyes as passengers began to file into the aisle.

"Meghan?" asked a woman in a southern twang.

Meghan shuddered; she looked exhausted, her clothes were messy, and her family still was not replying to her texts. The last thing she wanted to do was visit with someone from her hometown.

She smiled as a familiar face leaned down and waved at her from two aisles ahead. It was Joy Ford, her friend from high school. She and Joy had been cheerleaders together, and Joy embodied her name; she was one of the sweetest people Meghan had ever met.

"How are you doing?" Meghan asked. "It's been too long!"

"You would know if you made it back to our high school reunion last year," Joy chided her. "I'm just teasing; your mama told me you opened a business and that you were too busy to make it back to old Texas. No hard feelings though; I've always wished you the best, and I am so happy to hear your business is doing well. Your mama speaks so highly of you."

"She does? And what are you doing on this flight? Were you up north?"

"I was at a girls' weekend in Arizona," she informed Meghan. "We must have had the same flight in Phoenix. Oh yes," Joy told her. "She said it disappointed her that you didn't get married out of college like the rest of us girls on the cheer squad, but she is happy you are happy."

"Oh," Meghan replied, feeling disappointed that her mother seemed to still want her to be a proper southern belle. "So, how's married life anyway? I'll be there soon...."

Joy squealed as Meghan flashed her ring. "It's adorable, Meghan!" she told her as she eyed Meghan's ring. "I can tell it has character."

Meghan looked discretely at Joy's left hand. She had been at Joy's wedding and remembered Joy's ring was nice, but now, as she stood with her engagement ring on her hand, she realized Joy's engagement ring was monstrously large; it could have demanded its own zip code, and Meghan felt a brief flash of embarrassment at her simple ring.

"The side stones are from his family," Meghan shrugged as she entered the aisle and followed Joy out of the airplane.

"That's precious," Joy commented, slipping her arm through Meghan's when they reached the airport. "Say, have you heard the news about Trixie? She just inherited her daddy's oil company. And Mandy took over her mama's law firm! Diane is managing her mama's shampoo company, too. Everyone around here is doing well... including Fred James. Remember him? Well, of course you do! Freddy is about to become the richest fellow in town. His daddy is giving him his family business on January 1st! How exciting, right? I'm sure you'll be happy to see everyone and catch up since you are home for Christmas. How long are you home for, anyways?"

Meghan shook her head. "I don't know," she admitted. "I came home last minute. Mama told me my dad isn't doing well, and she begged me to rush home. I'm not sure what's going on, but I need to get home quickly..."

Joy's hazel eyes widened. "You should have said something and stopped me from gabbing," she gasped. "My car is waiting outside; my husband couldn't pick me up, but he sent his driver. Let me get you home!"

Joy and Meghan hurried to the car, and within the hour, Meghan was standing in front of the massive Texas estate where she had grown up. "See you soon," Joy waved as she sped off. "Tell your family I'm praying for them!"

Meghan took a long breath as she stared at the enormous antebellum plantation-style house. She remembered the last time she had stood on the wraparound porch, right before she moved to Los Angeles. Had it been that long since she had been home? She thought about how much she had changed, how much her life had changed, and she wondered what waited for her behind the double doors.

3

"SURPRISE!"

Meghan's jaw dropped; standing in the massive foyer of her parents' home were her mother, father, siblings, and their significant others. Her mother was beaming, and her father ran forward to wrap Meghan in a huge hug.

"What is going on?" Meghan exclaimed, feeling woozy as she smelled the distinct scent of her father's expensive cologne. "Daddy? I thought you were in the hospital! What are you doing home? What is everyone doing here?"

Rebecca, Meghan's mother, stepped forward and clapped her hands excitedly. "We knew this was the only way to get you home for the holidays!" she declared as Meghan gasped. "Your sisters and I played a little trick on you."

Meghan's dark eyes widened. "Daddy? You're okay? There was no emergency?"

Henry Truman shook his head, his eyes sparkling with mischief as he pulled Meghan close into his broad chest. "No emergency," he confirmed. "I just wanted to see all of my children home for the holidays, and your mama suggested this little scheme to get my baby girl here!"

Meghan pushed away from her father. "Does everyone know? Does Jack know? Was he in on this?"

Rebecca's face darkened. "No," she sighed. "We didn't want him to ruin the surprise."

Mandy, Meghan's younger sister, nodded. "Jack didn't come down here and ask us if he could marry you," she said snottily. "So we didn't think to include him in on this little surprise."

Meghan shook her head. "That's terrible," she murmured as she bit her lip. "He's worried sick about you, Daddy. You should have let him know what was going on."

"He should have shown up down here with you if he truly thought there was a problem," Henry countered. "Now, enough of this talk. Give your daddy a proper hug."

Meghan obliged, still irritated with her family for excluding Jack from the surprise, but aware that she needed to put on a happy face for the dozens of people gathered in the foyer. She didn't want to embarrass her parents with an outburst.

"We missed you, Meghan!" Molly, her youngest sister, shouted as she ran forward and grabbed onto Meghan's leg. "You haven't been home in so long."

Rebecca winked at Meghan. "See? It's about time you came home. All your sisters are so happy to see you."

"And happy to celebrate your engagement!" cried Myrtle, her favorite sister. Myrtle was eight years younger than Meghan, but they had always been close, and at twenty-one, Myrtle looked like a miniature version of Meghan. She had the womanly curves Meghan had developed as a young woman, and her shiny dark hair cascaded in loose waves down her back.

"Oh, Myrtle!" Meghan kissed her sister on the cheek. "You are lovelier and lovelier each day. I am so happy to see you!"

"I can't believe you're here!" Myrtle cried, her dark eyes filled with happy tears. "Let's see that ring!"

Meghan held out her hand, and four of her sisters rushed forward. "It's very... quaint," sniffed Mellie, the eldest of the Truman sisters. Mellie was technically Meghan's half-sister; Henry had been married briefly to Mellie's mother, who had passed away when she was only a baby. Mellie and Meghan had always had a tension between them; only two years apart in age, Mellie was highly competitive with Meghan, and she was jealous that the younger sisters tended to turn to Meghan for sisterly advice and counsel. Mellie was unhappily married to a stockbroker, and they lived in a Dallas penthouse that cost as much as ten houses combined in Sandy Bay. Mellie's wedding had been a wildly expensive and elegant social affair, and her ten-carat yellow diamond engagement ring was large enough to sink a boat.

"Thanks," Meghan replied stiffly as Mandy wrinkled her nose.

"Quaint isn't the right word," Mandy corrected Mellie. "I think more like... tiny."

"Mandy," Rebecca warned. "That's enough."

"I think it's beautiful," Myrtle said, her chin held high. "It's the perfect ring for Meghan: timeless and pretty."

"That's the perfect way to describe it," Meghan replied, grateful her favorite sister was on her side. "I am so happy with it, though to be honest, I love Jack so much, that I would have married him with a paper ring!"

"Ewww," said Mellie. "That would have been tacky."

"Enough," Rebecca growled. "Enough talk about rings. Let's help Meghan get settled in. We can visit with her in the parlor like proper hosts."

Rebecca waved over Stephanie, the family housekeeper. "Stephanie, please take Meghan's things upstairs. We'll be gathering in the parlor, so if you could put together some snacks and bring them in to us when you are done, that would be nice."

Meghan's face brightened. "Stephanie!" she cried as she ran to the housekeeper and hugged her. "It's so good to see you."

"You too, baby," Stephanie replied as she kissed Meghan on the forehead. "You are growing up to be such a beautiful woman. Your Mama tells me you are getting married, too? What a happy time."

"It is," Meghan agreed. "It sure is."

Fifteen minutes later, the Truman family had convened in the parlor of the family home. Henry sat in the overstuffed red leather chair in front of the fireplace, a small fire burning behind him. Rebecca sat beside him on the antique chaise lounge, her legs elegantly crossed at the ankles. The Truman siblings sat on two matching cream-colored couches, Meghan cuddling close to Myrtle as Stephanie served tea and finger sandwiches.

"We are so happy to have all of you home for the holidays," Henry's voice boomed. "What a sweet time to have all of my children here. We will celebrate Christmas together and the charity ball!"

"What charity ball?" Meghan asked. "Don't you two usually go to a ball each Christmas?"

Rebecca shook her head. "We do, but this year, things are different," she informed her daughter. "We are throwing a small gala here for the holidays. Your Daddy has been awarded the keys to the city for his service to the business community, and he is going to be honored here at home! We will host a fine party for all the right people because..."

"Because your Daddy might be running for office next year!" Henry interjected.

"You would make such a wonderful Governor of Texas," Mandy said daintily as Henry grinned. "Wouldn't Mama make such a pretty first lady?"

"She would," Mellie agreed, sitting primly, her enormous ring sparkling in the lights. "And we would make excellent First Daughters of the great state of Texas! The ladies at the Junior League would be so envious."

Meghan looked at her parents. They were traditional southerners, and while they could be overbearing, she knew they would lead Texas with grace and common sense. "I'm so happy for you, Daddy," she told him, a smile on her face. "I think you would make a fine Governor."

"Thank you, honey," he replied. "I will announce my candidacy at the ball with my family by my side. That's why we were so desperate to get you down here, baby girl. We wanted all of our children with us when we told the world of our plans."

She grinned. "Jack is planning to fly down this weekend," she announced. "I will call him and tell him there isn't an emergency, but he should still come for the ball."

Rebecca coughed awkwardly. "Are you sure you want to do that?" she asked Meghan. "The ball will already be crowded, and there will be plenty of handsome, interesting, successful young men there for you to visit with. Why don't you just tell Jack to stay home? You can see him over the New Year."

Meghan stood up. "He's my fiancé," she explained angrily. "He's going to be part of this family soon. He has every right to be here with us."

"Does he though?" Mellie countered. "If he couldn't fly down here and properly talk with Mama and Daddy about your engagement, I don't think he should be welcome in this house."

"We live a thousand miles away from here!" Meghan argued. "And Jack is a detective. His schedule is so unpredictable. Besides, he told me that last Christmas he mentioned proposing to me to Mama and Daddy, and Daddy was fine with it. Jack didn't think he needed to mention it twice."

"That was a whole year ago," Henry said gruffly. "And didn't you two break up between then and now?"

"Yes...." Meghan stammered. "But..."

"I would have appreciated better communication from him," Rebecca admitted. "But what's done is done. Meghan is engaged, and that's all there is to it."

"Exactly!" Meghan said firmly. "Jack will be part of this family, and if you can't accept that, I'm going home to Sandy Bay."

"No, don't do that," Mandy rolled her eyes. "You're being dramatic, Meghan. No wonder you went off to Hollywood. We're just giving you a hard time, and you know it."

"We're happy for you," Myrtle told her as she squeezed Meghan's hand. "Tell us more about your bakery, Meghan. I am so eager to hear about it, and I know everyone else is."

Meghan took a deep breath before sitting back down. "The bakery is my passion," she explained as her sisters nodded. "I am learning a lot each day, but I've really taken to baking."

"What things do you bake?" asked Millicent, another sister in her early twenties. "Cakes?"

"Cakes, scones, tarts, everything! Tarts have been my latest obsession," she admitted gleefully. "I've been trying to perfect my recipe in time for the holidays. I can teach you all to make some, if you'd like."

Rebecca chuckled good-naturedly. "No, dear," she said. "I'm the queen of tarts around this household. I'm the only one who gets to make them here."

"Fine, fine," Meghan laughed. "No tarts. But we could make an apple bake or a cinnamon twist roll. What do you girls think about that?"

Before the sisters could answer, Stephanie entered the parlor. "Ma'am? Sir? You have a visitor."

"Oh?" Rebecca replied with raised eyebrows. "We weren't expecting company, were we, Henry?"

Henry shook his head. "No," he agreed. "Stephanie, who is it?"

Meghan's jaw dropped as a familiar face walked in. It was Fred James, her high school sweetheart.

"Fred!" Rebecca exclaimed as Fred greeted her. He kissed her on both cheeks and then shook Henry's hands. "I heard you have a special guest," he said as he turned to greet Meghan. "Meghan, it is so good to see you."

Meghan's heart pounded as she stared into Fred's chocolate brown eyes. He was more handsome than ever; with his tall stature, muscular shoulders, and sharp jaw-line, he looked like a movie star as he stood grinning at her.

"Good to see you too," Meghan whispered. "What are you doing here?"

He shrugged. "I had to see you," he told her as her sisters gasped. "First loves are so special, and when I heard you were in town, I knew I had to see you sooner rather than later. Mandy told me about the plan to get you home, and I called up Mrs. Truman when I heard the news. Your Mama told me to drop by anytime, so here I am."

"Oh, did she?" Meghan asked. "It seems everyone knew about this surprise, except for me. And Jack, my fiancé."

"Ahhh, yes," Fred said. "I heard there was a fiancé. He's a security guard, right? Something in that field?"

"A detective," she told him flatly. "Jack is a detective."

"Where is Jack?" Fred asked. "He let you come down here alone?"

"Jack couldn't get off of work," Rebecca explained in amusement. "So poor Meghan is here all alone."

"She won't be alone for long," Fred assured her parents. "I'll look out for her while she's in town, mark my words."

4

Three days later, it was time for the Truman's ball. Meghan, who was staying in her childhood bedroom, did not feel motivated to dress up; upon finding out that Henry was in fine health, Jack had chosen not to fly down for the weekend.

"It's a lot of money," he had told her on the phone. "And since he's not in danger, I just don't think I can swing that kind of cash for such a short trip. I have to be back at work first thing Monday morning, and it just won't work."

"Please?" Meghan had pleaded. "I want to see you, and I think the time with my family would be good for us."

"Meghan, I'm still paying off your ring," he muttered. "And we are going to be paying for a wedding soon. I can't throw this kind of money away for a weekend trip."

"It's not like you are paying for our wedding," she argued. "My parents will pay for it."

"Regardless," Jack told her. "I just can't swing it, honey. I'm sorry. I wish I could."

Now, as Meghan stood before the floor-length mirror in her caramel-colored evening dress, she felt silly; what was the point of dressing up if her fiancé wasn't there to see her in all of her glamour and glory?

"You look gorgeous!" Myrtle cried as she opened the door and ran into Meghan's old bedroom. "That is your color, sis."

"Thanks," Meghan smiled as she surveyed her favorite sister's attire. Myrtle was dressed in a forest green long-sleeve velvet gown. A string of pearls was draped across her collar-bone, and she looked more grown-up than Meghan had ever seen her. "You don't look bad yourself, Myrtle."

"Is it too much?" her sister fretted as she examined herself in the mirror. "Mama loves the gown, but I'm afraid the color isn't right."

"It's stunning," Meghan assured her. "You look like a princess."

Myrtle grinned. "You do, too. But if we're princesses, Mama is the queen, and the queen has requested our presence downstairs. The guests have started to arrive."

Meghan sighed. "We had better get down there, then. Let's go."

The two sisters linked elbows and went into the long hallway. Formal portraits of their grandparents and great-grandparents stared down at them, and Meghan shuddered; she always hated the stiff, black and white pictures that seemed to watch whatever she did, and she wished she were back in Sandy Bay, cozied up with Fiesta and Siesta.

They rounded the corner. Mellie was shuffling up the grand staircase that was the centerpiece of the main hall of the house. "It's about time," she hissed at the pair of them. "Mama sent me to find you. It's time for you to be announced."

Myrtle rolled her eyes. "Everyone knows who we are," she told Mellie. "Why do we have to be announced? It's our house."

Mellie shook her head. "You don't understand formality, it appears," she huffed. "I've already been announced, but when you two come down the stairs, saunter; the master of ceremonies will say your name and relevant information."

"The master of ceremonies?" Meghan asked in confusion.

"You wouldn't understand," Mellie chastised her. "Clearly you don't go to too many nice parties anymore."

Mellie turned on her heel and scurried back down the stairs. "You go first," Meghan whispered to Myrtle. "Youngest first!"

"Ugh, you are the worst," Myrtle teased.

A deep voice boomed as Myrtle gracefully descended. "Presenting Myrtle Truman, daughter of Henry and Rebecca Truman. Myrtle is a junior at Southern Methodist University. She is majoring in elementary education. She aspires to be a second-grade teacher until she marries, and then, she looks forward to being a homemaker and mother."

"That isn't true," Meghan thought to herself as she saw Myrtle cringe. "We just talked about her future last night; Myrtle told me she wanted to be a researcher and study DNA at a university in Poland after she graduates. Mother must have written that little introduction."

Meghan realized all eyes below were on her, and she began slowly walking down the stairs, careful not to trip over the new pair of white kitten heels Rebecca had purchased for her the night before. "I wonder what mother will have them say about me."

"Meghan Truman, daughter of Henry and Rebecca Truman," the booming voice declared. "Meghan graduated Summa Cum Laude from the University of Texas-Austin, which also happens to be her parents' alma mater."

"That part is true," Meghan thought in amusement as she smiled politely.

"Upon graduation, Miss Truman moved to California, and later, the Pacific Northwest. Miss Truman is eager to return to her home state, Texas, and she looks forward to joining her father's company until she marries and becomes a homemaker and mother."

Meghan's eyes nearly bulged out of her head. "That part is not true." She forced a smile back on her lips, but after she reached the first floor and curtseyed to the hundred or so guests that were nodding at her, she went off in search of her mother. "She needs to hear a piece of my mind," Meghan glowered. "She didn't even mention my engagement. She's trying to rewrite history, and I won't have it."

She couldn't find her mother, but as she entered the large dining room, she bumped into her father. "Daddy, have you seen Mama?"

Henry shook his head. He looked handsome in his black tuxedo, and Meghan's heart melted as she saw how happy he looked. "I haven't, but didn't she do a nice job on the decorations, honey?"

Meghan nodded. Rebecca had done a nice job; the house was filled with glittering Christmas trees, hundreds of candles, red ribbon, and a life-size nativity scene sat in the corner of the parlor. The house had never looked more beautiful, and Meghan was happy it pleased her father. "She did," she agreed.

Two men walked up to her father and shook his hand. "Henry, the place looks amazing," the one on the left said, his brunette hair combed over and slicked back. "My wife has been in my ear all evening about it; she is burning with jealousy."

Henry laughed. "But Kyle, your wife planned this party! She made Rebecca's vision come true."

Kyle laughed. "You know how wives can be, though. All night long, all I've heard about is how Robin wishes we could throw a party like this."

Henry shrugged. "That sounds like a problem I don't want to be a part of," he joked. "Kyle, meet my daughter, Meghan. Meghan, this is Kyle Bourne, one of my business partners."

"It's a pleasure to meet you," Kyle said as he shook her hand. "What is it you do, Meghan?"

"I own and operate a bakery," she told him. "It's small, but I love what I do."

"A bakery?" he sneered. "That's cute. So you make cookies all day, huh? That sounds like the life, eh Henry? Bake some cookies, wear a little apron.... not like what we do!"

Meghan stared at him. "It's not as easy as it apparently sounds," she insisted. "I manage all operations, including our finances, scheduling, and more."

"Meghan is very proud of her business," Henry told Kyle and the other man who had not yet introduced himself. "We are happy she is happy."

"Come back to Texas," Kyle told her. "You can work with Fred and me and help your dad grow his business."

Fred stuck out his hand. "Fred James Senior," he said. "Nice to see you, Meghan. I remember when you dated my son, Fred James Junior. It's a pleasure to see you. You've grown up so nicely."

"Likewise," she replied stiffly. "I'm happy where I am. Sandy Bay is home, and my fiancé and I have no intention of leaving."

Kyle feigned annoyance. "Fiancé? No! I was hoping you were single. I think you'd make a nice little bride for my son."

"Henry, you didn't tell us she was engaged!" Fred said.

Henry crossed his arms. "It's a recent development," he apologized.

Fred turned to look at Kyle. "Besides, she wouldn't marry your son," he told him. "Your son can't even finish college. My son, however, is a very successful businessman, Meghan. Why don't you go see him? He's over there. I know he still holds a flame for you."

"My son is just as good as your son!" Kyle shouted, turning to push Fred.

"Excuse me? Did you just put your hands on me?" Fred yelled as he shoved Kyle back.

Meghan looked up at her father. "This is embarrassing," she hissed. "I'm going to find Mama."

She stormed off, her annoyance growing as she passed through the crowd. She heard the voice of the master of ceremonies again and groaned. "Would everyone please move to the parlor? The auction is about to begin!"

Meghan followed the crowd into the parlor and gasped. Rene Red, a famous author and psychologist, was standing in front of the fireplace with a microphone in her hands. "Good evening," she cooed. "I am the celebrity guest for tonight, and I will be hosting the auction."

"I love her work," Meghan thought to herself as she moved through the audience. "This is the only good thing to happen to me tonight."

Rene began the auction. Ten minutes later, Meghan's stomach churned as she heard Kyle bid on a pair of autographed baseball cleats. "I'll take 'em! Ten thousand dollars."

"Fifteen thousand!" Fred Senior called out.

"How does Daddy work with those two bozos?" Meghan thought as his business partners yelled back and forth. "They act like they are fraternity boys in college, not grown men running a successful business."

"Eighty-nine thousand!" Fred declared fifteen minutes later as Kyle stood silently.

"That's ridiculous," Meghan thought to herself. "That much money for a pair of baseball cleats? It's a charity auction, but still…"

All eyes were on Kyle. He said nothing, and his face paled.

"The winner is... Fred James Senior!" Rene told the audience. The crowd burst into applause, but then shared a collective gasp as Kyle fell to the ground.

"Is he just being silly?" Meghan heard a woman whisper to the person next to her.

"Why is he on the floor?"

"Maybe the stress of the auction got to him."

"Where is his wife? Someone should get Robin. She's here tonight, isn't she?"

"Where is Robin?"

Suddenly, a woman marched through the audience. "I'm a doctor," she told them. "Please let me through."

"That's Carmen Little, a neuroscientist," someone whispered. "She'll know what to do."

Dr. Little gently shook Kyle. Meghan saw the concern in her eyes.

"Ladies and gentlemen, please clear the room immediately," the doctor announced. "This man is dead."

5

The next morning, Meghan woke up with a knot in her stomach. She rolled onto her right side and clutched the lavender comforter close to her chest, wishing that the events from the previous evening had been a nightmare.

After the doctor had declared Kyle dead, mayhem had broken out in the Truman house; people screamed and ran for the doors, and only the arrival of the police ended the chaos. The officers had ushered Henry and Rebecca upstairs into a spare bedroom to interview them, and finally, the coroner arrived.

"What is going on here?" asked Michael, Mellie's husband, who had arrived late to the ball. "Meghan? Why are the police here? Have you seen my wife?"

She shook her head. "I don't know," she whispered to Michael. "Rene Red was running the auction, and then daddy's two business partners got into a tiff over a pair of baseball cleats. They were both bidding over them, and then Kyle, one of the business partners, dropped dead."

"He's dead?" Michael exclaimed, his face pale. "Kyle is dead?"

"You knew him?"

"We've met at some of your father's parties," Michael told her. "He and his wife came to our wedding. We were acquaintances. I can't believe he's dead."

"Honey!"

They both turned to look as Mellie rushed toward them. She threw her arms around Michael's neck and began sobbing into his chest. "The ball is ruined! Our family name has been tarnished by this scandal!"

Michael pulled away from his wife and scowled. "Kyle is dead, and you are worried about your reputation? Come on, Mellie..."

She wiped her eyes, careful not to leave a trail of mascara down her cheek. "It's a serious concern, dear," she argued, her eyes narrowed. "This ball was going to kick off daddy's candidacy for governor. You know that!"

"You are something else," Michael muttered as he turned on his heel and walked away from his wife.

"What was that about?" Meghan asked. "You and Michael seem--"

"We are madly in love and completely happy," Mellie insisted, though Meghan knew otherwise. "He is just stressed. He's had a busy quarter at the office."

"Sure," Meghan agreed half-heartedly. "I'm sure that's it."

A police officer walked up to them. "Meghan Truman?"

"That's me," she volunteered.

"Can we speak with you? We are trying to interview the entire family tonight."

"Of course," she told them. "Would you like to speak with her too? This is Mellie, my sister."

The officer shook her head. "No, your parents suggested we start with you."

"Okay?"

The officer nodded. "I'll escort you upstairs. We are just finishing our conversation with your parents."

Meghan followed the officer up the grand staircase, remembering that only an hour before, she had been announced to the party. She could hear her parents' raised voices when she reached the top of the stairs, and she cringed.

"This is your fault, Henry!" Rebecca screeched. "You insisted on throwing this big party, and now, everyone is going to link us to this death. How am I supposed to face the ladies at book club with something like this over my head?"

"Book club? You are worried about your book club?" Henry roared. "My reputation is on the line here, Rebecca. Do you even want to be the First Lady of Texas? Do you want to advance socially? Do you want me to run for President someday? I think you need to stop thinking about yourself and your silly book club and put on a supportive face! This could ruin my future in politics, dear, and I don't understand how you are missing that point!"

"Sir? Ma'am?" the officer greeted as she led Meghan into the room. "I've brought Meghan up to get her statement. Would you like to stay in the room with her?"

"I'm almost thirty," Meghan protested. "I can talk to you without my parents. I'm fine."

"We will be staying." Henry insisted. "Meghan, you will not speak to the police without us."

The officer nodded and gestured to a chair. "Have a seat."

Meghan sat, and the interview began. Meghan told the police she was visiting her family from Sandy Bay, and that she had only just met Kyle that evening. She had seen nothing suspicious during the auction, and she was upset that something terrible had happened in her home.

"Perhaps if you had been friendlier to Kyle, he wouldn't have dropped dead," Henry muttered as Meghan's dark eyes widened.

"What was that?" the officer asked.

"Nothing," Henry shook it off. "Meghan met Kyle earlier, and their meeting wasn't the friendliest..."

"He was rude to me, Daddy," Meghan countered angrily. "He was condescending and rude, and I think you know that too."

"Kyle just has--had--a different sense of humor," Rebecca offered. "Perhaps if you had known him better, you wouldn't have been so easily offended."

"And you would have known him better if you had visited home more..." Henry stated.

Meghan stood from the chair. "Why are you both turning this around on me?" she asked in disgust. "I own and operate a business, and I try to visit when I can. Don't try and blame me for the death of someone I just met. His rude comments and my chilly response didn't kill him, and I don't appreciate you insinuating that they did."

She looked at the officer. "Am I done?"

"Yes, thank you for your time."

Meghan stormed out of the guest room. She peered over the railing of the foyer and watched as the last guests left the house. "Some party this was."

After a fitful night of sleep in her childhood bedroom, Meghan made her way downstairs to the dining room. Several of her siblings sat around the dark oak table, and her father sat at the head, casually reading the Wall Street Journal and sipping his coffee.

"Good morning," he greeted as she sat down next to Myrtle. "Why the long face?"

She raised an eyebrow. "I'm upset," she told him, her voice flat. "Last night was a disaster, and I didn't appreciate the way you and Mama were talking about me."

"Don't be so sensitive, Meghan," Rebecca chided her as she glided into the dining room, still dressed in her blue velvet robe. "We all have to stick together at a time like this, and I suggest you adjust your attitude."

"Don't talk to me like I'm a teenager," Meghan fired. "I'm nearly thirty, engaged, and I don't appreciate being spoken to like a child."

"Calm down, Meghan," Henry ordered. "An officer is coming over this morning to talk to us again, and I suggest you put on a happy face."

"Why are they coming out again?"

Rebecca and Henry exchanged a look. "Kyle's death hasn't been ruled an accident," Rebecca intoned.

"It's suspicious?" Meghan asked. "Are they calling it a murder?"

"Don't get over-excited," Henry said. "You might scare your siblings."

Meghan sighed. "Fine, fine. I'll just focus on breakfast, then. Do you have any croissants?"

Rebecca shook her head. "Stephanie isn't here today, so we will order breakfast in."

Meghan rose from her seat. "I'll go get it," she offered. "I can run into town and get breakfast for everyone."

"No, no," Rebecca began.

"Let her go," Henry said dismissively. "It sounds like our Meghan needs to clear her head, and some time out in town might do her some good."

Meghan raced out of the room. "I'm taking your car, Mama," she called out as she walked into the four-car garage and started her mother's red Cadillac.

She pulled out of the garage and began driving down the long, familiar driveway. Meghan remembered walking down the winding pathway as a little girl, racing her sisters to make it to the bus first. The house was far from the main road, and Meghan wondered how her little legs had carried her so far each day.

She drove toward Peach Tree Grove, her hometown. The family home was only a five-minute drive away, but it had always felt longer when she was young. She smiled as she caught the familiar sights of the enormous marble library, the coffee shop on the corner of Main Street, and the bakery where she had tried her first croissant as a young lady. "It's good to be home," she breathed as she parked the car in front of the grocery store.

Graham's Grocery store was locally owned, and Meghan had always loved browsing the aisles for fresh ingredients. When she was little, she always begged Stephanie to take her shopping, and now, as she searched through the rows of produce, she was struck with the deep ache of nostalgia as she reminisced about simpler times.

"You look like you're lost in la-la land," a woman commented good-naturedly as Meghan nearly hit her with her cart. "Are you lost?"

"Sorry," Meghan apologized. "It's been a while since I've been here, and I was just thinking about coming to Graham's Grocery when I was a young girl."

"This place is a Peach Tree Grove staple," the woman affirmed as Meghan smiled at her. The woman was slender, with shoulder-length black hair that fell in spiral curls. "You look familiar... are you from here originally?"

"I am," Meghan told her. "My name is Meghan Truman. I'm Rebecca and Henry's daughter."

"Ahh, of course," the woman said, her eyes sparkling. "You look just like your Daddy. I should have known you were a Truman."

She blushed. "We all look alike, or so we're told," she said to the woman. "Last night at the party, ten people asked if I was Myrtle or Mandy."

"I heard your folks were hosting a grand party," the woman replied. "Was it a grand time? I've heard your mama is the best hostess in all of Texas!"

"It was fine, but we had some problems. My daddy's business partner dropped dead during the auction, and everything went to pieces."

"That's horrible," she cried. "Someone died?"

"He did," Meghan confirmed. "He was a jerk, that Kyle. I didn't like him, and I don't know how my daddy managed to deal with him. What a terrible business partner to have! Wait, how did you know it was Kyle? I think I've said too much..."

"Everyone knows he's one of your daddy's partners," she told her. "I just assumed. And don't you worry about me; I know when to keep my mouth closed."

She winked at Meghan and then walked away. "I hope I didn't make a mistake," Meghan thought to herself as she watched the woman go. "My stupid mouth. She seemed nice though, so I am sure it is fine…"

She finished her shopping and went home. When she walked into the dining room, she saw a police officer was talking to her parents. "What's up?"

"Detective, this is our daughter, Meghan," Henry introduced her as Meghan walked over and stuck out her hand.

"Nice to meet you," she greeted.

"Meghan?" he asked.

"Yes? I'm Meghan Truman."

He stared into her dark eyes. "I know," he said. "Meghan Truman of Sandy Bay. I know who you are."

6

Meghan's heart pounded as the officer stared at her. "You do?"

He nodded. "I thought your name sounded familiar. I'm Detective Doug Liman. I worked with your boyfriend, Jack, at a workshop in New Orleans a few months ago. He spoke highly of you, Meghan. I'm so happy to meet you in person."

Meghan blushed. "That's so kind," she thanked him. "I don't know if you keep in touch with Jack, but we've upgraded from boyfriend and girlfriend to fiancé and fiancée."

She flashed her ring at him, and he grinned. "That's amazing. Congratulations! Jack and I don't talk often, but he talked nonstop about his gorgeous, brilliant, perfect lady. I am so happy for both of you."

Myrtle shrieked. "Jack is such a doll! Mama, did you hear the things he said about Meghan?"

"Yes, dear," Rebecca replied, clearly unimpressed.

Mandy sidled up beside Meghan and batted her eyes at the detective. "I'm Meghan's single sister, Mandy," she giggled as she twirled her dark hair around her finger. "Nice to meet you, Detective Liman."

Meghan resisted the urge to gag at her sister's flirtation. Officer Liman was attractive; he wasn't tall, but with his green eyes, a buzz cut and bulging biceps, he was a type of handsome that Mandy couldn't resist.

"Nice to meet you, Mandy," he replied, winking at Mandy before turning back to address Henry and Rebecca. "Mr. and Mrs. Truman, I am here today to brief you on the investigation process as we move forward."

"How extensive is this process?" Henry asked wearily. "Are we talking a few hours?"

"Possibly a few weeks," Detective Liman informed them. "We will have forensic experts come out to take samples from the house."

"Samples?" Rebecca cried. "Of what?"

"DNA, evidence, things like that," he replied matter-of-factly.

"I don't recall giving the police permission to enter my home at their leisure," she argued. "I haven't even spoken with our attorney yet. Who says you can come into our home and take things?"

Henry shook his head. "Be quiet," he hissed at Rebecca. "You are causing a scene."

"Anyway," the detective continued. "We'll be requesting a few meetings with you in the coming days. We want to keep you informed, of course."

"The coming days?" Rebecca screeched. "But the holidays are here! We have family coming into town. How am I supposed to plan for our parties and gatherings with the police coming in and out?"

"Rebecca," Henry warned.

"No, this is ridiculous! All we did was to host a party. We had nothing to do with Kyle's death, and this man is treating us like we are criminals."

"Mom," Meghan cautioned. "He's just trying to brief us. He's trying to help our family. He isn't treating us like criminals. This is standard procedure. Jack makes calls like this in Sandy Bay when an investigation is happening."

"I don't care," Rebecca began to sob. "I don't care if this is standard procedure. I don't like it. I don't want the police in our home, especially not at the holidays."

"We really aren't all bad," the detective joked. "I promise we won't bite, ma'am."

Rebecca's eye twitched. "Do I look like I'm in the mood for jokes?" she shouted as the detective's smile disappeared.

Henry put a hand on his wife's shoulder. "Stop this. You sound like a petulant child, Rebecca."

She shoved his hand off. "Don't tell me what to do. I want this man out of my house now, and if you don't help me, I'll do it myself. I'm going upstairs to fetch my rifle!"

Meghan's jaw dropped. "Mama, stop," she pleaded, but it was too late.

Detective Liman pulled his handcuffs from his belt. "Ma'am, you have just threatened an officer," he said angrily. "I am going to have to take you downtown."

"Downtown?" Rebecca asked in horror. "Are you serious? Do you know who I am?"

"Mrs. Truman," he said patiently. "I know who you are. Rebecca Truman, wife of Henry Truman. I am aware that you both are important figures in Peach Tree Grove, but you cannot threaten an officer. We are going downtown together, and there is nothing more to be said about it."

"Now, see here," Henry interrupted. "My wife didn't mean to be rude. She is just upset. Surely you can make an exception for us? Just this once?"

"Don't let him take me!" Rebecca squealed as the detective snapped the handcuffs on her. "Henry, call our lawyer."

"I'm afraid I cannot make an exception," Detective Liman shrugged. "Mr. Truman, you are welcome to follow behind my squad car, or you can meet us later at the station."

"There's nothing you can do?" Henry demanded. "Nothing at all? Look, I understand that Rebecca was out of line, but surely you can do something."

Detective Liman sighed. "Here's what I can do," he began. "Either I can take her down to the station in my squad car, or the pair of you can follow behind me in your vehicle. Either way, she needs to be at the station. Do you understand?"

"That's so unfair," Rebecca wailed as Henry pursed his lips.

"We'll take it," he agreed before turning to his wife. "See what you've done? You need to hush your mouth, Rebecca, or it's going to be worse for you. The nice detective is doing us a favor by letting me drive you to the station myself. Stop crying, or it's going to get worse."

Meghan called the detective over. "Thanks for doing that," she whispered. "She's a little much sometimes, but I think it would have driven her over the edge to be hauled off in handcuffs."

He shrugged. "I'm trying to be better at picking my battles," he admitted. "And letting your mother and father drive to the station on their own seemed like a reasonable compromise."

Meghan's eyes twinkled. "Although, perhaps being hauled off in handcuffs would have given her the dose of humility she needs..."

Detective Liman laughed. "That'll have to be another day. I need to get out of here, but it was nice meeting you in person, Meghan. Congrats again on the engagement. I'll have to give Jack a call and wish him my best."

Meghan waved goodbye as Detective Liman left, her parents following behind him. She felt her phone vibrate in her pocket, and she was relieved to see it was Jack. She had spoken to him briefly the previous night and filled him in on what was going on, but as Jack had been at work, the call was short.

"Babe," she answered. "What a time to call..."

"Everything okay?" he asked.

"An old friend of yours is dragging my mom off to jail."

"WHAT?"

Meghan sighed. "That didn't come out right. Long story short, Doug Liman, a detective you met in Louisiana a few months ago, is looking into what happened last night. He came to the house, and Mama threw a fit. She threatened him, and now she has to go down to the station."

"Doug Liman? He works down there?" Jack asked in amazement. "Doug is a good guy. Sounds like your family will be in good hands. He'll make sure you're taken care of. Gosh, that poor guy never heard the end of how amazing you are when we were down at our workshop. I'll have to call him later. It's been a while since we've talked, but I want to make sure he's watching out for my wife-to-be."

She grinned. "Thanks, love," she told him. "You are the sweetest."

"I miss you," he mumbled. "Sandy Bay just isn't the same without you. Is there a chance you can get home early? Before Christmas?"

Meghan looked around the dining room. Mandy looked upset, and Myrtle was patting her on the back. “I don’t think so,” she admitted sadly. “With Kyle dropping dead in the middle of my parents’ grand party, there is just too much going on for me to leave. My family needs me, Jack. I hope you can understand.”

“I do,” he told her. “I do.”

7

The next day, Meghan sat with Joy at Maxine's, the quaint, but elegant tea shop on the square. The tea shop had been in business since Meghan's grandmother was a young woman, and it was a Peach Tree Grove favorite. Joy had asked to meet her there for tea and scones, and wanting to get out of the house for the morning, Meghan had obliged. As soon as the two women sat down across from each other, Joy's smile faded.

"They're calling it a murder."

Meghan's eyes widened at the news, though in reality, it was not news; Detective Liman had informed her parents the previous day that Kyle's death was ruled a homicide, but had advised the Truman's to keep that information to themselves.

"What are you talking about, Joy?"

Joy's eyes widened. "You know what I am talking about, Meghan. The party at your parents' place. Kyle's unfortunate passing. They are calling it a murder!"

Meghan shifted back in her seat. "Who told you that?"

Joy sat up straight. "I really shouldn't say," she began. "But I wanted to hear your thoughts."

"This doesn't seem like a polite public conversation," Meghan said cautiously. "And my parents told me I shouldn't speak of what happened to anyone…"

Joy laughed. "Oh, pish posh," she protested. "We're old friends! No one is here, anyway, so it's not like we'll be overheard."

Meghan looked around. The tea shop was empty, though she was surprised that Joy was eager to have such an uncouth conversation. Joy was the embodiment of refinement, and Meghan was shocked she would take part in anything other than small talk while in a public venue.

"Why are you asking me about this?" she asked, staring into Joy's face. "This doesn't seem like you..."

Joy threw up her hands. "I've started listening to true crime podcasts," she confessed to Meghan. "My husband thinks it's vulgar, but the stories of murders and kidnapping are so interesting to me. I took a few criminology courses in college, and sometimes, I guess who the killer is before they reveal it on the show."

Meghan raised an eyebrow. "That seems way out of your usual interest," she told Joy. "I thought you spent most of your time volunteering with your charity sorority and the Junior League."

"It's not like listening to podcasts takes up a lot of time," Joy said defensively. "Besides, they are the perfect way to pass the time when I'm driving; sometimes, I have to drive an hour round trip for events with the Junior League, and it's nice to have something to listen to."

"Gotcha," Meghan replied as she took a sip of her white, green tea.

"I think I know who killed Kyle," Joy murmured. "Do you want to know?"

Meghan shook her head. "The police will figure it out," she declared with confidence. "The truth always comes out."

Joy bit her lip. "I think you should know," she insisted. "Everyone in town thinks it was your father, Meghan, and when I put my thinking cap on and really consider all elements of the case, I believe your father is guilty of homicide. That's the legal way of saying murder. I learned that from one of my podcasts."

"I know what homicide means," Meghan snapped. "And I think that's a ridiculous accusation for you to make against my father, Joy. What on Earth makes you think he had anything to do with Kyle's death?"

Joy tossed her perfectly coiffed hair behind her shoulder. "There are several reasons I believe he had something to do with it," she replied matter-of-factly. "Everyone in town knows that your dad and Kyle had their ups and downs; most recently, they had a heated discussion in public over a business deal."

"A heated discussion doesn't lead to murder," Meghan insisted.

"Or does it?" Joy asked. "I don't know for sure, but according to all the podcasts I've listened to…"

"Enough about the podcasts," Meghan said firmly. "This is my father you're talking about, Joy, and this is really hurtful. You've known my father since you were little; he's driven you back and forth to cheerleading practices, he went on our camping trip for scouts, and he danced with you at your wedding. He teaches Sunday school every single week, and he volunteers at the children's hospital every Easter. Come on, Joy... do you really think my daddy would do something so evil?"

Joy hung her head. "I am so embarrassed," she muttered. "I guess I let my imagination get the best of me. My husband says I have too much time on my hands... I'm sorry, Meghan."

"It's okay," Meghan said graciously. "I get it, Joy; it can be exciting when big news happens in a small town. It's important to remember that real people's lives are at stake when things like this happen. If rumors start swirling about my daddy, who knows what could happen."

Joy reached into her pale blue handbag and retrieved a monogrammed handkerchief. She daintily dabbed at her eyes. "I'm so sorry," she apologized. "It was wrong of me to open my mouth and contribute to such a salacious rumor. I'm sorry for my poor choices, Meghan."

Meghan slumped in her seat. "It just stinks that this is happening," she moaned. "If you thought my daddy had something to do with Kyle's death, that means everyone in town is probably convinced he is some sort of killer!"

Joy's lip quivered. "This whole situation has made Peach Tree Grove seem ... darker. Not like it usually is around the holidays."

Meghan shook her head. "It doesn't really feel like Christmastime," she agreed. "I wish I could just go home to my life in Sandy Bay. I miss Jack, my jobs, and my business... maybe I should look at flights and just get out of here now. I know my family needs me, but this is too much…"

Joy frowned. "Meghan! You aren't really thinking of leaving town, are you? That will make you look suspicious to the police! Suspects should never leave town when a murder investigation is happening."

Meghan raised an eyebrow. "Are you back on your podcast stuff again? Joy, I'm not a suspect. I'm free to come and go as I please. Detective Liman, the guy working on the case, told me that I am in the clear."

Joy shrugged. "I just don't think it's a great idea to get out of here so quickly," she advised. "Your parents and siblings need you right now," she insisted. "How would you feel if something terrible happened, and someone important to you just left? What will Myrtle think if you leave now? Or your mama? Or Mandy?"

Meghan rolled her eyes. "Don't get me started on my mama and Mandy," she muttered.

"What was that?"

"Nothing," she said. "I'm just sick of staying at my house; it's too crowded with my whole family, and I need some time away."

"You could stay with my husband and me," Joy offered. "Our home has plenty of space, and I think you would love the third-floor guest suite!"

Meghan shook her head. "That's okay," she told Joy. "I'll be fine. I just need to take a walk or go for a run and clear my head."

The pair of old friends left the tea shop and walked around the block. Meghan's eye caught a large television that was mounted in the large window of the local radio station. "What is that?"

"It's for the news," Joy told her. "They installed it a few years ago. They want it to look like a fancy, big-city radio station, and fancy radio stations often have televisions with the news on."

Meghan peered at the screen and gasped when she saw a familiar face. "Oh my," she stammered. It was the stranger from the grocery store. She was being interviewed by Bob Brett, Peach Tree Grove's local news anchor.

"And what did Meghan Truman confess to you?" he asked the woman with a serious look on his face.

"She said that her father probably had something to do with the murder," the woman said. "She was flustered and nervous. I was just being friendly, and she spilled a lot of information!"

Meghan's heart sank. "Why would she say that?" she thought as she recalled her encounter with the woman. "I said nothing like that..."

"And there you have it!" Bob Brett stated as the camera panned to his face. "Henry Truman has been identified as the murderer by his own daughter! Stay tuned for updates and details!"

Meghan could feel her stomach rising. Her phone began to vibrate. It was her father. "Daddy?" she answered meekly.

"Get to my office," Henry ordered. "IMMEDIATELY."

8

Meghan ambled into her father's office building. His father had built it fifty years ago, and with its antique architecture, dark interior, and rich leather furniture, the place had always felt mysterious to Meghan. Now, as she approached the mahogany desk of the secretary in the waiting room, her heart was beating out of her chest, and she could hardly maintain her composure. Her father would be livid, and Meghan was fearful of his temper.

"I'm here to see my father," she told the receptionist, a young, attractive blonde man with huge dimples. "Henry Truman."

"Are you Meghan?"

"Yes."

"He left instructions for me to send you right back to his office. Do you need me to escort you?"

"I know where it is, but thank you for asking."

"No problem," the secretary told her. "He's expecting you, so please go on back."

Meghan turned to walk through a secured door that led to a dimly lit corridor. "This place seems scarier than ever... how appropriate," she thought darkly to herself as she wandered down the hallway and to the door of her father's private office. She gave it a hard knock.

"Come in," Henry answered.

Meghan pushed open the door and stepped inside. Her father's office was furnished with imported furniture from Japan; he preferred the clean minimalist style over his father's dark, antiquated taste, and the walls were bare except for two clean prints of Meghan's mother and the Truman children.

Henry was sitting at his black desk. The curtains were pulled over his wall to ceiling windows, and the room was lit by a single red lamp. "Meghan."

"Daddy," she began as she sat in the thin chair facing his desk. "Daddy, what they said on the news wasn't true! I don't believe you killed Kyle. It's ridiculous."

"Who was that woman?" he demanded. "Why were you talking to her?"

"She was a stranger at the grocery," she admitted. "I almost bumped into her, and she asked me a few questions. I answered them off-handedly, Daddy. I would never speak ill of you."

Henry shook his head. "I don't know what I believe anymore," he shrugged. "First, my business partner drops dead at my holiday party. Then, my own daughter slanders my good name on television. I don't understand, Meghan. Haven't your mother and I loved you enough? Haven't we supported you? What is the meaning of this little rebellion?"

"Rebellion?"

"Running off to California! Venturing to the Pacific Northwest! Opening a bakery! Meghan, you have a degree! You are from a wonderful family. You were a debutante! Why are you throwing that all away to rot in that little town of yours and settle being a detective's wife?"

"Daddy!" she gasped. "Is that what you and mama really think?"

"Is it different from that?" he asked. "Do you feel like you're living up to your potential?"

Meghan stood up and crossed her arms over her chest. "My bakery is one of the most popular establishments in the area," she cried. "And Jack is a good man who loves me and treats me well. I am happy living my life with him. Don't you and mama want me to be happy?"

Henry also stood. "We want you to be happy, but we also want you to use your head," he shouted. "Use that head of yours! You have the potential to do anything you want. You could be a lawyer, or make that bakery into a franchise. You can do anything you want to, Meghan, and your Mama and I can help."

"I don't want a franchise," she countered, her eyes flashing with fury. "I am perfectly content with my little bakery, my staff, and my life. This is the happiest I have ever been, and I think it is so sad that you and Mama don't see that."

Henry came around to the front of his desk. He reached for Meghan's hand and squeezed it. "You sure are a little spitfire," he praised her. "Just like your daddy."

Meghan stared at him. "What is that supposed to mean?"

"It means that you can always hold your own," he complimented her. "And that kind of passion is just what I need here at my company. Meghan, come home to Texas. Help me grow the family business. You are exactly who I want at the helm with me now that

Kyle is gone, and I couldn't think of a better person to take this company over when my time is through."

Meghan's jaw dropped. "What? You want me to what?"

"Come back to Texas," he repeated patiently. "This scandal will blow over; the truth always comes out when the time is right. Stay here with us and help me run the family business. With your business acumen, your integrity, and your passion, we will grow this business and reach new heights."

Meghan bit her lip. "Are you sure?"

"Absolutely."

Meghan ran a hand through her hair. "It's something I will have to think about, Daddy," she told him honestly. "I have a life in Sandy Bay. I have two employees who count on me. I have Jack."

"You think about it," he told her. "But know that I want you here. I have doubts about Fred James Senior, Meghan, and while sometimes in business, you have to swim with the sharks, I would rather run my company with someone I know like the back of my hand. That's you."

Meghan bit her lip. "I'll think about it and talk to Jack," she told him. "I'll need his input. He is my fiancé, after all."

"Of course," Henry said as he reached to pull Meghan into his arms for a hug. "Your mama and I like Jack, by the way. We just wish you were marrying someone local... someone we've known for a while. It's nothing against him, honey."

"I know, but you need to be nicer about him," she insisted. "I won't move here unless I know you and mama will accept Jack."

"I'll talk with your Mama," Henry winked at her. "You just let me know what you want to do."

Henry walked Meghan out to the lobby and hugged her goodbye. "Think about it," he whispered into her ear. "It'll be the right decision, I promise."

As Meghan turned to leave, she saw Dalton, a security guard at the company. She had known Dalton since she was a child, and she smiled as she waved at him.

"Is that Meghan Truman?" he teased as he walked over to her and patted her on the back. "You've grown up so much, young lady!"

"How are you? How are your wife and the family?" she asked eagerly. Growing up, Trish, his wife, always sent Meghan and her family cookies during the holidays, and Meghan had even babysat their children when she was in high school.

"Everyone is good," he told her. "Everyone except for your dad, it seems..."

Meghan surveyed his wrinkled face. "What do you mean, Dalton?"

He looked down at the floor. "Just between the two of us, there have been some shady folks coming in and out of this office," he murmured as Meghan's eyes widened. "I think your dad is in trouble; these guys look to be up to no good, and I'm worried that your dad is in over his head."

"Tell me more," Meghan asked.

Dalton looked at the receptionist who was watching them. "I can't say any more," he breathed as Meghan nodded. "Just keep an eye on your dad, okay? He's a good man, and I wouldn't want anything bad to happen to him."

9

The next morning, Meghan was sipping coffee at the dining room table when her mother came over and put an arm around her shoulder. "Good morning," Rebecca murmured as she brushed the messy hair from Meghan's forehead and kissed her. "How are you?"

"Fine," Meghan replied stiffly. She was still irritated with her parents, and she did not feel like exchanging pleasantries with her mother before she had finished her first cup of coffee.

"Can I ask a favor of you?" Rebecca asked as she sat down in the chair beside Meghan. "Stephanie hasn't come in for a few days; I have been calling her nonstop, but she isn't answering my calls."

"Okay?"

"Could you drop Marissa off at school this morning? I hate to ask, but I have to run down to your Daddy's office, and I need to leave in five minutes..."

Meghan raised an eyebrow. "Why are you going to Daddy's office?"

"Just to chat with him about a few things," Rebecca said dismissively. "Nothing to worry about."

Meghan nodded. "That's fine," she told her mother. "I can drop Marissa off."

Her mother clapped her hands together gleefully. "Thank you, Meghan! You are such a help. She is upstairs getting ready for school, so if you can fetch her when you are finished with your coffee, that would be great."

She scurried off, and Meghan finished her coffee, making sure she consumed every single drop. She felt exhausted, and all she wanted to do was get home to her life in Sandy Bay.

Meghan looked at the clock on the wall. It was nearly time to leave. She returned her mug to the kitchen, then went upstairs to find Marissa.

"Marissa?"

"In here!"

Marissa was in the bathroom closest to Mandy's old room. Meghan's heart lurched as she saw her little sister staring at her own reflection in the mirror, holding a straightening iron in her right hand. Meghan remembered spending too many hours in middle school, trying to straighten her dark wavy hair, not ready to accept it for what it was. It was such a relief when she finally gave up trying to tame her locks and embraced her natural look, and she hoped Marissa would soon have the same realization.

Marissa was stunningly beautiful. At fourteen, she had the olive skin and dark, exotic eyes of her sisters, but she had not developed their curves. Her frame was different from all the Truman girls; she was almost five inches taller than Meghan and Mellie, and her narrow hips and small shoulders made her appear delicate and dainty. A talent agent had approached her when she was younger, and she modeled for local boutiques and the occasional fashion show in

Dallas. Meghan could not believe how fast her sister was growing up, and she imagined that if any Truman sister had a real chance in Hollywood, it would be Marissa.

"I'm almost ready!" Marissa smiled, revealing a set of green braces.

"Green braces, huh?" Meghan laughed.

"They make my eyes pop," Marissa said defensively. "That's what Mandy told me."

"They do. Mandy is right," Meghan agreed. "I just forgot you had braces."

"They make me look so young," Marissa lamented as she applied a layer of pink lip gloss. "My agent is dying to have them taken off early, but we can't convince Mama. She says a year of braces won't kill me, and that I should just give soft smiles while I am modeling."

"Mama is right on that one," Meghan told her. "A year of braces isn't bad. Mellie had them for two years, and I had them for four! You are getting off easy, kid."

"Yeah, yeah," Marissa grumbled. She looked at her reflection, smiling and preening in the mirror. "Okay, I'm ready."

She walked out of the bathroom, and Meghan held out her hand to stop her. "Wait a second, Marissa," Meghan began. "Your skirt looks too short. That isn't the dress code length..."

"It's different now," Marissa argued, placing her hands on her skinny hips. "Private schools differ from when you attended!"

"I don't think so. Unroll your skirt, or I'll walk you into the school myself."

Marissa huffed. "I don't see why I have to listen to you," she moaned as she obeyed Meghan. "You aren't in charge of me."

Meghan shook her head. "Mama told me to take you to school, so for now, like it or not, I am in charge."

Meghan turned on her heel and walked to the garage with Marissa following behind. She unlocked the family's spare car, a white Audi. "Get in, we are running behind."

The sisters climbed into the vehicle, and Meghan turned on the radio. They drove in silence for a few moments, but finally, Marissa reached over to turn the radio down. "Can I ask you something?"

Meghan nodded. "What's up, sis?"

Her younger sister sighed. "How did you know you wanted to start your bakery?"

"It was the right thing to do, and I had a gut feeling," Meghan replied without hesitation. "I knew acting wasn't right for me, and I always dreamed of running my own business. It all fell into place, and I am happy doing what I do."

Marissa pursed her lips. "I know Mama wants me to be a fashion designer," she told Meghan. "She says it isn't ladylike to model past the age of eighteen, and to study fashion would be a natural transition. I just don't know how I feel about it."

Meghan kept her eyes on the road as she reached over to grab Marissa's hand and squeezed it. "If you don't know how you feel about something, that something might not be right for you."

"I don't think it is," Marissa agreed. "I enjoy modeling, but I could give it up tomorrow and be fine. It's just a fun activity for now. Fashion design just sounds boring. I don't like art, and I don't like clothes."

"Then it sounds like your instincts are right," Meghan praised. "Have you told Mama that?"

"You know how she can be. She doesn't listen when you aren't saying something she wants to hear."

Meghan laughed. "No comment."

Marissa's eyes filled with tears. "Help me, Meghan. I have been worrying about my future a lot; we had a career festival at school last week, and I feel clueless."

"You are fourteen," Meghan explained patiently. "You have all the time in the world left to try things, and your entire life to worry about the future. Find something you enjoy doing and focus on it. What do you do for fun outside of modeling?"

Marissa bit her lip. "I like learning about rocks," she said timidly. "We were studying geology in my science class, and my teacher explained how diamonds are really just rocks. It was so interesting! I started taking walks and collecting rocks after school. Mama doesn't know, though, so don't tell her. She wouldn't like for me to bring dirt into the house..."

"That's great, Marissa! Geology is a fascinating field," Meghan assured her. "If that's where your interest lies, don't give it up. Science and geology could really take you places."

Her sister grinned. "I knew you would have good advice. Thanks, Meghan."

They arrived at the gates of Blessed Hearts, the private school the entire Truman family had attended. "Thanks for dropping me off," Marissa thanked her sister as she got out of the car.

"No problem," Meghan told her as she got out of the car to wave goodbye.

She was hit by a wave of nostalgia; she remembered walking into the schoolyard each day, and her heart ached for the simplicity of childhood. As she daydreamed, a voice interrupted her. "You're a little too old to go to school here, aren't you?"

It was Fred James. "Hey," she greeted him. "What are you doing here?"

He pointed at a young man walking in through the gates. "My brother goes here," he explained. "I take him to school a few mornings each week."

"That's nice of you," she said absent-mindedly as she watched Marissa high five a group of her friends.

"My mom is really sick," he told her, his voice tinged with sadness. "She's been in and out of the hospital, so I try to help my family out as much as I can."

"I am so sorry," she said. "Your mother was always so nice to me. Please give her a big hug and let her know I am thinking of her."

"Of course," he agreed. "She loved you. She always asks how you are doing. She was so happy to hear you opened a bakery. She told me that she always thought you would end up being an entrepreneur."

She smiled. "Your mama always believed in me, even more than my mama, I think."

"She always thought of herself as your second mama," he admitted. "Y'all were always whispering and giggling when you would come over to the house. She thought we would end up together. As did I…"

Meghan shrugged. "We've all grown up," she stated matter-of-factly. "You, Joy, me…"

"Growing up doesn't change things," he countered.

"But for me, it did," she explained. "When I left Texas, I moved on, Fred. I'm engaged now, and my life in Sandy Bay is so happy."

He looked at her engagement ring and sneered. "That's not as big as a ring from me would have been. I always wanted to give you my great-grandmother's emerald-cut diamond. That would have looked so pretty on your hand."

She snatched her hand away. "I like what is on my hand. It means I am a taken woman, and there could never be anything between us again. Never."

Fred's eyes danced. "If there's one thing I've learned in life, Meghan," he drawled. "It's that you should never say never."

10

Meghan returned to the Truman family home and went upstairs to her childhood bedroom. She pulled out her cell phone to call Jack, but he did not answer. She was yearning for a taste of Sandy Bay, so she decided to see if Pamela was available. She dialed her number and was thrilled when Pamela opened the call in a video chat.

"Meghan!"

"Hey, you! How are you doing?"

Pamela grinned. "We're great here! We've been making delicious tarts for the holidays. I've been experimenting with pears and ricotta, and I think I've found the perfect combination. I can't wait for you to try them."

Meghan smiled. "That sounds incredible, Pamela. You always come up with the best recipes."

"Thanks!"

Meghan pursed her lips. "Are you at school? You shouldn't take my call if you're busy, dear."

"We have a half-day today," Pamela explained. "Parent-teacher conferences. I decided to pick up a shift, so I'm at the bakery."

Pamela held the phone away from her face, and Meghan could see the girl was in the dining room. "We're pretty slow today; we had a big snowfall last night, so the streets aren't great. Sandy Bay looks gorgeous, though!"

"Oh yeah?"

"They decorated downtown, and this year, they put up a sixty-foot Christmas tree in the square. I heard a rumor that they might install a skating rink too. I can't wait to see it. You'll love all the holiday lights and decor when you come home, Meghan. Speaking of which, when are you coming home?"

She lowered her eyes, trying not to cry. "I'm not sure," she admitted to Pamela. "I would love to be home right now; I miss you, and the bakery, and Jack so much."

"We miss you too!" Pamela informed her. "We miss you so much; Sandy Bay isn't the same without you. I can tell that Jack misses you so much too. Yesterday, he came into the bakery with your favorite peppermint hot chocolate from the coffee shop. He forgot you weren't in town, and he was so bummed when he remembered you were in Texas. The look on his face almost made Trudy and me cry."

"He brought hot chocolate for me?"

"He said it was something sweet for his something sweet," Pamela giggled. "He is so crazy about you."

Meghan slumped over. She was sitting at the pale oak desk where she had spent hours doing homework as a girl. A white framed bulletin board was above her; it was covered in old photographs, certificates from the cheerleading team, and academic ribbons. Meghan felt torn as she chatted with Pamela in her old bedroom. On one hand, she wished for the past, the quiet, easy times in her life when everything felt safe and simple. On the other hand, she was eager for her future in Sandy Bay, a future that included a wedding, her thriving business, and her many treasured friends.

"Meghan? I think you're spacing out."

"Sorry," she apologized as Pamela chuckled at her. "Lost in my thoughts. What were you saying?"

"I asked you how the visit to Texas is going. Jack told us it was a grand surprise, and that you had no idea your parents were hosting a ball at your house."

"That's true," she told her. "There was a ball…"

"Was it fun?" Pamela asked as Meghan cringed. Jack must not have told her what had happened.

"It was... eventful."

"What do you mean?"

She took a deep breath. "My family is having some issues," she explained. "There is a lot going on here, and I think my parents are struggling with some things. My daddy's business partner... died, and it's caused a lot of trouble for my family."

"Trouble? What kind of trouble?"

"Just... trouble."

Pamela wrinkled her nose. "I'm sorry to hear that," she said to Meghan. "If there's that much trouble, I think you should just come home."

"It doesn't quite work like that," Meghan lamented. "I'll try to be home as soon as I can though, I promise."

"While you're down there, can you do me a favor?"

"What kind of favor?"

Pamela's eyes danced with excitement. "Cowgirl boots are back in style, and I really want a pair," she told Meghan. "There's a pair I want online, but I can't afford the shipping. Could you pick up a pair for me while you are down there? I hear the best deals on cowgirl boots are in the south. You could just take the money out of my paycheck."

Meghan laughed. "A Pacific Northwesterner asking for cowgirl boots," she mused. "I'll find a pair of boots for you. You don't have to pay me. Consider them a holiday present."

"Are you serious?" Pamela screeched in amazement. "You'll get a pair for me? I won't have to pay?"

"They'll be a gift," Meghan confirmed, a grin on her face. "What do you have in mind?"

Pamela beamed. "I want a white pair," she began. "I'm a size nine. I'd love white leather, just like the Dallas Cowboys Cheerleaders wear!"

"Okay," Meghan agreed. "I can do that."

"And my name on them. In blue rhinestones!"

"So, a custom pair?"

"If you can?"

Meghan nodded. "I'll make it happen for you."

"THANK YOU!" Pamela squealed. "You are the best, Meghan!"

"I'm happy to do it. You're an amazing young lady, Pamela, and you have worked so hard this year. It'll be my pleasure to treat you."

They bid farewell and hung up the call, Meghan still smiling in amusement. Pamela reminded her so much of Myrtle, and it was nice to have a younger sister figure in her second-home.

As she put her phone in her red purse, there was a knock on the door. "Yeah?"

"It's your mama."

Meghan got up from the desk and walked to the door, opening it slowly. "Do you need something?"

Rebecca pushed her way in. "I need to vent."

Meghan shook her head. "I can't, Mama," she protested. "Why don't you talk to Daddy? Or Mellie?"

"I can't deal with them," her mother dramatically declared. "Your Daddy is driving me nuts, and Mellie is too busy with her husband to answer my calls."

Rebecca flung herself on Meghan's bed. "This is all just so stressful for me," she cried. "I feel so misunderstood; this scandal is wreaking havoc on our family name, and no one understands."

Meghan sighed. "Mama, how do you usually make yourself feel better when you are sad?"

"I go to my exercise classes, or I have tea downtown," Rebecca said. "But I can't even show my face in town right now. I'm too humiliated."

Meghan stared at her mother. "Why are you so embarrassed?" she asked. "We've done nothing wrong, right? Our family shouldn't be embarrassed if we have nothing to hide, right?"

Rebecca's face paled. "Right... right..."

"Mama?" Meghan asked. "Is there something you aren't telling me?"

Rebecca scowled. "Are you on my side or not, Meghan? You should have seen the way they treated me at the police station. They made me sit in a grimy waiting room, and I wasn't even allowed to have lunch!"

"They didn't let you eat?"

"They brought a boxed meal, but that isn't real food. I could have starved!"

"Oh, Mama…"

Rebecca's face darkened. "Don't be condescending, Meghan; if you had been dragged to the police station, forced to mingle with questionable people, and given a boxed lunch, you would be just as upset as I am. It's as if no one remembers that we are the Trumans! The Texas Trumans!"

Meghan shook her head. "I don't think they care if we're Trumans," she told her mother. "We aren't above the law, and we're just like everyone else."

Rebecca laughed. "We are not, Meghan. You are a direct descendant of one of America's founding fathers, Alexander Hamilton on my side, and on your father's side, you come from a line of English nobility."

Meghan raised an eyebrow. "Does any of that matter now? It's the twenty-first century, Mama…"

Rebecca sighed. "Our fine family heritage is clearly lost on you, Meghan. When I become the first lady of Texas, maybe then you will understand how important we are."

Meghan giggled. "You are clearly the most humble woman in Texas, Mama."

Rebecca stared at her, but then, her face broke into a smile. "You silly girl."

Rebecca reached to hug her. "I'm sorry we've been hard on you," she whispered as she stroked her hair. "We just miss you so much, honey."

"I know, Mama," Meghan murmured. "I miss you and our family too, but I also miss Sandy Bay."

Rebecca took her daughter's hands in hers. "This is home, Meghan. Texas is home. Home is where your family is."

Meghan shook her head. "Mama, your parents are back in Georgia, where you grew up. Your brothers and sisters are there, too. You moved here when you met Daddy at college. This is your home, just like Sandy Bay is my home."

Rebecca teared up. "I never thought of it like that," she admitted. "But Meghan, I just don't think Sandy Bay is where you are meant to be. I don't think Jack is your destiny. I don't want to hurt your feelings, but I have to be honest with you."

Meghan's shoulders slumped. "I can't do this anymore," she muttered. "I have to leave. I'm a grown woman, and it is clear that no one around this house respects my adult decisions. I've been here long enough. I am going home to Sandy Bay, and there is nothing that will stop me."

"Meghan, please," Rebecca pleaded. "Think about my feelings for a moment. I raised a beautiful, loving, sweet daughter. She was a cheerleader, and her high school boyfriend was just a darling. She made great grades, she was liked by all, and she was the prettiest debutante in her year."

"Okay…" Meghan said impatiently, unsure of where her mother was going with the conversation.

"She goes off to college, she graduated Summa Cum Laude, and then, she turns down a job offer from the finest marketing agency in Dallas. She runs off to Hollywood to become an actress. She's single, and as every year passes, she gets farther from a life as a wife and mother. Finally, she calls and says that she is leaving Hollywood."

"And?"

"And I was thrilled! I thought my girl would come home. I hoped she would reconcile with the love of her life, Fred. I thought she had some common sense. But no! She moves to a town she's never heard of and opens a bakery. She works in a kitchen like a common servant. She gets engaged to a public servant. What is a mother supposed to think, Meghan? You were bred for greatness, not to waste your years, and not to settle for someone who can never give you what you want."

Meghan's face darkened. She could feel her heart racing in her chest; she was furious at her mother's words. "Jack gives me what I want," she said through gritted teeth. "He gives me what I need: respect and love. I am happy with my life, Mama, and this is the last time I am going to argue with you about this."

Meghan reached for her duffle bag. "Don't be rash," her mother warned her. "Don't leave like this. I am trying to give you some feedback, as I would give any of my friends or your sisters."

She shook her head. "I didn't ask for it," she told her mother as she placed a sweatshirt in the bottom of the floral print duffle bag. "I'm done being disrespected. I'm done being made to feel like a fool in my own home by my own family."

Just then, Meghan heard a shout from downstairs. "What was that?"

"Rebecca!"

"It's your father," her mother sighed. "What could be wrong now?"

They went downstairs to Henry's office and found him slumped over at his desk. "Honey? What's the matter?" Rebecca asked as she ran toward her husband.

Henry held his phone in his hand. "I just got off the phone with my lawyer," he stammered, his face pale. "Fred James, my other business partner, is suing me."

11

Meghan leaned against the doorway and watched her parents talk frantically. "What do you mean?" Rebecca cried. "What is he suing you for?"

"The details are still unclear," Henry muttered. "But this is not good, Rebecca. This is not good at all. Our family's good name is under siege, and if we aren't careful, we could lose everything."

Meghan tapped on the door irreverently, still angry about her conversation with her mother. "Daddy? Sorry to interrupt, but I'm leaving."

"Excuse me?"

"I'm going back to Sandy Bay. I've had enough of Texas."

Henry stood up and pointed a finger at Meghan. "You are not going anywhere," he declared in a booming voice. "We need you here more than ever; we have to put on a united front as a family, and your participation is critical."

She shook her head. "No, I'm done, Daddy. I've done a lot for this family, and it seems no one cares or respects me."

Rebecca narrowed her eyes. "You are being so selfish."

"Your mother is right," Henry agreed. "Everything I have worked for is on the line. Do you want us to lose it all, Meghan? Do you want our family to go up in flames? Think of your sisters! Think of Marissa and Myrtle. Do you want to compromise their bright futures?"

Meghan's heart sank. She thought of her little sisters, and she knew that if her father lost everything, he would not be able to put the girls through school, help them with their careers, or assist them in the early stages of adulthood. She gulped, a knot in her throat, and she knew in her heart what she had to do.

"Well?"

"I'll stay," she breathed quietly.

"Thank goodness," Rebecca cried as she ran to hug Meghan. "I knew you would make the right choice."

Meghan slid out of her mother's embrace. "This isn't for you," she told her parents. "This is for the girls. This is for the family. This is not for you. I will stay here in Texas until these situations are resolved."

Henry smiled. "We'll take it. Thank you for making the best choice for our family, honey."

She nodded. "I want to help figure this Kyle thing out."

"Of course, love," her mother said.

"Who was the event planner for the party?" Meghan asked, her brow furrowed. "I want to get more information about the night, and I think speaking with the planner would be the most helpful."

Rebecca cocked her head to the side in agreement. "That makes sense," she replied. "I'm not sure how helpful the event planner will be though; Robin planned the party. She is... was... Kyle's wife."

Meghan frowned. "So this might be a difficult conversation..."

Rebecca shook her head. "Don't even think about talking to Robin," she ordered. "She is in mourning, and it would be so impolite to intrude on her."

Meghan looked between her parents. She nodded but knew in the back of her mind that she would talk to Robin, one way or the other.

Later that day, Myrtle asked Meghan to take a walk with her in the garden. "I want to come, too!" Mandy cried. "Don't leave me out."

"I guess I'll come as well," Mellie, who had just come over, chimed in.

The Truman sisters walked along the yellow brick path to the garden in the backyard. The garden was a masterpiece; Rebecca had spent hours designing its layout, and the different flowers matched perfectly. Each of the sisters was represented in the garden; for Meghan, Rebecca had planted yellow roses, for Myrtle, daisies, and so on. It was easily the most picturesque location on the property, and Meghan was excited to take a stroll.

"Isn't it nice that the flowers here never die?" Mellie gushed as she ran her hands over a shrub. "In Texas, our nice, mild winters are perfect for plants."

"The weather here is perfect," Mandy agreed.

"What about July afternoons?" Marissa replied. "I can't go outside in the summer months. Are you forgetting about that?"

Mellie huffed away, and Meghan patted Marissa on the shoulder. "I love that you speak your mind so freely," she praised as they rounded a corner and walked into the peony garden. "I didn't learn how to stand up to Mellie until I was in college, and here you are, doing it at fourteen years old."

Marissa flipped her hair. "Mellie is boring and grouchy. I don't need to take any trouble from her."

"What was that?" Mellie called out, turning around with her hands on her hips.

"Nothing!" Marissa replied innocently, turning to wink at Meghan.

Mandy began to shriek. "Marissa! That dead squirrel is still out here! Weren't you supposed to take care of it last week?"

Marissa's eyes widened. "I was hoping a coyote would eat it," she confessed to Meghan.

"Why were you supposed to pick up a dead squirrel?" Meghan asked. "Don't the gardeners usually take care of animal remains?"

Mandy held her head high in a haughty manner. "Someone snuck out on Thanksgiving," she tattled as Marissa sheepishly tucked a stray hair behind her ear. "Mama said that she had to clean up a dead squirrel as a punishment."

"If it was your responsibility, you need to take care of it," Mellie demanded. "That thing is smelly and an eyesore."

"It is disgusting," Myrtle added. "Marissa, can you just run to the garage now and grab a shovel? You could have it disposed of in ten minutes if you hurry."

Marissa shook her head. "No! It's gross. I'm not cleaning up a dead animal."

Mandy glared at her. "There are hundreds of flies on it," she stamped her foot on the yellow brick path. "Take care of it, now!"

Meghan held up her hands to stop her sisters from bickering. "Take it easy," she advised. "You can attract a lot more flies with honey, Mandy."

"I DON'T WANT TO ATTRACT MORE FLIES," Mandy yelled. "I WANT THEM GONE!"

Meghan shook her head. "That isn't what I meant," she corrected. "It's a saying. It means that you can be more successful and get what you want when you are nice. Maybe if you asked kindly, Marissa would have agreed to clean up the dead squirrel."

Before Mandy could reply, the Truman girls heard a commotion coming from inside. "Is that shouting?" Mellie asked worriedly. "What's going on in there?"

"I'll find out," Myrtle told them. She turned on her heel and spirited away, her sisters following closely behind.

When they reached the house, they collectively gasped as they saw their father being loaded into a police car. He was in handcuffs, and his face was contorted in pain. "I didn't do it!"

"You have a right to remain silent," the officer holding him said.

"Please! He didn't kill Kyle Bourne!" Rebecca sobbed as she ran out of the house. "Don't take him away."

The officer turned to Rebecca after guiding Henry into the police car. "Ma'am, you also have a right to remain silent! Anything you say could be used against you in a court of law. Your husband is under arrest for the murder of Kyle Bourne, and I don't want to take both of you downtown."

12

"His bail has been set at three million dollars? Fine. I'll write a check right now."

Meghan's eyes widened as her mother conferred with the family attorney on the telephone. The Trumans had been gathered in Henry's office for the better part of the evening, and Rebecca was working diligently to free her husband.

"And you think they'll let him come home tonight?" Rebecca asked. "Can I go pick him up?"

"Oh, I hope Daddy can come home tonight," Mellie cried as Mandy held her. "I can't believe Daddy is in jail."

"Do you think Daddy killed Kyle Bourne?" Myrtle whispered to Meghan.

Meghan took a deep breath. "I don't know," she admitted to her younger sister. "I would never tell Mama that, but if the police arrested him, there must be something going on that we don't know about."

Myrtle bit her lip. "I wonder just how much is going on that we don't know about..."

Rebecca angrily hung up the telephone. "They won't let me get him until the check clears. Who knows how long it will take for a three-million-dollar check to clear? What if we can't bring him home tonight?"

Marissa hugged her mother. "Daddy is strong, Mama," she assured her. "He is tough, and he will make it in jail for a night."

Rebecca continued to cry. Meghan knew there was nothing she could do to help, and she quietly left the room. She thought about what to do; she could go read in her room, or watch a television program, or....

"I have to find Robin," she thought to herself.

Within ten minutes, she had collected her purse and left the house. She took the keys to her father's Lamborghini, driving slowly down the long driveway hoping her sisters would not see her. She drove into town, squinting at the numbers on the houses hoping to find Robin Bourne's residence.

"That's it," she whispered as she drove by a modest Victorian house. She pulled into the driveway. The house was much less impressive than the Truman household, and she was surprised; if Kyle was her father's business partner, why was there such a discrepancy between his home and theirs? Had he not made as much money as Henry? Meghan pushed the thought away and climbed out of the car, discreetly walking to the front door.

The door was adorned with an antique knocker in the shape of a Cheshire cat, and she gave it a hard knock. She saw the light turn on, and her stomach churned; what if her meeting with Robin was a disaster?

A tall thin woman answered the door. "Yes?" she asked in a heavy Russian accent. "May I help you?"

"Robin?"

The woman shook her head. "Mrs. Bourne is at her office downtown. May I tell her you stopped by?"

"That's okay," Meghan said. "I'll find her."

She turned and returned to the car, determined to find Robin Bourne. She drove down the street, scanning each building downtown to find her office. When she finally saw the sign in the window of a small mint green building, she cheered. "Found you, Robin!"

Meghan parked the car and walked to the front door of the office. It was past seven in the evening, but the lights were on, and she walked right in.

"Excuse me?" a man's voice greeted her as she walked in. He was tall and handsome, but his face was drawn. "Can I help you?"

Meghan nodded. "I'm looking for Robin?"

"I'm Robin. Who are you?"

Robin appeared from behind a large desk. She looked nervous, and Meghan watched her exchange glances with the man. "What do you want?"

"I'll just get out of here," the man told Robin. He reached beneath Robin's desk and retrieved a cargo jacket. "Bye, Robin…"

Meghan was confused as she watched him leave. There was a strange, awkward energy in the room, and she felt as unsettled as Robin looked. "I'm Meghan Truman. Henry and Rebecca's daughter?"

Robin nodded. "You look just like them."

"Everyone says that."

"What can I do for you?"

Meghan sat down on the edge of a desk. "I'm so sorry for your loss, Robin."

"Thank you. I appreciate it. I'm very blessed to have support from my friends, family, and employees at this difficult time."

"Was that guy here one of your employees?" Meghan asked.

Robin raised an eyebrow. "That's not really your business, is it?"

Meghan shook her head. "I'm sorry," she apologized. "I was just curious. How are you doing?"

Robin shrugged. "I'm okay," she said, though her face did not show distress. "The funeral is Friday, so I am rushed to get my manicure, pedicure, and perm finished before then. I need to look my best before I see everyone Kyle and I have ever known gather in one place."

"You're getting beauty treatments?"

"I need to look my best at my husband's funeral, don't you think?"

Meghan pursed her lips. "I'm glad you're taking care of yourself."

Robin crossed her arms over her chest. She was thin and strikingly beautiful; with her waist-length black hair, porcelain skin, and tiny waist, she appeared to be quite younger than Kyle. "What are you doing here, Meghan? You don't have a card or a basket or a pot roast, all the usual things people have been bringing over to console me with. Why are you here?"

Meghan felt a knot in her stomach. She had a bad feeling about Robin, and she did not want to give too much information away. "I... I just wanted to tell you how sorry my family is for everything you are going through," she lied.

Robin rolled her eyes. "Everyone keeps telling me that," she lamented. "And everyone feels sorry for me. It's so boring and overdone. I just want things to go back to normal."

"My parents feel the same way."

"I hear your father was arrested for Kyle's murder? Is that why you're here, Meghan? To apologize?"

Meghan shook her head. "I just wanted to meet you...."

Robin shook her head. "I don't think your father killed my husband," she told Meghan breezily. "Kyle and Henry were attached at the hip; they were best friends and partners, and I know Henry would never hurt him."

"How do you think he was killed, then?"

"The police haven't confirmed anything," Robin began. "But they know it wasn't from a gunshot or a physical attack. My husband was such a type-A man, and I wonder if he had a heart attack during that dreadful auction. He was so tightly wound..."

Robin brushed a stray hair from her forehead, and Meghan noticed an enormous marquise cut sapphire ring on her right hand. "That's a lovely ring," she complimented as she waved her own engagement ring at Robin. "I just got engaged, and I feel like all I've been talking and thinking about is rings nonstop."

Robin blinked sweetly and smiled. "Isn't it stunning? I got it only recently, and I'm madly in love with it."

"I can see why," Meghan told her. "It looks like it was meant for royalty."

Before Robin could reply, the door crashed open. Three police officers stormed inside. "What's going on here?" Robin cried. "I think you've broken my door! It's practically off of the hinges. Officers, what is the meaning of this?"

The lithe, red-headed officer stared into Robin's eyes. "Robin Bourne," she began. "You have a right to remain silent..."

"Excuse me?" Robin demanded. "What are you talking about?"

"You are under arrest for the murder of your husband," the short male officer informed her. "His drink was spiked with poison, and we have evidence to suggest that you were responsible!"

13

"You watched Robin get arrested?" Henry gasped. It was the morning after the visit with Robin, and Henry had just returned from jail. Rebecca had been unable to bail him out until the next day, but finally, he was home with his family. He, Rebecca, and Meghan sat drinking tea in the parlor, and Meghan recounted the details of her visit to Robin's office.

"They stormed right in," Meghan told him. "She looked shocked."

Henry shifted in his seat. "Did she act suspicious? Do you think she did it? I love Robin; we've known her for years. But could she have had anything to do with Kyle's death?"

"I don't know," Meghan admitted. "But I think it's a good sign for you that they now have another suspect."

"I agree," Rebecca chimed in. "Moving forward, our efforts should be focused on keeping Henry's name cleared. We need to think of Robin as the enemy."

"That seems a little rash," Meghan argued. "We don't know if she did it."

"But we don't know if she didn't," Henry countered. "Your mother is right; Robin is the enemy now, so keep your distance from her. Until this issue is resolved, everyone outside of this family is the enemy. We have to keep a low profile until the truth comes out."

Rebecca kissed her husband on the cheek. "We'll stand by you forever, darling," she assured him.

"What did the police say to you when you were at the station?" Meghan asked. "Did they have any insights?"

"Not really," he told her. "They advised I keep a low profile and not to leave town. I'll be working at home for a while…"

"If only you hadn't spoken to that woman at the grocery store," Rebecca spat at Meghan. "That seemed to have made everyone think your father is guilty."

"It was an accident," Meghan said, shocked by how quickly her mother had become angry. "I won't say anything to anyone else."

"You had better not," Henry warned.

Meghan threw up her hands. "I shouldn't have come here," she told her parents. "I came as fast as I could when Mama told me you were sick, Daddy, and now, it's all gone to ruin."

Henry came to Meghan's side and slid an arm over her shoulder. "I'm sorry, dear," he apologized sincerely. "I'm just anxious about what's going on. It will all work out, though. The truth always comes out. I've always had good relationships with my business partners, and I had no reason to kill Kyle. I don't understand why Fred is suing me, but that will get smoothed over. It will all be okay."

Meghan raised an eyebrow. "Why do you think he is suing you?" she inquired. "Is it business related? What is his role in your business, exactly?"

Henry narrowed his eyes. "That's private company information," he said arrogantly. "It's complicated, and you wouldn't understand."

"Try me."

Before Henry could reply, there was a knock on the door.

"Come in," Henry called, and the door opened. A pale, mustached man crept in, and Meghan shuddered.

"Who is that?" she whispered to her mother, but Rebecca brushed her off.

"Meghan, we need some privacy," she announced as Henry nodded.

"Yes, Meghan, please see yourself out."

She obeyed, and she left her father's home office and ventured into the kitchen. She saw Dalton, the security guard, and she rushed over to greet him.

"Dalton! What are you doing here?"

He smiled. "Just dropping off a package for the boss."

Meghan leaned in close. "Do you know the man who just walked into his office?"

"Who? What does he look like?"

"He's very pale," Meghan explained. "He has a thick, creepy mustache. Large ears?"

The color drained from Dalton's face. "Was he short? With a slight limp?"

She nodded. "Yes! That's him."

He cringed. "That's Derrick Tulloch," he informed her. "Everyone around here knows Derrick; he's a local, and a convicted felon. He is trouble. Do you know what he's doing talking to your father in your own home?"

Meghan grimaced. "I have no idea," she told him. "No idea at all...."

14

While it wasn't snowing in Peach Tree Grove, the small Texas town's holiday spirit was undeniable. The town square was delightfully decorated for the holidays, and with string lights dripping off of the stately courthouse and surrounding buildings, a hot chocolate stand set up on the square, and rotating groups of singers and musicians who were constantly spreading holiday cheer with music, Peach Tree Grove was cheerier than the North Pole.

Meghan wanted to enjoy the holiday lights and decorations; it had been a stressful visit to Texas, and she needed to relax after trying so hard to support her family. Myrtle had suggested the sisters take a trip to the town square to take part in the town Winter Wonder Night, a night of caroling, treats, and cheer, and while she was exhausted from the week, Meghan had agreed.

Marissa led the way through the crowd as the Truman sisters oohed and aahed at the lights being turned on. Dark was falling, and the mayor of Peach Tree Grove had ceremoniously switched on the holiday lights as the audience applauded.

"This celebration is better than I remember," Meghan said to Mellie. "Was it this big when we were little girls?"

"I don't think so," Mellie agreed. She was dressed in a knee-length camel coat, emblematic of poise and wealth as she touted a designer bag that matched her red hat and gloves. It was a warm evening, and while Mellie's winter ensemble was unnecessary, Meghan had to admit that her sister looked beautiful. "We've always gathered here for caroling during the Winter Wonder Night, but they keep adding events every year. This year, there is shopping, too. They constructed a fake European Christmas market on the west side of the square, and there are a bunch of little shops and stands."

"I want to try the Belgian waffle hot chocolate," Myrtle exclaimed as they walked past a small stand. "Doesn't that sound delicious?"

"If you're hoping to look like a lump of coal," Mandy teased, pinching at Myrtle's sides. "Mama and Daddy said if they get this Kyle Bourne thing figured out, we can still go on our family trip to the Dominican over the New Year. You don't want to let your figure go quite yet, do you?"

Myrtle's eyes filled with tears. Meghan knew how sensitive her sister could be, and she intervened. "You're gorgeous, Myrtle," she gushed. "Skinny, curvy, hot chocolate, or no hot chocolate, you'll always be beautiful inside and on the outside."

Mandy rolled her eyes. "You always stick up for Myrtle," she muttered.

The Truman sisters passed a nutcracker building stand, a truck selling tinsel, and a booth offering meals for the homeless. "Isn't that Dalton?" Marissa asked, pointing at the booth. "And his wife?"

Meghan spotted them. Dalton, his wife, and Kitty, their youngest daughter, were spooning soup into bowls and giving them to people waiting in line. "That is them! Let's go say hello."

"Let's not," Mellie said. "They look... busy... and fraternizing with staff is uncouth."

Meghan shook her head. "You take this prissy southern belle thing too far sometimes," she told her sister. "You should be ashamed of the way you turn up your nose at people."

Before Mellie could speak, Marissa jumped in. "Y'all," she began, her eyes earnest. "Let's enjoy the night out as sisters. Don't fight, okay?"

Meghan pasted a smile on her face. "Of course. Sorry, guys."

Mellie turned away. "I'm going to go look at purses at that stand."

"I'll go with you," Mandy said.

The two sisters wandered off, and Meghan rolled her eyes. "I'm glad you two don't act like them," she praised Marissa and Myrtle.

"We want to be like you," Myrtle told her. "You're nice to everyone, and you are never mean to us."

Meghan pulled her sisters close for a hug. "This has been a hard trip home, but it's been worth it to have time with you two. This is the best Christmas gift I could ask for."

"For me too," Marissa agreed.

"Me too," Myrtle cried. "Come on, girls. Let's go say hi to Dalton."

They wandered over to the stand and greeted him. "Merry Christmas!"

Dalton's wife beamed. "The lovely Truman gals," she sang happily. "Y'all are getting so beautiful; it's so nice to see you."

"Nice to see you," the girls repeated.

Dalton picked up Kitty and held her up. "Our Kitty is eight now," he beamed. "Kitty, say hi to the girls. They've all babysat you before."

Kitty blushed as she wriggled out of her father's arms. "You've embarrassed her," his wife playfully chided. "Girls, do you want some soup? We're serving the less fortunate, but if you're hungry…?"

Meghan smiled. "That is so kind of you to offer, and how nice of you to volunteer at this time of year."

Dalton shrugged. "Helping others is what this time of year is all about," he explained as his wife nodded. "We want Kitty to know that even though we are of modest means, we are still called to serve those with less."

Myrtle put a hand on her heart. "That is so sweet," she gasped. "Can I help?"

Dalton chuckled. "Of course, Myrtle. Do we have an extra apron?"

"We do!"

Myrtle turned to Meghan. "Do you mind?" she asked. "I won't stay for long."

Meghan's face broke into a huge smile. "Go for it," she told her sister. "Marissa and I will be fine."

They bade farewell to Dalton, his family, and Myrtle, and then kept walking around the festive plaza. "Meghan," Marissa tugged at her sleeve. "Look, a dessert stand! Can we get a treat?"

The stand was a small table with four posts around it. The posts were painted to look like candy canes. Meghan nodded. "Of course. I want something sweet too, and Mellie and Mandy aren't here to be judgy."

They skipped over to the stand. "Wow," Marissa gasped as she looked at the row of treats. "Chocolate truffles, candle cane cookies, Texas winter pudding... can we get everything?"

"Y'all can't buy everything," the woman manning the stand laughed. "Or I'll have no more customers tonight. You Truman girls sure are precious though; can I offer you some reindeer sweet pretzels?"

She held up a pretzel twisted into the shape of a reindeer. A red candy sat in place of the nose. Marissa giggled. "This is adorable," she complimented. "I want two, please!"

Meghan looked at the woman. She was plump, with a thick waist and round cheeks. Her gray curly hair was cut in a bob, and she wore a small pair of wire-framed glasses. She looked like she could be Mrs. Claus, and Meghan liked how friendly she was. "Do we know you?"

"Everyone in town knows the Truman girls," the woman laughed. "You look just like your parents. Let me introduce myself to y'all, though; I'm Cindy Callaghan, the owner of the bakery in town."

"I own a bakery in Sandy Bay!" Meghan exclaimed. "I've been wanting to visit the bakery here, and it's so nice to meet you."

"The pleasure is mine," Cindy smiled warmly. "Actually, we've met before; I catered your parents' party. The one where that man..."

"Oh," Meghan's face fell. "I apologize I didn't remember you; that was a crazy night to say the least. You catered the event?"

"The treats," she confirmed. "Your mama and I sit on the board of the Women's Welfare League together, and she asked me to help out at the party. Little did anyone know that it would all turn out to be such a disaster. What a shame... that poor man..."

Meghan saw Cindy's brown eyes fill with tears. "It was a terrible night," she agreed. "But tonight is a happy night, so let's discuss happy things. Can I ask you a question about your reindeer pretzels? They are so cute."

"Of course," Cindy agreed, wiping a stray tear from her brown eyes. "They are a Peach Tree Grove tradition. The sweet dough was made popular by a baker in Houston, but his granddaughter, my mother, brought the recipe here."

"They are so good," Marissa praised, stuffing the second pretzel into her mouth, icing covering her lips. "Meghan, you should learn how to make them."

"You should!" Cindy squealed. "As a fellow Texan and a fellow bakery-owner, I feel like it's my duty to teach you how to make them. Please let me."

Meghan nodded excitedly. "I would love that," she told Cindy. "Are you free tomorrow morning?"

Cindy's eyes sparkled. "I am! Come by any time."

15

The next morning, Meghan crept out of the house before her family members woke up. She decided to jog into town to see Cindy; she needed some exercise, and it was a warm day with little humidity. She dressed in cream matching leggings and a purple sweatshirt and set off toward Peach Tree Grove.

She arrived at Cindy's bakery just before eight. Outside the front door, she could smell the same familiar scents of flour, sugar, and butter, and her heart ached for Truly Sweet. She hoped visiting a bakery would help her homesickness, and she knocked on the front door.

"Yoo-hoo!" Cindy answered it cheerfully. She was wearing red pants, a green sweater with a snowman on the front, and had a silver apron covering her torso. "So good to see you, Meghan. I'm happy you stopped by."

Meghan grinned. "It's good to be back in a bakery," she confessed as she followed Cindy inside. "Your place is adorable!"

The bakery was larger than Meghan's. It had painted white wooden floors, tall ceilings, and floor-to-ceiling windows on the east wall. It had a fresh, modern minimalist look, and while Meghan preferred a more antique aesthetic, she instantly felt comfortable.

"It was my dream to open my bakery," Cindy explained as she gave her a tour. "It was a slow start, but for the last ten years, we've had a lot of success. I did a massive renovation last summer, and it's brought in business from all over the state. It was worth every single penny."

Meghan raised an eyebrow. "A renovation? Can I ask how much that cost you? I don't mean to be rude, but I am curious. I've started thinking about ways to spruce up the bakery back home, and would love more information."

Cindy nodded. "It was a cool seven-hundred thousand," she informed Meghan. "But it was worth it, like I said. Martha Stewart's magazine came in last month and interviewed me! They took photos and tried my treats, and they wrote a nice article about the place in their December publication. Do you want to see it?"

Meghan gasped. "That is exactly the kind of publicity I want to attract someday," she told Cindy. "Tell me everything; how have you made this place such a dream?"

Cindy sat down at a long white wooden table. "Have a seat," she gestured to Meghan with her head. "Let's talk business. I wouldn't do this for any other Truman girl; to be honest, I find you nice and pleasant. A few of your sisters are pieces of work, and I'm impressed with your work ethic and humility. It's refreshing.

Meghan sat down across from Cindy. "Thank you for saying that," she replied sincerely. "I know Mellie and Mandy are a lot to handle, but we aren't all stuck up."

"I'm sure," Cindy winked. "By the way, would you like a tart? I've been working on a fresh batch, and I have some back in the kitchen."

She licked her lips. "That sounds amazing," she told Cindy. "I love tarts. I've been perfecting one of my recipes, but my mama won't let me bake them while I am here. She says that she is the queen of tarts and I need to let her lead the way..."

Cindy wrinkled her nose. "Sounds like we need to have a little bake-off," she declared with mischief in her eyes. "Between you, your mama, and myself, we could have a fun competition!"

"We could," Meghan agreed. "But my mama would never agree to it; she says competition is unladylike.

"Well then," Cindy chuckled. "Let me go grab a tart for you."

Cindy returned moments later holding a hot tart on a blue plate. "Dig in!"

"It's delicious," Meghan cried as she took a bite.

Cindy settled across the table from her, her face bright.

"So, what do you want to know about my business, Meghan Truman?"

Meghan quickly swallowed the tart. "How did you start this bakery? What is your biggest advice?"

Cindy rested her chin on her hand in a casual fashion. "I attended Harvard," she began as Meghan's dark eyes widened. "I studied business and economics. I know a thing or two about finance, and I always knew that I could start a successful company."

Meghan gasped. "How did you cnd up here? You went to Harvard?"

Cindy sighed. "My husband dragged me down here," she explained. "I'm from Houston originally, but after I went back to Harvard for my MBA, he insisted we return to Texas. I think he thought I was getting a big head when I told him it was my dream to work in New York or San Francisco. At the time, I was madly in love with him, and I agreed to come back down here."

"So then what happened?"

Cindy narrowed her eyes. "My husband left me," she said deadpan. "He left me for a fitness instructor; it was a messy affair, and he really sent me into a spiral."

"I am so sorry."

Cindy laughed. "It all worked out; I came out well in the divorce, and I was able to open this bakery without taking out any loans. I applied everything I learned in business school, and after three years, my income from the bakery was five times more than what my ex-husband made as a dentist."

"This bakery is that lucrative?"

"It is," Cindy confirmed. "If you are proficient in business, you can make any business a success. I've expanded my bakery multiple times now, and I finished franchising last year. I have locations in England, Connecticut, Utah, Hungary, Bolivia, Spain, and France, and I'm just getting started."

"But... but... you seem..."

"Like a modest little bakery owner?" Cindy laughed. "I know, I know. It's a fun role to play. In reality, I'm just a Texas girl with a Harvard education and some big dreams."

Meghan smiled. "You're the most interesting person I've talked with during my visit," she told Cindy. "I'm so glad we ran into you."

"The Winter Wonder Night is one of my favorite events of the year," Cindy told her. "No matter how big or successful our operation gets, we'll always have a stand there."

The two women continued chatting until Meghan's phone vibrated. "Should you answer that?"

"It's my mother," Meghan informed her. "I need a little break from Rebecca Truman at the moment."

Cindy giggled good-naturedly. "Don't we all need breaks from our mothers sometimes? Say, how is Rebecca doing? I'm sure this investigation is really stressing her out. I've seen a few things on the news, and I can't even imagine what your family is going through..."

"It's a lot," Meghan admitted. "She's struggling. I've been trying to get to the bottom of things myself; my fiancé is a detective, and I'd like to think I'm good at sniffing out the truth."

"I'm sure you are," Cindy agreed. "Have you talked with Robin? She planned the event, if I remember correctly. She coordinated all the vendors. Maybe she saw something?"

Meghan bit her lip. "My conversation with Robin wasn't great," she told Cindy. "She seemed on edge, and honestly, she didn't act like a grieving widow..."

Cindy raised an eyebrow. "What do you mean?"

"I just wonder how close she and her husband were," Meghan offered diplomatically. "There was a man there when I showed up to her office, and she didn't seem upset that Kyle had died."

Cindy shook her head. "That woman..." she muttered. "Robin Bourne has always had to have things her way. It wouldn't surprise me if she had something to do with poor Kyle's death; she's always been the vindictive type, and I'm sure that if he did something small like make the coffee wrong, she would have punished him."

Meghan shrugged. "I could see that," she replied. "We found out that Kyle died of food poisoning. I wonder if she put something in his lunch that day, or if maybe someone spoiled the food at the event?"

Cindy's face darkened. "You aren't saying that my treats killed him, are you?"

Meghan's jaw dropped. "Cindy, that is not what I meant at all," she assured her. "As one baker to another, I promise you; I have no doubt that your treats were incredible."

Cindy rose to her feet and crossed her arms over her chest. "I think it's time for you to leave, Meghan," she told her. "I've been accused of food poisoning once before, and it was a terrible hit on my business. I thought you were different than all of the Truman girls and that mother of yours, but I guess I was wrong. I'm not going to sit here and take insults in my own bakery from the daughter of a rogue businessman! I think you should leave at once."

16

The Trumans were seated around the dinner table. Stephanie had still not returned to work, but Meghan and her sisters had worked together to make a feast for the family; on the table were bowls of rosemary and oil drizzled sweet potatoes, prime rib, Caprese salad, and truffle butter. While making the dinner had been Meghan's idea, she was reeling from the end of her visit with Cindy; how had things gone so wrong?

"Meghan? I've asked you to pass the sweet potatoes like, five times now," Mandy complained as she snapped back to reality.

"Sorry," she muttered as she reached for the large red bowl. "Here you are."

The whole family seemed drained; Rebecca was staring off into space, Henry was working on his cell phone, and the Truman girls were irritable. No one was in the holiday spirit, but determined to bring some positivity to the table, Meghan started a conversation. "I think we should go around the table and talk about what brought us joy today."

Mellie raised an eyebrow. "Meghan, read the room; no one is in the mood for a team-building exercise. Daddy's being investigated for murder. Get a clue."

Myrtle shook her head. "Guys, Meghan is right; let's try to find the bright side! We have a lot to be grateful for."

"Like what?" Mandy snapped.

"A roof over our heads, nice clothes to wear, our educations…." Meghan began. "Think about Dalton and his family; they have much less than we do, yet they still volunteer and give back to others. We should take a cue from them, I think."

Rebecca stared at Meghan. "Are you lecturing us at a time like this?" she asked. "Your daddy is being investigated for murder, and you are trying to make us feel bad for not serving the homeless at an event in town? Really? Do you know how much money Daddy and I give to charity organizations each year? Do you know how much time I spend volunteering on charity boards? I think you need to hold your tongue, Meghan. This conversation has gotten quite rude."

Meghan stood up. "I'm not hungry anymore," she muttered as she walked out of the dining room.

She went to the family's dog kennel, a large room attached to the garage. Inside were the crates, food bowls, and toys of the family's three Great Danes. Meghan opened one of the kennels to remove Dave, a two-hundred-pound Merle Great Dane. "You and I are going on a walk, Davey-boy," she whispered to him as she attached his harness. "I need to burn off some of this angry energy."

She scratched Dave behind the ears, and he licked her face with his giant smooth pink tongue. "You've always loved me best, haven't you?" she cooed as she quietly opened the back door and snuck outside. Her parents had purchased Dave when she was a senior in college, and she had instantly taken to him; Meghan adored giant dogs, and once she had a house with a proper yard someday, she wanted one of her own.

"Let's go, boy," Meghan said as she gently tugged on his leash. The evening air was warm, and she took a long deep breath. She loved Texas and being home in Peach Tree Grove had brought back some sweet memories. She had enjoyed visiting with her sisters, seeing Joy, and venturing downtown for the Winter Wonder Night. She missed Sandy Bay, though; it was a strange, bittersweet feeling to be a grown woman in a place she loved, aching for a place she loved more. Meghan longed for a kiss from Jack, missed the daily routine at the bakery, and was in need of a long walk on the beach along the Pacific Ocean.

She was lost in her thoughts again, and she absent-mindedly left her family's property and began walking with Dave along a dirt road. Cows mooed in the fields alongside the road, and Dave barked happily at them. She was glad she had taken Dave with her; she needed company, but she knew she was not in the mood for human company.

Dave began to growl, and she watched as his tail went erect. The fur on his back stood up, and she looked around in concern, sensing the dog's frantic energy. "What's wrong, boy?" she asked him, kneeling down beside him to scratch his ears. "The cows are nice. Don't be afraid."

The dog began to bark furiously, and Meghan gasped as she saw two men come into view. They were in the field, and she could see they were shouting at each other. They were too far away to hear, but Meghan saw from their body language that the conversation looked to be contentious.

"We should go," she whispered to Dave. "Let's get out of here."

Before they could leave, one of the men turned and began running away. He ran right past her, and she crouched behind the dog. The other man followed and turned, stopping when he spotted her. "Hey, what are you doing? Were you spying on us?"

Meghan leaped to her feet and ran off in the opposite direction, not stopping to see if he was behind her. Dave's long legs flew over the dirt road, and they sprinted off toward the Truman house. Finally, feeling her lungs grow tight, Meghan came to a stop, and she was dismayed to hear footsteps behind her.

"Why are you following me?" she demanded as she turned around and saw the man come up to her. Her heart sank. It was Derrick Tulloch; the felon Dalton had warned her about. He stroked his mustache, and she felt her stomach churn.

"Why were you spying on us?" he asked as he stared into her eyes. "Ahhh, a Truman girl," he observed as Dave snapped at him. "You're lucky I recognized you, Miss Truman; if I didn't know your daddy, you would be in serious trouble..."

Meghan's dark eyes widened. "What do you mean?"

Derrick laughed. "Let's just say that I dish out pain for fun," he winked as Dave tried to break free from Meghan's grasp to attack the felon. "Like I said, you're lucky I recognized you as Henry's daughter. If you weren't a Truman, you'd be in for some real trouble."

17

As she darted back to the house, she wondered if she should call the police; Derrick's threat had been unsettling, but she wondered why her father was associating with a felon. She didn't want to get her father into any more trouble, but she was unsure if the family's safety was at risk.

She turned a corner and padded through the field, climbing over a wire fence and reaching her family's front yard. She spotted Rebecca sitting on the white wicker porch swing, and she waved as she guided Dave toward the house.

"Hey, Mama," she called as Dave wagged his tail happily at the sight of Rebecca.

"Hi," Rebecca greeted her flatly, a blank look on her face. "What are you doing?"

"Dave and I went for a walk," she told her mother.

"Your clothes are filthy," Rebecca commented, and Meghan looked down at her stained jeans and ripped sweatshirt. She must have torn the shirt as she cut through the field to return to the house.

"It was a long walk," she offered half-heartedly. "What are you up to?"

She freed Dave from his leash, and he went to lie at Rebecca's feet. "I'm just taking in the evening air," she told her daughter. "Just thinking about some things."

"What things?"

Rebecca sighed. "What you mentioned at dinner," she began. "About being grateful for what we have and giving back. I was thinking about the ways your daddy and I give back to the community, and I just wonder if it's enough."

Meghan raised an eyebrow. "Is that all that is on your mind?"

Rebecca said nothing, and Meghan sat next to her and took her hand. "What's really going on, Mama? What is Daddy involved with? I know that something strange is going on...."

Rebecca shifted uncomfortably. "I don't know," she admitted. "He's been acting odd, and I can sense that something is going on. I just don't know what to say to him. I don't know if it's my place..."

The back door opened, and Rebecca nearly fell out of the chair. "You frightened me," she chided Henry as he walked out onto the porch. "Your footsteps are so quiet."

"Sorry," he apologized as he leaned down to kiss her forehead.

"I need to go take care of some things," Rebecca told him as she rose from the chair and scurried inside.

Henry took her place and sat next to Meghan. "She ran off in a hurry," he mused. "What were you two talking about?"

Meghan shrugged. "Nothing," she lied as he wrapped an arm around her shoulders. "Nothing important."

Henry reached down to scratch Dave's enormous head. "Good boy," he murmured. "Dogs sure show us the simple pleasures in life," he said. "They are happy from the little things, like scratches and walks. It's a good lesson for us, isn't it?"

"It is," she agreed.

"Do you remember when our house was being refurbished and all of us were stuffed into that little rental house downtown?" he asked.

"Kind of," she told him. "I was pretty young."

"It was before Marissa and Myrtle were born. You, Mandy, and Mellie were here though, and the five of us, plus our dogs at the time, were stuffed into two bedrooms. Your mama was distraught, but when I think about that time, it was one of the happiest in my life."

"Really, Daddy?"

He nodded. "Things were simpler then. My company was smaller, and life was just easier. That year, celebrating Christmas in that little house, only exchanging a few presents, forgoing our holiday parties and events... it was a wonderful time. I wish we could have that again."

Meghan snuggled closer to her father. "I remember making gingerbread houses with you in that little kitchen," she said as he stroked her wavy hair. "That kitchen with the banana-colored wallpaper! Mama hated it."

"That house wasn't quite her cup of tea," he chuckled. "She was furious that we didn't rent a luxury condo for the season, but I thought a house downtown would be more fun with you girls."

"It was! You bought all the supplies for gingerbread houses and surprised us after school. Mama was so angry about the mess, but we had the best time. We did so many things together as a family back then."

"It was a good time, wasn't it?"

"I wouldn't mind returning to simpler times," she whispered. "Daddy, what's going around here? What's happening with your business? I'm worried that you and Mama are in trouble, and I want to help. Let me help you..."

Henry turned to stare into her eyes. "Stay out of it," he warned, his eyes filled with worry. "It's not for you to know or find out. Stay out of it, Meghan, or we all could be in trouble."

18

Meghan went upstairs to her childhood bedroom. She flung herself across the four-poster bed, sick of the turmoil brewing. She pulled her cell phone out of her pocket and called Karen Denton, one of her dearest friends from Sandy Bay. She had met Karen when they both lived in Hollywood, and despite their considerable age gap (Karen was in her seventies), they become close. Sandy Bay was Karen's hometown, and it had been Karen who convinced Meghan to move there with her.

"Meghan! How fabulous to hear from you. Jack told me you ran off to Texas to be with your family for the holidays. How are things down in the south?"

Meghan smiled at Karen's cheerful voice. Karen had more energy than anyone Meghan knew; she still ran marathons, practiced yoga daily, and had a schedule of volunteering and traveling that kept her very busy. "I'm okay. This visit hasn't been exactly what I thought. I'm ready to get back to my normal life in Sandy Bay, if I'm being honest... my family has been acting so odd; something is going on here, I just know it. It feels more like a Halloween horror story than a quiet Christmas holiday..."

"I'm sorry to hear that," Karen cooed. "It can be an odd experience to visit home as an adult. Hang in there, sweetie. You'll be back up here soon."

"I hope so," Meghan told her. "I don't have a ticket yet, and my parents want me to stay down here until after Christmas."

"You'll make it work, I just know it," Karen confidently declared. "And, if you don't, you'll have some company soon; I just signed up for the Dallas Downtown Decathlon, and I'll be competing on Christmas Eve!"

"What?" Meghan cried. "You'll be in Texas for Christmas? You must come to my parents' house after the decathlon and spend the holiday with us. I insist!"

"I was hoping you would say that," Karen chirped. "From what you've said, your parents' place sounds amazing, and it will be cheaper than a hotel. I'll rent a car and make my way to your hometown after the race. That's if I can still walk. This decathlon will be a challenge for this old bat."

"You know you'll do well," Meghan countered. "It will be so great to see you."

They chatted for a bit longer, and after they said goodbye, Meghan's phone rang. It was Joy. "Shopping day?" she asked when Meghan answered. "Like old times? I feel like you could use some retail therapy with everything that is going on…"

"I could," Meghan agreed. "I need to get out of this house. It's a little late, but I think I can sneak away."

"I'll come pick you up," Joy told her. "See you in fifteen minutes."

Joy arrived on time. Meghan watched through her window as she guided her white Tesla down the driveway, and she bounded down the stairs, hurrying so no one would stop her. She ran outside and jumped into the car. "How's it going?"

Joy grinned. "My husband's holiday bonus just came in, so I have some money to burn! It was more than we expected, and I am excited to shop until I drop."

Meghan bit her lip. She knew life with Jack would be modest, that he would never have excessive holiday bonuses, but as she sat in the Tesla with Joy, she realized she didn't care. She didn't need fancy vacations or designer handbags. All Meghan wanted was love and respect, and she had no doubt that Jack would give her those things until he took his last breath.

Joy drove toward the outskirts of town. The Peach Tree Grove Mall had been built while they were in high school; it was a modern building, with massive glass walls and contemporary architecture, and while it housed dozens of designer boutiques and expensive shops, it was considered an eyesore by locals.

"Here we are, just like when we were teenagers," Joy remarked as she parked. "Remember when we would sneak out of lunch to come here? I was always afraid we would get caught. My mama would have been so mad."

Meghan giggled. "My mama would have supported it. She always wanted me to shop more!"

The women entered the mall. While the outside was ugly, the inside was beautiful; the three-story building was covered in Christmas lights, and Christmas trees glittered in every corner. The stores were decorated for the holidays, and Meghan felt a burst of holiday spirit that she had been lacking when she heard a children's choir singing 'O Holy Night', her favorite Christmas song.

They shopped for two hours, both women finding bargains and holiday gifts, and for the first time in nearly ten days, Meghan felt at ease. It felt nice to spend time with an old friend, and the beautifully decorated shopping mall made her hopeful that she could still find the spirit of the season.

"I need to check out the stockings," Joy insisted. "My mama wants a pair of tartan stockings to wear to church; let's go to the shop downstairs."

They took the escalator downstairs, and Meghan heard the children's choir begin singing, 'All I Want for Christmas is You'. She gasped as they descended; at the bottom of the escalator, she saw Fred James beaming at her. "What is going on?" she asked Joy. "Is Fred waiting for us?"

"What?" Joy asked, pretending to be confused.

"Was this a setup?" Meghan asked incredulously. "Did you and Fred plan this?"

Joy said nothing, and when they reached the bottom, the choir came to surround them in a circle. Joy backed into the crowd, and Fred took Meghan's hand, escorting her to the middle of the circle. Meghan's jaw dropped when he bent down and kneeled before her. "Meghan Truman, you are the love of my life," he declared as her dark eyes widened. "I don't want to let you go again; it's a sign that you showed up here for the holidays, and I want to spend every holiday with you."

Fred pulled out a blue velvet box from his suit pocket. He popped it open, and the crowd gasped. An enormous princess cut ring resting on a plump blue cushion sparkled in the light, and Meghan placed a hand over her mouth in an attempt not to scream. "Marry me?"

She could feel everyone staring at her; Fred was looking into her eyes with a hopeful look on his face, Joy was clapping in the background, the choir watched in awe, and shoppers stopped to line the railings of the overlooks and shout. "Say yes! Say yes!"

A large television hanging above the food court flashed with a breaking news announcement. Everyone turned to look, and Fred gasped.

"Fred James Senior has been declared dead after a hit and run," the news anchor announced. "Police are trying to contact relatives, but at this time, we are unable to get a comment from his wife or family."

Fred's face paled. "My father is…"

Meghan pulled him up from his feet and hugged him. "I'm so sorry," she whispered in his ear as Joy tried to shoo the crowd away.

Fred pushed her away. "This is your fault," he glowered, pointing a finger in Meghan's face. "Your father did this!"

"What?" she cried. "My father? What does he have to do with this?"

Fred glared at Meghan. "Your father is a fraud and a murderer. He killed Kyle Bourne, and now, he's killed my father. He was behind this, and I will kill him for taking my father's life!"

19

"You're going to kill it! Use those legs. That's right! That's right! MURDER it! Kill that routine, Marissa!"

Meghan watched as Mandy coached Marissa in her dance warmup. The Truman sisters were waiting backstage at Marissa's winter dance recital; Rebecca refused to attend as she did not want the other parents to whisper about the family scandals, and the sisters had agreed to accompany Marissa.

"I don't think I can do this," Marissa cried, wiping tears from her cheeks. "Everyone is staring at our family. I'm scared that they all hate us. What if they boo me? Mama says people are really mad at Daddy, and I don't want them to be mad at me."

Meghan squeezed Marissa's hand. "Don't be scared," she told her sister. "You've modeled dozens of times. Just don't think about what anyone else is thinking; if you focus on your dancing, you will show everyone how lovely you are."

Marissa sniffled. "Thanks, sis," she hugged Meghan. "I'll see you after the show."

She waved goodbye, and she, Myrtle, Mellie, and Mandy went to find seats in the audience. The program began, and they watched excitedly as Marissa entered the stage, her head held high. "She looks gorgeous, doesn't she?" Mellie commented. "She certainly is the most beautiful sister."

"Hey!" Mandy squealed. "What about me?"

"Shhhh!" Mellie hushed her. "This isn't about you. This is about Marissa. Watch her dance."

Meghan's heart warmed as Marissa held her arms gracefully over her head, then twirled five times in a row. She thought of her future children, imagining herself and Jack sitting with hands intertwined at their sons' and daughters' recitals and events. She smiled. She was excited to marry Jack, and even more excited at the prospect of having a family with him. She wondered if their children would take after him, with icy blue eyes and blonde hair? Or would they have her olive skin, wavy, thick locks, and sturdy builds?

Intermission started, and she excused herself to go to the restroom. After using the toilet and washing her hands, she pulled out a stick of pink lip gloss and applied it, licking her lips as she finished.

"Meghan Truman?"

She turned around and frowned. It was the reporter, the same one who had interviewed the woman from the grocery store. "You..."

"I've been wanting to meet you," the reporter greeted her.

"I wish you had made an effort to meet me sooner," Meghan grumbled. "That one-sided interview you let that woman give about my family and me? It was rude and hurtful. I wish you had called me to verify your facts."

The reporter pursed her lips. "I'm sorry about that," she said sincerely. "We were on a deadline, and my boss wanted me to air the footage immediately. You are right; I should have reached out to you. It was wrong not to tell your side."

Meghan was surprised by the apology; most people rarely responded well to feedback, but she was pleased that the reporter had taken her seriously. "Thanks."

The reporter sighed. "I've been wanting to talk with you," she told Meghan. "There are some strange things going on around here, and I've heard that you have some experience solving mysteries?"

"Who told you that?"

The reporter smiled. "I did some digging into your life in Sandy Bay. I'm Patty, by the way."

"Patty, nice to meet you."

Patty raised an eyebrow. "Meghan? I've been investigating some shady dealings of top business people in the area, and I was wondering if I could leverage your experiences in solving mysteries to help me solve my case?"

Meghan crossed her arms in front of her chest. "What exactly do you have in mind?"

20

"I cheated on you."

Meghan's heart pounded as she answered Jack's phone call. "What?"

"With Jackie," he told her. "You were gone for so long, and I was lonely."

She screamed as she ripped the engagement ring from her finger and hurled it at the wall. "How could you do this to me? I thought what we have meant something to you!"

"It did," Jack whispered. "But I've thought about it, and I'm in love with Jackie now, Meghan. It happened so fast, but I couldn't help myself. I love her."

Meghan hung up the phone, shocked by Jack's confession. She dialed Jackie's number. "How could this happen?" she screeched when Jackie answered.

"I don't know," Jackie said. "I didn't mean to leave the oven on. I stopped by to heat up my holiday ham for a party, and I forgot to turn it off. Truly Sweet is burnt to the ground, and there's nothing I can do. I am so sorry."

Meghan's stomach dropped. "I was talking about you and Jack," she said slowly. "What do you mean, Truly Sweet is burnt?"

"Jack told you?" Jackie screamed. "He told you about us? He promised he wouldn't!"

"Jackie! Tell me the truth! What happened?"

Jackie wailed, and Meghan hung up the phone. She flung herself out of bed; she had to get back to Sandy Bay that day, and she needed to pack. Jack had cheated on her, her business was ruined, and there was nothing she could do about it from Peach Tree Grove, Texas.

She ran to the bathroom to pack up her toiletries and screamed when she saw her reflection in the mirror. Her cheeks were covered with deep, cystic acne pocks, and she nearly threw up as she looked down. She appeared to have gained fifty pounds overnight; her stomach bulged out from beneath her pajama top, and her ankles were as thick as her thighs. "What happened to me? What is going on here?"

"Meghan? Meghan?"

She sat straight up in bed. Myrtle was tapping on her shoulder, a worried look on her face. "Are you okay? You were screaming."

Meghan sighed in relief. She was drenched in sweat, but she realized that she had been having a nightmare. Jack still loved her. The bakery was operating. She was not fifty pounds overweight. "I was having a bad dream," she told her younger sister. "You can go back to sleep. I am fine."

Myrtle nodded and left her bedroom. Meghan couldn't fall back asleep; it was one-thirty in the morning, and she tossed and turned as she tried to get comfortable. Finally, she started looking through her phone at pictures of herself and Jack. She laughed at a picture of

Jack making a silly face at her; Jack had the best sense of humor, and she loved laughing with him.

She found a picture of Jack holding Fiesta and Siesta while his dog, Dash, sat across his lap. Meghan missed her fiancé and her dogs dearly, and she couldn't shake the deep feeling of melancholy that filled her chest.

She dressed in sweatpants and a jacket and walked quietly downstairs. She decided to take Dave for a walk, but as she passed her father's home office, she noticed a light was on. She leaned against the door and heard his voice.

"Please, please, please," Henry begged.

The door was slightly ajar, and Meghan peeked in. Henry was on the phone, a dark look on his face. "Please," he pleaded.

"Who is he talking to at this hour?" she wondered. "And not talking to... begging."

Meghan held her breath as she listened to her father. Finally, he hung up the phone. She wondered if she should confront him. When she saw him burst into tears, she decided she could wait no longer.

"Daddy," she said as she stormed in. "What is going on?"

Henry wiped the tears from his face and stood up straight. "Nothing," he lied. "I'm just working late."

She shook her head. "I heard you on the phone," she told him. "You have to tell me what's going on, Daddy. I want to help."

Henry sighed. "It's the business," he admitted, his shoulders slumping. "Kyle, Fred, and I got into some business we shouldn't have gotten involved with."

"What do you mean?"

He buried his head in his hands. "I thought we were dealing with an investment company; Kyle told me it was the right move to make, and I believed him. We contracted with a company, but it turns out, it was a Ponzi scheme."

"Oh Daddy," Meghan breathed.

"There's been an investigation going on for several weeks, and Kyle, Fred, and I knew they were onto us. I truly didn't mean for things to get out of hand, dear. I didn't know that we were dealing with a scam."

"What does Fred say? What did Kyle say?"

Henry glowered. "I wonder if Kyle killed himself to escape the consequences," he muttered. "There surely will be consequences, and now, Kyle and Fred James Senior will get off scot-free."

"Who else is involved? Did Fred plan this? Was he the mastermind?"

"I don't know," he told her, staring into her dark eyes. "We have a fourth business partner; I don't know who he is, but Kyle has worked with them and facilitated their membership in our business. They were the one's pulling the strings, but with Kyle and Fred dead, I have no idea how to tell the police who this fourth person is. I have no information, and I sound like a fool."

Meghan watched as her father's face crumpled. "What are we going to do?" he lamented to Meghan. "The fourth partner has been watching us; I've received multiple threats from an anonymous person, and I'm sure it's the fourth partner."

"Are we in danger?"

Henry nodded. "I believe so."

Meghan bit her lip. "Daddy, how many people did the Ponzi scheme affect? Maybe it's one of the victims who is lashing out at you? Couldn't you get the police to investigate them?"

Henry's eyes widened. "Oh honey," he murmured. "It wasn't just a few people who were defrauded," he informed her. "Our company stole from over sixty-five hundred people."

Meghan's jaw dropped. "Daddy…"

He shook his head. "I don't know what's worse, dear," he lamented. "The death of my two best friends, being sued by Fred, my family being in danger, or the reality that I could be dead soon, or in prison for a very, very, very long time."

Meghan stared at her father. "I don't think you should feel sorry for yourself," she told him as she placed her hands on her hips. "There are sixty-five hundred families who won't be enjoying Christmas this year because of what you and your partners did."

Henry stood up. "Meghan, I swear, I knew nothing about this."

"It's your company, Daddy! Even if that is true, the police will never believe it."

"Kyle was my best friend," Henry pleaded. "He suggested the investment company, and I went along with it. It seemed legitimate, and I trusted him."

"Just like all of those people trusted you with their money. Just like I trusted you to keep our family safe."

He hung his head. "I've failed you," he muttered. "And your mother and sisters. And now, I don't know how to make this right."

"You have to make it right," she demanded. "You have to fix this."

"How? What would you do?"

She sighed. "You have to confess to the police," she started. "And tell our family what you did. Mama is worried sick, and the girls are worried about you."

"Derrick has been threatening me," he told her, his face weary. "The fourth partner has been paying him to come around and threaten me. Derrick told me that if I go to the police, he'll kill me."

She shook her head. "There are ways to protect witnesses and informants, Daddy," she assured him. "Don't listen to Derrick. If you go forward to the police, they will help us. They could lessen your sentence."

"I don't know if I can do that..."

She stared at him. "You have to," she told him. "Think about the girls. Think about Mama. Do you want to be caught in these lies, afraid that Derrick will hurt us?"

His eyes filled with tears. "Of course not."

"The truth will set you free," she promised. "The truth can be hard, and doing the right thing can be painful, but if we're going to survive this, you have to tell the truth."

21

They formulated a plan; Henry would go to the police the day after Christmas and tell them everything. Meghan had wanted him to confess that night, but he persuaded her that it would be nice to give the family one last normal Christmas together.

It was four in the morning when they finished their conversation, but Meghan felt relief as she hugged her father. "Thank you for helping me," he whispered as they hugged in his home office.

"I don't think I'm going to be able to get back to sleep after this," she admitted.

He smiled at her. "Let's get out of here," he suggested. "I'll take you to one of my old haunts from before you were born. It's a twenty-four joint that's known by a lot of people. We haven't had time together since you've been home, and it will be fun."

"It's too early, Daddy."

He winked. "You just told me you won't be able to sleep! Humor your old Daddy with a little adventure."

She agreed, and they went to the garage and hopped in the Cadillac. He drove downtown and parked in front of Roy's, a dive bar. "Here?"

He nodded. "This was where Kyle, Fred and I used to come for darts after work," he told her. "Before we made it big. I hope you like it."

He led her inside. Though it was early in the morning, the bar was crowded, and a singer crooned carols into a microphone. They sat at the bar. "What do you want?" Henry asked.

"Just water," she replied.

"I need a beer after our conversation," he joked. "Actually, make that two beers," he told the bartender.

The bartender served them, and they sat for a while, chatting and listening to the singer. The front door opened, and Meghan shivered as a chilly breeze hit her. Then, she realized Derrick had walked in. "Daddy!" she whispered frantically.

Derrick sauntered over and took a seat next to them. "Surprised to see a pretty little Truman girl here," he sneered at Meghan. "Henry, are you here to do some business with me? Get this girl out of here if you want to talk business."

She sat up tall, trying to appear unafraid. "I'm my father's daughter, and anything that affects him, affects me."

Derrick cackled. "Henry, this girl is a riot. Now tell me, have you come to your senses? Are you going to give my client, the fourth partner, access to your database of clients?"

Henry's face darkened. "Derrick, I'm just not sure..."

"Stop," Derrick ordered. "We've talked about what will happen if you don't do what my client requests. You don't want anything to happen to your daughter, do you? Look at what happened to Kyle and Fred. It would be sad if there were three suspicious deaths in Peach Tree Grove within the month, wouldn't it?"

Henry wrinkled his nose. "I will," he assured Derrick, though Meghan suspected he was bluffing. They had agreed that he would hold Derrick off as long as he could until he could tell the police everything that had happened.

Henry put a hand on Derrick's shoulder. "I need to see your boss," he murmured. "You are going to get in trouble by traipsing into a bar; you're violating your parole, if I am correct. Your boss and I need to speak directly. We made a deal that your boss would meet me in person before Christmas, and yet, they haven't held up their end of the deal..."

Derrick winked. "You'll meet my boss," he promised. "In fact, my boss is here right now. Look!"

Meghan's heart beat furiously in her chest as she and Henry watched from the window as a black car with tinted windows pulled into the parking lot. A figure stepped out, and Meghan could not see their face.

"My boss has arrived," Derrick announced to them.

Cindy Callaghan walked through the door, and Meghan peered behind her to try and see Derrick's boss, the fourth partner. Cindy walked up to the bar and handed Derrick an envelope. "There you are," she whispered. "Thank you for your work. Now, get out of here."

Derrick obeyed, and Cindy took his place. "Cindy?" Meghan asked. "What are you doing here? Do you know him?"

Cindy laughed. "Haven't you figured it out by now?" she asked.

"Figured what out?"

She flipped her hair behind her shoulder and rolled her eyes. "Henry," she said matter-of-factly. "I'm the fourth partner. Now, are you ready to go all in on this deal? I know you've been trying to put this off, but I'm tired of waiting. Go big or go home... or... you'll go where Kyle and Fred went."

Meghan could hardly breathe. Her chest tightened, and she watched as her father's face fell. "You're the fourth partner?"

Cindy scowled. "Didn't you just hear me? You stupid girl. Yes, Meghan. Do you really think someone with an MBA from Harvard would settle to just own a silly little bakery?"

"You said you franchised it," Meghan said weakly.

Cindy giggled. "I sure gave you more credit than you deserved," she told Meghan. "I was sure you were on to me; that's why I invited you to my bakery. Now I know how dumb the Trumans' really are."

Cindy pulled out a shiny black gun and pointed it at Henry. "Now, Henry, you're going to meet my demands," she said with a sinister smile. "Or…."

Before Meghan could reply, a loud crash came from the front doors. "Stop right there, Cindy!" screamed Detective Doug Liman as he and three officers ran into the bar. "You are under arrest for the murder of Kyle Bourne and Fred James, and you are ordered to drop the weapon immediately!"

22

It was Christmas Eve, and the Truman house had never looked so beautiful; the house was filled with gold candles flickering, the fireplace in the parlor was roaring, and the Truman family was gathered together after attending a Christmas Eve church service.

It had been a busy week in the Truman household. After the police had taken Cindy away, Henry and Meghan had driven to the police station where Henry made an official confession as to everything he knew about Cindy, business fraud, and his part in the matter. The police had arrested him, but after spending two days in jail, he was allowed to come home for the holidays. It had been decided that Henry's cooperation was vital to prosecuting Cindy, and while the judge took Henry's passport, Henry was allowed to remain at home until his sentencing hearing in February.

Cindy, on the other hand, was facing serious consequences; the police had discovered that she and Kyle had been having an affair, and Cindy had convinced Kyle to make her an anonymous fourth partner in the business. She was the brains behind the Ponzi scheme, and she had manipulated Kyle into following her plan.

When Kyle decided to cut off the relationship to focus on his wife, Cindy had poisoned his drink at the Truman's party. Fred James had gotten wind of the situation, and she sent Derrick to kill him in the car crash. When the police reported this information to the Trumans, they felt grateful that Henry had survived the situation with only a short anticipated prison sentence.

The family sat by the fire. It had been difficult when Henry confessed his misdeeds to his wife and children, but they had gotten through it. Now, they were thankful to be safe, and happy to be together as they spent Christmas Eve as a family.

"Can we open a present?" Marissa asked as Stephanie passed around peppermint tea. Stephanie was back at work; she had had a case of the flu following the party, and she had been admitted to the hospital without the Trumans' knowledge. Everyone was happy to have her back, and Meghan was secretly relieved that Stephanie had not been involved in Kyle's death.

"No," Rebecca said. "We aren't doing gifts this year, remember? We donated our gifts to the less fortunate. The real gift is family time."

She slipped her hand into her husband's and squeezed. "Daddy might not be here next Christmas, so we are going to enjoy every minute of this holiday together!"

Their attorney had advised that Henry would likely be in prison for two years, but this sentence was generously light considering what Cindy would serve for murder, fraud, and more.

"Stephanie? Can we get more gingerbread?" Myrtle asked.

Stephanie nodded and returned to the kitchen, but came back a moment later. "There is a guest here," she announced.

Meghan glared at her parents. "If this is Fred James, I am going to be mad," she told them.

Henry laughed. "We are done trying to set you up with your high school boyfriend, I promise."

Stephanie smiled. "It isn't Fred..."

Everyone gasped as Jack walked into the room, an arrangement of poinsettias in his hand. "Jack!" Meghan cried as she ran to him and jumped into his arms, nearly knocking the flower arrangement onto Mellie's head.

"Merry Christmas," he greeted her with a kiss. "I couldn't go another minute without seeing you."

"How did you pull this surprise off?" she asked in amazement.

He beckoned at her parents. "They helped me."

Meghan's mouth opened. "You two helped him?"

"We know you wanted to spend the holiday with Jack, and we wanted to spend the holiday with our family," Rebecca told her. "Our growing family."

Meghan's eyes filled with tears. "I can't believe you're here."

He grinned. "I wouldn't miss Christmas with you for the world, babe. It's so good to see you."

Henry rose to his feet and strode across the room, reaching out his hand to shake Jack's. "We know you love our daughter," he said to Jack. "And we know you'll take good care of her."

Jack nodded. "It's my honor to take care of her, sir," he said as Meghan's sisters giggled. "I love her so much, and I can't wait until the wedding."

"Speaking of the wedding," Meghan chimed in as she stared into Jack's eyes. "I've been doing a lot of thinking, and I would like to have our wedding here, at our family home. The garden out back is the perfect place, and I want to get married here. Jack? What do you think?"

He shrugged. "That works for me, babe! Whatever you want."

She turned to her parents. "Mama? Daddy?"

Henry nodded, and Rebecca began to weep. "I was hoping you would ask," she cried as she hugged her daughter. Her sisters cheered. "A backyard wedding at our home will be the most beautiful thing anyone has ever seen!"

Meghan looked at her family, and her heart warmed. Her mother was crying tears of joy, her father looked more relaxed than she had seen him in weeks, and her sisters were smiling on the couch. Jack took her hand and squeezed it, and she felt overwhelmed with joy.

"A Texas wedding will be truly sweet," she declared as everyone smiled at her. "Truly sweet indeed."

The End

MISTLETOE AND DEADLY KISSES

1

Tracy opened her eyes and knew something was different. She got up from her sofa where she had fallen asleep while watching TV. She checked the front door in her one-bedroom apartment to make sure it was locked. She scurried into her kitchen. The correctly aligned knobs on her cooker showed her nothing was amiss there. Her bedroom looked just the way she had left it; the contents of her tote bag were scattered on her bed, a navy-blue, floor-length sequined gown hung from the opposite wall and Mr. Sydney, her Abyssinian cat, lay in the corner having a snooze. She walked back into her living room, exasperated as she surveyed the room to spot what was giving her a feeling that something was wrong. Then she saw it. Through a crack in her curtain, she caught a glimpse of a sight that always filled her with warmth and memories of her childhood. It was snowing.

She pulled her curtains wide open and noticed that the cars, lampposts and the sidewalk on her street were covered in snow. The small town of Fern Grove in the Pacific Northwest had been expecting the white stuff for a few weeks. The local weatherman had predicted it would be a white Christmas, but not a single snowflake had been seen in sight for the last three weeks. And now, it was everywhere. After a hard day working at her Aunt's flower shop, *In Season,* Tracy had arrived home and had a heavy meal of mac and cheese. She realized that the living room was unusually cold and figured it was what had made her on edge. Christmas was her favorite holiday of the year as it brought pleasant memories of quality time she had spent with her parents.

Her parents had died in a car crash when she was a teenager, and she had moved in with Aunt Rose and her husband, who was now deceased. Aunt Rose was more or less, the only mother figure she had known most of her life. Still, she remembered building a snowman with her dad who everyone said she resembled. She recalled opening up presents on Christmas Day while her parents recorded her reaction to her gifts on their camcorder. She remembered her mom presenting her with a hot cup of chocolate on nights when she had a runny nose. She sure would like some of that tasty treat. She opened the cupboard in her kitchen and was surprised to see that she was out of chocolate.

"Have you been having some chocolate while Mommy's been away working?" she said to her cat who had just sauntered into the kitchen.

"What can I do?" she murmured to herself. It seemed ridiculous to consider venturing out to the grocery store to buy chocolate, but the nostalgia she felt as she remembered Christmases long gone, made her grab her jacket and put on her winter boots.

"I won't be long now Mr. Sydney. I just need to pop to the shop and I'll get something special for you too," she said, as she wrapped a scarf across her neck.

As her feet hit the sidewalk, and she heard the crunch of snow under her feet, it brought more memories of her childhood. Tracy was fortunate to have a grocery store just around the corner from where she lived. She would get some chocolate, cookies, tea, milk and tuna for Mr. Sydney. She was looking forward to changing into a new *Wonder Woman* onesie pajamas she had gotten on sale during Black Friday and catching up on Hallmark movies. Tracy tucked her hands deeper into her jacket pockets and took broader steps.

A gust of wind that must have had its origin from the Pacific Ocean made her scrunch her nose. Maybe this late-night adventure wasn't so wise after all. She couldn't wait to get into the grocery store and enjoy some respite from the cold. As she got closer to the store, she could see what looked like little pebbles in different colors, which stood out underneath the street lights and against the snowy background. Perhaps it had fallen from an art and craft set from a passerby earlier that evening. She walked into the grocery store and was happy to see a familiar face behind the counter.

"Hi, Kim."

"Hi, Tracy. What are you doing out on such a night?"

"You can't have snow without chocolate, and I didn't have chocolate in my cupboard, so here I am."

"Couldn't it wait till morning? Not that I'm complaining. Hardly anyone has popped in since it started snowing."

Tracy rubbed her hands together and placed them on her cheeks which were cold as an ice block.

"I probably should have," she mumbled, feeling like a naughty child who had been told off for being impatient.

"It looks like I'll be closing early today. I don't think I'll be seeing much business in this weather and like you, I believe a cup of hot chocolate will be ideal in these conditions."

Tracy walked around the aisles, picking and throwing items into her basket that she had planned and not planned to buy. The store was adorned with Christmas decorations and a popular Christmas song was playing over the loudspeaker. She could hear Kim singing and humming along to it. As she bent down to pick some cookies from a lower shelf, she saw a trail of the same colored pebbles she had seen on the sidewalk, only this time, she realized that they were actually chocolate sweets. It seemed as if someone had hastily opened the chocolate bag and left evidence of their crime scattered on the floor.

"Kim, I believe you need to see this," she said, waving her hands in the direction of the counter. Kim stopped arranging a pile of magazines and shuffled towards Tracy.

"What's the matter now?" she said, as she approached her. Tracy pointed at the mess, which also included a ripped bag of peanuts.

"I knew that man was trouble," she said, putting her hands on her hips.

"What man?" she replied.

"There was this man who walked in with an oversized coat and a bushy beard like an Old Testament prophet. He wandered around the aisles asking for things we didn't stock. I didn't take too much notice of him as he had a soothing and kind voice. The kind of voice that could belong to a news anchorman."

"I'm so sorry," Tracy said, putting her hand on Kim's shoulders.

"I hate to say it, but this time of the year brings its fair share of weirdos," she said, walking back towards the counter. She retrieved a broom and dustpan and returned to where Tracy was still surveying the mess that had been made.

"Are you going to call the police?"

"I'm tempted to, but I feel like I'd be wasting their time over a bag of chocolate and peanuts," she said, as she shrugged her shoulders.

"Aren't you worried about your safety?"

"I'm a big girl Tracy. No chocolate-thieving scoundrel will stop me from running my business."

Tracy paid for her items and realized she'd have to carry two full bags of groceries home.

"You be careful out there Tracy. I'll soon be closing for the day."

Tracy thanked Kim and braced herself to go back into the snow. As she walked home, she couldn't decide if Kim was brave or foolish. If she witnessed a crime, no matter how small, she would seek to alert a law enforcement officer to report what she had seen. The way Kim brushed it off, seemed like it was an occurrence she was used to and a cross, she had decided to bear.

Tracy heard what sounded like a twig breaking under someone's foot. She stopped and looked under her feet. It definitely wasn't her. She looked behind her but couldn't see anyone. Was she hearing things? Tracy licked her lips and quickened her pace. She heard a few steps behind her but when she turned around, there wasn't anyone there. Her hands were trembling so she clutched her grocery bags a bit tighter. She stumbled over an uneven slab on the sidewalk. A red apple tumbled out of her grocery bag. She considered picking it up but knew she'd never forgive herself if something happened to her because she stopped to rescue an apple. Tracy could feel her heart pounding in her chest and as she exhaled, a misty cloud escaped from her mouth. She could hear footsteps getting closer and she could tell it was more than one person. She couldn't bear to stop and she couldn't dare to turn around.

"Ma'am."

Tracy had never been involved in an encounter with a criminal and she imagined that their voice would be rough and intimidating. The voice she had just heard sounded soothing and compelled her to stop. She slowly turned around and saw a man in an oversized coat, with a beard that covered his face which had snowflakes attached to it. She could see he had a Border Collie dog who looked as lost as its master.

"I didn't mean to frighten you," he said.

Tracy nodded.

"It's such a cold night and Rocky and I don't have anywhere to stay. I wondered if you could spare some change for us to get a cup of hot chocolate."

Tracy could feel a tear welling up in her eye. She put her groceries on some stairs. She reached into her back pocket and gave him a five-dollar bill which she had kept there earlier in the day.

"Thank you, Ma'am. God bless you. Let's go Rocky," he said.

She watched him turn around and walk in the opposite direction with his dog. Tracy picked up her groceries and almost ran all the way home, stopping to look back now and then.

2

The next day as Tracy walked to *In Season,* she noticed Fern Grove had woken up to discover what she had enjoyed the previous night. It hardly snowed this much in Oregon and seeing almost everything covered in snow was a rare sight this time of the year. Young teenagers were throwing snowballs at each other. Parents were building snowmen with their toddlers. Laughter and joy filled the air as the town reveled in one of the most prominent symbols of winter - snow. But Tracy wasn't feeling as joyful, as she recalled the events of last night. Who was that man? Was her life in danger? Was he the same person who had stolen sweets and cookies from Kim's store? It had taken her about an hour to calm down after she got indoors. Even though her apartment was warm, her hands were shaking and her teeth continued chattering for several minutes after she had entered her apartment. She peeped out of her window every few minutes to see if anyone was lurking outside her apartment. That night, her sleep was filled with nightmares of the strange man and his dog chasing her in a forest. She was so glad when she walked into the flower shop that morning. Her Aunt Rose and their young assistant, Tiffany, were already getting things ready for the day ahead.

"Hello, sleepyhead," Aunt Rose said, as she cleaned the surface of the counter.

"Good morning Aunt Rose. Good morning, Tiff," Tracy said, as she dumped her tote bag beside a table where they handled administrative stuff.

"Morning, Tracy. Have you seen the snow? I asked Aunt Rose if we could close the shop for a few hours to play... I mean enjoy the snow."

"Are you a five-year-old, Tiffany Evans?" Aunt Rose said, looking at the younger lady with a quizzical look.

"I can't remember when I saw this much snow Aunt Rose. Can you?" Tiffany said, looking at both ladies.

"Hmmmm..." Aunt Rose said, touching her chin and gazing into the distance. "I have to admit it's been quite a while."

"Can you remember seeing this much snow, Tracy?" Tiffany said.

Tracy, who was sitting behind a desk, had her hands clasped together and lost in thought.

"Tracy!" she said.

"Oh, I'm sorry. What did you say?" she replied.

"I was askng if you had seen this much snow?"

"Um... yes... no. I think."

"You sure haven't been yourself since you walked through those doors. Anything the matter?" Aunt Rose said as she walked towards her.

Tracy wasn't sure if she should share her encounter with the strange man and his dog with her colleagues. Her aunt could be a first-class worrier and she didn't want to spoil the pleasant atmosphere that the change in weather had brought.

"Oh, it's nothing. I probably ate too late yesterday," she said.

"I've told you to have your dinner early in the evening. Doctor Anderson told me it's one of the keys to a long life and a youthful body," she said, doing a twirl and flicking her hair which was pulled back into a ponytail.

For a woman in her seventies, Aunt Rose had body confidence that would make her a multi-millionaire, if she could bottle and sell it to women half her age. Even though she no longer lived under her aunt's roof, Aunt Rose sometimes treated Tracy like she was still in high school. Tracy knew her aunt meant well. She would share the events of the previous night with someone, but it wouldn't be Tiffany and definitely not Aunt Rose.

"Isn't it about time we put up our Christmas tree?" Tracy said, changing the topic.

"You're right. Mr. O'Neill made a delivery earlier in the week and I can't wait to put it up," Aunt Rose said.

"Ooh! I love decorating Christmas trees. My mom said we could put up ours this weekend. It's one of those events that really lets me know that Christmas is here," Tiffany said, grinning from ear to ear.

"I'm happy you're excited about putting up the Christmas tree Tiff," Tracy said.

"Do you know the origins of the Christmas tree?" she asked.

"Hmmm... not really. Care to enlighten us?" Tracy said.

"I was watching this documentary yesterday and it said they originated in Germany in the sixteenth century. The first Christmas trees were decorated with yummy delights like apples and gingerbread," she said.

"Well, while our Christmas tree won't have any edible items, it'll be a wonder to behold by the time we're finished," Aunt Rose declared.

The ladies spent the rest of the morning setting up and adorning their Christmas tree which was about seven feet tall. Aunt Rose usually had a small plastic tree which she put up at Christmas with electric lights she had gotten from the local hardware store. Tracy had insisted that as the premier flower shop in town, they had to have a signature piece that would attract people into their shop and hopefully generate business. Tracy had worked out a deal with their major supplier to buy Christmas trees in bulk which *In Season* would then resell to the citizens of Fern Grove. Tracy and Tiffany had dropped leaflets to announce this promotion in neighborhoods around the shop and Pastor Kevin Butler had announced it at the end of the church service at First Baptist Church, a few weeks ago. At first, there had been minimal uptake but since the beginning of the week, they had gotten a steady stream of orders and Tracy was confident they would have a record month on the back of the promotion.

"That looks amazing," Aunt Rose said, stepping back to admire the Christmas tree that was adorned with different colored baubles, small figurines of popular characters from animated movies and handmade felt decorations.

"Can I put on the lights Aunt Rose?" Tiffany said, holding the switch that would light up the Christmas tree. Aunt Rose nodded to confirm her consent.

"Now that really looks beautiful."

The ladies turned around to see that Pastor Butler had walked into the shop wearing a red Santa Claus hat. He was a huge man with a booming voice that filled any room he was in.

"How long have you been standing there," Aunt Rose said, opening up her arms to hug Pastor Butler as she walked towards him.

"Oh, long enough to love what I'm seeing," he said, as he embraced Aunt Rose.

"What brings you here on this fine morning? Wouldn't you agree it's the perfect day to play... I mean enjoy the snow... outdoors," Tiffany said, smiling and winking at him.

"I... um..." he said, looking confused.

"Don't pay attention to her Pastor Butler, she thinks she's still five," Tracy said, giving Tiffany a shoulder bump.

"Oh, well I have to admit I felt like a five-year-old when I woke up this morning," he said, winking back at Tiffany.

They all laughed.

"I'm here to find out if my Christmas tree has arrived," he said.

"Yes, it has," Tracy said, as she scanned the inventory list on the shop's tablet.

"Perfect! I'll send Jesse and Jeremy to pick it up later," he said.

"We'll have it ready for them," Tracy said, as she updated her inventory list.

"You know, I believe something's missing from your tree," he said, gazing at the Christmas tree.

"Really?" Aunt Rose said, putting on her glasses which were lodged in her blouse pocket.

"Yeah, just the way something seems to be missing from Tracy's demeanor this morning," he said.

"Why does everyone keep saying that? I'm totally fine. There's nothing..." she said, pausing when she saw Pastor Butler put a finger to his lips.

"You don't have to defend yourself, Tracy. I was only making an observation," he said, smiling kindly at her. "I have to be on my way now but expect the boys later today."

As Pastor Butler left the shop, a couple walked in, arm in arm.

"Good morning," he said.

"Good morning," Tracy replied as she moved behind the counter. "How can I help you?"

"I'd like a bouquet of roses for my special lady," he said, looking at the woman next to him, who gazed into his eyes.

"Is there a special occasion you're celebrating?" Tiffany asked, taking her place beside Tracy.

"Not really. Every day is a day of celebration with my wife by my side. I don't need a special occasion to celebrate this lady," he said.

"Stop it, Joseph," his wife said, her cheeks turning a light shade of red.

"But Eve you know it's true. I love you so much," he said, as he planted a kiss on her lips.

Tracy and Tiffany both put a hand to their chest as they gazed at the happy couple. Tiffany prepared a bouquet of twelve roses and handed it over to the man.

"This is for you Eve. You're my one and only," he said.

"Thank you, ladies," he said, as they walked out of *In Season*.

"He's so romantic. I wish for a husband like that when I get married," Tiffany said, staring at the swinging door.

"Be careful what you wish for," Aunt Rose said. "Not all that glitters is gold."

3

"Pastor Butler!"

Tracy had run after Kevin Butler when she spotted him walking past the shop an hour later. She had tried to laugh off his observation that she didn't seem alright. Her aunt had asked a few probing questions which she had found uncomfortable. Tiffany, being Tiffany, had tried to make light of the matter. It had dawned on her that if the people she loved and respected could tell that all wasn't well with her, then maybe it was worth unloading the cares of her heart to someone else. And the perfect person for that job was Pastor Butler. With his ever-present smile and ability to make people feel special when they were in his presence, she knew he'd have something to say that would calm her nerves that were still on edge.

"Pastor Butler!" she cried as she got closer to him, pulling her sweater over her fingers and exhaling in deep breaths.

"Oh, Tracy," he said, turning. "Did I forget something at the shop?"

"No, you didn't. I... um..."

"Is there something on your mind you'd like to share?"

Tracy nodded.

"The library's across the street. Let's go in there and you can tell me all about it," he said.

They crossed the road and had to dodge snowballs which some kids were throwing at each other. The Fern Grove Library was one of the oldest buildings in town and it showed its age in many ways. The musty smell of books from a bygone era was the first thing that greeted you as you walked through the doors. The long cracks in the walls that snaked from top to bottom were a reminder that once you finished your business, it'd serve you well to leave and not linger a moment longer.

There had been several offers to demolish and convert the land to residential or commercial use but each failed. Every successive mayor who had been in office had blocked such proposals. The one-story library represented a fabric of Fern Grove's past which its citizens were unwilling to wash away. There was hardly anyone around when they walked in. Tracy led the way to the corner of the room where they would be out of earshot of anyone who came into the library. As she sat down, Pastor Butler held her hands.

"What's the matter, Tracy?"

"Last night I met a man," she said.

"Oh," he said.

"And his dog," she whispered.

"Um... that doesn't sound out of the ordinary," he said, smiling at her.

"It's what happened before I met them."

"Ok."

"I went out late last night to Kim's store to get groceries..."

"In the snow?"

"Well, it brought back memories of my mom and dad when I was a little girl and..."

"You don't have to explain," he said, patting her hands.

Tracy took a deep breath and then exhaled slowly.

"I noticed the opened packets of sweets and cookies. Kim said there was a man who came in earlier that night that she suspected. Her description of this man fit a man who was stalking me with his dog. It scared the life out of me. I thought something bad... really bad, was going to happen to me," Tracy said with tears welling up in her eyes.

"I'm so sorry about your ordeal Tracy. The name of that man is Jonathan. I've seen him recently when I've had to make a late-night call."

Tracy ran her fingers through her hair as she relaxed her shoulders and sighed. Someone else knew the strange man.

"And he's not the only one."

"He's not!" Tracy said, her heart starting to beat faster.

"Yes. This time of the year and I don't know why but Fern Grove has its fair share of homeless people who just want a bite to eat and a place to lay their head."

"Oh," she said, tucking a stray lock of hair behind her ear. It had never crossed her mind that the strange man, Jonathan, was homeless and in need of help.

"I've actually had a few calls from people who've noticed several strange people in town. I let Jonathan sleep at the church a few nights ago with a friend of his but I feel like there's so much more we can do."

They both sighed.

"I know what we'll do!" Pastor Butler said, a big, fat grin plastered on his face. "Ok, I'm not sure it'll work but let me place a few calls and I'll call you later," he said, rising to his feet and scuttling out of the library.

Tracy watched him go and wondered what flash of inspiration had hit him.

* * *

THE REST of the day at *In Season* was quite eventful. Several customers came in to confirm if their Christmas trees had arrived at the shop. More people placed phone orders for flower deliveries over the festive season. Tracy and Aunt Rose spent some time figuring out their inventory and updating it on their database. Everyone who came into the shop was in awe of their huge Christmas tree that looked like it would belong in the foyer of a multi-billion-dollar company. There was one remark a few people kept repeating.

'Something was missing on the tree.'

Tracy, Tiffany and Aunt Rose gazed at the tree but couldn't quite put their finger on what that missing thing was. As she was closing up for the day, she got a text on her cell phone.

It was from Pastor Butler.

Please meet me at First Baptist. Maybe we can find a solution to the problem.

She wondered what Pastor Butler had up his sleeves. She immediately replied to say that she would come. As she walked towards the church that evening, a strong, cold gust of wind, made her stop to maintain her balance and served as a reminder why the homeless had to be supported; especially at this time of the year. She was surprised to see a few familiar faces as she walked into the basement room at First Baptist Church that was used for meetings.

Everyone was seated in a circle and there was one empty seat next to Pastor Butler which she took.

"Welcome everyone and thanks for coming to this meeting at such short notice," Pastor Butler said, as he swung his head to make eye contact with everyone in the circle. "The reason why we're here is simple. We have a problem in Fern Grove and we need to fix it."

Some people nodded their heads in agreement while others fidgeted as soon as he said, 'we need to fix it.'

"I'm not aware of any problem Pastor," Susan Gilmore said. She was the owner of a butcher shop in town.

"Of course, you do. Remember the guy who came to your shop the other day... and asked for some bones for his dog..." Pastor Butler said as he pulled his glasses further down his nose.

"Oh, that problem," she said, looking embarrassed.

"Yes, that problem. There are a few homeless people in Fern Grove and with this weather and the Christmas season upon us, I don't think that's right."

"But what can we do?" Luke said, who was the owner of the latest restaurant in town.

"You don't expect us to invite them into our homes?" Kim said.

"No... unless you want to," Pastor Butler replied.

"Are they dangerous?"

"Where did they come from?"

"Has someone informed the police?"

As these questions flew into the air, Tracy noticed that Pastor Butler had put his hand on his chin and was slowly shaking his head.

"Can we all be quiet!" Tracy said, standing up. She was surprised when her outburst was greeted by total silence. It was so quiet; you could have heard a pin drop. "I know having strangers in town can be disconcerting, but these people are homeless and like you and me, deserve a roof over their heads, clothes on their backs and food in their bellies. Did you have any ideas in mind Pastor Butler?"

"Um... yes I did," he said, sitting up straight as he waited for Tracy to take her seat. "I spoke to the owner of the *EndPoint Motel* about our situation and he said he'd be willing to house them."

A loud cheer and a spontaneous round of applause greeted this announcement. Pastor Butler raised his hands to quiet the small crowd.

"But it's going to cost us a fair sum to house them weekly. Norman has agreed to also provide food for them but like I said it'll cost us a bit."

"How much are we talking of?" Kim queried.

"Somewhere upwards of a thousand dollars a week."

"Then count me out," Kim said, as she picked up her purse and made her way to the exit.

"Kim!" Pastor Butler shouted. She stopped in her tracks and turned around to face him.

"I know it's not going to be easy but can you help make someone else's Christmas special," he said, looking at the people who represented the business community in Fern Grove.

"I will," Tracy said, raising her hand.

"Me too," Luke chorused, lifting up his hand enthusiastically.

One by one, everyone in the room lifted their hands and agreed to help Pastor Butler's initiative. Tracy began to wonder what she could do to raise extra funds.

4

The next morning, as Tracy walked to work, she thought about what *In Season* could do to raise more funds for the homeless initiative. Although the meeting had had a few tense moments, by the end, everyone was excited about doing something creative to help towards the cause. Her competitive gene had been awoken and she was determined to do something noteworthy. She saw Aunty Rose and Tiffany gazing at their Christmas tree when she walked into the shop.

"Good morning ladies," she said, placing her tote bag in its usual spot.

"Good morning Tracy," Aunt Rose said, walking over to hug her.

"Don't tell me you're still thinking of what to add to that Christmas tree. It's perfect," Tracy said, as she pulled away from Aunt Rose's embrace.

"I know but you know what they say. The customer can't be wrong. And not one or two but five people including Pastor Butler said it was missing something," she said, returning her gaze to the Christmas tree.

"How was your meeting at the church yesterday Tracy," Tiffany said, pausing from arranging a flower bouquet.

"It actually went well."

"What was it about?" she inquired further.

"Fern Grove has a problem."

"Problem!" Aunt Rose screeched as she deflected her gaze from the tree to Tracy.

"Yes. It seems there has been an influx of homeless people in town. I actually had an encounter with one of them the other night when it snowed..."

"Is that why you were all shaken up the next morning," Aunt Rose said, placing a hand on Tracy's right shoulder.

Tracy nodded.

"I hope he didn't do anything to you?" Tiffany whispered.

Tracy shook her head.

"It was just the fact that he seemed to approach me out of the blue. I thought he was stalking me but all he wanted was some spare change."

Tiffany hugged Tracy as Aunt Rose moved her hand up and down Tracy's back.

"It's okay ladies. It was just the most random thing to happen to me on a snowy day," Tracy said as she squeezed the hands of her colleagues. "It so happens that the stranger who accosted me was or is homeless. More tragic is the fact that there seem to be several homeless people in our town."

"Really?" Tiffany said, putting her hands on her hips. "I don't think I've seen any homeless people in Fern Grove."

"Apart from the fact that homeless people don't tend to wear a shiny badge declaring their status, it seems they tend to stay in the dark corners in town," Tracy said.

"What was Pastor Butler's solution to this problem?" Aunt Rose said.

"The solution is to house the homeless over the winter season at *EndPoint Motel*. Pastor Butler knows the owner who has agreed to house and feed them..."

"Why do I feel like you're about to say one of my least favorite words... but," Aunt Rose said, exhaling as she shrugged her shoulders.

"Not really but more like what needs to happen to make the solution a reality."

"So, in essence, a but!" Aunt Rose said, shaking her head. "C'mon spit it out."

"Every business owner in attendance was encouraged to help raise funds, about five thousand dollars, to support this initiative."

"That's a lot of money," Tiffany said, scratching her head.

"It is but if every business owner in Fern Grove pitches in, we can do it," Tracy said triumphantly.

"What can we do?" Aunt Rose said.

The ladies dispersed to different corners in the room. Tiffany wandered to the Christmas tree and was gazing at it.

"I know what we can do!"

"You do?" Aunt Rose and Tracy chorused, taken off guard by her sudden outburst.

"And I also know what's missing from this tree," she said, grinning from ear to ear.

"Don't kill us with suspense young lady, do share," Aunt Rose said, as she walked towards the Christmas tree. Tracy joined her there.

"Our tree is missing something at the top!" Tiffany said, clapping her hands.

A smile slowly spread across Aunt Rose's face as she and Tracy nodded in agreement.

"And we could put a mistletoe at the top and collect a donation of a dollar for everyone who kisses under it," she said, her eyeballs almost bulging out of their sockets.

"That's a brilliant idea Tiff," Aunt Rose said.

"I wholeheartedly agree," Tracy declared.

"Did you know that mistletoe symbolizes that life doesn't die," Tiffany said matter-of-factly.

"Interesting. I've always wondered where the tradition of kissing under the mistletoe came from?" Aunt Rose said.

"There are so many stories about that. Some people say it originated in ancient Greece and was done during marriage ceremonies as mistletoe stood for fertility. Others say it started with the Romans and enemies would make up under the mistletoe to represent peace," Tracy said.

"Wow! I work with some smart girls," Aunt Rose said as she patted both ladies on their backs.

They set to work. Tracy found some mistletoe in the storage unit at the back of the shop. Aunt Rose held a ladder in place, while Tracy careful placed the mistletoe with a red ribbon and berries near the top of the Christmas tree. Tiffany worked on a large poster that encouraged people to come and kiss under *In Season's* mistletoe if they wanted peace and fertility for the coming year. She drew a large one-dollar sign as the cost of the privilege and added all donations would go to charity.

Over the next few days, word about their proposition spread around town. At first, just a few people popped in to kiss under the mistletoe but after the third day, there was a steady stream of people that included grandparents, children with their parents, pets and their owners, workers, and even some members of the local police force dropped by; although, the object of their affection under the mistletoe were their badges.

Tracy was amazed to notice one afternoon that there was a line that stretched from the shop around the block. Tiffany prepared a playlist of popular Christmas songs that was on constant rotation and helped to enhance the holiday spirit. They had a small, red bucket at the counter which served to receive the donations. Tracy couldn't wait to find out how much they had raised when they handed the bucket to Pastor Butler.

One afternoon a familiar face walked through the door. Joseph Carter entered the shop with a lady on his arm who was definitely not his wife.

"Good morning ,ladies. You all are looking so lovely and I have to admit that tree is the best Christmas tree in Fern Grove," he said.

The lady on his arm chuckled in agreement.

"Thanks for your compliments Joseph," Tiffany said with a quizzical look on her face as she tried to remember if the lady on his arm was the same lady from the other day.

"C'mon Melanie, let's pucker up under the mistletoe," he said, leading her to the Christmas tree. They had a full kiss on the lips that made all the *In Season* ladies turn away in disgust.

Melanie, wearing a Christmas sweater with a big reindeer at the front pulled away from Joseph and cleaned her lips with the back of her hands.

"You're not going to get anything from Santa this year if you keep on being naughty," she said giggling like a baby who had been tickled.

"I'll give Santa a kiss if he was here right now and I reckon you deserve another one," he said as he pulled her towards him and planted another wet kiss on her lips.

Tracy could see Aunt Rose had gone red in her face and was close to breathing out fire if she could do that.

"That's enough kids," Tracy said, breaking up the lust birds.

Joseph put a five-dollar bill into the bucket.

"I'm sorry ladies. This little minx can't get her hands off me," he said as he walked out of the shop with Melanie.

"Who does that man think he is?" Tiffany said as she closed the door that had been left ajar.

"Don't think he's romantic anymore?" Tracy said.

"If I see that man in this shop again with another woman that's not his wife, I'm going to leave the shop and tell his wife," Aunt Rose said, folding her arms across her chest.

"Do you think we should stop the mistletoe challenge?" Tiffany said, looking at Tracy.

"You know, its crossed my mind but I don't think we should let one rotten egg spoil it for everyone else."

"I hope so," Aunt Rose said, as she arranged some carnations on the counter. "I wouldn't want us to be complicit in the breakdown of a marriage."

Later that evening on her way home, Tracy passed by Kim's grocery store to pick up some more chocolate. The packs she had bought before were gone and she loved the flavors Kim sold in her shop. Although Kim wasn't in the store, her assistant Juliette was there, arranging some fruits at the front of the store as Tracy approached the entrance. She was delighted to see that there was a red bucket on the counter, with a notice on it for customers to leave their spare change in it. As she turned the corner that led to the beverage section, she saw the last person in Fern Grove she wanted to see at that very moment. Joseph Carter. And he had seen her and was smiling in her direction.

"Hi, beautiful."

"Excuse me?" Tracy said, clutching her handbag.

"You know there's only me and you in the store. We could share our own kiss under these fluorescent lights. Shame they don't have mistletoe," he said, as he closed his eyes and puckered lips as if he wanted to give her a kiss. After a few seconds, he opened his eyes and started laughing when he saw the disgust on Tracy's face.

"What? I was just joking," he said, licking his lips.

"You're a fool, Joseph. You have a beautiful wife and a new born baby and you say and do all these nasty things behind their back."

"Hey, I'm just having fun. As long as they don't know, it won't hurt them."

"Well, one day they'll know. It'll hurt them and it'll hurt you," she said, as she grabbed three packs of chocolate and made her way to the counter, where she quickly paid and left the store.

That night in her apartment she cooked some mac and cheese and settled in front of her TV to watch some movies on the Hallmark channel.

She suddenly heard a loud noise which made her jump.

"Can you believe people are already lighting fireworks and it's not yet Christmas," she said, as she stroked Mr. Sydney, her Abyssinian cat.

She soon heard the sirens of an ambulance which caused her to go to her window to see what was happening. She noticed there was a small crowd on the street below as an ambulance slowly made its way up her road.

"I wonder what that's all about," she said, as she grabbed a jacket and rushed out of her apartment. On the street, she slowly made her way to where the ambulance had stopped.

"What happened?" she asked a lady with a brown trench coat.

"It seems someone was shot," she said.

"Oh no! Do you know who it was?"

"Someone said it was Joseph Carter. I think he's dead."

Tracy watched in disbelief as the body of Joseph Carter was stretchered into the back of the ambulance.

5

It was a rare start to the day. Tracy, Tiffany and Aunt Rose had all assembled at *Grind It Out,* a local coffee shop. Tracy always walked past the cafe on her way to work each morning and often popped in to grab a cup of coffee for her and an Earl Grey tea for Tiffany. As she walked past that morning, the smell of Arabica beans, which had permeated the area around the cafe, pulled her in.

She was surprised to see Tiffany in the line when she walked through the doors. Tiffany was there that morning as she had promised Tracy, she'd pick up their morning beverages. She reminded Tracy of this when she inquired. They were both surprised when they saw Aunt Rose walk in with an oversize gray coat that made her look out of place. The ladies always had some downtime before the hustle and bustle of the day began in earnest. But the location of their meeting this morning was rare.

"What are you doing here Aunt Rose?" Tracy asked.

"I'm here to get a cup of Camomile tea," Aunt Rose replied, pulling the winter jacket around her closer.

"But you never drink any hot drinks during the day," Tiffany interjected.

"Well, I woke up this morning with this funny feeling in my chest. My throat felt like it had sand particles lodged in it. And I felt a bit achy so I felt I'd grab a cup of hot herbal tea to chase away what was trying to jump on me."

"Aunt Rose, you should have stayed at home to recover. It looks like you may be coming down with something," Tracy said, a look of concern on her face.

"No. Never! I've been working for fifty-three years and I can count on my right hand the number of times I've missed work and none of them was because of sickness. I don't intend to start now," she said, shaking her head in Tracy's direction.

"That jacket looks cozy. Can I borrow it?" Tiffany said, stifling a giggle.

Aunt Rose playfully flicked her left cheek. "This cozy jacket belonged to my dear Frank. I knew I needed something extra this morning."

Aunt Rose had founded *In Season* with him a few years after they had gotten married. He was everything to her. A counselor, encourager, husband, lover, shoulder to cry on, soulmate, travel buddy but above all, friend. She missed him.

"Well, you definitely got something extra," Tracy said, with a mischievous look in her eyes.

"You can say what you want ladies, but I feel very warm in here and whatever was trying to get me down is finding another home," she said, shuffling along.

A little kid who was leaving the cafe with his mom tripped over Aunt Rose's jacket that had acquired a fair bit of real estate around her. He immediately got up to signify to his mom and Aunt Rose that he wasn't hurt.

"It seems your jacket is good at keeping you warm but getting others down," Tracy whispered.

"What was that Tracy?"

"Oh, nothing Aunt Rose. Hi Jurgen! Hi Helga!" Tracy said as she reached the front of the line.

She asked the other *In Season* ladies what they wanted and got it for them. When Jurgen asked her if they'd like the order to take away or have in the cafe, Tracy spun back to ask Aunt Rose and Tiffany.

"We should stay here and have it. I'm not one for drinking while I'm walking and don't fancy drinking cold tea," Aunt Rose said.

Tracy turned back to Jurgen and motioned to say that they'd like to have their drinks in the cafe.

They sat down by the window and spent a moment breathing in the smell of their hot beverages as they wrapped their hands around their cups.

"Did you hear what happened?" Tracy said.

"What?" Aunt Rose and Tiffany chorused.

"There's been another one."

"Another what Tracy?" Aunt Rose said.

"Another murder and you won't believe who it was?"

"Who was it, Tracy?" Tiffany mumbled, leaning closer to Tracy who sat opposite her.

"Joseph. Joseph Carter."

Aunt Rose shook her head in pity while Tiffany took a long sip from her cup.

"That boy was always trouble. Always trouble. But no one deserves for that to happen to them," Aunt Rose said.

"How did you hear about it?" Tiffany asked.

Tracy went on to tell them about the events of the previous night.

"I saw them place him in a white body bag before putting him in the ambulance."

"This is the worst thing that could happen at this time of the year. I wonder how Eve, his wife, is going to take it? I wonder if anyone has told her?"

"I'm sure after all this time, the police must have knocked on her door to give her the bad news. Speaking of time, we should be leaving," Tiffany said.

The other ladies looked at their watches and immediately drank the last bit of liquid in their cups. Aunt Rose took some time buttoning her jacket. The buttons reached down to her ankle and Tracy had to help her with the last two. As they walked out of *Grind It Out,* the cold chill from the distant Pacific Ocean made Tracy wish she had a blanket-sized winter jacket like her aunt. The ladies walked in silence as they made their way towards work. It seemed the drop in temperature made everyone walk a bit faster and mind their own business. The crunch of the melting snow beneath Tracy's feet was a sound she detested. She couldn't wait to get into a warm room.

As they walked past the library, Tracy noticed a figure who seemed lost and out of place. It was Eve Carter. She cut a forlorn figure as the world seemed to pass her by. Tracy noticed that she had a buggy with her little son in it. Oh boy. Tracy couldn't bear to imagine what she was going through. It seemed Aunt Rose and Tiffany had also spotted Eve. They collectively slowed down as they got closer to her.

"Hi Eve," Aunt Rose said.

"Hi," she replied.

"So sorry to hear about your loss," Tracy said.

Eve burst out crying. Tracy looked left and right. She looked at her aunt. She noticed Aunt Rose's eyes were red. Aunt Rose reached out and hugged Eve. Tiffany joined them. Tracy rubbed Eve's back as her shoulders rose and fell as she sobbed.

"Let me quickly run and open the shop. It's freezing out here," Tiffany said, as she ran ahead of them.

Aunt Rose hooked her arm through Eve's and they walked arm in arm. Tracy took charge of the buggy and followed behind them. It seemed everyone else they walked past was either too busy in their own thoughts or the discomfort of the weather to notice the most recent widow in town. Tracy was thankful that the shop was open when they arrived. Tiffany had already turned on the heater which was already making the place warm. Tracy pulled an armchair, reserved for Aunt Rose, to the warmest place in the shop and ushered Eve to it.

The kettle whistling in the background was evidence Tiffany was in the process of making something warm for Eve.

"How are you keeping dear," Aunt Rose said as she sat next to Eve and held her hands.

"Not too well. The police woke me up last night and gave me the bad news. Officer Wayne Copeland said someone shot my Joseph," she said, as she began to sob again.

Aunt Rose squeezed her hands. Tiffany set a pot of tea next to her.

"He was such a good man," Eve said between sobs.

Aunt Rose and Tracy exchanged a quizzical glance at each other.

"He was always there for me. I just don't know what I'll do without my Joe," she said, as she began crying a bit louder.

Aunt Rose reached out and hugged her. Tracy looked at Eve's son who was sleeping peacefully in his buggy. A tear rolled down her left cheek.

"How did you manage when you lost your husband, Mrs. Bishop?" Eve asked as she wiped her eyes and blew her nose with some tissue which Tiffany had given her.

"I won't lie to you, honey. The first few days are the hardest. But you'll get through. I know your mom, Juliette, will be a rock you can lean on at this time. It won't be easy, but you have to be strong for you and your little man over there," she said, wiping a tear that was trickling down Eve's cheek.

"I just don't know what I'll do without him. He made me laugh. He provided for us. My folks didn't like him much, but I guess with time they would have known him the way I knew him. Dependable and trustworthy."

Just then, a loud crash was heard from the little kitchen.

"Are you okay Tiffany?" Tracy shouted.

"I'm okay. Nothing to worry about," she yelled back.

"I'm so sorry. I must be making my way. You guys have a business to run. Thanks for the hospitality and kind words," she said as she rose.

Aunt Rose gave her another hug. Tracy followed suit.

"Let's go Hunter," Eve said, as she took control of the buggy and moved towards the door of the shop. "It's just going to be you and me now."

Aunt Rose and Tracy opened the door for her and watched for a while as she made her way down the street filled with people but alone in her grief.

6

"That woman doesn't know the man she married," Tiffany said as Aunt Rose and Tracy walked back into the shop.

Tracy flicked the switch to put on the Christmas tree and sat on a stool behind the counter.

"Either that or she's in serious denial," Tracy said.

"Or she's going through a very traumatic time in her life and we all need to extend some compassion and sympathy towards her," Aunt Rose said as she looked at both ladies.

"Dependable and trustworthy? Those are the last words I think anyone would use to describe Joseph Carter," Tiffany said, folding her arms across her chest.

"I believe we should focus less on her judgement now and more on her loss," Aunt Rose said, shaking her head.

"I'm sorry Aunt Rose. It just makes me so sad that that woman is suffering over a man who doesn't deserve her sympathy."

"Maybe not. But they were married and that woman is honoring the memory of her child's father."

They all stared at the Christmas tree which was flickering different colors in a pattern and frequency that was soothing.

"Let's get to work ladies. It's a new day," Tracy said.

Tiffany began placing flowers outside the shop to help attract business. Tracy began looking through the store's tablet that contained pending orders and deliveries for the day. The diary seemed thin for that day. She placed the tablet on the counter and placed the red donation bucket, which was behind the counter, on top of it. She had dropped what they had raised thus far with Pastor Butler the previous night. They had been surprised when they realized they had raised more than five hundred dollars. She wondered how much they'd be able to raise over the next few days. Aunt Rose tugging on her arms shook her out of her reverie.

"We need to stop this Mistletoe challenge Tracy," she said.

"No way Aunt Rose. We raised more than five hundred dollars in a few days. Do you know how much we could raise over this month if we keep this going?"

"I don't care. It pains me to think that our challenge in some way helped to put a strain on Eve's marriage and maybe led to Joseph's death."

"Don't say that Aunt Rose. We can't let one person's stupidity stop a good cause that'll help many people. Should every business establishment that Joseph walked into with a lady that wasn't his wife close down any profitable initiative they started? It's a shame that Joseph came here with a lady that wasn't his wife, but why should that stop some homeless person finding a home this Christmas?" she said.

"I just feel uncomfortable that some people could come here and exchange kisses. Kisses that could turn deadly," she said, leaning on the counter. "I really think we should stop it. Maybe we could think of something else to raise money."

The chiming of the bells above the shop door made them turn in that direction. A burly man dressed in black from head to toe walked in. He had so much facial hair, Tracy was sure he could smuggle something across the border in it. He didn't look like the kind of customer who frequented *In Season*. He looked vaguely familiar, but Tracy couldn't recall where she had met him.

"I just wanted to stop by and say thank you," he said.

Tracy remembered. He was the man who had approached her for change on the night it was snowing.

"Thank us for what," Aunt Rose said, rising up from her seat.

"Thank you for caring for the homeless," he said, taking off his hat.

"Oh.... I... we... it's the least we could do," Aunt Rose stuttered.

"You don't understand Ma'am. My name's Russell, but my friends call me Rusty. I used to be in the military, but after I was discharged for an incident that was partly my fault, my life went into a downward spiral. My marriage broke down and people I considered friends, deserted me. I started drifting from state to state and everywhere I went, I was reminded of my failings. Pastor Butler's been a good man to me, and yesterday, he said some good people in town had been raising money for people in my situation and he offered me a place at a local motel," he said.

Tracy brought a chair for him to sit on as he had been shifting from foot to foot.

"Thank you. He told me I didn't have to let the mistakes of yesterday stop me from having a better tomorrow. For the first time in a long time, I feel hopeful," he said, a smile breaking across his face.

Tracy could understand how he felt. After losing her job in a big investment bank in Portland, she never thought she'd able to get back on her feet. Successive rejections at job interviews only served to make her feel like the best part of her life was over. She had neglected her personal hygiene and would sometimes spend the entire day in her pajamas, eating ice cream, unless she had an interview to attend. She hadn't piled on too much weight in that period, but she despised the reflection she saw in the mirror. She hated going out in town and seeing people from her past life who'd inevitably ask her what she was now doing. She hated lying, but she always cringed when they offered her shallow words of comfort that couldn't build her self-image or replenish her fast dwindling savings account. She never knew an offer by her aunt to help out at her floundering flower shop would serve as the turning point in her life. At first, she thought it'd serve as a stopgap, but with each passing day, she had grown to love the job and enjoyed serving the people of Fern Grove. A year ago, she wondered if she had any skills to offer outside the walls of a corporate building. A year later, she was confident and hopeful she'd help her aunt turn her struggling business into a success.

The chiming of the bells above the door ushered a man dressed in an expensive suit and a little girl, dressed in a red winter jacket, into the shop. The man had an air about him that exuded confidence and wealth. This was the kind of customer *In Season* was used to welcoming. They had big smiles on their faces and the little girl had cute pigtails that reminded Tracy of a five-year-old picture of herself which she had recently discovered.

"Good morning ladies and gentleman. My name is Michael Diggs. I own a printing company in town. My daughter told me that her friend told her that you're raising money for a good cause and we just have to kiss under the mistletoe. Can we?" he said, holding unto his daughter who still had a big smile plastered across her face.

"Of course!" Tracy said. "You just have to do it by the Christmas tree."

"C'mon sugar," he said, as he knelt down by the Christmas tree. He closed his eyes and pointed to his cheeks. His daughter started giggling and place a big kiss on her dad's face.

"Thank you. Can I return the favor?" he said, looking at her with puppy eyes. She put her hands on her chin and stared into space like she was deep in thought.

"Okay, Daddy," she said, breaking into an infectious giggle that made the grownups in the room start laughing. Her dad lightly kissed her cheeks which made her laugh louder and the grownups laughed more.

"Where can I place my donation?" Michael said.

"Over here," Tracy replied, pointing to the donation bucket. He brought out a wad of cash and placed it in the bucket. His daughter brought out a few coins from her purse and put them in the bucket.

"Thank you," Tracy said.

"Thank you. Thank you both," Rusty said, as he rose up from his chair to shake Michael's hands.

"Who are you, sir?" Michael asked, a bit taken aback by the vigor with which Rusty shook his hands.

"Your donation is helping people like me, sir. I've been homeless for a while and your donation will get me off the streets."

"Oh. I'm glad to hear that. Is there anything I can do for you?"

"Not sure. I took an art course at college and my family and friends always said they loved my designs. I could maybe make some which you could help me sell," he said.

"I can do better than that. You can make them and we can sell them on my website. Plus, you can work in my office and get a decent wage. Here's my business card. Please pop over on Monday and we'll make your dream a reality," he said.

"Thank you so much. I can't believe this. Thank you, sir," Russell said, staring at the business card in his hands.

"Thank you, Daddy. I told you it was a good idea for us to come to *In Season*," the little girl said.

Tracy, Aunt Rose and Tiffany watched as Michael, his daughter and Rusty walked out of the shop.

"That was beautiful," Tiffany said, after they had left the shop.

"It sure was," Aunt Rose whispered. "Our little mistletoe challenge raised a bit more money and helped a homeless guy get a job."

"Do you still think those kisses are deadly Aunt Rose?" Tracy said as she winked at her aunt.

7

Tracy loved Christmas as it afforded her an opportunity to indulge. Indulge in eating. Indulge in binge-watching her cherished TV programs. And her favorite, indulge in shopping. Window shopping to be more exact. She loved going to the mall to feast her eyes on the various decorations in the shops. She enjoyed listening to the Christmas songs from carolers, at this time of the year, who were sure to provide a welcome distraction from her shopping.

She loved eavesdropping on the unusual conversations at this time of the year. She once stumbled on a woman trying to explain to her grandson that she couldn't go on a date with Santa Claus. The toddler had reminded her of her oft-repeated wish to find a man after grandad had passed away. The little boy felt Santa Claus, who he had just seen in a grotto, would make a good boyfriend. The dear old lady had to admit that she would like male company, but Santa Claus wasn't her kind of man. The little boy had started crying because he believed Santa would make the perfect granddad as he could give them gifts every day.

Tracy had promised Aunt Rose she would spend Christmas and Boxing Day with her. As she rummaged through her wardrobe that morning, she discovered she was low on socks and thermal wear. She fed Mr. Sydney and promised him she would get him a new cat collar if she spotted one. She had seen an ad on TV for a cat collar that had a GPS tracker that could be used to find your cat if they ever got lost. Mr. Sydney was the laziest cat she knew, but you never knew. If he ever decided to jump through one of the windows, she left open to air out her apartment after she had attempted to cook something exotic, she couldn't fathom where she'd begin her search. The only sticking point when she saw the ad was the price of the collar. She believed the holiday season would offer opportunities for her to get one at a better price. She made a mental note to look out for the collar when she got to the mall.

Infinity, a new mall in Greenwich, a town next to Fern Grove, was filled with people who were in the festive spirit and ready to spend some holiday dollars. Tracy was glad she was able to get a day off in the middle of the week. Before joining *In Season,* her aunt had worked six days a week and only closed on Sundays. Tracy could see how the monotony of coming into the same surroundings day after day, on her own, was detrimental to her aunt's well-being. She had previously run the shop with her late husband but since his demise, Aunt Rose had had to run the ship solo. The reminders of how life had been before Frank passed caused Aunt Rose to neglect the upkeep of the flower shop. Tracy had suggested they all had one day off apart from Sundays to recharge their batteries. It had at first seemed counter-intuitive to her aunt as she believed the one-day loss would mean a decrease in the shop's bottomline. However, the opposite had occurred. Tracy, Tiffany and Aunt Rose had always come back the day after their time off with a spring in their step.

Tracy aimlessly wandered from store to store trying not to get in anyone's way. At the end of the mall, she walked into a clothes shop that sold dinner and formal wear. An emerald green floor-length gown displayed in the shop's window pulled her in. She coasted from aisle to aisle looking for the emerald green gown that had caught her attention. The store was well lit and there were several ladies like her shopping but Tracy felt like someone was watching her. She turned around to see an elderly lady who had a figure Tracy would die for. The woman was too engrossed in comparing two knee-length gowns in burgundy and teal to be the person watching her. She turned around the corner and looked to see if there was an attendant that could help her find the gown she wanted. As she moved aside dresses on a rack, she could feel the hair standing on the back of her neck. Who was following her? It surely wasn't Rusty, the homeless man? He was a tall and huge man and she'd surely have noticed him as he walked through the store. Tracy quickened her steps and wondered if it was worth continuing her search in that store.

"Hello."

She felt a tap on her shoulder that almost made her scream. She turned around to see Melanie, the one-time bit on the side for the recently deceased Joseph Carter.

"Hi, Mel."

"What are you doing here?" Mel said, smacking her lips as she chewed gum.

Tracy looked around the shop and raised both her hands incredulously, widening her eyes as she gazed at Mel.

"Stupid me," she said, as she banged her forehead with her right hand and broke into an awful cackle. "Forgive me. I sometimes ask the most stupid questions."

"Can I help you, Mel?"

"Um, yes you can. I saw you talking with Eve Carter the other day..."

"And..."

"And I hope you didn't tell her about Joe and me?"

Tracy put her hands on her hips as she turned around to make sure that no one was within earshot. "That's the last thing I would do. Why were you with him, Mel? Did you know that he had a wife and child?"

"I knew but Joe was such a bad boy and I love bad boys," she said as she broke again into that awful cackle that made a young lady who was coming in their direction turn around.

"That's despicable behavior Mel," Tracy whispered. The comment wiped the smile from Mel's face.

"Where were you the night he was murdered?"

"What are you trying to say?" she said.

Tracy looked around as Mel had raised her voice. She regretted for a brief moment her brashness in confronting Mel in such a manner.

"I'm trying to say there's a young widow in Fern Grove whose husband has died and I wonder if you had anything to do with it?" she said.

Mel bowed her head.

"Honey, is everything okay?"

Tracy looked up to see a man in a purple spandex vest under a leather jacket walking towards them. He had a buzz cut and looked like he was preparing to compete in a Mr. Universe competition as he had muscles bulging from different parts of his body. He whisked Mel into his arms and gave her a long, wet kiss. Tracy felt like she could taste the contents of her breakfast that morning and looked around to see if there was a trash can, she might be forced to throw up in.

"Let's go, babe. I've been looking all over for you," he said, pulling her away.

As Mel walked past Tracy, she whispered, "I love bad boys. I don't kill bad boys."

Tracy watched as the slim, petite figure of Mel walked beside the herculean figure of her new catch. She had never seen such an odd couple. She was amazed that Mel had shown no remorse when Joseph's name was mentioned. And why was she interested in knowing if Tracy had mentioned anything to Eve? She shook her head and continued her search for the emerald green gown. As she got closer to the front of the store, she saw a woman with the gown she had been looking for asking the sales assistant a question.

Oh no!

She hoped the lady wasn't thinking of buying the outfit. As Tracy contemplated how she was going to convince the woman that the outfit did nothing to compliment the color of her eyes or figure, she felt a tap on her shoulder. Not again! She turned around to see a familiar face.

"Hi, Tracy."

It was Karen, a lovely twenty-something with strawberry blonde hair who worked at the latest restaurant in town.

"Hi Karen," Tracy said and hugged her.

"This is the second time I've bumped into you at this mall Tracy."

Tracy had done the flower arrangement for *The Grub,* the establishment where Karen worked when it had opened. It was owned by a young man named Luke. There was a murder that had occurred on the opening night of his restaurant and he had been identified as the primary suspect. Tracy was glad he was eventually acquitted when the murderer was found.

"It's my day off and I'm just doing some window shopping before Christmas," she said, flicking a stray hair behind her ears. "How's things at *The Grub?*"

"Things are very busy. It's my day off too and I'm so glad to be away from there. I love working there, but sometimes, it's good to be away from work. Do you know what I mean?"

"I totally understand."

"I heard about the mistletoe challenge at *In Season*. I might just swing by one of these days."

"Ooh. Is there anyone in your life?"

"Well, it's early days, but there is someone. Maybe I'll bring him along. You know you guys inspired us to do something to raise money for the homeless," she said.

"Oh, really? What did you guys do?" she asked.

"I was definitely not part of it, but Luke came up with the bright idea that if anyone could eat three hot chilis without drinking water for a minute, we would donate ten dollars to our donation fund."

"I thought the whole purpose of a challenge was to make customers donate?" Tracy said, scratching her head.

"I thought so too, but Luke had his own ideas."

"So how did it go?" she queried.

"Well, we had to cancel it," Karen replied.

"Why?"

"When Joseph Carter attempted to eat the chilis and almost passed out with his face as red as Rudolph's nose, we had to stop the challenge."

Both ladies burst into a belly laugh. Tracy noticed that Karen's eyes were watery and her face had gone a deep shade of red. Tracy, for once, forgot she was in a public place and joined Karen as they both supported themselves as they laughed. Tracy paused and touched Karen's arm.

"You do know he's dead."

"Who?" she said, covering her mouth.

"Joseph Carter."

"Oh no. He was such a good customer and always had nice things to say to me although they sometimes bordered on being flirty. His wife must be so distraught."

"Yeah, Eve isn't taken it too well."

"Eve? His wife's name or the lady who came to the restaurant with him wasn't called Eve."

"Oh, let me guess. Was her name Mel," Tracy said, scrunching up her nose in disgust.

"No. Her name was Norma," Karen said.

8

As Tracy went about her business the next day at *In Season,* she pondered over what Karen had said to her. She couldn't believe that Joseph was cheating on his wife with two women. It seemed like almost everyone in town knew Joseph was a cheating scoundrel but his wife. There must have been signs for Eve to know or at least suspect, that Joseph wasn't the man she thought he was. She wondered how Eve would feel when she eventually knew the truth. Would the blow be softened by the fact that the object of her misplaced affection was now six feet down under? Maybe she knew but simply refused to accept the reality of a broken relationship.

Tracy knew the feeling. She had been involved in a serious relationship once upon a time that ended really bad. The man of her dreams, the man she thought she'd spend the rest of her life with had left her high and dry. She had met David Baker while she was at college and they had both graduated together. His piercing rugged looks, strong ambition for success and gentle way with people, had endeared him to Tracy's heart. Sadly, the qualities that endeared him to her, were what also captured the attention of his boss. She had seduced him with the promise of a globetrotting lifestyle and a fast track on the corporate ladder. If he played ball with her, she'd provide many opportunities to be the man she believed he could be. David had sacrificed their relationship for his blind ambition to be a corporate titan. After their relationship had broken up, David traveled to Europe and she hadn't heard from him. It had taken awhile for Tracy to date again and she wasn't sure she was ready to get into another long-term relationship.

A loud sneeze made put an end to her reminiscing and alerted her to the presence of a customer in the shop. Not just any customer. It was handsome Detective Warren Copeland.

"Hi Tracy. Hope this isn't a bad time?" he said, with his hands in his pocket.

Tracy had recently been on a date with Detective Copeland at a charity event he had organized on behalf of the local police force. It wasn't what you would call a typical date as they had to cater for the less privileged in the community and Tracy had helped to serve and make them feel special. She didn't mind as she loved making people smile and feel appreciated. Prior to that, her only close encounter with Detective Copeland was at a salsa class she had gone to on a whim and bumped into him. He had been her dance partner and she discovered the detective had good feet and a warm personality. She had never dated an officer of the law but was ready to see if things would evolve with him.

"Um... no... I'm sorry. I was just lost in thought. How can I help you?" she said.

"I just popped into *Grind it Out* and remembered that you liked your Americano coffee with cream so I got one for you," he said, extending his offering to her.

So, he remembered.

"Oh, thanks Warren. I needed that," she said, as she grabbed the cup from him and took a sip. "You seem a little tired," she said, noticing the bags under his eyes.

"I am very tired. This Joseph Carter case is driving me nuts," he said.

"Oh, anything you can share?" she said, clumsily batting her eyelashes.

Just then a message came on his radio.

"I think there's something in your eyes Tracy. I'm sorry but I have to go. I'll pop round later," he said as he darted out of the shop.

Tracy watched him go and gazed at the swinging door.

"Hmmm... is it confirmed," Tiffany said, as Tracy turned to see she was staring at her with a goofy smile on her face.

"Is what confirmed?"

"That you guys are now a couple," she said, a big smile flashing across her face.

"Tiffany when... if we become a couple, you'll probably be the first to know."

"Please don't keep the good officer waiting," she said.

"Waiting for what?" Tracy said, folding her arms across her chest.

"Waiting for you to say I do. I can't wait to be on your bridal party," she said.

"Tiffany! I've not been on a proper date yet with him and you're already thinking of a bridal party. You've been watching too many romantic movies."

"Guilty as charged," she said, lifting her hands up. "But I do have to say, you two would make a great couple."

"I don't know if to say thank you or mind your own business."

"I'll take both," she said, as she hummed the *Going to the Chapel of Love* song.

"This is the place!"

Tracy turned to see that Mel and her new body-builder boyfriend had walked into the shop. She was the last person Tracy wanted to see.

"Jimbo, we don't need to be here," Mel said, as she attempted to drag him out of the shop but with hands the size of an oak tree, it was an exercise in futility.

"My buddy Leo told me he kissed his girl under the mistletoe in this shop and donated a dollar. He said it was the best dollar he ever spent," he said, as he moved towards the counter.

"Hi Mel," Tracy said.

"Um... hi Tracy," Mel said, with her head bowed.

"Hey, I know you. We bumped into you at *Infinity* the other day," he said, as he grinned to reveal a gold tooth. "You didn't tell me your friend worked here Mel."

"Yeah Mel, why didn't you tell..."

"Jimbo," he said.

"Why didn't you tell Jimbo I worked here?" she said.

"You're such a joker Tracy," Mel said, breaking into a cackle that was so irritating.

Jimbo placed a dollar in the red donation bucket and pulled Mel towards the Christmas tree. He planted a kiss on Mel that Tracy could tell she didn't like. He pulled away and flexed his muscles.

"You're really bad for me but I love you so much," he said. "Do you know how I met Mel?" he said, turning towards Tracy. She shook her head. "I met her a few days ago at the local gym. There she was, all lonely and pretty and trying to lift weights. I showed her how it's done," he said, kissing his biceps.

Tracy could see Tiffany, who was positioned behind them, pretending to puke. She had to control herself from chuckling.

"I think it's time we left," Mel said.

"If my girl says it's time to go, then it's time to go," he said, grabbing her hand and almost dragging her out of the shop. Tracy and Tiffany shook their heads in pity and disgust as they watched them go.

"It's a good thing Aunt Rose wasn't here to witness that," Tracy said.

"True. By the way, where's Aunt Rose?" Tiffany said.

"She finally succumbed to the flu that had been ailing her. A few days off will do her a world of good."

The day went by without much drama. A few customers came in to pick up their Christmas trees. Tiffany shared with Tracy a Christmas playlist she had created on Spotify. It contained many Christmas classics and it was fun to see customers sing along when they came into the shop. Christmas without music just wasn't Christmas.

A few minutes before the shop was due to close for the day, a familiar face peered behind the door.

"It's me!"

It was Detective Copeland.

"What brings me here?"

"Well, me remembered, me said, me'd get back to you. So, here is me," he said, winking at her.

Tracy smiled and turned around to make sure Tiffany wasn't in the shop at that moment. Thankfully, she was out back sorting a late order.

"Well, it's always nice to have me... I mean you pop over."

He gave a bow in response. He looked around and grabbed a stool that was next to a wall that had pictures of floral designs and sat down, letting out a big sigh.

"Was that hunger or tiredness or restlessness?" she said laughing.

"It's all of the above," he replied, taking off his jacket.

"You were just about to say something about the Joseph Carter case before you left..."

"Hmmm... you're always asking me about cases I'm working on." he said, shaking his head as he looked at her.

"Well, I'm just curious to know that the law enforcement agency in town are doing all in their power to find a killer."

"You know what I think?" he said, a serious look etched on his face.

"What?"

"I think you need to join the force."

"Me? No way!"

"You should think about it. You seem to have a way of asking the right questions and being in the right place at the right time."

Tracy had helped Detective Copeland solve a few cases in her own little way since she returned to Fern Grove.

"I won't promise you that I'll think about it because I won't. But I'll be happy to help with any cases you might have in any way that I can," she said as she switched off the light on the Christmas tree. "Speaking of which, how's the murder case for Joseph Carter going?"

He sighed again.

"That bad?"

"We've arrested someone."

"Who?"

He looked around to see if anyone was nearby.

"His wife, Eve," he whispered.

"No!" Tracy said, as she covered her mouth in shock at her outburst and the new revelation.

"Please don't tell anyone... I'm sure it'll soon be common news in this small town but she's a strong suspect."

"Why?"

"That I can't tell," he said, bidding her farewell as he walked out of the shop.

9

Tracy was waiting at a local salon to get her hair done. She fixed an appointment with Becky Sue who owned the aptly named *Becky Sue Styles* hair salon. Becky Sue had worked in Hollywood on the hair and makeup department of a popular TV show for several years. She had returned to Fern Grove in the last few years after her father took ill. Tracy had always had this impression that people who came from or worked in Hollywood were loud, phoney and materialistic. Becky Sue was none of these. She treated every client who walked into her salon like they were an A-list celebrity. People came from towns around Fern Grove to get their hair styled by Becky Sue. Although her prices were Hollywood, the service and transformation one went through after getting styled by Becky Sue and her team was worth it.

Tracy tried to occupy herself by reading magazines while she waited her turn but she just couldn't concentrate on any article. Her mind was on Eve. She was the last person Tracy thought would be a suspect in this murder case. Eve's grief on the morning they had bumped into her seemed genuine. Was she faking all those tears? If the police had arrested her then surely there was a good reason for that. But what if they were wrong? Tracy had stayed in Fern Grove long enough to know that not every suspect arrested by the police was the actual perpetrator of a crime. She had firsthand experience of being wrongly accused and knew the anguish that could cause. If only Detective Copeland could share more with her. Tracy suddenly noticed that Becky Sue was standing in front of her and waving.

"Is there a problem Becky Sue?" she said.

"Of course, there's a problem Tracy. Your phone's been ringing the whole time. Now I love Santa Claus saying ho-ho-ho but after the seventh time, it gets a little bit disturbing," she said smiling.

"I'm so sorry," she said, as she looked around the salon to see that all eyes were on her. "I wonder who it could be," she said as she fumbled in her purse for her mobile phone.

As she was searching her purse for her phone, it started ringing again. She could feel all eyes on her.

"Don't worry I've almost gotten it," she said as she hurried towards the salon's exit. She was able to press the 'Answer' button before it rang a fifth time.

"Hi, Isabel."

"Hi, Tracy. Did I catch you at a bad time? I've tried a couple of time to call you. I could call later."

"No that's okay. I'm in a hair salon and due to the noise here, I didn't hear when you rang," Tracy lied.

"How's good ol' Fern Grove and my award-winning florist entrepreneur?"

"Award-winning, not yet, florist entrepreneur... always trying to perfect that," she said, as she stepped aside to let a woman, who had wild hair like she had just come out of hibernation, through the door that Tracy was temporarily blocking as she took her call.

"It's so boring this time of year at CMB," Isabel said.

Isabel was Tracy's close friend and they had both worked at CMB Capital before she was shown the exit.

"I remember those days. I used to love all the parties organized by the firm at this time of the year."

"Well, this year, the official line was that there's no cash in the till to throw any shindigs. I'm seriously thinking of leaving Tracy."

"I thought you told me a few weeks back that things were changing. New management and all."

"Yes and no. We definitely have new management and they've promised to change but when that change becomes apparent is anybody's guess."

"It seems like you're serious about leaving."

"Its crossed my mind a lot in the last few weeks but I'm scared," she whispered.

"I don't know if they've truly stopped the cull but it's better to take your own future into your hands. The worst feeling in the world is to get called into an office and told your services are no longer required," she said.

"Anyway, how's Fern Grove? I sometimes wish I could swap lives with you for a day."

"Things are good. We started this charity initiative at the shop and we've raised quite a bit of money for a charity in town."

"That sounds fun. What's this initiative?"

"Tiffany had this brilliant idea that we could have mistletoe on the Christmas tree in the shop and customers could sneak a kiss under it and make a donation."

"So, have you and Detective Copeland been getting friendly under the mistletoe?"

"No!" Tracy screeched, looking around to see if anyone had heard her shout.

"Steady on Miss I-really-like-him-but-I'm-going-to-pretend-to-myself-and-everyone-else-that-I-don't."

There was an awkward pause in the air between the friends.

"Anyway, I don't think Warren's ready for a relationship now," Tracy whispered.

"Why?"

"He's knee-deep in a murder investigation."

"For a small town, Fern Grove does have its fair share of murder investigations. What's the situation this time?"

"A local, cheating scoundrel was found dead."

"I'm guessing not many people, at least decent people, are crying over him."

"Funny you should say that but his wife's actually in a state of despair. My aunt and I spent some time with her and she's really mourning her husband. But guess what's recently transpired?"

"Ooh, the plot thickens," Isabel said.

"There's been a recent arrest and guess who they arrested?"

"Don't tell me... his wife?"

"How did you know?" Tracy said, moving the phone away from her ears and looking at it.

"Did I ever tell you that I took a course in criminology at college?"

"No, you didn't."

"You should tell Detective Copeland that you have a friend who can help with his case but I charge though."

"What's your fee?"

"Considering the referral will be coming from you... my fee is that he asks my dear friend out!"

"Bella!" Tracy yelled. She listened as Isabel laughed on the other end of the phone. One of Becky Sue's assistants motioned to Tracy that it was her turn.

"Gotta run. I'm next."

"You take care and remember to deliver my message to Detective Copeland."

"Bye Isabel," Tracy said as she hung up and shook her head at the phone. She missed her friend.

When Tracy got home that night, she spent a bit of time admiring her new look in the floor-length mirror. Becky Sue and her team had tamed her wild curls and given her a girl-next-door look in the process. They had done a fabulous job in styling big spiral curls that bounced off her shoulders. The curls at the front of her head were transformed into bangs that ended right above her eyebrows. If only there was someone to admire her or somewhere chic, she could go to.

She remembered the emerald green gown she had gotten from the *Insanity* shopping mall. After she had finished her conversation with Karen, she had asked the shop assistant where she could find the same emerald green gown that was on the mannequin out front. The assistant had smiled and fished out the emerald green gown from a rack behind her. She said it was the last one in the store as the one on the mannequin had some irreparable tears. Tracy rushed to her bedroom and got the dress out of her closet. She changed into it and put on some matching green earrings which she had inherited from her mom. She sashayed out of the room and did a catwalk up down her corridor, gazing at her image in the mirror as she twisted to see how the gown fitted her figure. It was perfect. Mr. Sydney purred in agreement as he looked up at her.

"Mommy looks the business, doesn't she?" she said, bending down to stroke him. Something melodic caught her attention just then. It was coming from her window. She tiptoed towards it and peeped behind the curtain. In the street below, were a group of carolers singing *Silent Night*. Tracy could see that a small crowd was gathering around the singers.

"I need to get a front-row seat for this Mr. Sydney," she said, looking at her cat who had climbed onto the ledge of the window. "Wanna come?"

He bolted away.

"Don't you have the Christmas spirit boy? Okay, I'll tell you all about it when I get back."

She grabbed her winter jacket and put on her boots and rushed out of the door. When she got to the street, the crowd had grown. Tracy squeezed through the crowd to the front where she could sing in tune with the carolers.

Silent night, holy night
All is calm, all is bright
Round yon Virgin, Mother and Child
Holy infant so tender and mild
Sleep in heavenly peace
Sleep in heavenly...

She felt a tap on her shoulders. She looked around and saw Warren Copeland looking at her. He was wearing a black and red Christmas sweater that had a gingerbread man on it that said *'Christmas broke me.'*

"I didn't know you could sing," he whispered in her ear.

"I didn't know you liked Christmas songs," she replied.

They both sang the last verse of the song together.

"What song should we sing next?" the lead singer asked the crowd.

"How about *Feliz Navidad*?" someone shouted from the back.

"I don't think I know that one," he replied.

"Of course, you do," a lady standing next to him said as she nudged him in the ribs. Tracy assumed she was his wife. "It's the song that has the lyrics *I wanna wish you a Merry Christmas* at the end."

"Oh, that song... how could I forget. Let's take it away," he said.

"I love your new hairstyle Tracy," Warren said, a gentle smile playing across his face.

"Thank you," she said, her cheeks turning a deep shade of red.

"I would have dressed up if I knew I was going to bump into you here," he said.

As the crowd swayed from side to side as they sang the *'I want to wish you a Merry Christmas'* part of the song, Tracy noticed that Warren had his arm across her shoulder. She leaned into him. Something felt good about this.

10

The next morning, Tracy woke up feeling good. At first, she couldn't pinpoint what was making her feel giddy. Was it her bargain purchase from *Insanity* that she saw hanging on the wall, opposite her bed? Or maybe it was the fact that Christmas would be in a few days and she'd be spending it with Aunt Rose and a few relatives who were coming from out of town? Or maybe it was the fact that they had raised so much money for the homeless? While all those things were worth celebrating and being proud of, she was sure it wasn't what was making her have a big smile on her face that morning. A smile. Yes, she remembered what was giving her this smile. It was Detective Warren Copeland.

After the carolers had finished their Christmas rendition, Tracy had walked Warren back to his squad car parked at the end of the road. Then he had walked her back to the front of her apartment. She then walked him back to his squad car. They repeated this about twelve times. Through it all, she had gotten to know a bit more about Warren Copeland. He had decided to join the police force after his parents were killed in a hit and run accident. The perpetrator was never found. A young fifteen-year-old Warren had promised himself he'd join the police force and become a detective to solve homicides. He never wanted someone else to go through what he went through. He originally came from Washington state and moved to Fern Grove after his training on the police force. It wasn't his original plan to move to a small town but fate had its hand in the trajectory of his career path. A shortage of officers in the Fern Grove police force plus a pending mass exodus of soon-to-be-retired officers had a big part to play in his move to Fern Grove. A senior officer who was his mentor had advised him to take the opportunity in a small town and learn the ropes from seasoned professionals who'd have a lot to share. Warren intended to stay in Fern Grove for a year but a year had turned into two and two into four. Before he knew it, he had spent over a decade in Fern Grove... and he loved it. He had fallen in love with the town and the town had fallen in love with him. He loved how each case was not just another random item on his tray but linked to real people he knew.

Tracy got to discover that he had almost been married twice but, on each occasion, it had been called off by the bride-to-be. It had left him disillusioned with dating. Tracy had asked if he was now ready, to which he had smiled, and nodded. They ended the night midway between her apartment and his car. Underneath a streetlight, as light snow began falling, they had exchanged numbers and kissed. The kiss. Tracy now knew what was making her giddy.

When she felt this way, it was hard for her to eat or do anything worthwhile. The best remedy for this predicament was sweating and the only way she knew to get a good sweat was to go jogging. She quickly changed into her tracksuit, brushed her teeth and made sure Mr. Sydney had some water to drink when he awoke.

The air that morning was crisp. Perfect weather for running. She put on her headphones and started jogging, as she listened to an inspirational playlist she had built on her phone. She decided to try a new route which wouldn't go through the nearby beach. At that time in the morning, the streets were almost void of any human activity. During a lull in the track she was listening to, she heard the waves of the Pacific Ocean pounding in the distance. Tracy loved her life at the moment. The only thing that cast a shade over this time in her life was the death of Joseph Carter. Unlike other murders that had occurred in Fern Grove, it seemed the common consensus was that Joseph had it coming. Apart from his wife, it seemed hardly anyone was sympathetic towards his demise.

Tracy had known some womanizers in her time but Joseph's philandering ways appeared to have affected most people in town. As she turned a corner to a street that had an upward incline, she noticed a lady was struggling to pick up the contents of her grocery bag which had fallen on the sidewalk. She hurried along to pick up two apples that were hurtling towards her.

"Here you go," she said, extending the apples to the lady who was kneeling down with her back towards Tracy. The woman turned around and Tracy wished she had used another route. It was Melanie.

"Oh... thanks Tracy," she said.

"Not a problem. What are you doing out this early in the morning?" she asked.

Melanie fell to the sidewalk in a crumpled heap. She buried her head in her hands and her heaving shoulders told Tracy what sort of state she was in. She looked up and down the street and couldn't see another soul within distance. She sat beside Mel and put her arm around her.

"What's the matter, Mel?"

"He dumped me," she said between sobs.

"Oh, the bodybuilder guy?"

"Yes, Jimbo dumped me," she said, looking up at Tracy and wiping her eyes.

"I'm sorry to hear that Mel. Did you like him?"

"I thought I did but he was only using me."

"Using you for what?" Tracy asked, zipping up her tracksuit top as a cold wind blew up the street.

"He used me to get to know about Joseph."

"I don't understand... but Joseph's dead," Tracy asked, with a skeptical look on her face.

"Yes, but Jimbo stole a black book that contained all Joe's contacts," Mel said, clapping her hands in exasperation.

"Oh... what profession is Joseph in... I mean, was Joseph in?" she said.

"He supplied medicinal supplements to people in the area. Jimbo was trying to fill the gap with Joe's passing. Now that he got what he wanted, he doesn't have any time for me," she said, burying her head in her hands again.

"Medicinal supplements? Mel, I honestly think you deserve more. I don't mean to judge as I haven't been in Fern Grove that long but I have to say your reputation isn't that good."

"Really?" she asked.

Tracy nodded her head. "Joseph... Jimbo... and whoever else was on the scene before I came."

"I swear there were only two other guys... Justin and Javier," she said, putting her hand on her chest.

Tracy cleared her throat and held Mel's hands. "You deserve more Mel. I heard you used to have a business?"

"Yes, I ran it with my mom but things haven't been easy. We run a cleaning business and serviced private and domestic residences. You can ask anyone around town; we had a great reputation."

"Well, what happened to this great reputation?"

"Javier happened to our business. He went back to Columbia after we dated for over two years. I thought he was going to be my one and only. My mom advised me over my relationships but I thought I knew better."

"You need to listen to your mom and pour your energy back into your business. It'll make her happy and make your customers happy but above all, you'll regain a sense of worth and joy as you see your service improve the lives of others."

"Thank you," Mel said as she wiped a tear that was trickling down her right cheek.

"Gotta run now but you take care and think about what I said," Tracy mumbled as she got to her feet and started jogging.

She found it hard regaining the pace she had before she ran into Melanie. She wondered what type of medicinal supplements Melanie was alluding to when she said Joseph supplied certain people in the area. The sun was coming up and its rays on Tracy's face gave her a renewed energy as she quickened her pace. She had assumed that Joseph had come to his untimely death at the hands of a woman whose heart he had broken. After her chat with Melanie, she began to wonder if it had come at the hand of a disgruntled business associate or dissatisfied customer. She began to wonder if the police had considered these other angles in their investigation?

As she approached a grocery store, which she had never visited, she remembered that she had almost run out toothpaste. She'd had to squeeze the last bit out that morning. She walked in and was amazed at how big it was. There was a big sign outside saying *Essentials* in neon lights. She couldn't remember any news about a new store opening in town. It looked small from the outside, but as soon as she got in, she noticed that the place was quite large.

"Can I help you, madam?"

She turned around to see a teenage boy with lots of freckles and pimples on his face, smiling at her.

"I wonder if you could tell me where I could find some toothpaste?" she said.

"It's at the end of aisle two. Do you want me to take you there?" he said.

"Nah, I'll be fine. How long have you guys been open for?"

"We just opened last week. Not a lot of people in Fern Grove know that we exist," he said.

"I see. Thanks for your help..." she squinted to read the name on his name badge. "Kyle. If I need any help, I'll come find you."

She walked along the first aisle taking in all the store had to offer. She turned around the corner and spotted the section for toothpaste. She had never seen that many varieties of toothpaste on offer at a store. There were so many packs of toothpaste, Tracy thought the shop could have the tagline, '*we specialise in toothpaste because that's an essential*.'

Her original intention was to pick up just one pack of toothpaste and be on her way. However, the collection of toothpaste made her think of buying more than one would be economical. There were *'2 for 1'* signs under each brand of toothpaste. Tracy had two favorite brands which she wanted to purchase. She wasn't sure if she'd get the *'2 for 1'* deal if she took two different brands. She walked towards the front of the store to find Kyle but he was nowhere in sight. She looked down the first aisle but he wasn't there. The second and third aisles yielded nothing. Wasn't there anyone else in this store? When she looked down the fourth aisle, she saw an attendant at the end of the aisle who seemed to be stocking up. She hoped the attendant would confirm that the deal applied to two different brands.

"Excuse me, can I ask you a question?" Tracy said.

As the lady who was kneeling by the baby food shelf turned around, Tracy realized she wasn't stocking up and she wasn't an attendant. It was Eve Carter.

11

As Tracy looked down at Eve, she couldn't help but notice that her eyes were red. The kind of red that would suggest someone had either been crying, had been deprived of sleep or was really angry. Maybe she was experiencing all three.

"Eve, what are you doing here?"

"I could ask you the same," she said, as she put some baby food jars in her shopping basket.

"I was jogging and popped in when I remembered I had run out of toothpaste. Is everything okay?"

"No, everything's not okay," she said as tears began to stream down her face.

Tracy began to wonder if she was wearing something that attracted crying women that morning. She bent down to lift Eve up who was struggling.

"The police think I killed my husband," she said, once she got to her feet.

"Ma'am were you looking for me?!"

Tracy looked up to see Kyle waving at her. He or someone in a security room somewhere must have seen her searching for him.

"I was. I'll be with you in a moment," she said, as she turned to face Eve. "Have you finished?"

Eve nodded.

"Then let's go. We can talk all about it outside."

The ladies moved towards the counter to pay for their items. Kyle confirmed that any brand of toothpaste would qualify for the deal. Tracy hurried to the toothpaste shelf and picked four packs. When she paid for them, she stuffed the toothpaste packs in every available pocket.

As they walked out of the store, Tracy realized where she was. The red signage for *Grind It Out* confirmed that she was in familiar territory. She had never approached this side of town from the angle she had taken.

"If you have some time, we could walk over to the coffee shop and have a chat," she said, smiling at Eve, who nodded.

"Who's looking after your baby?"

"My mom moved in to stay with me after what happened," she said.

"I see. I hope they won't miss you too much."

"They'll be fine. I just wanted to leave the house for a while as it reminded me of everything wrong that's going on in my life right now," she said, clutching her grocery bag closer to her.

Although Eve was wearing a thick, green winter jacket with a hoodie, Tracy noticed that Eve was having a bad hair day as it was tangled in an unholy mess. She opened the door when they got to *Grind It Out* and allowed Eve to walk through first. The coffee shop was almost empty apart from a couple who were sitting by the window. Tracy was surprised to see that Helga; the co-owner of the shop wasn't behind the counter. Jurgen and Helga were the German owners of *Grind it Out*. They were part and parcel of the Fern Grove community and their thick German accent was the only thing that confirmed they weren't born and raised in the town.

"Good morning, Jurgen. Where is everyone and where's Helga?" Tracy asked.

"Honestly I don't know but one thing I can guarantee you is that it won't be like this for long. Sometimes, it's like everyone in Fern Grove has the same alarm clock and move at the same time. Helga's come down with something so I'm all by myself today. How can I help you ladies?" he said.

"I'll have an Americano. What would you like Eve?" Tracy said, turning around to look at Eve who was behind her.

"I'd like a cup of tea," she whispered.

Tracy relayed her order to Jurgen who went about preparing them. She silently hummed along to a Christmas song that was playing through the speakers in the coffee shop. Eve was staring out of the window with a lost look on her face. Tracy wondered what was going through her mind. Jurgen passed over a tray that contained their order and Tracy found a place for them towards the back of the coffee shop where they'd be out of earshot of the couple who were sitting by the window.

"Thanks for paying for my drink, Tracy."

"Not a problem. My pleasure," she said, tilting her head in Eve's direction.

"I've had the worst forty-eight hours of my life," Eve said, wrapping her hands around her cup of tea and blowing at the steam that was escaping from it.

"What's been going on?"

"The police hauled me into their station for questioning. They kept me there for almost the whole day and kept on asking me the same questions," she said, as she removed the hoodie that was covering her face.

"Why do you think they brought you in?" Tracy asked.

"I don't know. All I know is that they came back to my house and said I had to hand over the clothes I was wearing on the night Joe was killed as they wanted to test it for gun residue," she said, as she took a long sip of her tea.

Tracy digested this new bit of information as there was a moment of silence between the two ladies.

"I'm really sorry to hear about your loss Eve."

They looked up to see Jurgen by the table next to them, putting the chairs in place and cleaning the table.

"Thanks, Jurgen," Eve mumbled, as she stared at the cup in front of her.

"He was a good customer and always came here with..."

Eve immediately looked up at Jurgen. Tracy could see that Jurgen had a look on his face like a deer caught in headlights.

"Came here with who?" Eve sneered.

"Came here with... um... friends. I think friends from his office."

"Jurgen!" someone shouted who was waiting to be served.

"Excuse me, ladies," he said, as he scuttled away.

Tracy noticed that Eve's eyes were full of disdain as she watched Jurgen withdraw.

"I hate that man," Eve hissed.

"Jurgen? Jurgen's a great guy," Tracy protested.

"Not him. Joseph Carter. My dead husband."

"Oh," Tracy said, as she took another sip of her coffee.

"The police told me that Joseph had been involved with other ladies. He was cheating on me, Tracy! Did you know about this?"

"No way. I'm so sorry to hear about that," she said, taking a long sip of her coffee and avoiding Eve's eyes.

"They told me his death might have come at the hands of someone he was involved with or someone related to someone he was involved with," she said.

"I don't know how investigations work but I'm sure the murderer will eventually be found."

"How are you so sure?"

"Well, isn't that their job?"

Eve shrugged her shoulders.

"I went out to a charity event recently with some members of the Fern Grove Police Department, and they struck me as hard-working and dedicated to their jobs. They came across as being thorough and taking great pride in the work they did in the community," Tracy said, as she pushed her almost empty cup away from her.

Eve sighed.

This was a part of Eve that Tracy wasn't familiar with. Granted, she hadn't known Eve for a long time but in the few interactions she'd had with her, she had always come across as gentle and kind. Today was different. Maybe it was the treatment she received at the police station. Maybe it was the revelation that her knight in shining armor wasn't a defender of the union they had promised to keep. Maybe it was the uncertain future that lay in front of her. Whatever it was, it was making Eve erratic and bitter.

"I need to start going home. I'm not dressed appropriately for this weather," Tracy said, as she rubbed her palms together.

"I'm sorry Tracy. Can you please wait while I finished my tea?"

Tracy nodded, smiling at Eve. "So, what next?"

Eve sighed. "I honestly don't know," she said. "Although Joseph was a cheating, lying scoundrel, he was still the father of my boy. I'll speak to Pastor Butler and seek his advice on funeral arrangements."

"That's a good idea," she said, as she reached out to touch Eve's arm.

"It's crazy how one minute you think you're living with the love of your life with a bright future to look forward to and the next minute you discover he's not only dead but wasn't what you thought he was. I wonder if it was my fault?" Eve muttered as she gazed into the distance.

"Don't say that Eve. I don't think it's right to burden yourself with the guilt that any of Joseph's actions, and the events leading to his death, might be your fault."

"I loved him so much but everyone told me to avoid him," she said, as tears began to trickle down her face.

Tracy got up and pulled a chair close to Eve. She wrapped her arm around Eve as she sobbed. Tracy noticed that the cafe was beginning to fill up and certain people were looking in their direction.

"Tracy!"

She twisted around to see who had shouted her name. It was Melanie and she was weaving her way around tables and chairs, waving a glove in her hand.

Tracy moved her head from left to right in a quick motion to warn her not to advance further.

Melanie must have either not seen what she was doing or interpreted it to mean something else as she continued making her way towards them. Eve's head was still on Tracy's shoulder by the time Melanie got to their table.

"This fell out of your pocket when we met earlier today," Melanie said, panting as she tried to catch her breath. "Who's that?" she said, pointing at Eve.

Eve slowly raised her head as she made eye contact with Melanie "You!"

12

The tension in the air reminded Tracy of an animal documentary she had recently watched. It had shown the moments before two chickens engaged in a fight. They would dispassionately circle themselves as they eyed each other. The staring competition would be temporarily broken as they pretended to peck at something on the ground. You knew a fight was imminent when the chickens stood as tall as possible with their wings spread apart as they tried to eyeball their rival down. All hell was sure to break loose if neither bird backed down, as they would proceed to start pecking the other, accompanied by beating each other with their wings.

As Tracy watched Eve and Melanie stare at each other, she knew something ugly was inevitable.

"You! What's your name again?" Eve hissed.

"My name's Mel. Why do you ask?"

"I'm Eve Carter. The wife of Joseph Carter. The dead Joseph Carter. I heard you were fooling around with him."

"I was. Only because I heard you couldn't give him a good time."

Eve grabbed her almost empty cup of tea and poured the remaining contents on Melanie. It was only a few drops but because Melanie was wearing a white winter jacket with a fake fur hoodie, the damage was striking. Melanie shoved Eve in the chest, who backed into a table where an old couple was sitting. The force with which she made contact with their table caused one of the mugs to fall to the ground and smashed into pieces. Eve steadied herself and lunged at Melanie. Both ladies tumbled to the floor and started clawing at each other, reaching to pull each other's hair. As Tracy looked around at the crowd that was building around the fighting ladies, she wasn't sure if she was really seeing what she was seeing. Was she back in high school or in a respectable coffee shop?

"Hey!"

The shriek momentarily stopped their attempt to tear the other's head off as they looked at the figure whose command had made the crowd part like the Red Sea. Jurgen walked towards the ladies who were scrambling to get up and retain any sense of decency they had.

"You will not turn my cafe into a wrestling ring. If you have any problem with each other, please take it outside. Now!" he said, pointing at the door.

Melanie rolled her eyes at Eve as she hurried out of *Grind It Out*. A few people gave her dirty looks as she walked past them. Eve picked up her grocery bag and put her hand on her neck, which had the visible mark of a scratch. She winced in pain.

"I'm sorry Jurgen," she said, as she walked out of the cafe with her head hanging down.

Tracy picked up her black glove, which she noticed was underneath one of the tables. Funny how something so small and inconsequential could be the trigger to cause such a ruckus. She stuffed it into her pocket and dashed after Eve. As Tracy's feet landed on the sidewalk, she noticed Eve looking at her with her face scrunched up.

"You knew her, didn't you?"

Tracy scratched her head. The last thing she thought she'd face when she left home that morning for a jog was an inquisition. She slowly nodded her head.

"Did you see her with Joseph?"

"Eve, please don't do this to yourself."

"Did you?" she whispered.

"I did."

"I thought you were a friend. I can't believe you knew Tracy. It seems all of Fern Grove knew Joe was playing me but me. I feel like such a fool," she said putting on her hoodie over her face as someone exited *Grind It Out*.

"We can't reverse the hands of time but maybe this is an opportunity to move on and start afresh," Tracy said, reaching out to touch Eve's shoulder. Eve recoiled at Tracy's touch.

"Yes, maybe it's time for a fresh start," she said, as she picked up her grocery bag and started walking away.

Tracy thought about following her but as she looked at her watch, she knew she was already going to be late for work that morning. Any giddiness she had woken up with that morning had well and truly disappeared.

* * *

As SHE WALKED towards *In Season,* she replayed the events of an eventful morning. She had encountered two women who were hurting. In a way, they were both suffering from the same pain of rejection. One had been rejected by a man who was no longer alive to feel the venom of her disappointment. The other had been rejected repeatedly by men who saw her as an extra-curricular activity. The common denominator between both ladies was a man they had both loved was gone... for good. Despite Eve's protestations and Melanie's swift move to the next man, Tracy sensed that deep down both of them were mourning for Joseph Carter's demise. Still, was it possible that one of them had discovered the duplicity of his ways and proceeded to make him pay?

"You're late!"

She looked up to see her aunt with a broom in her hands as she walked through the doors of the flower shop.

"I'm so sorry Aunt Rose, you won't believe the morning I've just had," she said, as she hurried to put her tote bag away.

"Hi Tracy," Tiffany said, appearing from behind the counter.

"Hi, Tiff."

"Okay. I'm listening," Aunt Rose said, motioning her hands at Tracy.

She proceeded to tell her Aunt and Tiffany the events of her morning and her fateful encounter with the ladies plus the fight at the cafe.

"Oh my, how come I don't have such types of mornings?" Tiffany said, pouting in an over-dramatic way.

"Eve must really be hurting," Aunt Rose said.

"Melanie's hurting too," Tracy added.

Aunt Rose rolled her eyes.

"She really is Aunt Rose."

"Sometimes your heart is too kind. What would you do if she did that to your man? Would you still be sympathetic towards her?" Aunt Rose said, folding her hands across her chest.

"Um... maybe not..."

"Maybe not? Are you kidding me Tracy Adams?" she said, as she dropped her hands to her sides.

"But what if Melanie was your friend or a daughter?"

Aunt Rose paused for a moment before she responded. "Well, I would have warned her long ago, if I knew of her reckless ways, to desist and do the right thing. I wouldn't condone such nonsense."

"But what if that friend or child confessed to the error of their ways and wanted to start over. Wouldn't you give them a second chance?" she said.

Aunt Rose shook her head. "Tracy, I hear what you're saying. I've lived longer than you and I've seen women like Melanie break up marriages. That girl is trouble."

Tracy was a big believer in giving people second chances. Maybe she was naïve, but she couldn't understand why her aunt couldn't extend an iota of grace towards Melanie.

"You know, this whole mistletoe idea was wrong."

Tracy turned around to see her aunt staring at the Christmas tree which had an oversized mistletoe at the top.

"Here we go," Tracy whispered under her breath.

"Did you say something Tracy," Aunt Rose said, still staring at the top of the Christmas tree.

"Nothing ma'am."

"Like I was saying. This mistletoe challenge or whatever you call it was a bad idea."

"I disagree, Aunt Rose," Tiffany said.

"Who asked your opinion little missy?"

"I'm sorry Aunt Rose but my mom works as a reporter at the local TV station and she did a piece on one of the homeless guys who's been a beneficiary of the donations that have been pouring in from local businesses. He's now reunited with his family and has enrolled to take a course in engineering."

The serious gaze that had enveloped Aunt Rose's face softened.

"I know you think our mistletoe challenge had a part to play in the breakdown of Eve's marriage but I don't think that was our fault and I think the good we've done far outweighs any bad," she said, as she clutched a bouquet of carnations that were on the counter.

Aunt Rose ambled towards the back of the shop and settled in her armchair.

Tracy followed after her.

"Is something the matter Aunt Rose?" Tracy said, as she crouched by her aunt and placed her hands on her knees.

"This whole thing with Eve brings back memories."

"What memories?"

"Memories of when Frank... your dear Uncle Frank cheated on me," she said, as she looked away into the distance.

Tracy raised her hand to cover her mouth, her eyes widened.

"Yes, Uncle Frank and I weren't always a wonderful couple. I caught him kissing a lady who had wandered into town and needed a job. It was in that very corner," she said, pointing to a corner of the shop that was at the end of a row of shelves that had an arrangement of flowers. "I told her she had to go. Frank assured me that it was nothing but I couldn't trust him for a long time. He finally earned my trust and I grew to love him again but it took time."

Tracy held her aunt's hands and squeezed them.

"I just feel guilty knowing that in some way, our mistletoe challenge might in some way be encouraging bad behavior," she said, as she smiled at Tracy. "Sometimes, people take advantage of your kindness and what was meant for good can sometimes be twisted for evil purposes."

"I understand," Tracy said. Tiffany came over and rubbed Aunt Rose's shoulders.

"Ok. Enough of this mushy stuff, we have a shop to run," Aunt Rose said, as she rose from her chair.

The tinkle of a bell above the shop door alerted them to the presence of a visitor.

"Good morning... or should I say good afternoon ladies," Pastor Butler said.

"Wow! It's almost one. How time flies. Afternoon, Pastor Butler," Aunt Rose said.

"Hi, Pastor Butler," Tracy and Tiffany chorused.

"I just came here to personally thank you. There's a report that's going to go out tonight about the transformation of a young man who was homeless has undergone. He'll be reunited with his family and he's going back to school. The TV crew made me look good but all of that wouldn't have been possible without your support," he said.

"The pleasure has been all ours," Tracy said, beaming from ear to ear.

"But we have a problem," he said.

"A problem?" Tracy replied, the smile immediately disappearing from her face.

"Yes, a problem and one I hope you can help me fix," he said.

13

Later that day, Tracy made her way down the stairs to the basement room at First Baptist Church. As she walked into the room, she saw the same set of faces she had seen about a week ago. A lot had changed in a week. Gone was the hesitancy and fear about helping Pastor Butler help the poor. Tracy could see Kim, the grocery store owner, chatting with a few other local entrepreneurs. She had encouraged her customers to donate the change from their shopping. Jurgen and Helga were by the water fountain having a drink of water. They had hosted a jazz night at *Grind it Out* and donated all the proceeds to the initiative. Stella, a local dog walker, had made special dog collars, which she sold to her clients. There was a collective sense of pride and fulfilment in the room. Tracy wondered what the little bit of problem was that Pastor Butler alluded to earlier in the shop. She didn't have to wonder too long as he entered the room and beckoned for everyone to take their seats.

"Welcome everyone and thanks for coming at such short notice. First of all, thank you," he said, his lips quivering. "When I called you here about a week ago, to share this burden about the homeless that was on my heart, I didn't know what the response was going to be. I have to admit that I was a bit scared," he paused and looked around the room.

You could hear a pin drop at that moment.

"I prayed and asked God to help me with the funds to carry out this project. You guys are the answer to that prayer," he whispered, a tear rolling down his cheek.

Someone started to clap in the room and it spread like wildfire. Everyone was soon on their feet, high fiving each other and shaking Pastor Butler's hands. Pastor Butler made a gesture for everyone to take their seat.

"I'm sure you've heard about all the transformed lives, the donations you helped to raise, have changed. Please don't stop. Maybe this Christmas, we can ensure there's no homeless person on our streets," he said, as he looked left and right at the circle of people seated around him.

Everyone nodded in agreement.

"Well done, Pastor Butler. I believe I speak for everyone when I say it has been a pleasure raising funds for your initiative. Is there anything else?" Kim said, looking at her watch.

"As a matter of fact, there is," he said, slowly exhaling. "While I've enjoyed leading this initiative and seeing first-hand the impact it's making, I have to admit it's taken me away from my duties here at the church."

Someone made a screeching noise with their chair as they shifted from side to side. Almost everyone turned to where the noise came from.

"I'm sorry," Jurgen whispered, waving his hand.

"That's ok. We need to change some of these chairs. What was I saying?"

"That your duties were being neglected here at the church," Tracy said.

"Yes, thanks Tracy. I only noticed the other day that I haven't confirmed the order of service for Christmas Day and the church's visit to the Children's Hospital hasn't been finalized."

"Is there anything we can do to help?" Helga asked.

"Well, there is one thing that takes quite a bit of my time," he said, as he clutched both hands.

Almost everyone leaned in to hear what Pastor Butler would say after a pregnant pause that seemed to last forever.

"I would be most grateful if someone could handle the collection of the funds and help us open a bank account so there's clear accountability and we can track and trace where the funds came from," he said, looking around. "Anyone interested in helping out?"

Tracy noticed that some people shifted in their seats while others tried not to make eye contact with Pastor Butler as he scanned the room.

"I'll do it," Tracy said.

"You will? Oh, thanks Tracy. Thank you," he said.

Stella, who was sitting next to Tracy, gave her a pat on the back.

"I have to admit that was the biggest challenge I was facing," Pastor Butler said.

"Will that be all pastor?" Kim said, making it obvious she was looking at her watch.

Pastor Butler chuckled. "That will be all. Although I have a surprise for you all," he said, rising up as he dashed to a corner of the room. There was a table that had a cloth over it. Pastor Butler pulled away the cloth to reveal an array of finger foods that included meat pies, sausage rolls, chicken wings, spring rolls and sandwiches.

There were loud oohs and aahs as the smell of the spread filled the room.

"Please come and tuck in," Pastor Butler said, motioning for everyone to join him at the table.

There was a mini stampede as people rushed to grab their share of the tasty delights on offer. Tracy found it amusing that Kim, who had been itching to leave, was the first person to get to the table. Tracy spent the evening getting to know a few of the other business owners in Fern Grove. She was happy to share with them the mistletoe challenge, and how *In Season* had received several large donations.

"There's something about this time of the year that really lends itself to giving," Luke said, to a small group that had gathered around the water cooler.

"I couldn't agree more with you," Kim replied, between mouthfuls of a cheese and ham sandwich.

Tracy felt a tap on her shoulder and turned around.

"Can I see you for a brief moment," Pastor Butler said.

She followed him to the window on the other side of the room that had a view of the church's garden.

"Thanks once again Tracy, you're a lifesaver," he said, slightly tilting his head.

"My pleasure," she replied.

"What I need you to do is go to Union Bank on the High Street to open an account. There's a lady there, I believe she's new in town. What's her name..." he said, beating his forehead with his hand. "It'll come to me. She was very helpful the last time I was there. This folder contains all the documents she'll ask for," he said, handing over a black paper folder.

Tracy couldn't remember the last time she had opened a bank account but the folder felt light. She opened the folder and reviewed the contents.

"How soon can you visit the bank?" he said.

"Um... as soon as you'd like," she replied.

"How about tomorrow?"

"Hmmm... okay. I'll just have to tell Aunt Rose that I'll be in slightly later than normal."

"Great. That is absolutely fabulous. If anything pops up, you can call me."

"Will do."

"Ooh... look at the time. I need to go and prepare for a Bible study class in an hour," he said, bolting out of the room as he waved to the people who were still around.

The next day, Tracy walked into Union Bank at nine-thirty a.m. She grinned as she caught a glimpse of herself in a large mirror in the bank. While a pinstriped navy-blue pantsuit didn't look out of place in a banking establishment, she would definitely be sticking out like a sore thumb at *In Season* if she went in dressed like that. She made a mental note to dash back home after her appointment. She had texted Aunt Rose the night before to let her know that she would be coming in late as she had to open an account for the charity initiative Pastor Butler was spearheading.

"May I help you, Ma'am?"

She turned around to see a tall lady with blonde hair and a cheerful countenance before her. She picked up a twang in her accent that wasn't familiar to that area.

"Hello, I'm here to open an account on behalf of Pastor Butler and the First Baptist Church," Tracy replied.

"Oh, I've been expecting you. My name's Norma Templeton. Please follow me," she said.

The name rang a bell but Tracy couldn't remember where she had heard it. She followed behind her and noticed that the bank was almost empty apart from a few staff members who sat behind their desks staring at computer screens. It made her realize how much she liked working at *In Season*.

"Please take a seat," she said, waving at a chair in front of her desk.

Tracy took her seat and brought out a black folder from her tote bag. She handed it over to Norma.

"Oh, thank you. This must be the documents we require to open the account," she said, grabbing the folder from Tracy.

Norma put on her glasses and began thumbing through the paperwork. Tracy tried to guess her age. There was a zip about her that made her look like she could be in her late twenties but some crow's feet around her eyes, made it more realistic that she'd be in her late thirties or early forties.

"This all looks in order. Let me make a photocopy of the key documents," she said.

She got up and took a few steps to a printer that was positioned near the window. Tracy had walked past Union Bank on several occasions but had never had reason to walk in. The bank was small compared to the banks in Portland. Each staff member had a personal area that was segregated by a transparent glass partition. Tracy noticed that Norma's area seemed to be a bit bigger than her colleagues. The printer made a humming noise as Norma stood next to it tapping her manicured fingers, painted in red nail polish, on its surface. Each copy appeared to take forever to process.

"I noticed a certain twang to your accent," Tracy said, hoping to break the awkward silence that had built up between them.

"You noticed? Guilty as charged," she said, raising her hands and laughing. "I'm actually from the Mid-West. I was transferred from my branch in Nebraska to Portland. The manager here is on maternity leave, so I'm covering for her."

"Do you live in town?" Tracy asked.

"Oh no. I'm here twice a week. I moved to Portland about three months ago. Still getting to know the lay of the land and its people," she said, as she picked up the last copy that had been spewed out by the printer.

"Made any friends yet?" Tracy asked.

"Well, apart from my colleagues here and a few customers, I haven't really gotten to know many people," she said, sitting on her chair. She leaned close to Tracy who sat across her desk and raised her left hand to cover the side of her face. "To be honest, working here at Fern Grove can be boring," she whispered. "But please don't tell anyone I said that."

"Your secret is safe with me. I'm sure there must be something you like about our little town," Tracy said.

"Well, interacting with customers can be the highlight of my day as I get to know their goals and challenges," she said, gazing towards the ceiling. A smile suddenly broke across her face.

"There's this one customer who's taken me out to lunch on three occasions."

"You see our town isn't that boring. At least you get to go to nice restaurants," she said.

Norma nodded. "I have to say I was impressed with the restaurant he took me to. The menu was quite exotic. I thought I was in an upscale restaurant in Portland."

"So, how's things with this customer?" Tracy said, winking at Norma.

"Well, it's funny you should ask. After his third visit here, I knew he wasn't really interested in financial advice. He was sweet and charming. The strange thing is he hasn't been returning my calls," she said.

"What was his name?" Tracy asked, hoping it wouldn't be who she thought it was.

"His name was Joseph. Joseph Carter," she said, grinning at Tracy.

14

"Phew!"

As Tracy walked out of First Union Bank, she was so glad that the mystery man who was wining and dining Norma Templeton was Joseph Carter and not Wayne Copeland. She could feel her heart almost bursting out of her chest as she awaited Norma's response to her question. She just didn't know what she would have done if Norma had revealed it was Wayne. She had burst out laughing when Norma had mentioned Joseph's name. She had to quickly check herself when she noticed the puzzled look on Norma's face and lie when Norma asked if she knew Joe. She hated lying. Was there something wrong with her she thought? Wayne Copeland was having an effect on her even in his absence. She was surprised he hadn't called after the other night. Maybe things were super busy at the police station. She couldn't remember the last time she had this much butterflies in her tummy.

Norma had made her sign a few documents which would give her the right to make withdrawals and pay in deposits when she wanted. She applauded Tracy for her contribution to Pastor Butler's initiative and said she had some ideas of how Union Bank could be a more vocal and supportive presence in town. The meeting ended with Tracy asking Norma to stop by *In Season* when she had the opportunity.

After changing into a more comfortable attire, she raced to *In Season*. If there was something Aunt Rose disliked, it was lateness. And lateness was something Tracy had been working on in the last few months. She knew her aunt extended some grace to her in that department as she made up for it in so many other ways. Still, if getting in at eleven a.m. would spare her a lecture from her aunt on the virtues of punctuality, she was willing to arrive at the shop out of breath but on time. When she walked into the shop, she quickly grabbed an apron and started attending to the customers. With Christmas just a few days away, it seemed there was a huge demand from customers to get the last bit of flower arrangements, Christmas trees, seasonal cards or accessory before the big day. After an hour of non-stop activity, the last customer paid for their item and left the shop.

"My, oh my! I've never known the shop to be that busy," Tiffany said, wiping a bead of sweat that was forming on her forehead.

"Not surprised," Aunt Rose replied. "It's always this way a few days before Christmas."

"Will it get worse?" Tiffany inquired.

"I don't know but I'll say cherish every spare moment you have."

"Roger that. I'm going to grab some water from the back. Would you guys like some?"

"Definitely," Aunt Rose said.

"Me too," Tracy bellowed as Tiffany walked away.

"How was your appointment at the bank?" Aunt Rose asked.

"It was okay. Thanks for giving me the time to do that," Tracy replied.

"Is Cheryl Martins still there?"

"Cheryl? Um... I didn't meet a Cheryl Martins. I was attended to by Norma Templeton."

"Oh, she must be new," she said as she rearranged a bouquet of carnations that were out of place on the shelf.

"Here you go," Tiffany said, as she handed a cup of water to each lady.

"Thanks, Tiff," Aunt Rose said.

Tracy mumbled her gratitude to Tiffany as she had just gulped some water.

"I went into Kim's grocery store this morning to pick up fruits and I overheard her talking with Tom, the handyman," Tiffany said.

"What were those busybodies saying?" Aunt Rose said.

"Kim seemed to think it was Eve who did it."

"Eve? You saw her here the other day. I don't think she knew her husband was fooling around," Aunt Rose said.

"What if she knew and that made her do it," Tracy countered.

"That was exactly what Kim said. She said if her husband cheated on her, she would kill him and wait for the police to come and arrest her," Tiffany said.

"Hmmm... that's cold," Tracy said.

"Tom thought maybe it was one of Joseph's business partners. It seems he had his fingers in a lot of pies around town. Apparently, some of them were illegal," she said.

"Mel revealed to me the other day that Jimbo..."

"Who's Jimbo?" Aunt Rose asked.

"Um... the guy she came into the shop with the other day," Tracy said.

"I don't think I was in the store when she came in with a Jimbo."

"That was the day you were sick and didn't come in," Tiffany said.

"Mel shared with me that this Jimbo guy only befriended her because he wanted Joseph's black book which he stole from her," Tracy disclosed.

"That girl is trouble," Aunt Rose hissed.

"I think she can and wants to change," Tracy said, putting her hands behind her back.

"Ha! Can a leopard change its spots? No! Can an old dog learn new tricks? I don't think so. The sight of that girl makes me angry. And her mother is such a nice lady," Aunt Rose said, as she took a big gulp of water.

"She did mention her mom when I bumped into her the other day. I don't think I've seen her before," Tracy said, putting her finger on her chin.

"Celia Blair is a good woman. Sometimes I wonder how she ever had a daughter like Melanie. She was formerly on the police force but began running a cleaning business when she had an early retirement. I'm not sure if it's still active. She has two daughters, Melanie and Joanna. Joanna stayed in New York after finishing university there. She might be around this Christmas."

"Hmmm... I didn't know Melanie had a sister," Tiffany said.

"Joseph must have done something really nasty to whoever killed him," Aunt Rose said.

"I don't think there's anyone in this town who has something good to say about him," Tiffany said.

"You'd be wrong on that front," Tracy replied, shaking her head.

"Who would have something good to say about that dirty scoundrel... may his soul rest in peace," Aunt Rose said.

"Norma. Norma Templeton. She's the interim bank manager at Union Bank. It seems Joseph had taken her out to lunch on a couple of occasions. Sadly, she doesn't know he's passed away and wonders why he isn't returning her calls."

"You should have told her Tracy," Tiffany said, tugging at Tracy's sweater.

"I just couldn't bring myself to do it. She seems like such a nice lady and is only in town twice a week. She'll eventually know but I sure won't be the bearer of such bad news."

"What bad news?"

The ladies turned around to see Detective Warren Copeland, by the door of *In Season*.

"Detective Copeland you really have to stop doing that or I'll have to report you to the police," Aunt Rose said, pointing at him.

"It'll be my pleasure to introduce you to him... um, I mean them," he said with a glint in his eyes.

"Well, after the introduction, can you close that door and come on in," she said, rubbing her exposed upper arms.

"Yes ma'am," he said, as he walked into the shop and took off his leather gloves.

"So, what brings you in here today," Tracy said with a straight face. She flashed a quick glance over what she was wearing.

"I'd like to have the biggest bouquet of your best flowers and the biggest Christmas card you have here," he said, casting his eyes over the rack of cards in the corner of the shop.

"Ooh... who's the special damsel worthy of this special gift," Tiffany said, nudging Tracy who was standing next to her.

"Actually, it's for the staff and kids at the Children's Hospital on Beckham Street. Sorry to disappoint you, Tiffany," he said.

"None whatsoever taken," she said, with a mischievous smile across her face.

"Tiffany can you prepare the biggest bouquet for Detective Copeland and I'll select a card that I know he'll be happy with," Tracy said.

Tiffany went to a shelf that contained a variety of flowers that included carnations, roses, chrysanthemums, daisies, tulips, lilies and orchids. She selected a variety and ensured that the colours balanced out. She took them to a preparation table and began her arrangement. Tracy made her way to the rack that had the greeting cards. She had to walk past Warren on her way as the room narrowed towards that area of the shop. As she tried to walk past him, he moved to the right. Tracy wrongly anticipated which direction he would move and moved in the same direction. He quickly moved to his left and Tracy followed suit.

"Are you trying to dance with the customer or get a card for the customer?" Aunt Rose said, bemused by the pantomime show playing out in front of her.

"Yes ma'am! I mean, no ma'am. Warren, will you please step aside!" Tracy said, as she walked past Detective Copeland who had held his breath, in an attempt to make himself as flat as an ironing board, as she walked past.

Aunt Rose and Tiffany tried to suppress their giggles as they watched the impromptu drama unfold before them.

"Will this do?" Tracy said, waving a very large Christmas card.

"That looks perfect," he said, moving towards the counter where there was more room.

Tiffany made the final touches to the bouquet she had been preparing that comprised of red roses, yellow carnations, green chrysanthemums and white lilies. She wrapped up the bouquet and taped a sachet of flower food to it.

"The wonderful people at the hospital will love this arrangement," Tiffany said, as she presented the bouquet to Detective Copeland.

"Wow! That is so beautiful. I never knew you were that good," he said, admiring the bouquet and smelled it.

Aunt Rose cleared her throat. "She's trained by the best," she said, pointing to herself.

Everyone in the shop laughed.

"You know, I'm just noticing that there's a mistletoe at the top of your Christmas tree," he said, staring at the top of the tree.

"For a man in your line of work, I'm really disappointed that you hadn't already noticed that," Aunt Rose said, winking at him. "And you know why we have it up there, don't you?"

"Um... you'll need to enlighten me," he said.

"Tiffany came up with the idea that customers who came to the shop could make a donation if they kissed under the mistletoe," she said.

"Ah... I see. Can I make a donation?" he asked, looking at Aunt Rose who had joined Tiffany behind the counter.

"Well, before you make a donation, you have to kiss someone. Tracy will you be willing to help the good Detective," Aunt Rose said, struggling to keep a serious face.

Tracy sighed. "Okay Detective Warren but just on the cheek," she said, pointing to her cheek that had turned a light shade of red.

"Just the cheek, I thought you'd be happy to..."

Tracy hit him on his arm. "Just the cheek Detective!"

"You all saw that. You're witnesses to Tracy's assault on a police officer," he said, as he puckered up to kiss her.

Tracy closed her eyes as she waited to receive the kiss from him. Suddenly, she felt something warm on her lips. Detective Copeland had kissed her on her lips. For a brief moment, she responded by kissing him back before she remembered that she was in a public place with her aunt and their assistant watching. She opened her eyes and saw them clapping and cheering.

She felt happy and embarrassed at the same time.

15

Tracy woke up the next morning feeling happy with herself. She had dreamed of getting married to Warren in an exotic location overlooking a lake, with snow-capped mountains in the distance. As she rolled out of her bed, still groggy from a good night's rest, her eyes latched onto a digital calendar that was on her bedside table. Christmas was just around the corner and Tracy couldn't wait. She had always spent Christmas in Fern Grove with Aunt Rose and Uncle Frank, before he died. However, this would be her first Christmas in Fern Grove as a resident since she moved to college. Something about it felt different. Perhaps, it had to do with the fact that she saw her aunt almost every day at *In Season*. Her aunt was just that person she could rely upon to cook up a storm on Thanksgiving and Christmas. A person to share the highlights of her achievements at work and in former years, school. Aunt Rose had a front-row seat to witness all of Tracy's high points and low points. In a way, she didn't mind as she loved how they were there to be a rock for each other. When Tracy moved back to Fern Grove, she had initially stayed at Aunt Rose's place. It just didn't feel right.

After living independently for over seventeen years, having to take instructions from someone else on how to navigate her domestic surroundings was, to be blunt, annoying. The turning point had been the day Aunt Rose had washed her favorite sweater and ruined it. She knew her aunt meant well and wanted to help but infringing on her personal space and property was one gesture of kindness too many for Tracy. Furthermore, after spending the entire day with Aunt Rose at the flower shop and then the whole evening at home together, they both knew some form of separation would be ideal for their relationship. She had found an apartment on the other side of town that was still a bearable walking distance from *In Season*. She was looking forward to spending time with Aunt Rose over Christmas and meeting relatives who were coming from out of town.

Sitting on her bed that morning, she mentally tried to recall everything she'd need for her short stay.

Clothes, check.

Toiletries, check.

Entertainment, check.

Late-night beverage, hmmm... she wasn't sure if Aunt Rose would have the types of beverages she loved drinking before going to bed. She loved having either chocolate or lemon and ginger herbal tea to wrap up a long day. She darted to her kitchen to see if she had any spare beverages. She noticed the chocolate tin was still half full. That would be enough for her and anyone else who wanted some. Sadly, the packet that contained her lemon and ginger tea bags was empty. It seemed trivial to want to replace it but Tracy knew it was often the seemingly trivial things, to others, that was a big deal to her. She tip-toed over Mr. Sydney who had fallen asleep in her corridor. She wondered why he wasn't in his wicker basket that had soft cushions? Didn't he know it had cost her a lot of money?

She grabbed her jacket and bounded down the stairs of her apartment. She was glad when she remembered she had agreed to come in a bit later to *In Season,* so she could pack her things. As she walked towards Kim's grocery store, she remembered the night Joseph Carter was killed. It seemed like it happened an eternity ago but it had just been a few days. She wondered if the season had anything to do with the police not making any headway with the case. He might not have been everyone's cup of tea but someone killing him to settle a score was surely not right. Like her aunt would say, two wrongs don't make a right.

She walked into the grocery store and was greeted by a popular Christmas song, *I Saw Mommy Kissing Santa Claus*. She stopped for a brief moment and started tapping her feet. She always mused over the lyrics of the song whenever she heard it. Did the child in the song know that his intention to tell his dad that he saw mommy kissing Santa Claus could potentially break up his family?

"I see someone's in the Christmas spirit."

Tracy turned to see Kim smiling at her. She must have put on a show as Kim started mirroring her moves.

"Sorry Kim, that song always gets me. It's one of my favorite Christmas songs," she said.

"It's one of the things I love about this time of the year. Listening to Christmas songs," Kim said, arranging a box of sweets on the counter. "What brings you to my grand establishment this early in the morning?"

"I'll be spending Christmas with Aunt Rose and I wanted to pick up some herbal tea. Do you have ginger and lemon?" she said, moving away from the entrance of the store.

"I not only have ginger and lemon but I also have apple and cinnamon, chamomile tea, hibiscus tea, green tea, ginseng tea, lemongrass tea... you name it, we have it!"

Tracy chuckled, taken aback by Kim's glee that morning. Maybe it was the season.

"Where can I find them?" she asked.

"Oh, at the end of the last aisle. You can't miss them," she replied.

Tracy walked along the aisle Kim had advised and when she got to the end, she saw that she was true to her word. It seemed every type of herbal tea under the sun was stocked on the shelves in front of her. She picked a box of ginger and lemon. The red box for strawberry and raspberry looked inviting, so she added that to her basket. She had never tried blackcurrant and blueberry, so she added that too. As well as peppermint and cranberry and mango tea. She didn't plan to buy this much tea but she was looking forward to trying them out. She felt someone behind her trying to squeeze past as the aisles were narrow.

"I'm sorry, let me remove my basket from the way," she said, before she recognized who she was making room for. It was Melanie.

"Hi Tracy," she said.

"Hi Melanie," she replied. "We seem to keep bumping into each other. Are you stalking me?"

"Oh, no! Not at all," she said as her eyes grew three sizes bigger.

"I was just kidding," Tracy said, giving her a playful punch on her shoulder. She noticed that Melanie was wearing overalls beneath her knee-length wool jacket.

"Going to work?" she asked.

"Yes, I am," she responded, biting her upper lip. "The chat we had the other day really made me think. I'm tired of wasting away my life and want to do something special with it."

Tracy couldn't help but take another glance at what she was wearing.

"Well, I'm not going to become the next President of the United States but I want to start where I am," she said, folding her hands across her chest.

"And where would that be?" Tracy enquired.

"Helping my mother in her cleaning business."

"If you don't mind me asking," Tracy said, looking around to make sure no one was within earshot. "What was the turning point for you apart from what I said?"

"My younger sister is coming home this Christmas. Joanna's graduated from med school and is now working as a junior doctor in New York. She's coming back to Fern Grove for the first time in two years. The realisation that she's making something of her life while I'm wasting mine hit me like a ton of bricks after we had our chat and that little event at *Grind It Out*," she said, biting her lower lip.

"I wouldn't call what happened at *Grind It Out* little. You both behaved like two silly school girls without any manners."

"I'm sorry you had to see that, Tracy. I don't know what got to me when I saw Eve," she said with her head bowed down. "I think seeing her at the police station on the day I was called in for questioning and how she looked at me like I was a piece of dirt really made me angry."

"Can I ask you a question, Mel?"

"Yeah, go ahead," she said, lifting up her head to look at Tracy.

"Where were you the night Joseph died?"

Melanie took a deep breath and exhaled through her mouth. "I was singing on that night."

"Singing? What kind of singing?"

"I used to be in the choir at First Baptist..."

Tracy rolled her eyes.

"You have to believe me. I used to be in the choir many years ago."

"How many years ago?"

"Um... when I was twelve," she whispered.

"That doesn't qualify. That's too long ago," Tracy said.

"Anyway, the choirmaster then formed a group that sings around town during Christmas. He invited me to sing along with them. I don't know if you've heard or seen them?" she said.

"I have and they're very good," she said, recollecting the other landmark event that had occurred on the night she had heard the carolers.

"I was with them on that night. Joe and I fought the day before. He told me I was beginning to bore him and he didn't have time for me," she mumbled.

Tracy could tell a part of Melanie still missed Joseph.

"Can I ask you another question?"

"Sure," she replied.

"Who do you think killed Joseph?"

"I don't know. It could be anybody. I know he had some dodgy dealings going on but I was never a witness to them. Maybe it was his wife, Eve," she said.

"Eve? I don't think Eve would do such a thing," Tracy said, running her hands through her hair.

"Maybe not. But if she did, I would understand. If I were in her shoes, I probably would do it," she said.

Tracy found her choice of words odd. There was an uncomfortable silence between them.

"Ooh... I have to run," Melanie said, looking at her watch.

They both made their way to the counter and paid for their items. They zipped their jackets as they braced themselves to get back in the cold. As Tracy bid Melanie farewell, as she was walking in the opposite direction, she wondered if there was anything Melanie had said, that contained a clue as to who killed Joseph Carter.

16

Tracy couldn't shake off a question that had been bouncing around in her mind, 'Who killed Joseph Carter?'

It was a question that was beginning to occupy too much real estate in her mind. All she knew so far was that he was killed by a gunshot and his wife had been arrested by the police as a likely suspect. When she met Eve the other day at the new grocery store, she hadn't revealed much. Was there something the police knew that she didn't about Eve? There were also the extra women in Joseph's life like Melanie, Norma and any others which she didn't know of. Could it be that one of these ladies in a moment of rage had done the unthinkable? After spending time with Mel, her gut told her it wasn't Melanie. Norma just seemed too professional and career-driven to sabotage all of that by committing a heinous criminal offense.

From what she had gathered from her chat with her at the bank, she had accepted Joseph's invitation for a business lunch on the premise that he would switch his business account to Union Bank. By the third date, she had her doubts about his true intentions but loved his charm and wit. If the killer wasn't one of Joseph's romantic pursuits, then could it be a business associate? She still wasn't sure what he did apart from the tidbit that Mel had shared about him distributing medicinal supplements. She was surprised that this Jimbo character who had stolen Joseph's black book from her was not a bigger target in the murder investigation. She would ask Melanie when she saw her next if she had informed the police of Jimbo's theft.

She turned her attention to the items she had bought from the grocery store. Aunt Rose would be delighted with the assortment of herbal teas she had purchased. She wasn't sure where exactly she had acquired her like for herbal teas from, but it was something anyone who spent some time with her was aware of. As she turned the corner, she saw a woman who seemed to have walked into a lamppost and was furiously rubbing her forehead. She noticed the lady's baby buggy which was next to her slowly rolling backwards. She hurried to make sure the woman didn't suffer a double tragedy.

"Are you okay," Tracy said, as she wheeled the buggy nearer to the lady.

"No, I'm not okay," she said, rubbing her head.

Although the lady's back was turned towards Tracy, she would recognize that voice with her eyes closed. It was Eve Carter.

"What happened Eve?" she said.

Eve slowly turned around to look at Tracy. She removed her hand from her forehead and Tracy could see a bump growing on it. It was as if someone had stuffed a beach pebble in Eve's skull.

She sighed as she winced in pain. "I was reading a text message from my mom when I ran into this stupid pole," she said, kicking the guilty, lifeless object.

"That really looks bad," she said, as she caught another glimpse of the bump. "We need to get a cold compress on that before it becomes the size of a tennis ball," she said.

"Oh, no! Is it that bad?" she said, her eyes blinking rapidly as she felt the errant protrusion begin to throb.

"Um... I've seen worse. Do you live nearby?" she said.

"Yeah, just down that street," she said pointing at a street on the opposite side of the road.

Tracy realized two things at that moment. Eve's house was close to hers and ominously, it was near to the spot where Joseph had met his untimely end. She pushed the buggy that had Eve's sleeping son. She could tell Eve was in a lot of pain by the steady stream of grunts and sighs she let out. The street Eve had pointed to was a cul-de-sac, a road which had a dead-end but with a circle for turning around at the end.

Tracy had grown up in a cul-de-sac and she liked and disliked them. She liked them because they were a safe place where she could ride her bike with her friends and play under the watchful gaze of her mom without the flow of traffic you would experience on a normal road that had cars moving in either direction. She disliked them as parking your car could be a nightmare. If a neighbor had a party with lots of guests, you could find people either parked on your driveway or restricting you from leaving your driveway.

Eve hurried to the second house on the street and fidgeted in her pocket for her keys. She eventually found them and opened the door to her home. Two things struck Tracy as she walked in, the smell of mac and cheese and pictures. There were pictures in almost every corner she could see. Pictures frames that lined the wall going upstairs. Watercolor pictures of Eve and her deceased husband and son on the living room door. As they walked into the living room, she discovered there were more pictures. An opportunistic burglar invading that home would be left in no doubt who the victims of their crime were. Eve flung her jacket on a long leather couch. She walked to a large, antique gold mirror on a wall beside French doors that led to a garden. She twisted her head in different angles as she looked at the bump.

"We need to take care of that. Looking at it won't help. Where's your kitchen?" Tracy said.

"It's over there," she said, moving her hair to the side to get another view of the bump.

Tracy walked into the kitchen and saw more pictures. The size of the kitchen, with all the fancy cookery and gadgets on display, made Tracy realize how small her kitchen was. She couldn't help but notice the white and red theme Eve had going on in her kitchen. She saw a big pot on the stove and couldn't resist opening it to see what was inside. She inhaled the aroma of mac and cheese as it wafted into the air. She was tempted to grab a fork and have a taste but knew it would be overstepping her boundaries. She slowly put the lid back on the pot, hoping she'd have the opportunity to taste the food she had just seen and smelled. She opened a white fridge freezer and looked for something that would act as a cooling agent for Eve's bump. She found a bag of mixed vegetable that was almost frozen. It would be perfect. She rushed back to the living room and saw Eve still by the mirror examining her head.

"Please come over here, Eve," she pleaded.

Eve walked over and they both sat on the long couch. Tracy pushed Eve's hair to the side and placed the frozen bag on her bump. She let out a slow groan, flinching as the cold bag made contact with her skin.

"Just hold it there for a while," Tracy urged, making sure Eve had control of the frozen bag before she let go.

Tracy walked over to the buggy to see if Eve's son was still sleeping. As she peeped into his buggy, she could tell he was fine as his chest slowly moved up and down.

"Thank you," Eve said.

Tracy spun to see Eve with a smile on her face and the bump downgraded to the size of a mini pebble.

"That looks so much better," Tracy said, sitting next to Eve.

"It does?" she said, getting up to check it out in the mirror.

Tracy pulled her back on to the couch. "You'll just give yourself a headache if you keep looking at it," she said.

"Okay," she said, contorting her face in frustration.

"I have to say you have a big and beautiful house," Tracy said, nodding slowly in appreciation of the splendor before her.

"It was all Joseph. He loved big things. He loved good things. He made this a home for us," she said, gazing at a picture of her and Joseph on the mantelpiece.

"If you don't mind me asking, what's up with all the pictures?" she said.

Eve chuckled. "Ow..." she said, applying the frozen bag back to her forehead. "Photography was something that brought Joseph and me together. We both studied photography at college. Well, he actually studied fine art but he had a few classes in photography," she said.

"I see," Tracy mumbled.

"I met him for the first time at an electronic shop when I went in to return a faulty camera. He pretended to be a sales assistant and showed me what was wrong with the camera and the correct model to buy," she said, gazing into the air as she recalled this fond moment in her past. "I went into that shop with a faulty camera but left with the memory of a person who shared my passion for photography. I was amazed when someone tapped me on the shoulder on the bus as I was going home and it was him. We started a relationship then, that's had its highs and lows but has been very eventful," she said, wiping a tear that was rolling down her left cheek.

Tracy hugged her as she could tell Eve was about to break down. She quietly sobbed in the crook of Tracy's shoulder. Eve composed herself and cleared her throat.

"I'm so sorry about that. I have to admit that I miss him," she said, another tear escaping from her red eyes.

"No need to apologize. I can't imagine the roller-coaster of emotions you must have been through in the last few days," she said.

Eve slowly shook her head. "You can say that again."

"I know it's none of my business but I've been thinking of the events surrounding Joseph's death and who would have wanted him dead," Tracy said, adjusting the scarf that was around her neck.

"I've been thinking about it since it happened," Eve said.

"Can you remember what happened the day he passed away?" she said.

"Um... it was like any other day. Joe went to work while I stayed at home with Hunter," she said.

"What does Joe do?" Tracy asked.

"He's a property manager and oversees the maintenance of several commercial buildings in town," she said.

"Wow, it must pay well," Tracy said, looking around the living room.

Eve shifted on the couch, flicking a strand of hair behind her ear. "Ehm... both our salaries made this possible."

"So, did you hear from him that day? Did anything unusual happen?" she queried.

"Nothing unusual that I can think of. The day after he died my house was broken into and I noticed this gun under my bed which I reported to the police. They seemed to think it was the murder weapon and that I planted a murder weapon in my own house," she said, her eyebrows arched.

"Oh wow! I wasn't aware of that," she said.

"You should have seen the state of this house Tracy. It was an absolute mess. If there's any consolation, a cleaner came here to clean the house after I came back from the police interrogation. She said Joseph had hired her a week before. With Hunter being so demanding, I have to admit that I have neglected my domestic duties," she said, flashing a shy smile. "That was very much like Joseph to think of how he could make my life easier," she said, putting her hand on her chin.

"Anything else you can think of?" she said.

"Nothing really. My mind keeps going back to that moment when the police knocked on my door that fateful evening to share the bad news," she said, setting the frozen pack on a side table.

There was a brief moment of silence between both ladies. Tracy was thinking of what she would tell her aunt when she saw her. Would she believe that she had bumped into Mel and Eve again?

"It might not make much difference but I remember something," Eve said, as she got up and dashed out of the living room. Tracy could hear her bounding up her stairs. She wondered what Eve had remembered. She came back into the room panting. She flashed a large gold earring at Tracy.

"I saw this a few days after Joe died," she said.

Tracy took the earring from her and inspected it. "Who do you think it belongs to if it's not yours?"

"Hmmm... maybe it belongs to my mom. She loves gold. Not many people have been in the house since Joe died. I was going to ask the cleaner when she came back," she said.

"Do you think it belongs to the cleaner?" Tracy said.

"Maybe. I don't know. I was going to ask her when she came next." she said.

"Why don't you call her and ask her?" she said.

"I don't have her number. Remember it was Joe that hired her," she said, taking the earring back from Tracy. "Maybe it belongs to one of the police officers who came to search my house."

Just then, Tracy's mobile phone vibrated. She pulled it out of her pocket and unlocked it. There was a message from Aunt Rose that simply said, *'Where are you?'*

"I have to be going Eve. Maybe the earring belongs to the cleaner or a policewoman or maybe your mom knows something about it," she said.

"Yeah... maybe," she murmured.

As Tracy rushed out of Eve's house, she wondered what excuse she'd give to Aunt Rose and if the earring had anything to do with Joseph's death.

17

As Tracy raced back to her house before she went to work, she tried to remember all that she had heard that morning. It appeared Melanie was looking to turn a new leaf but was it genuine? Eve had been emotional when she recalled the memory of her deceased husband but was it a smokescreen to hide something sinister?

Was it Norma?

Was it Jimbo?

Or someone she didn't know?

At that moment, she wished she was a police officer so she could in some way contribute towards the resolution of this murder investigation. When she got home, she was annoyed to realize that Mr. Sydney spilt his bowl of water on the floor. If she didn't take care of his mess now, she knew it could be worse and was an accident waiting to happen. She had a shower, dressed up and made sure that the contents of her suitcase were complete. She noticed Mr. Sydney peeping to look at her as she packed. Even though she was looking forward to spending time with Aunt Rose and believed she'd have a good time, she was aware that things didn't always pan out the way you wanted them. For that reason, she planned to use Mr. Sydney as an excuse to leave her aunt's house if for any reason the company or atmosphere wasn't right for her. As she looked at Mr. Sydney who was lying down by her bedroom door, Tracy bent down to stroke his fur.

"I'm sure you're wondering where mommy's going. Well, mommy's going to spend time with Grandma Rose. Wanna come?" she said.

Mr. Sydney purred.

"Okay then. Change of plans," she said, letting out a loud sigh.

Mr. Sydney had just offered her the perfect excuse if her aunt queried her lateness that morning. Aunt Rose wasn't the best at looking after pets, especially cats and would understand the attention she had to lavish on her cat before she left for a few days.

The shop was fairly busy as she walked in and she evaded her aunt's stare as she went to put away her bag. It was the last day the flower shop would be open before Christmas. Most people had already gotten their Christmas trees and any floral arrangements they needed for loved ones. Most of the sales they made that morning were for seasonal and birthday cards. Tracy had always felt sorry for people who had their birthdays on Christmas Day as she felt their big day would be overshadowed by the holiday festivities. Aunt Rose had told her she was eager to close the shop early so she could go home and start the preparations for Christmas. Tiffany had also intimated that her mom expected her to chip in towards cooking as she was tired of carrying the burden for feeding Tiffany and her four brothers plus her husband all by herself. It was agreed that they'd close the shop early and this had been advertised on the shop window for the past two weeks. They had also told customers who had made orders that they'd be closing early on that day. As the day wore on, less and less people walked through the door and the ladies of *In Season* kept on glancing at the large rustic metal wall clock, willing the time to go faster.

"You know, I prefer it when it's busy in here," Tiffany said.

"Me too," Aunt Rose replied.

"Is there anything we can do to make the time go faster?" Tracy said.

The tinkle of the bell over the door was the reply to her question. Tracy was surprised to see Norma Templeton walk through the door.

"Norma? Hi. What are you doing here?" Tracy said.

"Hi, Tracy. It's been dead at the bank today and I began to think about what I could do to make the time go faster," she said, putting her finger to her chin and gazing at the ceiling. "Then I thought why don't you go and see local businesses and let them know what Union Bank has to offer them."

"So, in other words, you were bored and we were the answer to your boredom," Tracy said, grinning and shaking her head.

"Yes! I'm guilty," she replied, flashing a pair of very white teeth as she laughed.

"Let me introduce you to my Aunt Rose who founded this flower shop with her husband many years ago," she said, pointing to Aunt Rose. Norma stretched her hand and shook Aunt Rose's hand vigorously.

"And our wonderful intern extraordinaire, who makes the best floral arrangements," she said, pointing to Tiffany who was already in line to receive a handshake from the bank manager.

Tiffany's head began bobbing after Norma's handshake which lasted a tad too long.

"So great to meet you ladies and I've heard so much about your shop. Where's your husband, Ms. Rose?"

"He's dead," she replied.

"Oh, I'm so sorry," Norma said.

"No need to be, it's been quite a while but I still miss him," she said, patting Norma's upper arm.

Tracy was so glad that her aunt had rescued what could have been a particularly bad situation.

"By the way Tracy have you seen Joseph Carter?" Norma said.

"You knew that creep too?" Aunt Rose shouted.

"Creep? What do you mean? " she asked, her hands flying to her chest.

"He's dead," Tiffany said.

"Dead? Tracy, did you know about this? Is it true?" Norma said, looking at Tracy, her eyes bulging.

"Yes," she whispered.

"Oh..." she said, her lips quivering. She turned around and walked out of the shop.

Like the air escaping a burst balloon, the festive cheer at *In Season* disappeared and was replaced by a deathly silence.

"Hi everyone!" Melanie said, as she walked into *In Season*.

Everyone wasn't interested in her loud greetings.

"What's wrong with everyone today? You guys look like you're attending a funeral. Its Christmas in a few days! Even the bank manager looked like she's attending the same funeral," she said.

"You know her?" Tracy said, holding the edge of the counter.

"Who?" she replied.

"The bank manager... Norma Templeton?" Tracy said.

"Oh, her... um... yeah I know her. My mom's been trying to get a contract with Union Bank," she said.

“To do what?” Tiffany asked.

"To clean," she said, unbuttoning her winter jacket to reveal cleaning overalls.

"Melanie, I'm not ready for your drama. How can we help you?" Aunt Rose said, switching glances between Melanie and the clock on the wall.

"My mom sent me in here to get two bouquets. It's also our last day and we wanted to give them to our best customers," she said, oblivious to the sharp tone in Aunt Rose's voice.

"That's good," Aunt Rose deadpanned. "Any particular flowers you were thinking of?"

"Um... not sure. The two customers are really special to us so please give me your best."

"Tiffany, please arrange two bouquets for Melanie," she said.

"Sure, Aunt Rose. I'll put something together that'll make your customers know that you really value their business," Tiffany said, grinning at Melanie.

"Ooh... thanks Tiff," she said, smiling back at her.

Aunt Rose and Tracy busied themselves cleaning and putting away things. Tiffany selected some yellow roses, lilac freesias, green carnations and white chrysanthemums. She carefully positioned each stalk so the colors would beautifully offset each other. Melanie was left standing at the counter, staring at the black and white photo of Aunt Rose and her deceased husband.

"I don't mean to trouble you ladies but the atmosphere in here is so un-Christmas. Can you at least play Christmas songs?" Melanie said.

Tracy looked at Aunt Rose, who sighed and slowly nodded her head. Tracy walked over to the portable radio they had behind the counter and flipped it on. A popular Christmas song started playing over the speakers.

"That's what I'm talking about... Christmas!" she screeched.

Melanie started doing a robotic dance that was totally out of sync with the song playing. Tracy started laughing at the absurdity of Melanie's dance moves. Melanie seemed unconcerned with the attention her actions were attracting. Tracy's mild chuckling turned into a belly laugh when Tiffany joined her on the dance floor and started imitating her moves.

"That's the spirit, Tiff," Mel said, happy to have a partner. She motioned for Tracy to join them.

"I'm fine where I am," she said. She did a quick move, raising her right hand towards her face and bringing it back down to her elbow and repeating the same move with her left hand. This attracted a cheer from Melanie and Tiffany. Tracy noticed that Aunt Rose had stopped cleaning and was smiling. Then she saw it. Melanie was wearing the gold earring which Eve had shown her earlier. Tracy switched off the radio.

"Hey, why did you do that?... I actually liked the song that just started playing," Melanie said, moving from side to side.

"Melanie, where were you the night Joseph died?" Tracy asked.

A dark look replaced the jovial one on Melanie's face. "I've told you before and I'm sick and tired of telling you. I was singing and I have witnesses to prove it. Do you think I killed him?" she snapped, folding her arms across her chest.

"Melanie, what's taking you so long?"

Everyone looked towards the door as a short woman with a stocky build walked in. Tracy could see, through her unbuttoned jacket, that she was wearing the same type of overalls as Melanie.

"I'm sorry, mom. Just trying to enjoy the Christmas spirit which some people are desperate to kill," she said, casting an evil glance at Tracy.

"Hi, Celia," Aunt Rose said, walking towards Melanie's mother. "I haven't seen you for a while."

"It's been quite busy. Not that I'm complaining. At least lil madam over there has offered to join me to grow our business," she said, hugging Aunt Rose. "Wow, that Christmas tree is huge."

As she spun her head to look at the Christmas tree, Tracy noticed that Celia was wearing the same gold earring.

"Goodness gracious!"

"What now?" Melanie said, sneering at Tracy.

"Is there a problem here?"

Detective Warren Copeland had just walked into *In Season*. He had two cups of coffee in his hands. The smile on his face vanished when he saw the petrified look on Tracy's face.

"Yes, there is a problem Detective Copeland. I have some information that could help you with the murder investigation."

18

The residents of Fern Grove had to digest the fallout from the Joseph Carter murder investigation along with roast turkey, mashed potatoes, cranberry sauce, pecan pie, prime rib and more at their dinner tables that Christmas.

Tracy noticing the gold earring worn by Melanie and her mom, Celia, was the trigger that set things in motion towards the murder investigation's resolution. It was the hot topic across town as families gathered to celebrate Christmas. The murderer was someone no one was expecting.

As Tracy walked into *In Season* on the first working day of the new year, she wasn't surprised to discover that it was still a hot topic of discussion.

"I still can't believe Celia did it," Aunt Rose said, shaking her head.

"I know! I thought so too," Tiffany replied.

"What made you think it was her Tracy? I know you told me before but I'm still trying to wrap my head around all of this," Aunt Rose said.

"It had to do with some things Eve told me on the day I visited her. She mentioned that she was interrogated by the police after she reported an intrusion into her house and discovered a handgun, tucked away under her bed. She also mentioned that she had found a gold earring which matched what Melanie and Celia were wearing," she said.

"But how did it all link back to Celia?" Tiffany asked.

"Apparently, Celia owns a cleaning company that hires quite a few unsavoury characters. Joseph was aware of this and facilitated a lucrative contract for her to clean the buildings he managed for a kickback in return. When Celia refused to continue paying the agreed kickbacks, Joseph threatened to expose her."

"Oh no," Tiffany said, covering her mouth.

"That's not the worst bit. Sadly, Melanie innocently informed her mom of Joseph's movements. She knew his exact whereabouts and he was on Glover street, where Melanie said he usually walked through at that time of the evening. After she shot him, she broke into his house to plant the murder weapon which Eve later found," Tracy said.

"I still don't understand how Celia's earring ended up at Eve's house," Aunt Rose said.

"She got too clever for her own good. She knocked on Eve's door a few days after the murder and claimed that her husband had hired her to clean her home. Eve believed her as she looked the part and she knew her husband would have connections to cleaning companies in his line of work. Celia's intended to clean any trace of her fingerprints or anything that would come back to incriminate her in the crime. I guess in the midst of her actions, she must have lost her earring," Tracy said.

"Wow! Good thing you visited Eve and she showed you that earring," Tiffany said.

"What about Melanie?" Aunt Rose said.

"I understand she's left town," Tracy said. "The shame of knowing that her mom would soon be a convicted killer was too much for her. I feel sorry for her as she seemed to have turned a leaf for the better."

"Any other news related to the case?" Tiffany asked.

"The latest development was that Jimbo... the muscle builder guy she kissed under our mistletoe was arrested for possession of illegal substances. Looks like the medicinal supplements he was alleged to have been distributing were not so medicinal," Tracy said.

The ladies all exhaled as they considered the untimely events that had occurred in their town and the characters involved.

"I listened to our messages before you came in Tracy and there's one from Norma, the bank manager. She apologized for her reaction the other day and said she'll visit one of these days," Aunt Rose said.

"So, do you have any resolutions for the new year?" Tiffany said as she tied an apron.

"Not to be involved in any murder investigations in Fern Grove," Tracy said.

They all laughed.

"What can we do today? I reckon it's not going to be a busy day," Tracy said.

"Well, we can take this Christmas tree down. We'll have to come up with other ways to raise money for the homeless. By the way, Pastor Butler said to congratulate you all. He said our last donation helped to secure shelter for a family of six over Christmas," Aunt Rose said.

"Yay! That's great to hear. Now how do we tackle bringing this tree down," Tracy said.

The ladies all gathered around the tree, looking at it from top to bottom.

"Am I interrupting anything?"

They turned around to see Detective Warren Copeland had walked into the shop. He was dressed in blue jeans, a red flannel shirt and a white t-shirt.

"Happy New Year Warren," Aunt Rose said.

"Happy New Year Rose, Tiffany... Tracy," he said.

Tracy had talked with Warren on a couple of occasions over the Christmas break. They had arranged to meet up but an incident at the station had made them cancel that rendezvous.

"Are you thinking of taking down that Christmas tree," he asked.

"We can't keep a Christmas tree up past Christmas," Aunt Rose said.

"Before you take it down, can I do something," he said.

The ladies looked at each other, wondering what the Detective had up his sleeve. He slowly walked towards Tiffany, paused, and walked past her. He made eye contact with Aunt Rose but walked past her when he got to her. He then walked towards Tracy and stood in front of her.

"Tracy, there's been something I've been meaning to say to you for the past few days. I think I'll go crazy if I don't say it. It's been eating me up..."

"What do you want to say?" Tracy said, looking into his blue eyes.

"Will you be my girlfriend?" he said, holding her hands.

She smiled and looked at her aunt and Tiffany.

"Don't look at us. Answer the man," Aunt Rose said, beaming.

"Yes," she whispered.

He took her face in his hand and kissed her. Aunt Rose and Tiffany looked on as they saw their colleague melt into the arms of a man they knew loved her.

"You know, all things work together for good," Tiffany said.

"Now that's a word in season," Aunt Rose replied.

Tracy leaned into Warren as they hugged each other and then they kissed again under the mistletoe. It was the perfect start to the new year.

The End

RED ROSES AND BLOODY NOSES

1

There are certain things which can trigger an emotion deep within you that is hard to explain. As Tracy gazed at the sight in front of her, she knew it had stirred something within her. Tracy never tired of coral peonies; she loved how the bold, unforgettable color spilled out from the dainty petals, and she wished they were always in season. They were usually only available in the late spring and early summer, but she sometimes dreamed of the way they moved, as though they were delicate powder puffs. Each April, when the skies finally cleared and the last snow melted from the cold ground in the Pacific Northwest, her spirits lifted as she thought of the dozens of bouquets of peonies she would buy to fill her vases and brighten her home.

Today though, on the first Monday of December, Tracy was surprised to find a bouquet of coral peonies waiting for her when she arrived for work at *In Season,* the quaint flower shop owned and operated by her beloved Aunt Rose. "Aunt Rose?" she called out as she spotted the bouquet on the counter with a card bearing her own name attached. "Are these for me?"

Aunt Rose appeared from the back room, her hair piled atop her head in a messy bun. "They are," she grinned.

"Are they from you?" Tracy asked in confusion. Though Aunt Rose owned the flower shop and likely could have gotten a deal on any flower she wanted, Tracy knew peonies still would have been pricey.

Aunt Rose shook her head. "Not from me..."

The front door opened and Tiffany, the teenage apprentice Aunt Rose and Tracy mentored, shuffled in. "Morning," she muttered as she rubbed her eyes.

"Good morning," Aunt Rose greeted her brightly. "Did you forget your cup of coffee this morning? You are looking droopier than a dahlia in December!"

Tiffany groaned. "No flower jokes right now," she insisted. "I'm still waking up."

Aunt Rose's big eyes sparkled. "I have some hot chocolate brewing in the back," she informed the adolescent. "Go fix yourself a cup."

Tiffany perked up. "Hot chocolate? My mom *never* lets me have it at home. She says it's a cavity in a cup. I'll have as many cups as you'll let me, Aunt Rose."

She skipped to the back, and Aunt Rose chuckled. "It's a good thing to know the way to her heart is through hot chocolate," she commented as Tracy picked up the bouquet of peonies and examined the blooms.

Tracy turned to her aunt. "These really aren't from you?" she questioned.

"I told you they weren't. Read the card!"

Tracy unclipped the card from the stem of the bouquet and read the note. "It's from Warren," she smiled as she scanned the note.

"Ooooo, your boyfriend!" Tiffany squealed as she bounced back into the front room with a steaming mug of hot chocolate in hand. "I wish I had a hot detective boyfriend to send flowers to me. You're so lucky, Tracy!"

Tracy indeed considered herself lucky. About two years ago, she had been let go from her job in Portland. She found herself nearing forty with no romantic interest, no children and no future. It was only when her Aunt Rose had invited her to work at *In Season,* located in the small town of Fern Grove, that Tracy's luck had begun to look up. Tracy had packed up her beloved apartment at Broadstone Reveal, a modern building in downtown Portland, and moved down the coast to the small, charming town where she had grown up with her aunt and her late husband, after the death of her parents.

Upon moving to Fern Grove Tracy had met Warren Copeland, a handsome local detective. After a few months of playing hard to get they were finally a couple. Warren was all she had ever wanted in a significant other, He was kind, considerate, reliable and successful in his career. She was thrilled the holidays were coming and they would soon be spending their first Christmas as a couple.

Aunt Rose took the peonies from Tracy. "I'll get these settled in a nice vase," she told her niece as Tracy nodded. "Flowers like these deserve a gorgeous vase. I know just the one I'll put them in."

Aunt Rose bustled to the back room in search of a vase, and Tracy smiled. She had been through so much. Being let go from her prestigious job in Portland had been a devastating blow. Now, leaning against the counter of the flower shop, listening to Christmas carols and watching the snow beginning to fall outside, she was sure everything had worked out the way it was supposed to. She was happy. She enjoyed the quiet, low-key work of her job at her Aunt Rose's flower shop. She loved spending time with her aunt, and she was in a relationship she was proud of.

"What do you think?" Aunt Rose asked as she reappeared, proudly displaying the arrangement of peonies tucked into an antique red vase. "I thought this was festive, and I love how the red makes the coral pop."

"It's gorgeous," Tracy complimented. "Thank you for popping it in the vase."

"It's the least I can do for my favorite niece," Aunt Rose winked as she turned to Tiffany. "We need to chat about your hours over the next few weeks," she commented as Tracy turned and started to work on making a flower arrangement that was supposed to be picked up that afternoon."

"My hours?"

"Yes," Aunt Rose affirmed. "With the holidays coming up, I wanted to see what your plans were. We'll be busy around here, and I need to know if I can schedule you for your normal shifts."

Tiffany retrieved her phone from her pocket. "Let me check my calendar."

Aunt Rose rolled her eyes. "You kids and your cell phones," she clucked.

"I can do my normal hours," Tiffany informed her as she glanced at the cell phone. "I don't have any major plans."

"No trips out of town to see your extended family?" Aunt Rose asked. "That used to be my favorite part of the holidays. On Christmas Eve, my parents would get us all bundled up in our winter coats and hats, and we would make the long drive down to Crescent City to see my cousins and aunts and uncles."

"Crescent City?" Tiffany inquired. "Where is that?"

"Northern California," Tracy chimed in, thinking of her own parents telling these stories about their extended family holiday get-togethers. "It's a town right on the coast, pretty close to Tolowa Dunes State Park."

Tiffany wrinkled her nose. "Never heard of it," she shrugged. "The only place I want to go in Cali is LA! When I graduate, maybe I can get an agent and start a modeling career there."

Aunt Rose nodded. "Maybe. But in the meantime... tell me about your favorite parts of the holiday season. Does your family have any special traditions?"

Tiffany thought for a moment. "This sounds silly," she began. "But during the holidays, my parents make us wear red and green pajamas every single night."

"That's cute!" Tracy commented. "Holiday pajamas are adorable."

Tiffany narrowed her eyes. "It was cute when we were babies," she corrected. "But I'm a woman now. I don't want to wear matching pajamas with my family. It's so embarrassing."

Tracy shot a look at Aunt Rose. Sometimes, Tiffany could seem much older than her age, but now, as she complained about her parents' traditions, she sounded like the teenager she was.

"Do you have any traditions you enjoy?" Tracy asked. "Like baking cookies or sledding?"

Tiffany grinned. "We do have one good tradition," she explained. "Every year, on the twenty-third of December, my parents buy us new outfits and we go out to a fancy dinner to celebrate everything our family has accomplished that year. We rotate on who gets to pick the restaurant, and this year, it's my turn! I'm going to pick Vida, that really nice new place on New York Street. They have a set menu for the holidays, and it looks amazing."

Aunt Rose beamed. "That sounds like a lovely tradition," she praised. "It's so special to spend time with the ones you love most."

"Good morning, ladies!"

Pastor Butler, the local minister, strode into the shop, his lips curled up into a smile beneath his thick mustache. "I hear you were talking about the holiday season?"

"We were sharing our favorite things," Tracy told him. "What's your favorite thing about the holidays?"

He laughed. "Jesus is the reason for the season," he said matter-of-factly. "But I *also* enjoy Christmas cookies and hot chocolate!"

Tiffany looked down at her mug. "Speaking of hot chocolate, I need a refill."

She scurried to the back room. Tracy blinked up at Pastor Butler. He was a huge man; Tracy was only five foot two, and he towered over her. She practically needed a stepstool to make eye contact with him. "Can I help you with something today?"

He shook his head. "I just wanted to pop in and ask you a question," he smiled at the group. "Do any of you like to sing?"

Aunt Rose and Tracy simultaneously pointed at Tiffany as she walked back into the room. "She sings all the time," Tracy laughed as Tiffany gave a dramatic hair flip. "She's always humming or singing when she works."

"I do not," Tiffany said, looking bashful.

"She was in her high school choir," Aunt Rose chimed in. "She has a lovely alto voice; she had a solo at last spring's concert. It was a real treat to hear her, Pastor. Tiffany's rendition of *You're My Best Friend* by Queen was all anyone in town could talk about for a week!"

The teenager blushed. "It wasn't that great," she argued.

Tracy chuckled. "Why are you being shy all of a sudden?" she asked.

"I'm thinking of retiring from my singing," Tiffany announced dramatically.

"And why would you do that?" Aunt Rose exclaimed with a worried look in her eyes. "Your voice is a treasure, dear."

Tiffany looked down at her shoes, slumping her shoulders. "I didn't get the big solo in the Christmas choir show last year," she muttered, her face falling. "They gave it to Irina Kravtchouk instead."

Tracy put her arm around her shoulder. "You had the spring solo," she told Tiffany. "It was Irina's turn to shine. Couldn't you be happy for her? Just a bit?"

"I guess," she sighed. "I was just embarrassed by it all. I thought I did such a nice job on the audition. Now I'll never get to sing the main part in *O Holy Night* in front of a crowd."

Pastor Butler cleared his throat. "Actually," he announced. "That's part of why I came over here today."

The three women turned their heads to face him.

"Oh…" Aunt Rose said.

He smiled. "The church choir concert is next week, and unfortunately, several of our singers have caught a nasty bout of the flu. I need to fill their places, and I wanted to ask if you gals had any interest."

"I can't sing," Tracy declared. "My voice sounds like I attacked my cat, Mr. Sydney."

"I'm sure that isn't true," the pastor protested.

"She's right," Aunt Rose laughed. "Tracy really can't sing. Neither can I. We were blessed with some wonderful gifts, but the gift of song is not one of them, Pastor Butler."

He looked at them with pleading eyes. "Could you still be part of it?" he asked, turning to Tiffany. "We'll be doing *O Holy Night*, you know. And Rhonda, our soloist, is one of the sick ones…"

Tiffany's eyes grew large. "Really?"

"Really."

She turned to Tracy and Aunt Rose. "Let's do it, ladies! It will be fun."

"All the money goes to charity, too," the Pastor added. "Don't you want to do a nice deed this holiday season? Come join the choir and lift your voice and heart in song!"

Tracy bit her lip. "We have a lot going on here, Pastor Butler," she said. "The holidays are one of our busiest seasons."

"Can we think about it and get back to you?" Aunt Rose asked kindly. "We'll need some time to review our schedules. Maybe we could work something out."

"I'll be there for sure," Tiffany smiled, batting her eyelashes at the Pastor. "I should start practicing the solo."

Tiffany rushed out of the room, belting the lyrics as she went.

"I think you've made her day," Tracy chuckled. "Thanks for asking us, Pastor."

Aunt Rose smiled. "We'll let you know."

He tipped his hat at them and waved goodbye as he turned to leave the flower shop. "Have a blessed day!"

Aunt Rose and Tracy waved goodbye as he turned on his heel and left. "He is such a good man," she sighed as Tracy raised her eyebrow. "He is so devoted to this community, and he is so caring."

"Do you have a crush on the pastor?" Tracy teased.

Aunt Rose shook her head. "Come on, now," she told Tracy. "You know my heart belongs to your late Uncle Frank."

The front door opened and a woman with thick auburn curls walked in. "Good morning," Tracy greeted her. "How can we help you?"

The woman batted her eyelashes. "I need some flowers," she began as she eyed a display of crimson amaryllis flowers in a vase. "I have a loved one in the hospital, and I want to bring something pretty to brighten up the hospital room."

"No problem," Tracy smiled. "Do you have a preference on the type of flower?"

"Red roses," the woman told her without hesitation. "Roses of the deepest red color, please."

Tracy reached into the refrigerated back case holding several buckets of roses. "What about that?" she asked. "It's a sangria red, and it's one of our most popular red roses."

The woman wrinkled her nose. "No," she declined. "I want something deeper. Like...the color of blood."

Tracy laughed. "You're funny," she chirped as she placed the rose back in its bucket, but when she turned around, she saw the woman wasn't kidding. "Oh," she stammered. "So... a blood red rose?"

"Exactly."

Tracy peered into the case. "What about this one?" she asked as she retrieved a thick red rose from the next bucket. "We got these in from a dealer in Shanghai. They're a bit pricey, but I think the color will be more to your liking."

"It's perfect," the woman sighed. "The perfect blood red rose. I'll take twenty-four in an arrangement, please."

Tracy's eyes widened; twenty-four of these roses would be quite pricey, but she was glad they were getting the business. "These will look lovely," she commented as she selected fresh calluna for the filler flower. "What do you think?"

"This will be the loveliest thing I've ever taken to the hospital," the woman remarked. "I often take flowers to visit with friends and loved ones. I think I've been over there fifteen times this year!"

"You're a great friend," Tracy told her as she chose a pale pink vase for the arrangement. "This pink will set off the color, don't you think?"

"It's gorgeous," the woman agreed. "You have quite an eye for flower arranging. I wish I had something like this to take over when I was last visiting the hospital."

Tracy placed the vase of roses on the counter and rang up the order on the cash register. "Who were you visiting last time?" she asked absent-mindedly, careful to push the correct buttons to properly ring up the arrangement.

"Tyler," the woman replied. "He had done a chivalrous deed, of course, but got hurt along the way."

"Tyler Foxley?" Aunt Rose asked.

"Yes! Tyler Foxley."

Tracy jerked her head up from the cash register and stared at the woman.

"Are you alright?" she asked.

Tracy nodded and moved to hand the woman the vase, but her hands were shaking, and she dropped the arrangement on the floor.

"Tracy!" Aunt Rose cried as she rushed over. "What are you doing?"

Tracy did not speak, and Aunt Rose turned to the woman. "I am so sorry," her aunt apologized as she fell to her knees and began gathering shards of the pink glass from the floor.

"It's no problem," the woman assured her. "I'm just glad the glass didn't get stuck in my shoes."

Aunt Rose frowned at Tracy. "Get her a new vase," she ordered, but the woman shrugged. "I'll just take the bouquet to go," she told them. "I need to be off, and surely the hospital has an empty vase I can borrow."

Tracy carefully retrieved the roses from the mess on the floor and wrapped them in white paper. "I'm so sorry," she apologized to the woman as she handed her the flowers. "Next time you come in, your arrangement is on the house."

"Thank you," the woman smiled. "It's really no worry at all. Have a nice day," she said as she turned and breezed out of the shop.

Aunt Rose raised an eyebrow. "What was that all about?"

Tracy's face was pale. She bit her lip, feeling her heart pound as she hung her head, not wanting to turn and tell her aunt the truth.

2

Tiffany bustled over to where Aunt Rose and Tracy had begun to clean up the shards of pink glass. "What was that all about?" she asked. "And who the heck is Tyler Foxley? Tracy freaked out when that lady said his name."

Tracy's face burned; she could feel her usually pale cheeks blushing a deep red, and she tried to slow her racing heart.

"Tyler Foxley is a saint and a sweetheart," Aunt Rose commented as she retrieved a dustpan from behind the counter.

"Like... a minister? Like Pastor Butler?"

"No," Aunt Rose said. "He's just an amazing man. He is Tracy's age, and he is just a doll. In fact, didn't you two run around together when you were teenagers, Tracy? Am I remembering that correctly?"

Tracy blushed. "I think that sounds familiar," she said, though she knew exactly who her aunt was referring to.

"I see that look on your face," Aunt Rose commented. "You *do* know him, don't you?"

"Not anymore," Tracy admitted. "We were sweet on each other as teenagers, but I don't know what became of him."

Aunt Rose raised an eyebrow. "If I remember correctly, you two went steady for a summer or two," she commented. "You two were attached at the hip!"

Tracy feigned disinterest. "It was a long time ago," she remarked. "I don't remember much about him. He was handsome though, but doesn't everyone think their first love is handsome?"

Tiffany perked up. "Wait... you've gone from telling us you don't really know him to admitting he was your first love? Tracy! Spill the details. Who is this guy?"

Tracy bit her lip. "He was my first real boyfriend," she confessed. "But it was about twenty years ago. It doesn't mean anything."

"It must mean something," Tiffany insisted. "Because your eyes are all dreamy and your face is red."

"No, it isn't," Tracy countered.

Aunt Rose held up her hands. "Tiffany, leave her alone," she ordered as she turned to her niece. "When's the last time you saw Tyler, anyway?"

Tracy shook her head. "Really, it doesn't matter," she told them. "We broke up before my senior year in high school, and we haven't spoken since. But I never forgot him..."

"It's been that long? That's nearly twenty years," Aunt Rose gasped. "Oh, my goodness. No wonder this feels so strange."

Tracy eyed her aunt. "When is the last time *you* saw Tyler?" she asked, struck by the odd tone in her aunt's voice. "It's not like he stayed around town."

Aunt Rose shrugged. "He left Fern Grove to attend college on the east coast," she explained. "A college called... oh, what's the name of it? It's named after a color. Gray? Blue? Burgundy? No matter. He's been back through town quite a few times, and he's stopped by the shop a few times."

Tracy's jaw fell open. "Wait," she told her aunt. "Wait, a second. You're telling me that Tyler went to *Brown*?"

"That's it!" Aunt Rose grinned. "I knew you would think of it, you clever lady."

Tracy shook her head. "So, Tyler… my Tyler… made it to the Ivy Leagues?"

"That's impressive," Tiffany commented earnestly. "My guidance counselor says the Ivy Leagues are the best of the best."

Aunt Rose tilted her head and closed her eyes. "He didn't stay at Brown long," she admitted, but Tiffany waved her hands.

Tiffany's eyes grew large. "You had better forget him," she hissed. "Tracy's real *boyfriend* is about to walk into the shop right now."

"What?"

The color drained from her face as Warren walked in, a smile on his handsome face.

"Hey," he greeted them as he stepped up to the counter. "What are you lovely ladies chatting about this morning? The detective in me tells me you look like you're up to something!"

Aunt Rose shook her head, an innocent look on her face. "Us? No! We're just chatting about Tiffany's... prom date! Yes, that's right. Tiffany was telling us all about her date to the prom."

Tiffany looked puzzled, but quickly caught on. "Yes!" she agreed. "My prom."

Warren cocked his head to the side. "Prom?" he asked. "Maybe I'm just a silly guy or something, but isn't prom usually toward the end of the year?"

"It *is* the end of the year," Tiffany declared. "It's almost New Year's Eve!"

He laughed. "The end of the *school* year? Isn't it a little early to have a prom date lined up, Tiffany and haven't you already graduated from high school?"

She shot Tracy a look and then dashed out of the room. "Ignore her," Tracy laughed, trying to seem calm and collected. "She doesn't know what she's talking about."

Warren smiled at her, leaning across the counter to kiss her. "I wanted to get our plans for the night squared away," he grinned. "I'll pick you up from your apartment at seven. Does that give you enough time to get ready?"

"That's perfect," she agreed. "Remind me, where are we going again?"

"Work thing," he told her. "My colleague is retiring, and the department is doing a send-off for him. It'll be a great chance to show you off to the guys and gals at the department."

"I can't wait and thanks for the flowers," she told him, her eyes sparkling with excitement at the prospect of being shown off by her handsome detective boyfriend. "It's a date!"

That evening, after work, Tracy excitedly prepared for the outing with Warren. She showered and blow-dried her hair, set out her favorite pair of lace up fashion boots, and carefully studied her closet as she tried to find the perfect outfit.

Tracy was short and curvy; she knew her hips, bust, and waist made her look feminine, but at only five foot two inches tall, her short torso made certain outfits very unflattering for her figure. She was always careful to avoid tight pants and boxy dresses, knowing these looks would draw unwanted attention to her curves.

For the date, Tracy selected a belted A-line dress the color of a ripe plum to wear over opaque beige tights. She brushed her hair out, running her fingers through it until it settled nicely on her shoulders. She put on her makeup, careful to draw on perfect black cat eyes on each eyelid, working hard not to smudge the eye-liner as she guided the pencil across the ridges.

Tracy was a realist. She knew she'd never become a supermodel, but she also knew she had a sensual figure, full lips, and never carried weight in her face. By all accounts she was an attractive woman. When Warren knocked on the door of her one-bedroom apartment, she walked proudly forward to greet him, confident she looked her best.

When she answered the door, she was dismayed to find Warren dressed in jeans, a long-sleeve t-shirt, and a black leather jacket.

"Hey," she says as she stood before him in her dress and makeup. "I didn't realize this was going to be so relaxed."

He smiled. "It's fine," he promised. "You'll be the most beautiful girl at the bar."

"The bar?" she cried. "Then I'm definitely changing. This is a nice dress. I'm not wearing it out to a bar."

Warren pulled Tracy in close, wrapping his arms around her waist. "Please don't change," he begged her, leaning in to kiss her forehead. "We're running late, and you really look great, Tracy."

She sighed, pulling out of his embrace and reaching for her coat. "If you say so," she agreed, pulling a tin of breath mints out of her coat pocket and popping one into her mouth.

When they arrived at the bar, Tracy was not pleased with what she saw and heard; it was cramped and dark, and loud rock music made it impossible to hear. "Are you having fun?" Warren asked earnestly as he took her hand and guided her through the entryway.

"WHAT?" she called out, unable to hear him.

He squeezed her hand, pulling her toward a small alcove filled with tables. Tracy spotted several of Warren's colleagues seated with drinks. It was a little less noisy in the alcove, and she felt her shoulders relax.

"Hey," Warren greeted the group, and Tracy gave a little wave. "You all remember my girlfriend, Tracy?"

She smiled. "Nice to see everyone."

Before anyone could respond, there was a crash. Tracy watched all the detectives and police officers glance around; the noise had instantly transformed each of them back into public servants, and they all abandoned their drinks and rose from the table.

"Tracy, sit down," Warren ordered her as another loud crash came from the main part of the bar. She heard shouting, and she shook her head.

"Are you going to check it out?" she asked worriedly.

"It'll be fine," he assured her. "I'll be right back."

Warren and the six officers left, but Tracy quietly followed along behind them. Someone screamed, and she craned her neck to see what was going on.

"Get out of here!" a man's voice boomed. "You've caused enough trouble at my bar for the night. Get out of here, or I'll pick you up and throw you out myself!"

Tracy rounded the corner and could see two men staring at each other. One had his hands raised in fists, and the other, the bartender, was scowling.

"Enough!" the scowling man called out. "Get out of my bar, or I'll give you a bloody nose."

Warren rushed over. "Take it easy," he ordered. "Or I'll be taking you both to jail."

The man holding his fists in the air lowered his arms. "I'm not doing nothing wrong," he insisted. "The jerk won't serve me."

The bartender frowned. "This guy and his friends are causing a commotion. Detective, can you tell them to settle down?"

Warren looked at Tracy. "Will you be okay if I step in?"

"Of course," she smiled pleasantly. "Go take care of business, honey."

Just then, there was a huge crash, and Tracy heard someone wailing. "Call for help!" a voice screamed. "Call 911!"

Warren kissed her on the head. "Love you," he murmured, and Tracy watched as her boyfriend ran toward the screaming.

She hadn't imagined her night being full of so much commotion. She just hoped it wasn't a sign of things to come.

3

Tracy returned to her seat, nervous as to what was going on.

Warren returned to the table a few moments later. "You okay?" he asked.

Her face was pale. "What happened? Are you okay? What was with the screaming?"

He sighed. "It was a bar fight gone bad," he assured her. "Nothing more. The bartender has a black eye, but other than that, no casualties."

He shrugged. "It's what I do. Have you had a chance to look at the menu? I'm starving?"

Just then, a server appeared. "Hey," he greeted them flatly. "Can I take your order?"

Tracy nodded politely. "I'll take the Cuban with a side of sweet potato fries."

"Got it," he wrote on his notepad. "And for you?"

"A burger, medium, and a side of loaded potato skins," Warren told him.

The server nodded. "Got it. Anything else for you guys? My apologies about the noise earlier. Not sure what that was all about, but I'm glad the place has settled."

Warren shrugged. "It's all good, man."

Their server returned twenty minutes later with their food and an update. "So, I asked the bartender what's up," he murmured as he set Tracy's sandwich down in front of her. "He said it was the circus folks again."

Warren's face darkened. "Seriously? Again?"

He nodded. "They're back for their winter show."

"I hate it when those clowns come to town," Warren frowned. "They always come into town and cause a ruckus; it's like they take their act into town and cause all sorts of trouble in Fern Grove. It's so irritating. I swear, Tracy, the next five cases I'll have will be with circus people."

"They come into town and get folks riled up," he agreed. "That guy who was fighting with the bartender, Bruce, earlier? His name is Brett Goff. He's the owner of the circus that's in town right now, and from what some guys in the kitchen told me, he is trouble with a capital T."

Warren nodded. "That's interesting. Thanks, man."

"Anytime."

Tracy watched as he walked away from their table. "I wonder what his vendetta against the circus people is all about," she commented. "Surely they aren't all bad."

Warren stared at her. "Tracy, the circus people show up in town, cause trouble, and leave," he explained, tilting his head back and looking up at the ceiling. "It's a total nightmare for all of us at the department; we get reports about them constantly, but there isn't much we can do when they skip town the next day."

She bit her lip. "Have you ever thought about how they feel?"

His eyes widened. "How who feels? The folks in town?"

She shook her head. "No. The people in the circus. Don't you think they have bigger problems to worry about than we do? Surely working in the circus doesn't pay much. I'm sure they don't have an easy life."

Warren laughed out loud. "That's rich," he snorted as he held a hand in front of his mouth to prevent Tracy from seeing the food that was close to spilling from his lips. "You are a riot, Tracy. A total riot."

She sat watching him, shaking her head. "I'm serious."

He stopped laughing. "Tracy, really? You want me to think about how they feel? They make my life miserable four times a year. I get stuck cleaning up after their mess, coordinating their arrivals and departures, and frankly, I'm sick of it. I wish they didn't come to town at all."

Tracy looked at him. "I think it's really rude of you to generalize them like that," she declared as she pushed her half-eaten dinner aside and folded her hands on the table. "It's not like every single person who has ever worked at a circus is a bad person. That isn't fair."

Warren cleared his throat, clearly uncomfortable with her confrontation. "Tracy, you don't know what it's like," he pushed back. "You don't have a clue about dealing with these people. It must be easy to sit in a comfortable flower shop all day and not have to deal with real problems."

Her stomach churned, and she rose from her seat. "Excuse me?" she countered as she put her coat on. "I think we're done here."

"Tracy, I didn't mean it…"

She glared at him. "See you later."

Tracy stormed out of the bar. Warren's lack of empathy for the circus crowd disturbed her, and she was frustrated that she had gotten all dressed up to go to a dive bar.

She walked down the street, shivering as she passed the Swizzle Stick, an upscale cocktail bar downtown. With dainty white string lights adorning the large picture windows in the front, the Swizzle Stick looked inviting and festive. "I'm already dressed... I might as well enjoy a drink this evening," she thought to herself as she walked in.

Tracy entered the cocktail bar and was pleasantly surprised to find Emily Maher seated at the bar. Emily worked at the local newspaper, and she was always dressed to the nines, exuding the elegance of a big-city reporter despite working and living in a small town. Emily was a bit stuck up; she had wealthy parents and a big personality, but Tracy liked her style and sense of humor. "Hey, lady," she greeted Emily as she took the empty stool next to her. "Waiting on a hot date?"

"The opposite," Emily sniffed before taking a long sip of her martini. "I was stood up; I was supposed to meet a cutie from the dating app I've been using, but he never showed up."

Tracy patted her on the shoulder. "I'm so sorry," she told Emily. "That's the worst."

Emily took another sip and then placed the empty glass on the counter. "What are you up to?" she asked. "You look nice, though that color of lipstick isn't quite the shade I would choose for you..."

She took the backhanded compliment in stride. "I was out with Warren," she told Emily. "But then we had an argument." She filled Emily in on the details, and Emily chuckled.

"You know you're telling this to the wrong person," Emily commented as Tracy ordered a gin fizz. "I hate circuses. I don't like dirt or animals, and I'm sure the people who work in circuses are just as disorderly."

Tracy laughed. "Yeah, you're probably not the person I should have told this to," she admitted. "But I was happy to see a familiar face here."

Emily raised an eyebrow. "So, what's the deal?" she asked. "Why are you like, a circus apologist or something? I don't think Warren is wrong."

Tracy shrugged. "I have fond memories of going to the circus when I was growing up," she explained. "I would always go to the circus with my family. It was a treat. I lived for the long afternoons under the tent, watching elephants do tricks, and stuffing myself silly with popcorn."

Emily blinked. "They abuse animals, you know," she told Tracy. "Circuses are breeding grounds for trouble. Sorry to burst your bubble."

Tracy nodded. "I know that happens sometimes," she sighed. "I think I was just upset to hear Warren sound so uppity and that he was ruining my nostalgia. I even had my first kiss at the circus in Fern Grove, you know. Happy memories."

Emily narrowed her eyes. "You had your first kiss at the circus?" she asked. "I didn't know that. With who?"

"I can't say," Tracy whispered. "I don't want it to get out."

Emily squared her body to face Tracy. "Tell me," she insisted. "I've had a horrible night and have been stood up. Please? Pretty *please?*"

Tracy heard Emily sing the last please; it sounded like she had enjoyed a few drinks, but Tracy noticed she had a lovely singing voice. "I should recommend her for the choir concert," she thought as Emily continued.

"Please?!"

Tracy giggled. "It *is* fun to see you beg," she teased. "Fine, I'll tell you. My first kiss was at the Fern Grove Traveling Circus Show during the summer of 1997."

"Oh my gosh," Emily commented. "I was only five years old!"

Tracy rolled her eyes. "Focus!" she ordered. "Anyway, my kiss was with my first boyfriend, Tyler. Tyler Foxely. He was a perfect gentleman and so handsome. I wonder whatever happened to him."

"I've never heard of him," Emily told her. "But then again, I don't know a lot of people your age."

"Hey," Tracy held up her hands. "I'm not that much older than you!"

Emily shrugged. "So, you're still thinking of this old flame, huh?"

Tracy nodded. "A little bit," she admitted. "I wonder what became of him. I wonder if he ever wonders about *me*?"

4

"Did you know the circus is coming?!"

Tracy groaned as Tiffany ran shrieking into the front room of the flower shop. She had been out too late with Emily; it was nearly two in the morning when the two women finally settled their tabs at the Swizzle Stick, and now, seven hours later, Tracy was suffering from an excruciating headache. Tracy had only had a cocktail, but Emily had consumed drink after drink after drink, and Tracy had to walk her home.

"I've never seen a teenager quite so enthused for the circus," Aunt Rose commented.

Tiffany winked. "It's not about the circus itself," she informed them as she straightened the collar on her red button-up shirt. "It's about the cute boys who come to town with it."

"Ahem," Tracy cleared her throat. "They aren't boys, Tiffany. The grown *men* who are in town and work at the circus are way too old for you. You're living in a fantasy world, dear."

Tiffany batted her eyelashes. "I'm almost eighteen, Tracy," she corrected her. "I'm nearly an adult. If I meet a cute circus guy who is in his twenties, it's not like we're too far apart in age to make it work."

Aunt Rose held up her hands. Her brows were furrowed, and a look of alarm crossed her face. "You stay away from those men," she told Tiffany. "Grown men and teenagers have no business mingling. If I get word that you've been running around the circus trying to find a boyfriend, I am going to march over to your school, talk with your Principal, and make sure you have detention for the rest of your life. Is that understood?"

Tiffany rolled her eyes. "This is why I can't tell you anything," she moaned. "You two act like my mother!"

Tracy smiled. "That's what happens when you reach a certain age," she informed the teenager. "You start acting like everyone's mother. Just wait and see: in ten years, you'll be wagging your finger at silly teenagers and threatening to call their mothers."

"No, I won't!" she promised.

"Okay," Aunt Rose winked. "We'll see."

Tiffany huffed to the back of the store; her face hot with anger.

"So, are you going to make a trip over to see the circus?" Tracy asked her aunt. "It sounds like it will be a good show."

"I don't think so," Aunt Rose shuddered as she turned and began clipping the stems of a bunch of carnations. "When I was younger, I had a bad experience with a clown. I wandered off from my parents and found myself in the clowns' changing area. Watching them put their creepy makeup on was horrifying! I never wanted to go back to a circus ever again."

Tracy nodded. "That sounds awful."

"I'll be going," Tiffany announced as she waltzed back into the room carrying a vase of fresh pansies. "To the circus, that is. My parents are taking my family tomorrow. That is, unless you two try to ruin it for me by getting me into trouble. I was just joking about finding a boyfriend at the circus, you know. You two take everything so seriously."

Tracy shot a look at her aunt. They both knew Tiffany had every intention of finding love at the circus, but if she was with her parents, she surely wouldn't get into trouble.

"Are you going?" Tiffany asked Tracy. "Will I see you there?"

She shrugged. "Warren texted me earlier and told me he had tickets for us," she mentioned, though neglecting to say anything about the spat they had the previous evening. His text had been brisk, and Tracy had not decided if she wanted to actually go with him or not, especially given their argument.

"A date night? How sweet," Aunt Rose chirped. "He is so thoughtful."

The phone rang, and Tiffany answered it. She greeted the caller and then put her hand over the phone. "It's for you," she mouthed at Tracy.

Tracy took the phone. "Hello?"

"Hey," Warren said. "How are you?"

"Fine," she answered icily. "You?"

"Great," he replied curtly. "Look, I can't make it to the show tonight. Sorry. I have work to finish up at the station. You can take the tickets, if you want. I'll leave them at the front desk."

"Cool."

There was a long pause.

"...you're welcome?" Warren said testily.

Tracy sighed. "Thank you," she said. "Thanks for the tickets."

"I wanted to make it up to you for last night," his voice broke. "I'm sorry I was such a jerk."

"Just forget about it," she sighed. "I'll be by soon to get the tickets."

She hung up the phone. Tiffany and Aunt Rose were staring at her, both with confused looks on their faces.

"That didn't sound too lovey-dovey," Aunt Rose remarked. "Did Date night not go well last night?"

Tracy rubbed her tired eyes. "I don't want to talk about it," she stated flatly.

"Come on," Tiffany prodded.

"Tiffany," Tracy said sharply. "ENOUGH."

After her shift was over, Tracy ran home to change clothes, abandoning her work outfit for a comfortable pair of jeans, a white turtleneck, and a red vest. She gave her beloved Abyssinian cat, Mr. Sydney, a kiss on the head before darting out the door to the police station.

As she approached the police station, she was shocked to see a man dressed in a clown suit standing outside. "TICKETS!" he shouted as passersby gave him curious stares. "Buy your tickets!"

She eyed him as she ascended the steps of the police station, and he caught her gaze. "Ma'am! Tickets for the circus! I've got 'em. You wanna buy?"

"No thank you," she said as she gently pushed past him and entered the police station. She picked up the tickets from the front desk. She thought briefly about popping into Warren's office to say hello, but decided against it, still feeling angry about their disagreement.

That evening, Tracy found herself feeling sad to be attending the circus alone. As she approached the fairgrounds, she watched as a pair of women around her age, clearly a pair of good friends, greeted each other by the ticket booth. "I should have invited Emily," she thought, amused by how much fun they had had at their impromptu girls' night the previous evening. "Maybe she would have come," she thought as she approached the ticket line.

"Tracy!"

She turned to see Tiffany running toward her. "Hey!"

"Hey," Tiffany greeted her. "Can I sit with you inside? My family is being so annoying."

Tracy waved to Tiffany's mother, who was watching Tiffany with an angry look on her face. "Did you ask your mom?"

"Yes," Tiffany nodded.

Tracy followed up by texting Tiffany's mother, and when she agreed, she turned to Tiffany and smiled. "All good."

They waited in line, both chatting about the acts they'd hope would be at the circus. "Look at the tent," Tiffany pointed as the line moved closer to the entrance. "It's huge!"

The tent *was* massive; it was a green and white striped pole tent with three points. They could hear laughter and applause coming from inside, and as they waited in line, their anticipation grew. "Almost to the front," Tiffany commented excitedly as the line moved and they took another step forward.

"Excuse me," a male voice said, and someone brushed past Tracy, cutting the line and darting into the tent. She glowered at him and realized the man looked like Tyler Foxley.

"Hey," she called out, but he walked away quickly. "That was weird," she said under her breath. What was Tyler Foxley doing at the circus?

"Jerk!" Tiffany called out. "People can be so rude!"

Tracy nodded. "Yes, they sure can."

Tiffany tugged on her coat. "It's chilly," she complained. "I wish this line would move faster."

Tracy smiled. "Patience, my dear."

"That's what your aunt always says," Tiffany told her. "You two are so much alike."

"I wish she were here," Tracy sighed. "Everything is always more fun with Aunt Rose."

Suddenly, the line began to move rapidly, and before they knew it, two clowns ushered them inside.

"Wow!" Tiffany shrieked as they followed the line. The inside of the tent was filled with twinkling lights strung from the three main poles. Between the poles were three separate stages, and metal bleachers had been built around the perimeter, giving guests views of each of the three stages. "This is just like in the movies."

Tracy and Tiffany found a pair of seats and sat down. "Do you see that?" Tiffany pointed as the lights flashed and then went low. "I think it was an elephant."

Tracy scanned the tent. She saw dozens of people she knew from town; it seemed that nearly everyone had come to the circus that evening. Though she was still annoyed with him, she wished Warren were sitting beside her, holding her hand on the chilly winter evening.

"LADIES AND GENTLEMEN," an announcer began. "Welcome to the time of your life! The biggest night you'll ever live. WELCOME TO THE CIRCUS!"

The show began, and for the next hour, Tiffany and Tracy, along with the rest of the crowd, were delighted by the impressive show of animals and performers. "This is the coolest thing I've ever seen,"

Tiffany whispered to Tracy as a costumed woman holding a leopard cub appeared, dangling from a rope attached to the tallest pole.

At the conclusion of the show, Tracy and Tiffany rose to their feet and gave the performers a round of applause. "That was sweet," Tiffany praised, and Tracy agreed. It had been a spectacular show; with colorful lights, music, and an array of interesting spectacles, the hour had flown by.

The performers all stepped forward to take their final bows, and the announcer came back on over the speakers. "And finally, give a warm round of applause to our owner, Brett Goff!"

The crowd roared, but no one stepped forward.

"BRETT GOFF!" the announcer repeated, and suddenly, there was a scream.

A tall woman wearing a gold tutu rushed onto the main stage. "He's dead!" she wailed as the crowd gasped. "Brett Goff is DEAD! Somebody *murdered* Brett!"

5

The next morning, Tiffany, Aunt Rose, and Tracy closed the flower shop for the day; the town was in chaos after the murder of Brett Goff, the owner of the circus, and the police had issued a stay-at-home order for everyone in town. The three ladies decided to have a quick business meeting on a telephone call instead of trying to go into work.

"Good morning," Aunt Rose greeted them as Tracy and Tiffany hopped on the call. "How are you two ladies doing?"

Tiffany sighed. Tracy knew Tiffany had been shaken by the events of the previous night; the girl had clasped Tracy's hands as soon as the murder had been announced, and she didn't let go until Tracy delivered her safely back into the care of her worried parents.

"I'm like, traumatized," Tiffany moaned. "Someone was *murdered* right before our eyes!"

Tracy shifted on the emerald green couch in her apartment, trying to get comfortable as Mr. Sydney perched on her knees. "It wasn't quite before our eyes," she gently reminded Tiffany. "We didn't see anything."

Tiffany scoffed. "But we were *there*, Tracy," she countered. "We were sitting only steps away from a murder. Who knows, it could have happened right below the bleachers where we were sitting. Can you even imagine that?"

Aunt Rose took control of the conversation. "I'm just glad you two weren't hurt," she told them. "I heard there was rioting in town last night, and I was worried sick. They're saying a group of angry clowns tried to set fire to the town hall, Tracy."

Tiffany shrieked. "This town isn't safe anymore," she complained. "Murders? Arsonist-clowns? What's next?"

"It's all going to be okay," Aunt Rose assured her. "This will get sorted out. Fern Grove has a very capable police department and detective. Tracy would know."

Tracy frowned. She had barely heard from Warren since the debacle at the circus; she had called him when she returned home the previous evening, but he had only sent a short text.

Heading to the circus now. Stay home. Stay safe. XO.

"What does Warren think happened?" Tiffany asked. "Did he give you any info, Tracy? My friends think he was fed to a tiger. Isn't that gruesome?"

"I was also wondering what happened," Aunt Rose chimed in. "Tracy, did Warren have any updates?"

She bit her lip. "I don't know," she admitted, her voice slightly breaking on the last word. "I haven't really heard from him."

"You haven't really heard from him?" Tiffany asked. "But there was a riot!"

"We texted," Tracy said defensively. "But I imagine that he is very, very busy trying to get to the bottom of what happened."

"She's right, Tiffany," Aunt Rose added. "Warren has a very important job keeping our community safe. I'm sure he's been working his tail off to find out what happened."

"Okay, okay," Tiffany said. "I just want to find out what happened. It's just crazy to have something like this happen in our town. Tracy, are you *sure* Warren didn't say anything? Did *you* see anything last night? I keep wracking my brain to relive last night, but nothing seemed out of the ordinary."

Tracy's eyes widened. She *had* seen something out of the ordinary at the circus; she remembered the man who had cut her in line looked like Tyler, her ex-boyfriend, and she had thought that was strange, but she didn't want to share that with Tiffany.

They finished their call and Tracy leaned back against her sofa. She felt exhausted and frustrated; she was relieved to have the day off of work, but she felt like Warren was angry with her. "I need a pick me up," she thought as she scratched Mr. Sydney behind his small ears.

Just then, she heard a ping from her phone. It was a text message from Aunt Rose.

Stay-at-home order lifted. I'm going into the shop, but I am giving you and Tiffany the day off. Go do something nice for yourself! Love, Auntie.

Tracy pursed her lips. What should she do with her day? She considered staying in her pajamas and watching holiday movies all day, but then decided against it; she knew staying at home alone would only make her feel sad.

"I know what I'll do!" she said aloud as she stood up and stretched her arms overhead, enjoying the gentle crack of her neck. "Time for some coffee!"

Tracy picked out a pair of bootcut jeans from her closet, pairing the pants with her favorite taupe ankle boots. She threw a silver mock neck sweater on, adjusting it so the front tucked into her beige belt and accentuated her figure. She bundled up in her knee-length belted white felt winter coat and added a matching beret.

Feeling pretty as she left her house, Tracy decided to treat herself to a cup of coffee at *Grind it Out*, her favorite coffee shop. It was a bitterly cold day; snow was falling as she made her way downtown, and Tracy looked forward to the warmth and taste of the peppermint mocha latte she was planning to order.

As she entered the coffee shop, she waved hello to Jurgen, the owner. Jurgen was an immigrant from Berlin, Germany, and he spoke in the most charming accent.

"*Guten morgen*!" Tracy greeted him in German as she sidled up to the counter. "How are you today?"

"*Mir geht es gut*," he replied. "I am well. A little shaken from that stay-at-home order and all the drama from last night, but doing better now."

Tracy nodded. "It's crazy to think that something like that can happen in our town," she said. "Have you heard anything about it?"

Jurgen, who was usually in the know about the comings and goings of everyone in town, shrugged. "I heard it might have been poison," he murmured as Tracy raised her brows. "But who knows? Clowns are a bad omen in Germany; did you know that? Back home, we detest clowns. It's bad luck to have one cross your path. I hate to say it, but when I heard the circus was coming to town, I had a bad feeling, Tracy."

She nodded. "Clowns can be creepy," she agreed. "In other news, I want to place an order for a holiday-themed drink. Your peppermint mocha has been a favorite of mine the last few weeks, but I'm feeling like something else today. Do you have a recommendation?"

He thought for a moment, his blonde eyebrows crossing. "Have you tried the eggnog smoothie?"

"Not a fan," she said politely. "Anything else?"

"Let me think," he told her. "What are your favorite holiday flavors?"

"Cinnamon, sweet cream, and coffee," she replied.

He grinned. "If you'll step out of line and give me five minutes, I'll make up a custom drink for you based on those choices. What do you think?"

"Deal!" she beamed.

Tracy stepped out of line and let the woman behind her approach the counter. She heard the woman order, and then saw her step to the side after paying. Tracy's heart began to pound. The woman was wearing black leggings, knee-high black boots, and an oversized sweatshirt with a circus emblem on it. Was this woman going to start problems in the coffee shop?

The woman felt Tracy's gaze on her, because she stared right into Tracy's eyes. "Hey," she said curtly. "What are you looking at?"

Tracy forced herself to smile. "I was admiring your boots," she lied. "I've been looking for a nice pair of boots like that, and I was wondering where you got those."

The woman scowled. She looked to be around Tracy's age, and she had long glossy dark hair that hung in ringlets, and she ran a hand through her hair as she awkwardly shifted back and forth. "You were staring at my sweatshirt, weren't you?"

Tracy nodded. "You caught me. I was just curious about the circus. With what happened there last night, and all the commotion in town..."

The woman narrowed her eyes at Tracy. "Look," she began. "You don't know what you're talking about. The rumors about arson and riots? It's all a bunch of lies. We're good people, you see; our circus is full of hard-working, reliable, decent folks. It isn't our fault that society labels us as no-good."

Tracy bit her lip. "I'm so sorry for all the trouble you've been through here," she said earnestly. "It sounds like it's been bad for all of you, especially the man who died..."

The woman reached up and blotted her eyes with a handkerchief she had retrieved from the pocket of her sweatshirt. "Did you know him well?" Tracy asked gently.

The woman stared into Tracy's eyes. "He was only my *husband,*" she said sharply.

6

"Tyler Foxley!"

Tracy jerked her head toward Aunt Rose's shriek. They were back to work the next day, and Tracy had been trimming the stems of a bouquet of crocus when the front door opened and Aunt Rose started shouting with excitement.

She looked up as Tyler Foxley strode into the flower shop, a wolfish grin on his face. He looked as handsome as ever; at five foot ten, he was brawny and fit, and it was evident he spent serious time in the gym. His dark blonde hair spilled out of a backward baseball cap, and Tracy's heart began to pound when he turned to her, his eyes widening.

"Tracy!" he greeted her as he stepped inside. "It's been a minute. How are you doing? You look incredible. I heard you were back in town."

Tracy smiled politely. "I'm well, thanks," she told him. "I'm working here with my aunt. What's new with you?"

Aunt Rose ran around the counter to give him a hug. "You look wonderful, dear," she complimented him. "This town just isn't the same without you. What have you been up to since you've been away? The last I heard, you were in medical school in New York? Or was it that you were getting married in the Seychelles? Gosh, Tyler, now that I think about it, the last I heard of you, you were headed to become a ski instructor in Aspen!"

Tyler shrugged. "It didn't work out," he admitted. "None of it did. But that's okay. When one door closes, another always opens," he smiled.

"That's the spirit!" Aunt Rose cheered. "Always an optimist. Trying new things is a gift, and it is so lovely that you love to put yourself out there."

Tyler glanced at Tracy's left hand. "Tracy, what about you? I don't think I've seen you since we were eighteen. Surely you have a couple of kiddos? A lucky fella?"

Before Tracy could answer, Tiffany interjected. "Tracy is a wildly successful businesswoman," she announced as she sashayed into the room. "She helped Rose restructure the shop's marketing and communications campaign, and business has been booming ever since."

"Is that so?" Tyler asked, his eyes dancing in amusement as the brazen teenager stood next to Tracy and stuck her nose in the air.

"Tracy has been a big help," Aunt Rose agreed. "She has really elevated the way we do business."

Tracy smiled. "You know I'm happy to help you."

Tyler looked at Tracy. "I'm back in town for a bit," he told her. "Work has brought me to Fern Grove, and I've been catching up with my family and old friends."

"That's wonderful," Aunt Rose commented. "What kind of work?"

"The circus," he said cautiously. "Surely you've heard about the circus in town?"

Tracy's eyes widened. "Oh, my goodness, Tyler," she breathed. "Are you okay? We've heard it's been chaotic over there, especially with that guy dying."

Tyler shook his head. "It's a lot more relaxed than it sounds," he promised. "I know it sounds wild and crazy to work for a circus, but the crew is incredible, and I've really found some good friends there."

Tracy peered at her former flame with curiosity. "So... what exactly do you do in the circus?" she asked.

"That's a great question," he beamed. "I handle most of the operations; I earned a bachelor's degree in systems and operations from the University of Kentucky, and I'm putting it to good use. It's a critical role for the company, and I'm happy to be doing it."

"But... what does that even mean?" Tracy blinked. "You... operate what, exactly?"

Aunt Rose shushed her. "Don't be rude," she chided Tracy. "I'm excited to hear Tyler is doing something he enjoys. I always liked you, Tyler, and it is such a joy to see you all grown up and handsome."

Tyler puffed up his chest. "I'm hoping I'm handsome enough to convince your pretty niece to go out with me," he grinned. "Just as friends, of course. Tracy, what do you say about grabbing a bite with me tonight? Over pizza or something? We can catch up. I want to hear all about your life here."

Tracy wrinkled her nose. It was one thing to think about seeing Tyler Foxely again, but it was another thing to see him here, in the flesh, inviting her out. What would Warren think? And would she get into trouble for being associated with a circus person?

"I don't know," she told him. "I'm just not sure that's a great idea, Tyler."

"Come on," he pleaded with a smile on his face. "For old time's sake."

She bit her lip. "Why don't you tell me more about operations, or whatever you do over at the circus?" she suggested. "Did you know that guy who died?"

Tyler cocked his head to the side. "Let me tell you all about it over dinner, 'kay?"

She shook her head. "Come on, Tyler. I'm just dying to know more about life at the circus. Was that Brett guy your boss?"

"Tracy," Aunt Rose warned her. "Enough. You're being rude. Whether Tyler knew the man or not, it's still a tragedy that he died, and you shouldn't be peppering him with questions."

Tyler winked at Aunt Rose. "I'll let her pepper me with all the questions she wants if she agrees to come out with me," he told her. "I'll get out of the way—I know you ladies need to work. I just wanted to come over and say hello."

He waved goodbye, and as soon as he left, Aunt Rose glared at Tracy. "What was that all about?" she asked. "You seemed quite rude with Tyler. He is so kind and handsome, and you were so dismissive."

"I didn't like him," Tiffany declared. "He seemed arrogant."

"Is that why you came to my rescue with the businesswoman comment?" Tracy laughed. "Thanks for that. I really did appreciate it."

"Any time!" Tiffany told her. "When my ex-boyfriend, Malcolm, came sniffing around trying to find out about what I've been up to since he dumped me last spring, my friend, Mona, told him I've been working part-time as a model and am going to study abroad in Paris."

"Is any of that true?" Aunt Rose asked.

"Obviously not," Tiffany laughed. "But it never hurts to let your ex think you're better off without him."

Later that evening, Tracy arrived home, looking forward to a quiet evening watching Chums, her favorite television show. She had ordered in, and was expecting a delivery from the local Thai restaurant, and she couldn't wait to have a relaxing night eating her favorite foods and laughing at the characters she loved so much.

Just as she changed into her pajamas and settled in front of the television with a fried spring roll in hand, her cell phone rang. "That had better be Warren," she grumbled as she picked up the device. "I haven't had a real conversation with him in forever."

She was secretly dismayed to hear the voice of Isabella, one of her good friends. Isabella was happily engaged, and while Tracy had wanted to talk with her boyfriend, she knew a conversation with Isabella would raise her spirits.

"IT'S OVER," Isabella wailed as Tracy answered the call.

Tracy was confused. "What's over?" she asked, trying to speak and swallow the large piece of spring roll in her mouth.

"OUR ENGAGEMENT," she cried. "The wedding is off."

Tracy's eyes widened. Isabella's engagement was off? First, a murder in town, and now, her friend, who had been happily betrothed, was no longer getting married? What was going on?

The two women talked things through for nearly two hours, with Isabella detailing the breakup, the process of calling off the wedding, and the money she had lost on vendors who would not be refunding her deposits. "It's a nightmare," she moaned as Tracy nodded sympathetically. "But I will be happy again one day," she declared. "I won't let him steal my joy. Say, you are in a happy relationship. Tell me how things are going with Warren. I need some cheer in my life."

Tracy gritted her teeth. Things were *not* going so great with Warren; between their fight and lack of communication over the last few days, she was feeling uneasy about her relationship. Besides, it had been a shock to see her ex-boyfriend back in town, and she was still reeling from the surprise of seeing him at the flower shop.

She relayed all this to Isabella, who laughed. "So let me get this straight," she began. "I have no one who loves me anymore, and you have *two* guys after you?"

"It's weird," Tracy told her friend as Mr. Sydney appeared and crawled into her lap. "I had always imagined seeing Tyler again, but now that he's shown up, I feel odd."

"Do you have feelings for him?" she asked.

"For Tyler?"

"Yeah! The cute circus guy who stole your heart and first kiss as a teenager? Come on, Tracy. There is some major history there."

Tracy was silent. Her friend was right, but she knew she owed it to Warren to be totally committed to him. She *was* his girlfriend, and this wasn't high school. They were all adults now, and she needed to act like a mature woman who knew what she wanted.

"Just don't give Tyler the wrong idea," Isabella warned her. "If you are feeling weird about seeing him, listen to your gut instincts. You don't want to lose what you have with Warren over some guy from the past, do you?"

Tracy felt her stomach drop. She didn't want to compromise her relationship with Warren, but she *was* curious about Tyler.

"Tracy? Do you?"

Her attention returned to the phone call. “No,” she said softly, though she didn’t quite believe herself. “Of course, not…”

7

"And fifteen pounds of baby's breath, please! Don't forget this time!"

The next day, Aunt Rose bid Tracy farewell as she headed off to the market with a list of supplies in hand. It was Tracy's turn to run errands, and while she rarely wanted to get stuck doing the shopping as she loathed crowds and busy stores, Aunt Rose's gushing about Tyler was driving her nuts, and she was eager to escape the flower shop for a while.

Tracy headed to the large indoor farmer's market housed in the local elementary school gymnasium every weekend. She carried two large recyclable shopping bags and was ready to pick through the vendors selling filler flowers. The shop was nearly out of the inexpensive greenery, and Tracy hoped to purchase enough to last through Christmas.

As she entered the gymnasium, she waved hello to Greg, the president of the city council. He was manning a booth filled with flyers and signs encouraging residents to run for city council, and his wife, Lydia, sat next to him. "Nice to see you," Tracy called out to the couple. "Busy day today?"

"Not quite," Lydia told her. "The big crowds were here this morning, but things are beginning to calm down."

"Thank goodness," Greg sighed in relief. "The noise in here gets to be too much for me when it is too crowded."

Tracy said goodbye and walked over to a booth where a mother and daughter were selling hot chocolate. "I'll take one," Tracy told them as she fished for a dollar from her purse.

"Hey!"

It was Emily Maher.

"How are you feeling?" Tracy asked. "You were having a rough night at the bar."

Emily blushed. "So sorry about that," she apologized, batting her eyelashes. "It's so rude to get wasted in public like that, and I was such an embarrassment. Thanks so much for walking me home, Tracy."

"It wasn't a big deal," Tracy assured her. "We've all had our nights. You should have seen me on my twenty-second birthday. I was drinking gin and juice like it was my job. That was when I was young and restless."

Emily shuddered. "I can't even think about drinking," she told Tracy. "Anyway, what are you up to? Just browsing?"

"Errands," Tracy explained. "Hey, I've been meaning to ask you something."

"What's up?"

"The other night at the bar, you sang a little," Tracy began.

Emily giggled. "If I remember correctly, we sang karaoke at the bar for an hour," she corrected Tracy. "I really embarrassed myself, didn't I?"

"Not at all," Tracy promised. "In fact, your singing was so lovely, that I wanted to recommend you for the Christmas choir program at Pastor Butler's church. He needs people to volunteer to sing, and you would be fantastic."

Emily wrinkled her nose. "I don't know about that," she told Tracy. "I'm Jewish. I don't know how my Bubbe–my grandmother—would feel about me singing Christian songs in a church. She's very proud of our heritage, and I would hate to make her feel uncomfortable."

Tracy nodded. "I didn't know you were Jewish!" she smiled. "That's so cool. I didn't know Fern Grove had a Jewish community."

"It doesn't," Emily told her. "I drive up to Portland to go to my Synagogue. It really makes it difficult to meet the nice Jewish boy my mother prays I will marry someday."

Tracy laughed. "Well, if you change your mind, Pastor Butler would love to have you."

"*Would* he?" Emily asked. "How does he feel about letting a Jewish woman sing Christmas songs?"

Tracy smiled. "Pastor Butler is a good man," she promised her friend. "With a huge heart. I think he would welcome you with open arms."

They chatted for a bit longer, and then Tracy looked at her watch and gasped. "The time," she told Emily. "I have to run."

"Wait!" Emily requested. "You didn't tell me about that guy."

"Warren?"

Emily shook her head. "No, the ex-boyfriend. Taylor? Tanner?"

"Tyler."

"Yeah! You brought him up at the bar. I want to hear more."

Tracy shook her head. "Nothing to hear, my friend."

Emily raised an eyebrow. "Are you sure? Your face is red. I'm looking to write a piece about the circus people for the newspaper, and he could be my in. Can you connect us?"

"I don't think so," Tracy sighed as she turned and waved goodbye. "See you later, Emily."

She bolted to the flower stands. She wasn't ready to indulge Emily's intrusion into her past. There were three sellers today, and she eagerly tore into their inventory of greenery. She studied a bucket of baby's breath, and as she moved on to a bucket of hoary stock, she heard someone call her name. Tracy turned to find Tyler Foxley smiling at her.

"Hey, stranger," he greeted her warmly. "How's it going?"

She smiled politely. "Fine. I'm just picking up some things for my aunt. How are you?"

He shrugged. "I'm picking up some shifts at the vegan food stand," he told her. "The circus has been shut down while the police are investigating, and I need to make a few bucks."

She glanced down and realized he was wearing a green apron. "Oh," she replied. "I didn't realize you were vegan."

"I'm not," he laughed. "But I'll do anything to make a buck."

She laughed. "I remember that last summer we had together, you worked what, fifteen jobs?"

"Five," he corrected her good-naturedly. "I bagged groceries at the market, washed cars for my dad, did some shifts at the hardware store, walked dogs, and helped at the pizza shop."

"How do you remember all of that?" she asked in amazement.

"I remember everything," he winked, and she felt her heart pound.

"How are things over at the circus?" she asked, quickly trying to change the subject.

His face darkened. "It's been hard," he confessed. "No one is making money, and the police have been jerks to us."

She raised an eyebrow. "What do you mean?"

He shrugged. "They've been really gruff and rude during the investigation," he informed her. "It seems unnecessary. They seem to have a lot of biases against circus performers and crews, and their treatment has reflected that."

Tracy's face darkened. She hated injustice, and while she had been skeptical about the circus workers given the situation she had witnessed at the bar with Brett Goff, she agreed it was unfair to generalize everyone.

"What specifically have they done?" she asked. "I have some... connections at the police station. Maybe I could help?"

He smiled. "That would be really nice, Tracy. Thank you. Well, for starters, the police officers have been really rough with our people. They've used a lot of force and been really rude... lots of foul language."

"That is awful!" she declared. "Has there been someone leading the investigation? Like a head officer or something?"

"Warren something," he told her, and the color drained from her face.

"Warren?" she stammered.

"You know him?" he asked.

Before she could answer, a little girl holding a golden retriever puppy on a leash ran up to her and tugged on her coat. "Miss? Miss?"

Tracy bent down to kneel at eye level with the girl. "Hi!" she greeted her, rubbing the dog's soft ears. "Cute dog."

"Can you take our picture?" the little girl asked. "This is my new puppy. Isn't she cute?"

Tyler's eyes lit up. "She's perfect," he told the little girl. "What's her name?"

"Goldie," the little girl grinned.

"Did I hear that someone needed a photo taken?" a voice called out from behind them. A woman dressed in a tracksuit walked over. "What a gorgeous family you four are! A handsome daddy, a pretty mommy, and an adorable daughter and puppy?! You four are just precious. Get together, and I'll get the shot you want."

Tracy's smile vanished from her lips. "Excuse me," she told the woman. "So sorry for the misunderstanding."

"Misunderstanding?" the woman asked. "I heard you wanted someone to take a photo. Let me help. Every adorable family needs a cute photo, and this is a great shot."

"No," Tracy said, standing up and backing away, feeling uncomfortable as people started staring at her. "We aren't a family. I'm sorry. I have to go."

Tracy turned on her heel and darted away, leaving Tyler, the little girl, woman, and shoppers all staring at her as she rushed out the door and into the chilly morning air.

8

"You forgot the baby's breath!" Aunt Rose scolded Tracy as she returned to the flower shop.

Tracy's stomach churned. The scene at the farmer's market had been so embarrassing; the passerby had thought she and Tyler were a *couple,* and now she knew Warren was allegedly mistreating circus workers during the investigation. Could the day be off to a worse start?

"I'm going to have to go back myself," Aunt Rose complained as she eyed the two empty bags on Tracy's elbows.

"I'm sorry," she apologized. "I got distracted. I bumped into Emily Maher and chatted for too long. I shouldn't have made you wait. I'm sorry."

Aunt Rose studied her face. "What's the matter?" she asked, her eyes filled with worry. "You look like you saw a ghost, Tracy. Is everything okay?"

Tracy felt her cheeks burn. "I saw Tyler at the farmer's market," she told her aunt.

"Tyler? What a doll. Wait, a second... why did that upset you?"

Tracy gulped. "I don't know," she admitted, and her aunt put her arm around her shoulder.

"Honey, it's normal to feel awkward around your first love," Aunt Rose assured her. "I always felt that way when I saw Jesse."

"Jesse?" Tracy cried. "Who's Jesse?"

"My first boyfriend," her aunt replied matter-of-factly. "He was your late Uncle Frank's cousin, actually."

Tracy's jaw dropped. "Your first love was Uncle Frank's cousin? Aunt Rose! That's crazy."

Her aunt chuckled. "We were kids, dear," she told her. "Just like you and Tyler were kids when you spent time together. Young love is important, but that doesn't always make it real love. What you have with Warren? That's real love: two independent adults caring for each other, respecting each other, and sharing their adult lives."

Tracy sighed. "I don't feel like Warren and I have real love. At least not lately," she confessed. "Ever since our argument, things have been strained between us. It just hasn't felt the same."

Aunt Rose nodded. "And I'm sure it doesn't help that Tyler swooped into town and stirred up your memories and teenage feelings," she offered. "Look, cut yourself some slack," she insisted. "Things with Warren will get better. Tyler will leave town sooner than later, too, and things will go back to normal."

"I hope so," she told her aunt.

"Just make sure you don't lead Tyler on," Aunt Rose warned her. "I think it's fine to be polite, but don't be too friendly. You wouldn't want him to read into anything that isn't there."

"You're right," Tracy told her aunt. "I definitely will not be having dinner with him, that's for sure!"

"Dinner with whom?"

Tiffany appeared from the back room. "Tracy, did you forget the filler flowers?"

Aunt Rose laughed. "Tiffany, don't act like your ear hasn't been pressed against the wall this entire time. I know you, and I know you've been eavesdropping."

Tiffany blushed. "Who, me?"

Aunt Rose gave the teenager a playful swat on the behind. "Yes, you. You know she forgot the filler flowers. It's fine. We'll get by."

Just then, a girl around Tiffany's age walked into the flower shop. She had dark curly hair and wore a red headband. "Hi," she waved as she approached the counter.

"Can we help you with something?" Aunt Rose asked as Tiffany eyed the girl.

She nodded. "I want to buy a bouquet of red roses to send to someone," she announced.

Tracy smiled. "That's so sweet. Who is it for? Your mother?"

The girl shook her head, sending her dark curls shaking. "No, it's for myself."

Tiffany raised an eyebrow. "You're sending flowers to yourself?"

"Yes," the girl grinned. "It's all part of my plan. I have two boys who like me, but both of them are too shy to make the first move. I am going to send myself flowers and tell each boy. I'll pretend like the other boy sent the roses. Maybe it will make them make a move already."

Aunt Rose frowned. "I don't know if that's the best plan," she advised.

"Why not?" Tiffany laughed. "I think it's genius. I should have done this before myself!"

Aunt Rose pursed her lips. "Honey," she addressed the girl. "Love is patient. True love waits. Can't you be patient and wait a bit longer for one of these young men to confess his feelings for you? Wouldn't that be easier and less expensive than buying yourself a bouquet?"

The girl placed her hands on her hips. "My mom tells me to go out and get what I want," she declared. "So, I'm trying to do that."

The girl looked at Tracy. "What do you think?"

Tracy scrunched up her nose. "I don't like it," she told the girl. "It feels... tricky. Manipulative. Getting into the habit of manipulating feelings isn't good. I know it's hard to be patient, but I think my aunt is right. Be patient, and the right person will come around when the time is right."

The girl rolled her eyes. "I guess you're right," she groaned. "Well, who can I send these flowers to if I don't send them to myself?"

"What about your dad?" Tiffany asked. "Maybe if you send flowers to your dad, he'll be in a good mood and raise your allowance"

"Oh, I can't do that," the girl replied nonchalantly.

"What? No allowance?" Tiffany wondered.

"Nope. No dad."

Tiffany shifted awkwardly. "Sorry," she offered. "Does he live far away or something? We do ship flowers to faraway places, you know."

The dark-haired girl looked Tiffany in the eyes. "I don't think I could afford that shipping. My dad is dead. He was murdered at the circus a few days ago."

9

"Oh my gosh," Tracy gasped as the girl's eyes widened. "We are so sorry to hear that."

The girl's shoulders slumped. "I think I'm still in shock, to be honest. It's easier for me if I make jokes about it."

Tracy rushed around the counter to give the girl a hug. "We'll find the killer," she promised the girl. "The good people of Fern Grove will not let this stand."

"Thanks," the girl sighed. "I'm Linda, by the way."

"I'm Tracy," she told her. "This is my Aunt Rose, and Tiffany."

"Nice to meet you," Linda said kindly. "I had better be going," she told them. "Thanks for talking with me. It's nice to meet some normal people for once; my mom and the rest of the crew at the circus are going crazy with Dad passing away."

"Come back anytime," Tiffany told her. "Maybe we could hang out sometime?"

"I'd like that," Linda told her. "Maybe you could come visit me at the circus."

"We'll have to arrange that," Tracy smiled as Linda waved goodbye.

When the front door closed, Aunt Rose gave Tracy a look. "What was that all about?"

"What do you mean?"

"All that talk about finding the killer."

Tracy shrugged. "I feel terrible for the girl," she told her aunt.

Aunt Rose looked Tracy in the eye. "Honey, I know you mean well," she began. "But I don't think you need to get tangled up in any circus business. It isn't your place."

Tracy tilted her head to the side. "Isn't it, though?" she asked. "Linda reminded me of myself as a girl; I got the feeling that she doesn't seem like she belongs anywhere. She seems lost and alone."

Aunt Rose frowned. "You felt like that as a girl? You had a family who loved you, plenty of clothes and toys, and a lovely home."

Tracy pursed her lips. "But when my parents died, I felt so alone, Aunt Rose," she whispered. "I felt as though I didn't belong anywhere anymore."

Aunt Rose's face paled. "I forgot," she murmured as she came over and wrapped her niece in a hug. "You are *family,* Tracy. Your parents trusted us to love you with all of our hearts, and we did. We took care of you when they died and never looked back. Wasn't that enough?"

Tracy smiled. "I know that now," she told her aunt. "But I certainly struggled with it for a while. But no matter; I just related to Linda a bit, that's all."

"You have a big heart," Aunt Rose praised her. "You're always trying to do right by others. I love that about you. I just don't want you to get caught up in anyone's troubles or drama right now. There is enough going on around here with a murderer on the loose..."

That evening, Tracy took the long way home from *In Season*; the air was unusually warm for a December day in the Pacific Northwest, and she wanted to soak in the pleasant weather as she strolled through the streets of Fern Grove.

She passed a crowd of people heading into the elementary school gym; the farmer's market was still open, and she decided to have a peek, hoping to pick up a delicious treat or something fun for dinner.

As Tracy walked in, she felt her cheeks flush; the air inside was hot and stuffy, and she quickly removed her winter hat in hopes of cooling off. A jazz quartet was playing Christmas carols on the stage in the corner, and she smiled as she felt the Christmas spirit rising within her heart.

Tracy passed a vendor selling tamales, and she bought two that were stuffed with goat cheese and sweet red Peruvian peppers. "This will be so delicious," she cried as the seller wrapped them up in pale yellow parchment paper and placed them in a bag.

Her next stop was the fruit stand; Tracy eyed the bright yellow gooseberries, and she selected twenty-five of the juiciest, most plump berries to take home. "These will be delicious in a smoothie," she thought as the seller popped the berries into two plastic cartons and handed them to her.

Holding her bags tightly, Tracy wound through the sea of vendors and shoppers, finding herself staring at a display of original paintings set up near the exit. "Do you like them?" the artist asked as Tracy nodded. The oil paintings were of two slender figures posing on what looked to be a blue velvet couch. They wore low-heeled black shoes, maroon tights, and their faces were painted white. White Shakespeare collars were wrapped around their necks, and their faces were pale, painted a shade of cream.

"What are they doing?" Tracy asked, her eyes filled with wonder. "Are these supposed to be guys doing a Shakespeare play or something? Hamlet? That's the play you aren't supposed to say the name of aloud, right?"

The artist shrugged. "I don't know about plays," she told Tracy. "But you have the era correct; these are clowns from the Elizabethan era. I was inspired to paint them by the circus in town. Are you interested in purchasing a painting?"

Tracy gulped. "Clowns?" she asked, ready to be done with all things related to the circus. "I see. Well, have a nice day."

She turned on her heel and walked away quickly, nearly plowing down a small girl who was standing nearby. "Oh!" Tracy exclaimed. "I am so sorry." One carton of gooseberries spilled out of her bag, and she dropped to her hands and knees to pick them up.

She realized it was the girl who had asked her to take a photo of her. "I remember you," Tracy smiled. "How are you today?"

"I'm here with my daddy," the girl grinned as she bent down to help Tracy. "He's looking for snacks to take home with us."

Tracy scooped the gooseberries into her hand. "These are no good," she murmured as she sadly held the round yellow berries.

"What are those?" the little girl asked as she peered at a gooseberry she had picked up from the floor. "They look like tomatoes."

"They do," Tracy agreed as she threw the berries and empty container into the trash. "They're gooseberries. Want to try?"

The little girl nodded, and Tracy reached into the bag and revealed the carton that was still intact. "Ta da!"

She opened the container and pulled out the fattest gooseberry. "Try it."

The little girl took it from Tracy and popped it into her mouth. Her eyes lit up as she chewed. "It's so yummy," she moaned as she held out her hand to Tracy. "Can I have another?"

"Mille? What are you doing?"

A young man who looked to be around thirty ran over, a look of panic on his face. "You know you shouldn't take food from strangers. Mommy and I have taught you better than that."

He took the little girl's hand and pulled her close to him.

"I am so sorry," Tracy apologized. "I didn't mean to break your rules. I'm Tracy. Your daughter is adorable. I accidentally ran into her, and she was helping me pick up the berries I spilled. I just purchased them from that vendor over there."

His expression brightened. "Sorry to come off so strong," he said as Tracy smiled at him. "She wandered off, and the next thing I knew, I saw her hanging out with a stranger. It's a scary world, you know? You just never know what kind of crazies will be out there trying to hurt your kid."

Tracy nodded. "No worries, I get it," she assured him. "My boyfriend, Warren, is a detective in town. I hear stories from him all the time..."

The little girl's father grinned. "You're Warren's lady? I know him; I'm a few years younger, but we were in the same fraternity at Oregon State a million years ago."

"Small world!"

He nodded. "I had best get this one home," he nodded at his daughter. "Take care! Happy holidays."

Tracy watched as the man scooped his daughter up, placing her on his shoulders and bouncing her as they walked out of the farmer's market. She was struck with deja vu, thinking of a similar visit to the mall she had had with her father when she was a little girl. She had wandered off, getting lost in the food court, and her father had been so relieved to find her safe an hour later. Now, as a grown woman, she missed her dad and felt nostalgic as she remembered the magic of the holidays spent with her parents during childhood. Her parents had always made Christmas the most special time of the year, and she would be forever grateful for her idyllic childhood.

Her heart sank as she thought of Linda, the young lady who had just lost her dad. "She's gotta be hurting," Tracy thought to herself as she took a deep breath. "I think she needs a friend."

Disregarding her aunt's warning, she left the farmer's market and started walking toward the circus.

10

As Tracy walked through town, the sun was beginning to set, and the air was getting chillier. She hoped she would not run into Tyler; she was going to drop off the tamales to Linda and her mother, and that was all she wanted to do.

Tracy walked toward the edge of town. The circus had set up its tents and trailers at the fairgrounds, ten minutes walking outside of Fern Grove, and Tracy could hear noises and music before she could even see the circus itself.

As she approached, she saw a lot of activity; people were dashing in and out of mobile homes, tents were being raised, and workers were hastily picking up trash and debris from the grounds. "What's going on?" she asked a woman sitting in the ticket booth reading a magazine. "Is it always this crazy?"

The woman eyed her suspiciously. "Are you with the cops?"

"No," Tracy promised. "I'm just dropping off dinner for Linda and her mother."

The woman's face fell. "Poor Amy and Linda," she lamented. "Amy is now a widow and Linda is half of an orphan. What a tragedy."

Tracy raised an eyebrow. "Are there any updates about the case?"

The woman placed her magazine down. "Not about the murder," she said, snapping her gum loudly. "But the police let us know that we can resume the circus in a few days. They're supposed to give us the all-clear on Sunday."

"Wow," Tracy commented. "That's so soon."

The woman narrowed her eyes at her. "Who did you say you were, again? A friend of Amy's?"

"A friend of Linda's," she corrected. "Can you tell me where to find her?"

"They live in the big RV next to the pretzel stand," the woman told her. "The red one with the sides pulled out. You can't miss it."

"Thank you so much," Tracy called out as she walked away, determined to find Linda.

She arrived at the RV and knocked on the door. "Linda?" she called out. "Are you in there?"

She could hear voices coming from inside, but no one came to the door. "I wonder if it's unlocked," she thought as she reached out to touch the front door. She gave it a gentle shake, placing her hands on the doorknob and applying pressure. The door popped open. Tracy bit her lip. Should she go inside? She didn't want to startle them, but Linda *had* invited her to visit her at the circus. She took a deep breath and pushed the door open, quietly stepping inside.

The RV was dark. Tracy glanced around and her jaw dropped; there were clothes and shoes everywhere, and not a single surface of the RV was cleared. It smelled of thick, floral perfume, and she nearly gagged as the smell invaded her nostrils.

"How can anyone live like this?" she wondered as she looked up and saw a small loft built into the ceiling. "That must be where Linda sleeps…"

The RV was not dirty, but it was the messiest place Tracy had ever been. She could barely walk across the floor; it was covered in costumes and circus props, and she could hardly believe Linda could live in such a stressful environment.

Just then, she heard shouting from the back room. A sliver of light was visible from the crack under the door, and she slowly walked in that direction, hoping to hear what was going on.

"I don't want to do it," a woman's voice declared. "The deal feels shady, and I can't do shady anymore."

"Amy, come on," a man pleaded. "You know it's the right thing to do. Brett is out of the way, and you can do what you want at last. Take a leap with me, Amy. You know you want to."

"What were they talking about?" Tracy wondered. She felt her heart pound in her chest, and she knew it was time to leave. She didn't know what she was overhearing, but it did not sound good.

"I don't know," she heard Amy tell the man as she turned to leave.

"Maybe this will change your mind," he said matter-of-factly. "It's time you knew the truth."

Just then, Tracy heard the door open.

"Hey!" Linda greeted her as she walked inside and flipped on the light. "Tracy? What are you doing here?"

Tracy felt the color drain from her face. "Umm... I brought dinner for you and your mom," she told Linda as she held up the bag of tamales. "I thought you could use a pick-me-up, especially with all you two have gone through lately."

Linda grinned. "That's so nice of you! Can you hold up the bag? Just like that?"

She whipped a cell phone out of her pocket and aimed it at Tracy. "Are you taking a photo?" Tracy asked in amusement.

"I'm making a movie," Linda replied. "My dad got this phone for me before he died. I'm going to use the film feature to make a movie about his life and everything that happened when he died."

Tracy shook her head and held her hand in front of her face. "Wait. I don't want to be in it. I didn't even know your dad."

Linda lowered the phone. "But you brought me dinner when he died," she protested. "Please? Can I just put a little clip of you holding the bag in the film? It will be so cool."

The door opened and Amy came out of the bedroom. "What are you doing?" she hissed at Linda. "I told you to stay out of here tonight; I have a business meeting. And what are *you* doing here?"

Tracy waved, trying to seem relaxed and casual. "Hey! How are you? I met your daughter in town and wanted to drop off dinner for the pair of you. I'm so sorry for your loss, Amy."

"Thanks," Amy eyed her suspiciously. "Look, that's real nice of you, but I'm in a meeting. Can you two keep it down?"

"Sorry," Linda apologized. "Sorry, Mom."

"I was just leaving," Tracy assured her. "Nice to see you again."

Amy cocked her head to the side as though she were about to say something. "AMY!" the man's voice called out, and she hurried back to the bedroom, slamming the door behind her.

"Who's that?" Tracy whispered to Linda. "That guy?"

"No idea," Linda told her. "Sorry my mom was in such a mood. She is... was... usually the nicer of my parents."

Tracy bit her lip. "What do you mean?"

"My dad was a bit of a bully," Linda revealed. "He would get angry and scream at my mom and me. She would wind him up—she knew just how to make him mad. But he couldn't control his temper, and sometimes, he would break things."

Linda gestured at the mess on the floor. "They had a fight right before he died. I don't know what it was about, but he was so angry that he tore this place apart. That's why it's such a wreck in here."

Tracy's eyes widened. "Are you serious? Oh, Linda..."

"I'm used to it," Linda smiled. "Not a big deal. Sometimes, I would take advantage of it, to be honest... I wanted this phone so badly, and I got my dad really mad at me last week. He screamed and yelled and even pushed me, but he felt guilty after, and he bought this for me."

Tracy's stomach dropped. "What did your mom do about it?"

"She hated him," Linda told her as she opened the bag of tamales and took one out, smelling it and grinning. "This smells amazing."

"Go ahead and eat," Tracy told her. "Please."

The teenager tore into the tamale. "Do you really think your mom hated your dad?"

"Everyone did," Linda told her. "But my mom hated him the most. They only got married because she got pregnant with me. She never wanted to do the circus thing. She was raised with money on the East Coast."

Tracy's jaw dropped. "How do you know all of this?"

Linda shrugged. "It's a small trailer," she stated. "There are no secrets in a space this small... or in a family as messed up as mine."

11

That night, as Tracy walked home from the circus, she could not get Amy Goff out of her mind. What was Amy talking about with the mysterious man back in the RV?

Linda's words haunted her. "...my mom hated him the most." Did Amy Goff have something to do with her husband's murder?

She was lost in thought as she made her way through the fairgrounds, and she was shocked when she bumped straight into a man holding a pizza box.

"Hey!"

Her heart sank. The man holding the pizza box was Tyler, and she had walked right into him. "Hey," she replied weakly. "What's up?"

He stared at her. "I could ask you the same thing," he said, his eyes large with curiosity. "What are you doing over here, Tracy?"

She sniffed, the cold air biting her cheeks. "I was dropping off some food for the family of the deceased," she explained. "I met Linda at the flower shop, and she seemed like she needed a friend..."

His face lit up. "She is such a sweetheart," he praised. "But I worry she'll get into trouble, especially now that her Daddy is gone. Linda has a big heart *and* a huge brain; she received a perfect score on the ACT."

"Wow!" Tracy exclaimed. "That's a huge deal. Is she heading to college soon?"

Tyler frowned. "I don't know," he admitted. "For circus kids, college isn't really an option. I heard Brett was *livid* when he found out she took the ACT, let alone aced it. Everyone said he went ballistic."

"Because she took a test?" Tracy wondered. "I don't get it."

He shrugged. "Linda was being groomed to run the family business," he explained. "And she would have been great at it. She is so smart, and she has a great sense of humor. You never would have known she was Brett's girl."

Tracy wrinkled her nose. "Why can't she go off and do what she wants? Isn't she free to do that now that Brett's dead?"

"I don't know what they're going to do with the circus," Tyler sighed. "Who knows, they might shut this whole thing down. Maybe I'll be out of a job sooner than later. Do you think your Aunt would let me come work at the shop?"

Tracy felt the heat rise to her face. "I'm just joking," he assured her, laughing as she let out a sigh of relief. "I can see you wouldn't be a fan of that..."

She nodded. "I think it's best to leave the past in the past," she said firmly. "Hey, how is the investigation going?" she asked. "Any news?"

Tyler furrowed his brow. "The police have been all over this place. They've interviewed everyone. People are even joking that they're going to interview the animals next. It's nuts."

She put her hands on her hips. "That's good though, isn't it? The sooner they speak with everyone, the sooner they'll solve this thing."

"I don't know," Tyler said curtly. "It seems like they're unnecessarily picking around in our business for nothing..."

She stuck her nose in the air. "I think you all just need to comply with the police," she countered. "Figure out what happened, get back to normal."

He grinned. "The show will be getting back to normal soon," he promised her with excitement in his voice. "The police are going to let us resume the circus on Sunday."

"I heard."

"How would you like to have a front row seat to the dress rehearsal we're doing Saturday night?" he asked. "I know a guy who can get you in."

He winked at her, and she pursed her lips. "I don't know, Tyler," she told him. "It seems like a bad idea."

"What? You don't like the circus? Or the *guy*?" he teased, and she couldn't help but to blush.

"It's complicated," she declared. "You wouldn't understand."

"Maybe you could *help* me understand?" he suggested with a twinkle in his eye. "At the circus. Saturday night. Come on, Tracy. Live a little! And besides, I always see you out and about all by yourself. Word around town is that you and that detective boyfriend of yours —yes, I know about him—are in a little fight. Wouldn't you like to make him jealous? Come sit at the rehearsal with me! It'll get him all riled up, and he'll come running to you like a child runs to the Christmas tree on Christmas morning."

She stared at him. Tyler was always scheming, and she didn't want to get caught up in one of his plans. Then again, she *wouldn't* mind making Warren jealous; they were still barely communicating after their fight. He kept claiming he was ridiculously busy at work, and while she knew he was assigned to the murder case, he could at least spare five minutes and give her a phone call on his lunch break.

"Think about it, Tracy," Tyler smiled. "You come spend time with me at the circus, you get a free show, your boyfriend comes to his senses, and we all go home happy…."

It *did* sound easy enough. "Okay," she agreed. "Okay. What time does the rehearsal start?"

"I'll pick you up at seven," he told her, giving her a dramatic bow before walking away. "Get excited!"

Tracy watched him walk away, feeling her chest tighten. Was she making the right choice? Would she regret attending the dress rehearsal with Tyler, her former boyfriend? Would Warren even care about her seeing the show with someone else? She pondered these questions as she resumed her walk back to town, weighing her options and finally deciding that she had made the best choice.

Having given the tamales away to Amy and Linda, Tracy stopped by the grocery store to pick up a few things to make dinner. She thought about preparing an elaborate meal, but eventually settled on making cauliflower crust pizza with vegan cheese and organic tomato sauce. "Yummy *and* healthy," she thought cheerfully to herself as she perused the display of fresh cauliflower.

As she examined the bulky heads of cauliflower, she spotted Kim, the owner of the grocery store, who knew almost everyone in town, stocking tomatoes in the section next to her. "Hey, Kim," she called out, happy to see a familiar face after what had turned into a strange evening. "How are you doing?"

Kim smiled. Her blonde hair was twisted into a bun atop her head, and she rose from the display of tomatoes and made her way to Tracy. "I'm well," she greeted her. "Happy that stay-at-home order is through and things are getting back to normal."

Tracy nodded. "The flower shop was closed down for the order," she told her. "Though I'm sure Aunt Rose mentioned it."

"She did," Kim agreed. "Say, your fella works at the police department. Any leads on the murderer? I'm just dying to know who did it."

Tracy shook her head. "No idea," she apologized. "Warren keeps his work to himself, mostly. Just between the two of us, I'm wondering if his wife did it," she whispered to Kim. "She seems like no stranger to trouble, that's for sure."

"I've heard that!" Kim told Tracy. "I've heard Mrs. Goff was an odd duck. But it sounds like they all were, really. That Brett Goff really did some damage to Bruce's bar, you know."

"I was there!" Tracy told her. "I saw them fighting. Bruce was so angry."

Kim narrowed her eyes. "Brett Goff came in here the day he died," she murmured as Tracy's eyes widened. "He told me Bruce had threatened him with a lawsuit, and that he had done so much damage to the bar that Bruce was going to have to close down for a week. Can you imagine? He was boasting about it, too! Who brags about that kind of behavior?"

"I don't know," Tracy sighed. "It sounds like he certainly didn't make a lot of friends during his short time in Fern Grove."

"No, he didn't," Kim agreed. "Well, it was good to see you, honey. Take good care of yourself. And stay away from that circus. Those people are *bad* news, Tracy."

12

The next morning, Tracy was still thinking about Brett Goff as she walked to work. The weather was terrible; it had snowed the night before, and the sidewalks were perilously icy. She shivered as a gust of cold wind nipped at her face, and she treaded carefully through the thick, wet snow as fast as she could.

Tracy could not get Amy Goff out of her mind. After tossing and turning all night thinking about the murder, she had finally gotten up and started writing in her journal about the events of her second trip to the circus. She was careful to add as much detail as possible, and as she recounted the tense exchange with Amy, she could not shake the deep gut feeling that Amy knew more than she was letting on.

She was shocked to open the door to *In Season* and see Amy Goff herself standing in front of the counter with Linda at her side. "Good morning," she greeted them, forcing herself to smile. "What brings you ladies in today? Are you shopping for arrangements for the funeral?"

Linda's face fell. "I'm so sorry," Tracy quickly added. "That was insensitive. I should have let you tell me why you two came in."

Amy shoved Linda toward Tracy. "Can you watch her for a bit?" she asked tersely.

"Watch her? What do you mean?"

Amy tapped her foot on the tiled floor. "I mean what I said. Can you keep an eye on her? I don't think she needs to be sitting alone in an RV all day."

Tracy looked at Tiffany, who was manning the front counter. "Um…."

"I have to go to the bank, and she can't come with me," Amy added. "Please? As a favor?"

Tiffany glanced down at her watch. "Aunt Rose isn't coming in today," she muttered. "What would she think?"

Before Tracy could respond to Amy, the widow took off, leaving Linda behind her. "I'll be back at five," she called out as she left the shop, hurrying onto the street.

"Well," Tracy began. "It's nice to see you, Linda. What was all of that about, if you don't mind me asking?"

Linda shrugged. "No idea, but I would rather be here than at the fairgrounds. Some guys are creepy over there."

Tracy's face softened. "You can hang out here as long as you'd like," she assured the teenager. "With Aunt Rose out today, we would really benefit from your help. Do you mind if we put you to work?"

Linda's eyes shined. "I can help with the flowers?"

Tiffany laughed. "If I can do it, anyone can! Come on, I'll take you to the back and help you get ready."

Tiffany led Linda to the back, and when they reappeared ten minutes later, Linda was dressed in a red smock, her dark curls pulled back into a braid. "You look great," Tracy complimented. "Let's get to work. Tiffany, can you show her how to remove dead winter berries from a bunch? I think that would be a good place for her to start."

"Aye, aye, Captain!" Tiffany mock saluted, and the two teenagers turned to a bucket brimming with bright red winterberries.

The three ladies had the best day together; Linda proved to be great company, and she was a natural at working with the flowers. By lunch, she had moved on to trimming the stems of camellias, a difficult winter flower to work with, and by early evening, she was creating original flower arrangements.

"You have a knack for florals," Tracy complimented as Tiffany nodded. "A gift, really! Is this your first time working in a flower shop, Linda?"

"It is," she smiled as she fluffed the petals of a primrose. "I love fashion and design; I always thought I wanted to be a fashion designer, or an interior decorator."

"I think you'd be better off as a florist," Tiffany chimed in.

"I think you would do well," Tracy agreed.

At five sharp, Amy Goff strode back into the shop. She was empty-handed, and her face was flushed. "Did you have a nice time?" she asked Linda as she glanced at the flower arrangement she was working on.

"It was a blast," Linda told her mother. "Look at what I made."

Tracy smiled at Amy. "She has a real gift," she told the teenager's mother. "Please don't ever let her hesitate to come back here. She was a pleasure to have around."

Amy nodded. "So are you going to pay her for her work?"

Tracy raised an eyebrow. "What?"

"Are you going to pay her," Amy asked. "From what I see, Linda worked for you all day. The least you can do is pay her."

"This woman has some nerve," Tracy thought to herself as she stared at Amy. "She drops her daughter off here without warning, abandons her for the day, doesn't check in, and now, she expects me to pay her?"

"Linda isn't on the books here," Tracy said, forcing an apologetic tone. "And she was not hired by our owner, Rose Bishop. Linda's help was appreciated, but as I see it, she volunteered here today. She didn't work. At least, not officially."

Amy's face was drawn. "Fine," she replied curtly. "Well, while we're here, we need to discuss arrangements for the funeral. We might as well get that out of the way."

"What will you be needing?" Tracy asked kindly. "Roses? Calla lilies? Carnations and daffodils are pretty standard for funeral arrangements."

"Whatever is cheapest," Amy laughed.

"Mom!" Linda cried. "That isn't nice. Daddy left us all of that money. I want to get him nice flowers."

Amy hushed her daughter. "We'll take a wreath for the casket and two decent arrangements for the aisle. Is that better?"

Linda nodded. "I guess…."

"How much do I owe you?" she asked Tracy.

"With the wreath, that will be four hundred even."

Amy gave her a dark look and then pulled out her checkbook. "That scoundrel didn't do anything for us while he was alive," she muttered as she wrote the check. "But at least he took out a nice little life insurance policy. Linda and I won't be lacking for *anything* anymore."

She ripped the check from its book and handed it to Tracy. "There. That settles it. Please have it sent to the fairgrounds on Friday evening. The service is scheduled for Saturday morning."

She looked down at Linda. "Say goodbye."

"Thank you so much for having me," Linda gushed, pulling out her phone and waving it at Tracy. "I got some awesome footage of us working in here today. I'll have to show you sometime."

Amy led her daughter away, and Tiffany let out a nervous laugh. "That woman was a piece of work," she commented as Tracy shook her head. "She was so nasty!"

"Yes, she was," Tracy agreed, thinking about Amy's comment regarding the life insurance policy. How much had the policy been for? Were they swimming in money now? She was even more suspicious of Amy now; the cushy life insurance policy seemed like a great reason to get rid of a husband she hated.

The front door opened and she gasped.

"Hey, stranger."

It was Warren. Dressed in his uniform, he walked hesitantly up to the counter and offered her a weak smile. "Nice to see you."

She nodded. "You too." It was the first time seeing him since their argument, and she felt nervous.

"I'll leave you two alone," Tiffany told them as she scurried off to the back.

Tracy looked into his eyes. "What's up?"

He shifted awkwardly. "Can we talk today?" he asked, his face pale.

She raised an eyebrow. “Aren’t we talking right now?”

He shook his head. “I think we should get together in person,” he told her. “Tracy, we *really* need to talk.”

13

"Can I get you something to drink?"

Tracy nodded as Bruce approached her at the bar. "Gin mule, please, Bruce."

He smiled at her. "Are you waiting on someone?"

She looked down at the counter and nodded. "My boyfriend, Warren."

Bruce smiled. He was a stocky man with a lined face, but his smile was dazzling; he had perfect white teeth that gleamed in the darkness of the bar. "I know Warren. Good guy. You're a lucky girl."

She sighed as he walked away. She did not feel so lucky; she and Warren had decided to meet at seven at the bar, but it was nearly eight, and he still had not shown up. She didn't know what he needed to talk with her about; they needed to clear the air after their fight, but she was worried there was something more serious going on.

Bruce returned with her drink, laying the copper mule cup in front of her with a grin. "A gin mule for the pretty lady."

She smiled weakly. "Thank you," she told him as she pulled the cup toward her, admiring the mint leaves sprinkled on top. "This mint looks fresh; where did you get it? We haven't been able to find fresh mint since the early frost back in October."

He peered at her curiously. "The early frost? You must know a thing or two about plants, huh?"

She nodded. "I work at *In Season*," she explained, and then took a long sip of her drink. "My aunt, Rose, owns and operates the store."

Bruce did a double take. "You're Rose's niece?" he asked in surprise. "Of course, you are! You look just like her; I went to high school with her. Rose is a sweet lady. How is she doing, anyway? I'm so sorry about your uncle Frank. I heard she took it pretty hard."

"She did," Tracy agreed. "She's doing well, thank you for asking. I think every year helps a bit."

"It always does," Bruce agreed. "My wife divorced me a decade ago. It's a little different from having a spouse die, of course, but it hurts nonetheless. But like you said, every year, it gets a little better."

Tracy smiled. Bruce was calm and cordial, so much different from the angry version of him she had seen the other night when Brett Goff was tormenting him. She even thought he was handsome, in a rugged way. She wondered if he was seeing anyone; he looked to be about Aunt Rose's age, and she knew her aunt would like his bright smile.

"So, what's the hardest part of owning a bar?" she asked curiously. "Aunt Rose tells me the hardest part of owning a flower shop, or any business, is dealing with people. Do you feel the same way?"

He nodded emphatically. "Absolutely," he told her. "People can be the hardest part of this gig. Rude customers, lazy staff members, drunkards who don't know their limits... it can be a lot."

She looked into his eyes. "I was here the night that circus guy went off," she chimed in. "That guy who was murdered. What was his deal?"

His face darkened. "Brett Goff," he hissed as she recoiled.

"Did you know him well?" she asked quietly.

She could see the color rising in his cheeks. "Did I know him well," he muttered as he folded his arms over his chest. "I'll tell you what. Take my advice: don't *ever* trust a person who runs around with the circus. They'll do you dirty, and they won't think twice about it."

She raised an eyebrow. "What do you mean?"

Bruce's eyes narrowed. "Don't worry about it," he muttered. "I just can't stand circus people, that's all."

A female customer waved him over, and he turned to Tracy, his face dark. "Gotta help her. Sorry. Enjoy the drink."

She watched him as he walked away, puzzled by the fact that he still harbored a grudge against the circus community. She understood Brett had been a nuisance when he was last at the bar, but she assumed Bruce dealt with such incidents regularly.

"Hi, stranger."

She swiveled around on her barstool to find Tyler standing behind her, a beer in his hand. "Tyler, I'm meeting someone," she told him as she glanced around the bar. "I can't talk right now."

He disregarded her statement and sat down on the empty barstool beside her. "You can't spare five minutes for an old friend, Tracy? That isn't like you."

She groaned as he sat down. "What? Waiting on that boyfriend of yours?"

She said nothing, and he laughed. "I guess that's it, isn't it? Where is the good detective tonight? Did he stand you up?"

Tracy felt her stomach sink. "I guess he did," she admitted. "He's over an hour late…"

Tyler frowned, the line between his eyebrows deepening as he stared into her eyes. "I'm sorry," he said softly, putting a hand on her shoulder. "That's really rude of him."

"It's fine," she insisted, brushing his hand away. "I got to enjoy my drink and chat with Bruce. It's nice to have time to yourself."

Tyler raised an eyebrow. "Oh, don't be like that, Tracy," he sighed. "I can still read you like a book, you know. I can tell you're upset. What's the deal with him, anyway? Why did he stand you up?"

She straightened her posture, sitting primly at the bar. "That is none of your business," she declared. "I don't run around town sharing my relationship troubles with everyone."

"So, you're having relationship troubles?"

She could have kicked herself. Tracy knew she needed to keep her mouth shut; Tyler had a way of getting information out of people, and she did not want him to have any details about her problems with Warren. "Tyler, enough," she said firmly. "Enough about me. What are you doing here?"

He rested his elbows on the bar. "I just needed a pick me up," he told her. "Well, maybe seven or eight pick me ups, if I'm honest."

He chugged the last of his beer and slammed it on the counter. "Time for another! Bartender?"

A female bartender arrived with another cold beer. "Thanks," he winked as she slid it toward him and passed her a five-dollar bill. "Keep the change."

Tracy eyed the empty bottle and shifted her gaze back at Tyler. "You've had eight beers already?" she asked incredulously. "That's a lot, Ty…"

Tyler winked. "You know I can handle it. Remember that night at Calder's farm the summer before junior year? I shot-gunned twelve beers in an hour."

"...And then threw up for the next two days," Tracy finished. "I don't think it's something to brag about, Tyler. We're adults now."

He sat up straight, mocking her prim posture. "Forgive me," he apologized facetiously in a fake British accent. "I forgot. Tracy left town, worked at a bank, and is now Queen of all things adult."

She gave him a playful shove, a smile creeping onto her face. Tyler was funny; she remembered how he had kept her in stitches when they were teenagers, and after the last few days, it felt good to laugh. "Stop it."

He smiled. "See? You always liked my jokes."

"Hey," Bruce called out from across the bar. "You need another mule?"

She held up her hand and shook her head. "I'm good, thanks."

Tyler peered at Bruce. "I heard he got into it with Brett right before he died," he said, his eyes narrowing.

Tracy nodded. "He's the owner of the bar, and it sounds like Brett was being out of hand."

Tyler's eyes widened. "Are you serious? Brett did not get out of hand often. He was the most even-tempered guy at the circus."

She shrugged. "I didn't know him," she told Tyler. "So, I don't know what to say..."

Just then, Bruce reappeared before them, his eyes flashing with anger. "You need to get out of my bar before I force you out," he growled, baring his teeth. "You've messed with the wrong guy."

Tracy blinked. "What?" she asked Bruce. "Messed with you? I'm just sipping my drink."

He glared at her. "Not you. HIM."

He pointed at Tyler. "Circus trash needs to go back to where he came from," he demanded, stomping his foot on the hardwood floor. "I won't have someone like him in my bar."

Tyler rose to his feet. "Excuse me?"

"Bruce," Tracy interrupted.

Bruce pointed to Tyler. "He's one of those circus fools, isn't he? I can tell by the look of 'em; he is one of those circus fools, no doubt."

Tyler rose from the barstool. "And what if I am? What if I am one of those circus fools? What are you gonna do about it?"

Bruce scowled. "I'm going to kick your butt out of here, or worse."

Tyler laughed. "Worse, huh? Are you going to do to me what you did to your own *brother*, buddy?"

Tracy stared up at Bruce, her eyes wide with shock. "What?" she cried. "What are you talking about, Tyler?"

"His brother," Tyler said matter-of-factly. "Brett Goff was this guy's brother. He kicked his own brother out of his bar, and he couldn't care less about the fact that his flesh and blood is *dead*."

14

Tracy saw Bruce's hands ball into fists, his jaw clenched and his face red. "Get out of here," he repeated as Tyler's jaw dropped. "Now."

Tyler crossed his arms over his chest. "And who do you think you are?" Tyler asked. "You can't order me out of here just because I work at the circus, like your brother. You're just a bartender. You can't do anything to me!"

Bruce took a step toward them. "It's a good thing this bar is in the way," he muttered, jerking his head to gesture at the bar. "Or I would pick you up right now and toss you out."

Tracy moved to stand in front of Tyler. "Bruce, he wasn't causing trouble. In fact, he was just leaving."

Tyler shook his head. "I'm not going anywhere," he announced loudly as patrons of the bar turned to stare at them. "You can't discriminate against me because of where I work. It just isn't right."

Bruce laughed. "I don't care what you think," he declared. "You are circus trash, and I don't want circus trash in my bar. Get out of my bar, or you'll be sorry."

"How sorry?" Tyler mocked.

"Sorry."

"I doubt it," Tyler added, lunging across the bar and wrapping his hands around Bruce's neck.

"TYLER!" Tracy screamed, moving out of the way so she would not be in the way of their fight.

Bruce and Tyler rolled on the floor behind the bar. People were screaming, and glass was breaking as glasses rattled on the countertop and fell, breaking into jagged shards.

"Get off of me!" Bruce demanded as Tyler climbed on top of him and began swatting at his face. "Get off now."

Tyler laughed in his face. "I won't have you treat me like trash," he yelled, leaning in close to Bruce. "When you're the one on the floor like a piece of trash at the bar. Look at you now, buddy. Helpless!"

Tracy ran around to the side of the bar and stomped her feet. "Stop!" she cried. "Stop it. Tyler, get off of him."

"Stay out of this," he replied, and she pulled out her phone.

"I'm going to call the police if you don't get off," she told Tyler. "I'm calling the police, and they will arrest you, Tyler."

"It's too late," a woman across the bar called out. "I already called. They're on their way."

Tracy felt an ache in her gut. She didn't want Tyler to get into trouble, but he had undeniably crossed a line.

"Please," Bruce begged as Tyler straddled him. "Please let me go. I can't get enough air."

Tracy ran toward Tyler and gave him a big push, removing him from Bruce's body. He was shocked as he went flying through the air, and while Tracy was surprised she had tackled him with such force, she was proud of herself for stepping in and saving Bruce.

"TYLER!" she screamed as he lay on the ground, slowly sitting up to rub his head. "Enough. You have crossed a line."

"Tracy," he said, slurring the last syllable of her name.

"You're drunk and you're out of control," she told him, rising to her feet and dusting herself off.

"Tracy!"

Warren rushed in, a worried look on his face. "I'm so sorry I'm late. Are you okay? What's going on here? I got a call on the radio that there was an emergency, and I came right over."

She glared at him. "It's been handled," she declared, pointing at Tyler. "I got him to back off."

Warren eyed Tyler as Bruce sat up and called for him. "Warren, that man attacked me," he told the detective as Warren surveyed the scene. "These folks are all witnesses."

Tyler stood up and walked right up to Warren. "So, you're Tracy's hotshot detective boyfriend, huh?"

Warren puffed up his chest. "And you are?"

"He's the drunk idiot who started the fight," Bruce told Warren. "He attacked me and should be charged with assault."

Tyler laughed. "He asked for it, Detective."

Warren glanced over at Tracy. "Did you see what happened?"

"Every part of it," she sighed. "And you would have too if you hadn't been an hour late."

Tyler grinned. "So, you're the fool who stood up my girl."

"Your girl?" Warren scowled. "Excuse me?"

Tyler reached over and gave Warren a push. "Step aside, detective. I think it's time I got myself home."

Warren shook his head. "You just put your hands on an officer," he warned Tyler. "You need to stand here and tell me what happened, or I'll have to take you in."

Tyler's eyes danced. "I'll show you what it means to put hands on an officer," he chuckled, and he reared back and punched Warren in the nose.

"Tyler!" Tracy screamed. "What are you doing? Stop it!"

Bruce ran over and grabbed Tyler's arms; he was flailing about so much that it was easy to subdue him. Warren quickly sprang into action; he retrieved a pair of shiny silver handcuffs from his belt and fastened them on Tyler's wrists.

"What?" Tyler choked as the handcuffs clicked into place. "What is this for?"

"For assaulting an officer and a citizen," Warren informed him before reading him his Miranda Rights. "Now, let's go to the car. Try not to make a scene."

Tracy's eyes widened. Warren's nose was gushing blood, but his eyes were steely and cold as he steered Tyler outside and placed him in the back of his patrol car. Her heart pounded as he got into the driver's seat, turned the sirens on, and sped off into the night.

15

"...And there was blood *everywhere.*"

It was bright and early the next morning, and Tracy, Aunt Rose, and Tiffany were standing at the counter of *In Season,* sipping coffee and catching up before they opened the doors for the day.

"What did Warren say?" Aunt Rose asked, her face filled with worry. "Is Tyler alright?"

Tracy shook her head. "Warren took him to jail," she informed them.

"Not poor Tyler," Aunt Rose hung her head. "That boy never stood a chance."

"Poor Tyler?" Tiffany cried. "He socked Tracy's boyfriend in the face. What do you mean, poor Tyler?"

Aunt Rose bit her lip. "Everyone around town loves dear Tyler," she began. "Because sometimes, when parents can't be there for their children, it takes a village..."

Tracy cocked her head to the side. "What are you talking about? Tyler grew up with both of his parents; I remember his mom worked a lot, but his dad was always home when we would hang out at his house…"

Aunt Rose shook her head. "Mr. Foxely had his demons," she continued, shrugging her shoulders. "Think about the story you just told us, Tracy. You mentioned Tyler was guzzling beers left and right…"

Suddenly, Tracy knew what her aunt meant. Her face paled. "Mr. Foxely was an alcoholic?" she slowly pieced together as her aunt nodded.

"It was a well-known secret," Aunt Rose sighed. "And with Mrs. Foxely out of town for work so frequently, it meant everyone around took Tyler under their wing. He was raised by this town, which is why we all adore him. It's just such a pity that he's succumbed to the same darkness as his father. What a shame."

Tracy stared at her aunt. "I didn't know that about his family," she revealed, her face drawn. "Why didn't you tell me?"

Her aunt raised an eyebrow. "What was I supposed to do? You two were teenage sweethearts, but everyone knows young love rarely makes it. I'm sure if you two had kept dating seriously, it would have come up, but you had a good head on your shoulders, and I always knew I could trust you. Tyler was always such a gentleman, too; I trusted him completely when he was a boy, and I didn't have any concerns."

Tiffany frowned. "It's super sad Tyler fell into the same path as his dad. Does that happen to everyone?"

Aunt Rose shook her head. "That's the beauty of life and human nature," she told them. "We all have our choices, and we are all free to make those choices. It can be hard though, when the role models you have don't show you the best paths. While we are all free to make our own choices, if all we've ever seen is chaos and dysfunction, sometimes, it's all we know how to choose..."

Tracy hung her head. "I feel so bad for Tyler," she breathed. "He just seems so... lost."

"I know," Aunt Tracy said, putting a hand on Tracy's back. "It's hard to see people we've cared about in a downward spiral. All we can do is pray and hope he finds his way...."

There was a loud knock at the front door, and Tiffany scowled. "Can't they read the sign out front?" she complained as the knocking grew louder. "We don't open for ten more minutes."

"HEY!" a voice called from outside. "Hello? I see the lights on in there; let me in."

Tracy shook her head. "Let's just leave it," she told her aunt. "We have ten more minutes to drink coffee and talk. I'm not ready to start the day yet."

Her aunt smiled. "Let's bank on some good karma," she countered. "We'll open ten minutes early, and maybe that will cause something miraculous to happen today."

Tracy's hopes for the spectacular were dashed when Tiffany went to unlock the door and Amy Goff strutted in, a sour look on her face.

"Good morning," she greeted her half-heartedly. "What can we help you with today, Amy?"

"I need a bouquet to take to the hospital." Amy crossed her arms over her voluminous bosom and glowered at her. "He's in the hospital, you know? That fight really messed him up."

"What? It was just a bloody nose!" Tracy cried.

Amy narrowed her eyes. "Not your detective boyfriend. *Tyler*. Tyler is in the hospital."

Tracy's eyes grew large. "What are you talking about?"

Amy put her hands on her hips. "He got a concussion when that bartender attacked him," she explained, her lips drawn in a thin line. "Now he's in the hospital."

Tiffany tilted her head to the side. "You said Tyler attacked the bartender," she called over to Tracy.

"He did," she murmured as Amy glared at her.

"Sounds like you need something cheerful to take to him," Aunt Rose interjected, selecting a premade bouquet of bright yellow daisies from a bucket below the counter. "What do you think of these?"

"How much?"

"They are fifty-dollars, but since I know Tyler, they're on the house," Aunt Rose smiled kindly. "Please give him our best."

Amy flashed a bright smile. "Free? Great. Thanks, ladies."

She snatched the flowers from Aunt Rose and sashayed out of the flower shop, swaying her hips as she walked outside.

"That woman has more attitude than anyone I've ever met," Tracy complained, but Aunt Rose shushed her.

"She's been through a lot," her Aunt protested. "Give her a break. We all need a break sometime."

Just then, Tracy's phone vibrated in her pocket. She pulled it out to find a text from Warren.

Don't want to worry you, but I am in the hospital, Tracy. I woke up with a killer headache, and the doctor at the station advised I go in for a concussion test. I'll be here all day. Just wanted to let you know. XO

She gasped. "Warren's in the hospital," she told them, rereading the text.

"Don't you mean Tyler?" Tiffany asked.

"Tyler AND Warren; Warren just texted me that he might have a concussion."

Aunt Rose pursed her lips. "Concussions are serious," she said gently. "Why don't you get out of here and go to him at the hospital? Warren probably would like some company…"

She shook her head. "I don't want to get in the way…"

"You won't be," Aunt Rose assured her. "Go to him, dear. I think it would mean the world to him if you were to go be there to support him. Why don't you take some flowers to him? You can drop some off for Tyler and then give something nice to Warren."

"Can I pick out Tyler's flowers?" Tiffany asked.

"I thought you didn't like him?" Tracy replied, but Tiffany blushed.

"He was arrogant, but he was really cute," she giggled, and Tracy laughed.

"Fine. You pick out some flowers for Tyler, and I'll make up an arrangement for Warren."

Aunt Rose nodded. "The flowers for Tyler will be from me, of course, and you can take a nice arrangement to Warren, free of charge."

She went about creating a small, but elaborate arrangement for Warren. She filled a tall glass vase with bright purple Algerian Irises, adding some winter honeysuckle to balance out the color palette. She tied a yellow ribbon around the stems, pleased with her handiwork.

"Ta da!"

They turned to see Tiffany's bouquet; a bunch of dazzling violets mixed in with delicate winter aconite flowers. "Lovely," Aunt Rose complimented the teenager. "Well done!"

Flowers in hand, Tracy set off toward the hospital, eager to make things right with Warren and be there to offer support. As she crossed the street, she spotted a familiar face and waved. "Pastor Butler!"

He turned and smiled. Dressed in a long green winter coat with a matching feather in his fedora hat, he looked quite dapper as he peered at her from across the road. "Hi, Tracy!"

She darted over to him and gave him a quick side hug. "Nice to see you, Pastor," she greeted him. "How are you today?"

He shrugged. "Can I speak frankly?"

"Always!"

He cast his eyes downward and sighed. "Today is not an easy day for a man of the Lord," he told her as they walked down the street.

"What do you mean?" she asked.

"I just finished finalizing funeral arrangements with Mrs. Goff, that widow of the circus owner," he explained. "It is never fun to do funerals, Tracy."

Tracy nodded. "I can imagine it's so difficult," she agreed. "How are the Goffs today? Isn't Linda the sweetest?"

His face brightened, his mustache twisting up with the movement of his lips. "She is a doll," he agreed. "Her mother was... rough. But Linda was charming and had the nicest manners. She even took a photo of us on her cell phone. She added those silly filters, and it made me look like a deer. I had antlers on my head! Can you imagine? These kids and their technology... it's incredible!"

Tracy grinned, thinking of Tiffany posing and preening for filtered photos on her own cell phone. "It's amazing what technology can do," she agreed. "Linda loves taking videos and photos on her cell phone. She told me she was going to turn it all into a piece about losing her dad. Isn't that sweet?"

"It's very touching," he affirmed. "What a dear girl. It's just such a shame her mother is so cold and dare I say... calculated."

"Calculated?" Tracy asked. "What do you mean, Pastor?"

His face paled. "I shouldn't have said anything," he muttered, glancing at his watch and then back at Tracy. "I am late for my next appointment. You take care now, okay?"

She watched as he strode away and wondered what he had meant. Pastor Butler never spoke ill of anyone, and she was curious about his observations of Amy Goff. What had Pastor Butler noticed about her? Had Tracy's concerns been correct? Could Amy Goff have been cold and calculated enough to murder her own husband? Tracy did not know the answer, but she was determined to find out.

16

When Tracy arrived at the hospital, she walked up to the nurse's station and asked for Warren's information. "He has been admitted and placed in room K342," a bright-eyed male nurse informed her. "It's just down that hallway and to the left."

"Thanks," she waved as she turned on her heel and set off down the long corridor.

She hated being in hospitals; it reminded her of when her parents passed away, and she was filled with dread as she squinted beneath the excessively bright fluorescent lights. Hospitals brought back feelings of angst and melancholy, and she hoped Warren would not have to stay very long.

She arrived at his door and gave it a light knock. "Come in," she heard him call out, and she walked inside, pasting a smile on her face.

"How are you?" she asked, shocked to see him dressed in a gown and laying in a hospital bed.

He sat up and stretched his arms over his head. "I'm honestly fine," he laughed as he registered her concern. "My headache was bad, and the police chief doesn't mess around when it comes to concussions. They did some testing and determined I have a grade two concussion. The department requires anyone who gets a grade two concussion or above to stay overnight in a hospital, so here I am."

"Here you are," she repeated softly. She walked to his side and placed the two flower arrangements down on the bedside chair before giving him a kiss on the forehead. "Your nose is looking better; the last time I saw you, you were gushing blood."

He shrugged. "It wasn't broken, thank goodness. The concussion is the only real issue. I feel fine. I'm just trying to take it easy and relax; it's technically a paid day off work, so I've been relaxing, eating snacks, and taking naps all morning."

She grinned. "That sounds like your kind of Heaven."

"It is now that you're here," he told her, reaching over to take her hand. "I've missed you, Tracy."

"I've missed you too," she murmured. "I'm sorry we've been off lately; I want things to get back to normal."

"And I want to apologize for my nasty attitude about the circus folks," he told Tracy. "It was out of line. They aren't all bad, and I should have had more grace."

Tracy looked at him with awe. "Where is this coming from?" she asked in amazement. "You were so against them."

He shrugged. "They've had me take a walk around to stretch my legs and make sure my concussion wasn't too serious. They walked me through the children's wing, and I saw a family of circus folks."

"What happened?"

"This child was laying in a bed with her family surrounding her. Her leg was in a cast. The parents tended to her with such love, and the doctor came over with a silly clown nose on her face to make the kiddo laugh. It was such a sweet moment, and I realized I had been putting all the circus folk in the same bucket… they aren't all bad. Some of them are parents who just want to make a living. There are certainly worse things to do, aren't there?"

Tracy smiled. "I'm so glad you see it that way," she sighed in relief.

"Me too," he agreed. "I should have had empathy from the start. And I shouldn't have been so terse with you. I want things to be normal again. No, not normal. Better! Truce?"

"Truce."

He lifted himself out of the bed and reached for her, pulling her toward him and taking her face in his hands. He gave her a long, hard kiss on the lips, and Tracy felt shivers down her spine. "I've missed that."

He grinned at her. "I can't believe you got to see me in action," he chuckled as Tracy wiped smeared lipstick from his upper lip. "That guy really went at me, didn't he? I realized he was drunk, but he still had some serious fight in him."

Tracy's face darkened. "It was pretty ugly."

"He just wouldn't let up," Warren continued. "I wanted to give him a warning and let him off, but once he hit me, it was done. I couldn't let that stand."

"I get it," she told him. "You had to do your job."

Warren glanced beside her at the two flower arrangements. "Did you bring those for me?" he asked excitedly. "Both of them? That's so nice of you, Tracy."

She shifted awkwardly. "One is for you," she told him.

"And the other?" he asked. "What, do you have another boyfriend in the hospital or something?" he joked.

"If only you knew," she thought darkly as she forced herself to smile. "Don't be silly. One is for a friend of my aunt's who is here. She asked me to drop them off."

"You are such a sweetie," he praised her, but she felt the burn of guilt wash over her body. She had just lied to her boyfriend about Tyler; what was she doing?

A young nurse popped into the room. "Warren? We need to do another MRI," she chirped pleasantly as he groaned. "The last one was inconclusive, and we need more information about the type of concussion you are experiencing."

Warren rolled his eyes. "You people and your MRIs!" he moaned good-naturedly. "Okay, Clarice. Can I say a quick goodbye to my girl, here? Tracy, this is Clarice, my nurse. She's been watching over me all morning."

Clarice gave a friendly wave to Tracy before leaving the room. "She seems nice," Tracy commented absent-mindedly. "I guess I'll go."

She gathered the other flower arrangement and stood up. "See you soon."

"Wait!" Warren cried. "You aren't going to give me a kiss? I thought we made up."

"Sorry," she smiled weakly, walking back over to him and kissing him on the cheek. "Love you, Warren."

"Love you too, Tracy."

She left his room and returned to the nurse's station. "I need to see Tyler Foxely," she whispered to the male nurse, looking around to see if anyone saw her. "What room is he in?"

The nurse stared at her. "He's that jailbird they brought in, right? I'm not sure if I can let you see him. We don't usually allow visitors for inmates."

"Please?" she pleaded, holding up the flowers. "I just want to drop these off to him. I'll leave right after."

The nurse thought for a moment and then gave Tracy a nod. "Make it quick. He's in room K035. It's down the opposite hallway of the *first* guy you saw."

She noted the judgement in his voice, but thanked him anyway. Tracy turned around and hurried off to find Tyler, her step quick. When she reached his door, she gave it a gentle knock.

"Leave me alone," Tyler groaned, but she walked in any way.

"Hey," she greeted him, holding up the flowers. "I brought you something."

Tyler stared at her. "What are you doing here?" he asked angrily. "Your boyfriend took me to jail, and now I have a concussion. Isn't that enough agony for one 24-hour period?"

Tracy shrugged. "I just wanted to check on you, Tyler."

He rolled over in the hospital bed, facing away from her as she stood in the doorway with the bouquet. "These flowers are for you."

"I don't want them," he scoffed. "Your boyfriend really did a number on me, Tracy. It wasn't fair. I was drunk and totally out of it, and he had the advantage."

"I'm not sure that's how it went," she countered as she drew closer to the bed and placed the flowers on the nightstand.

"Oh yeah? It's not like you saw it," he argued.

"Actually, I did," she told him. "I was there, Tyler. You were talking to me at the bar. You were pretty drunk. I can't believe you don't remember me being there."

She saw his face turned a shade of crimson as he turned over to face her and propped himself up by his elbow. "I was smashed," he admitted. "Wasted. It happens sometimes when I'm angry; I can get so drunk that I forget everything."

She shook her head. "That isn't good, Tyler."

His eyes flashed with anger. "Yeah? Well, neither is your boyfriend putting his hands on me," he declared. "He didn't have to give me a concussion. I should sue the police department and make a buck or two or three million off of him. Your man did a number on my head, that's for sure, and he should have to pay."

Tracy shook her head. "Tyler, you were the one who attacked Bruce," she told him sternly. "You started the fight. Warren had to do his job."

Tyler rolled his eyes. "He didn't have to hurt me. He wanted to hurt me. He knew I was your ex-boyfriend and he wanted to punish me for it."

Tracy furrowed her brow. "He doesn't know," she insisted as she crossed her arms over her chest. "Warren doesn't know that you and I used to be boyfriend and girlfriend. He has no idea."

"He does now, Tracy."

They both turned to look at the doorway where Warren was standing, his eyes dancing with rage.

17

Tracy could not believe what had just happened in the hospital; how could things have gone so wrong? One moment, she and Warren had made up after a few distant, awkward days, and now, he was surely furious with her.

"I shouldn't have gone to see Tyler," she scolded herself as she walked out of the hospital, her head hung. "Or been sneaky about it."

The cold winter air stung her eyes as she stepped outside. She blinked back tears. Tracy was not usually a crier, but the stress of the day was rapidly catching up with her, and she could feel her eyes water as she thought about what to do next.

"Hey!"

Her thoughts were interrupted by a familiar voice. "Tracy? Are you okay?"

Emily Maher was walking toward her with a concerned look on her pretty face. She was dressed in an ankle-length white belted coat with a matching hat and ivory boots, looking like the definition of elegance as she hurried over to Tracy.

"Yeah," Tracy faked a smile. "Why?"

Emily stared into her eyes. "You look like your cat just died, and you're leaving the hospital," she said. "What's going on? Are you sick?"

Tracy shook her head. "I was just visiting friends in the hospital," she explained. "What are you up to?" she asked, intentionally changing the subject. "You look great, too. That's a gorgeous outfit."

Emily's eyes shined. "Thanks," she told Tracy. "Monochromatic looks are my favorite, as you know. They are so fun to pull off."

"I don't know if I could wear just one color," Tracy observed, looking down at her outfit. "I think I'm too short and would look like a crayon."

Emily laughed. "No," she protested. "No way. You could definitely pull off a monochromatic look. How tall are you?"

"Five-two," Tracy revealed. "But I always buy tall shoes. It helps."

Emily studied Tracy's figure. "I think a pale peach outfit would look lovely with your complexion," she decided. "Warm colors would be the most flattering for your frame and height."

Tracy nodded. "What about green? That's one of my favorite colors. My dad used to say my eyes looked spicy in green. I don't know what he meant, but it always seemed like a good thing."

Emily wrinkled her nose. "Green isn't my favorite color," she admitted. "But sage would suit you. We should go shopping sometime. Our girls' night out at the bar was such an unexpected treat, and I would love to get together again. What do you think, Tracy?"

Tracy smiled. "Do you have time right now? I could really use a little shopping excursion to take my mind off things..."

"I can't do it right now, unfortunately," Emily frowned. "I'm trying to work on a Christmas story for the newspaper, but I'm not having much luck finding examples of holiday spirit in town..."

"Really?" Tracy asked. "Usually, Fern Grove is brimming with holiday spirit."

"I know," Emily agreed. "But that murder really put a damper on people's spirit and joy. It's sad, really. I've been asking around, and no one wants to be interviewed or put in the paper. I don't want to let my boss down, but it's been so difficult."

Tracy thought for a moment. "What if you pick a theme?" she suggested. "A theme relating to Christmas and the holidays, but keep it very open and flexible. I think that could be helpful."Emily's face lit up. "A theme? I didn't even think about that," she grinned. "I think that could be a really helpful idea, Tracy."

"I'm glad you like it."

Emily bit her lip. "What are some appropriate Christmas themes?" she asked earnestly. "I don't know a lot about the intricacies of the holiday... do you have any suggestions?"

"Hmmmm," Tracy wondered aloud. "There's always the theme of giving, but that seems a bit..."

"Overdone?"

"Exactly," Tracy agreed. "You could try peace? Hope? Love?"

Emily made a face. "Those are a little generic—no offense. I want something that captures that attention of readers. Something a little... provocative."

Tracy giggled. "I've never framed Christmas as being provocative before," she chuckled as she tucked a hair behind her ear and shifted. "Wait, I know!" she squealed. "What about the idea of forgiveness?"

Emily cocked her head to the side. "Forgiveness? Wait a second, Tracy. I took a class on Biblical literature in college. I *read* the Christmas Story in the Bible. I don't remember anything about forgiveness, though. Are you thinking of a different part of the Bible? Like when Jesus was crucified?"

Tracy shook her head. "No, hear me out. The Christmas story itself doesn't have blatant themes of forgiveness, but the holidays are all about being kind, showing love, and connecting with the people you love. Christmas is about joy and love and righting wrongs and telling the truth."

Emily raised an eyebrow. "Are you sure you aren't just recapping the plot of Love Actually?" she asked in a joking tone.

"I'm serious," Tracy insisted. "I think the idea of forgiveness would really resonate with people. Everyone has had a situation in their lives where they had to show or be shown forgiveness, and I'm sure some of those situations have happened around the holidays."

Emily nodded her head, her drop pearl earrings shaking with her movements. "That does sound pretty interesting," she admitted. "I'll have to give it some thought."

Tracy smiled. "I think it would be great for the holiday spirit."

Emily's eyes widened. "Speaking of the holiday spirit," she began. "I went to the Christmas choir rehearsal," she informed her friend.

"You did?" Tracy asked in shock. "I really didn't think you would do it. What did you think?"

"It was lovely," Emily beamed. "That girl who works at the flower shop, Tiffany, was there, and everyone went out of their way to make me feel included. I emailed Pastor Butler and explained that

I'm Jewish, and he was totally fine with that. He told me that God welcomes all, and I felt very much at home."

Tracy's heart warmed. "Pastor Butler is a good man," she breathed happily. "I am so glad you had a good time. You have such a pretty voice, Emily, and it's nice of you to share it with the world."

Emily batted her eyelashes. "You really think so?"

"I do," Tracy confirmed. "Did Tiffany get to sing the solo in *O Holy Night*?"

Emily nodded. "She knocked it out of the park. Her alto voice is so lovely, especially for someone her age."

"I wish I could sing," Tracy lamented. "My mother used to sing to me before bed every night. She had the voice of an angel, and I can still remember it."

"What would she sing to you?" Emily asked kindly. "Lullabies?"

Tracy shook her head. "Even better—classic rock!"

Emily groaned. "My mom was obsessed with REO Speedwagon," she told her. "She would crank their music in the car every time she took us to school. She loved blaring *Time For Me To Fly* when my brother and I would get out of the car. It was so embarrassing."

Tracy thought of her mother's raspy voice. "She loved Stevie Nicks," she explained to Emily. "She sounded just like her, in fact; now, every time I hear the song *Dreams* or *Landslide,* I think it's my mom saying hi to me."

Tracy's stomach churned as she remembered her mother singing into a fake microphone as she danced around the kitchen with Tracy. "She loved Stevie Nicks," she repeated quietly, feeling her eyes water and her face burn.

"Oh, Tracy," Emily said. "I'm sorry. I didn't mean to make you sad by talking about our mothers. Please forgive me."

"See?" Tracy forced herself to laugh. "Forgiveness. You could write about this moment for your story."

Emily's face fell. "I don't think I want to do that," she murmured.

Tracy wiped her eyes. "I'm fine," she lied, feeling the familiar ache in her belly she experienced every time she thought of her mother.

"You are not fine," Emily countered, reaching to take Tracy's shaking hands in hers. "You're sad and you're cold—I can feel you shivering. Let's get out of here and go to the grocery store."

"The grocery?"

Emily nodded. "You need a hot soup. Hot soup cures everything, you know!"

"I've never heard that one before," Tracy smiled weakly. "You are full of surprises, Emily."

"I know," she winked at her, and then linked her arm in Tracy's. "A nice soup will fix you right up. Do you like carrot soup? Or we could get supplies to make tomato soup. My favorite is butternut squash soup, but I know some folks don't love that…"

Tracy grinned, happy that they had moved on from talking about their mothers to discussing their favorite soups. "Chicken noodle has always been my favorite," she told Emily.

"Perfect! Then we will get some chicken, noodles, broth, and a few vegetables to sprinkle in," Emily chirped. "I am an expert in picking out fresh vegetables. Let's go!"

Tracy nodded, but she glanced behind her to take one last look at the hospital she had just left. Her heart sank as she spotted dark figures staring at her from two different windows. It was Warren and Tyler. She held up a hand to wave, but neither man waved back.

"Who are you waving at?" Emily asked.

"No one," Tracy lied, bringing her hand down. "It was no one."

18

"Stop attacking me!" Tracy screamed, flailing her arms and trying to get away.

Mr. Sydney was determined to be a nuisance; his green eyes were dilated, meaning he was ready to pounce again, and Tracy swatted at his behind. "What is the matter with you? You're angry with me too, Mr. Sydney?"

He wrapped himself around her ankles and nipped at her calf. "Stop it," she cried as she held up a pan in front of her face. "Mr. Sydney, your mother is trying to make a nice soup dinner, and you are making her life difficult right now," she warned him as he hissed at her. "Go away."

He sprang forward, biting her hand, and she reached for a glass of water sitting on her kitchen counter. She held it up as a threat, and when he pounced again, she dumped it on the naughty cat. Mr. Sydney screeched, shaking his body wildly before darting into the next room.

"What has gotten into everyone these days?" she wondered as she returned to the stove and resumed cooking dinner. "First Tyler, then Warren, and now, Mr. Sydney…"

She shuddered as she recalled the scene at the hospital when Warren had caught her in Tyler's room.

"What is going on here?" Warren had asked as Tyler smirked. "Tracy, what is happening? You told me you were dropping off something for your aunt's friend. This is the guy who was fighting at the bar."

"That wasn't untrue," she insisted, rushing over to her boyfriend and clutching his hands. "Aunt Rose suggested I deliver something to Tyler. He is a friend of Aunt Rose."

"I think you and I have too much of a history to just be friends," Tyler chimed in, and Tracy shot him a dirty look. "Come on, Tracy. Fill him in."

Warren pulled his hands away from Tracy and crossed his arms over his broad chest. "Explain," he demanded, narrowing his eyes as Tracy gritted her teeth.

"Tyler was my childhood sweetheart," she began as Warren eyed her suspiciously. "We went steady for a few summers, but we broke things off before I went off to college. It was totally innocent, Warren. We were just two young kids…"

"...two young kids in love," Tyler added. "And now, we're just two soulmates who have found each other again."

Tracy turned to glare at Tyler. "Enough," she ordered him, and he sat back in the hospital bed, his hands folded.

"We aren't soulmates," she told Warren. "We aren't *anything*. Tyler works for the circus, and he's been around town. Before this, I hadn't seen or heard from him in twenty-years, Warren. I promise."

Warren glowered at her, and she put her hand on his chest. "Warren, I love you. Tyler is a *stranger* to me. You are my love."

Warren looked into her eyes. "Why didn't you just tell me about him?" he asked, his face filled with hurt. "You could have let me know your ex was in town. Why the secrets, Tracy?"

She hung her head. "I don't know," she muttered. "It didn't seem like something to say over a text, and we haven't seen each other in a few days...I should have let you know."

Tyler rolled his eyes. "Can you two take the love fest elsewhere? This is gross to watch."

Warren nodded. "I was just leaving."

Tracy gasped as he walked out of the hospital room. She ran behind him and tugged at the hospital gown. "Warren, please," she begged. "Please don't walk away. Let's talk about this."

He shrugged her off. "I don't want to talk about this right now," he declared. "We promised each other we could always be honest and true, Tracy. I know you didn't mean to deceive me, but I feel pretty hurt right now. I think you should get out of here. I need to be alone."

Now, as she stood in her kitchen, she felt a deep pit in her stomach. Would things ever be the same between them again? When had Tyler turned into such an antagonist? Had he been like that when they were teenagers?

Her cell phone rang. She hoped it was Warren, and was disappointed when it was her friend, Isabelle on the phone.

"Hey girl," she greeted her. "How's it going?"

Isabelle huffed. "You know, just the same stuff. The wedding is still off and my life is *over*. Otherwise, things are fine."

Tracy stifled a laugh. Isabelle had a flair for dramatics, but it was clearly not an appropriate time for a chuckle at her expense. "I'm so sorry," she told her. "How are you holding up?"

"My therapist says I'm doing great," Isabelle said stonily. "What's new with you?"

Tracy bit her lip before diving into the story of dealing with Tyler and Warren at the hospital.

"Wait," Isabelle interrupted. "They were both there for the same thing? That's crazy."

"It is," Tracy agreed, and then told her about Warren walking into the hospital room and finding her at Tyler's bedside.

"Girl, this is the kind of drama I've been *needing*," Isabelle laughed. "Drama that isn't mine. Tell me more."

Tracy described the anger on Warren's face, and the way Tyler had chimed in. "Tyler sounds like a total jerk," Isabelle lamented. "I can't believe you dated him."

"I don't think he was always like this," Tracy told her. "At least, I don't remember him acting like this."

She finished her story and Isabelle laughed. "I didn't think anyone's situation was worse than mine," she began as Tracy raised an eyebrow. "But yours sounds pretty bad right now. An ex, an angry lover, and a murderer on the loose in town? Yikes, Tracy."

Tracy gripped the phone tightly. "If you were me, what would you do?" she asked. "About Warren?"

Isabelle sighed. "You have to give him time," she advised. "His ego is probably hurting."

"His ego?"

"The male ego is exceptionally fragile," Isabelle continued. "Trust me, my ex-fiancé's was practically made of glass. Warren's ego is probably in pieces from finding you with an ex-boyfriend, and he needs time to let it recover."

Tracy nodded. "So, give him time... and then?"

"Avoid that Tyler guy at all costs if you want things with Warren to work out," Isabelle suggested. "He sounds toxic and a little dangerous. You've gotta stay away from him."

They moved on to another topic, but Tracy could not stop thinking of what Isabelle had said. "He sounds toxic and a little dangerous." Tyler had gotten drunk and attacked Bruce, and he didn't seem to have any remorse. He even joked about the situation, and Tracy could tell he had a serious drinking problem. What if Tyler's demons were darker than she knew? Tyler worked at the circus, and Brett *owned* the circus... could Tyler have had something to do with Brett's murder? Was her ex-boyfriend a killer?

The next morning, she was awakened by the sound of her cell phone ringing. She opened her eyes and reached for her phone. It was Warren!

"Warren?" she answered. "Hey."

"How are you doing?"

"I've been better," she admitted. "Warren, I am still so sorry--"

"Stop," he insisted. "Tracy, I thought about what happened, and I want you to know that we are okay. I know you, and I trust you, and I'm sorry I got so upset. I was just fired up after that guy was acting like a jerk and being in the hospital made me feel so vulnerable. Anyway, I'm sorry. I hope you can forgive me."

"Forgive you?" she cried. "No, forgive me!"

Warren gave a little laugh. "It's a good sign when two people both want to be forgiven," he commented. "I'm out of the hospital and back at the office, but let's get together later. I need to see your beautiful face."

"It's a date," she agreed, and they hung up the phone after chatting for a few more minutes.

She ended the call and glanced down at her text messages, shocked to find ten new messages that came through overnight. "What on Earth?"

They were all from an unknown number, but she instantly knew who had reached out. She read the first two and then turned her phone over.

Tracy, I'm sorry your boy was mad. Forgive me. —T

Please, Tracy, I just want to be your friend. Sorry for the trouble I caused. —T

Tyler. She wondered how he had gotten her number. Had he asked Aunt Rose? Heeding Isabelle's advice, she blocked the phone number, relieved that he could no longer contact her.

It was Tracy's day off, and she started making a big breakfast. She and Mr. Sydney had ended their spat, and she smiled as he licked her toes. "Do you want eggs, bacon, or both?" she asked him, knowing she would make both for herself.

There was a knock on the door, and Tracy's eyes widened. "Tyler," she muttered. She wasn't expecting anyone, and she hoped it wasn't her ex-boyfriend at the front door. She threw on her blue cotton bathrobe and slowly answered the door. "Hello?"

Before her stood Bruce, the owner of the bar. He held his red baseball cap in his hands, and he hung his head as he stood on Tracy's doorstep. "Hey," he greeted her. "Tracy, right? Warren's lady friend?"

"Yes?"

"I just wanted to swing by and apologize for that scene at the bar," he told her. "I feel bad that you, a pretty patron, had to witness such a spectacle. I shouldn't have let that guy get to me."

She bit her lip. "You were really mad when he said he was a circus guy…"

Brett nodded. "I know," he agreed. "I shouldn't have let it get to me."

She smiled at him. "Thanks for dropping by," she told him. "Look, I'm sure it's hard to have circus people around. I bet that brings up a lot for you, especially when your brother…"

"What do you know about my brother?" he demanded, his eyes suddenly flashing with anger. "You don't know *anything.*"

She took a step back into her apartment. "I don't," she admitted. "You're right. But regardless, Bruce, I am sorry for the loss."

Bruce's face darkened. "Don't you ever mention my brother again," he demanded, sticking his pointer finger in her face. "That fool abandoned our family and ran off to join the circus. He didn't care at all how it hurt our Ma and embarrassed our Dad. Brett just did whatever he pleased."

She nodded. "That sounds really hard for you," she agreed.

"You have no idea," he glowered. "Brett ran off without even a goodbye to my poor Ma. He broke her heart. She died six months later, and he didn't even bother to come to the funeral. My Dad was never the same."

She hung her head. "That's awful."

"It is," he declared. "And he had some nerve to come around my bar like he did. He was always causing trouble. Anyway, I am done with circus folks, and done with those who fraternize with them, like you. Stay out of my bar. I'm not going to ask nicely next time!"

Tracy's jaw dropped as he turned and barreled away. He had gone from a pleasant gentleman to a jerk in less than ten seconds. She was reeling from his abrupt change in mood, and suddenly, she felt light-headed. Bruce had a temper; she had seen the way he taunted his own brother during their fight at the bar, and she could not believe how he had just unleashed his wrath on her. Could Bruce have killed Brett? Tracy had never considered it before, but now, as she stood in the doorway of her home after his visit, she could not shake the notion that there was more to Bruce than she knew.

19

"Linda!" Tiffany squealed as the two Goff ladies walked into the flower shop.

Tracy wished she shared the teenager's enthusiasm, but all she could do was stifle a groan at the sight of Amy Goff. "Good morning," she greeted them, forcing herself to smile politely as they stood in front of the counter.

"What kind of flower is that?" Linda asked, pointing to a dainty winter jasmine positioned at the forefront of arrangement sitting on the counter.

"It's a winter jasmine," Aunt Rose replied kindly. "The buttery yellow color is one of my favorites."

"Mine too," Linda grinned, taking out her cell phone and snapping a picture. "The color instantly makes me feel happy."

"Enough about colors and happiness," Amy snapped, tapping her foot impatiently as she placed her hands on her narrow hips. "We wanted to check on the flower arrangements for the funeral."

Tracy nodded. "Of course. They are coming along nicely; we're using a combination of winterberry holly, mahonia, and spring snowflakes. We didn't want the aesthetic to be reminiscent of the upcoming holidays, so we've been careful to avoid red ribbons and other festive trappings."

Amy raised an eyebrow. "You didn't mention red roses."

Tracy pursed her lips. "Red roses are not traditional funeral flowers," she explained kindly as Amy stared at her. "We actually try to avoid them for funerals; it's a standard trick of the trade."

Aunt Rose agreed. "I can show you a sample of the spring snowflakes," she offered sweetly. "Maybe that will put your mind at ease?"

"It won't," Amy declared. "I want blood red roses for my husband's funeral, and I'm not going to ask again."

Amy turned abruptly and stormed out of the flower shop. Linda looked embarrassed. "I'm sorry about my mom," she muttered, hanging her head and staring down at her snow boots. "She can be great when she's in a good mood."

"I'm sure she's lovely," Tracy lied through her teeth. "We'll take care of the arrangements, dear. Don't you worry about them."

Linda shrugged. "I just hope its everything Mom wants," she sighed.

Aunt Rose shot the girl a look of sympathy. "Honey, when my late husband passed, I was in a bad state," she explained. "I'm sure your mother will come around."

Linda stared at her. "She isn't upset because of the funeral," she chuckled. "My mom could care less about Dad being gone. She's just stressed out about the dress rehearsal. Now that she technically owns the circus, she's in charge, and we all haven't heard the end of it..."

Tracy's eyes widened. "The dress rehearsal," she said. "I forgot about that."

Linda turned to Tracy and Tiffany with a smile. "I actually dropped by to ask you two about that," she told them. "The dress rehearsal."

"What about it?" Tiffany asked.

"I want you two to come," Linda asked earnestly. "You two have been so kind to me, and it really means the world. I'm doing a special tribute for my Dad at the rehearsal, and I would love for you two to be there to see it."

Tracy blinked back tears. Linda was such a kind, thoughtful young woman, and her heart ached for her as she thought about what it meant to lose a parent at such a young age.

"I'm grounded," Tiffany told her apologetically. "So, I'm out. I'm sorry, Linda."

She nodded. "I get it," Linda assured her. "Being grounded stinks. Tracy? Can you make it."

Tracy gulped. "I'm not so sure it's a great idea for me to be around the circus right now," she carefully told the girl. "I hope you can understand."

Linda cocked her head to the side, looking at Tracy with pleading eyes. "Please? It would mean so much to me, Tracy."

She felt her heart pound. What if Warren found out? Would he be angry with her? Tyler was in the hospital, and after his stay, he would be taken to the jail, where he couldn't mess with her. Perhaps it wouldn't be a big deal to sneak over there for an hour.

"Okay," Tracy agreed, and Linda's face lit up. "I'll do it. I'll be there."

* * *

When it was time for the rehearsal, Tracy dressed in a pair of loose-fitting jeans, a black and white striped t-shirt, and a fitted blazer. She wanted to look nice, but low-key, and she nodded at her reflection in the mirror as she surveyed her appearance before leaving the apartment.

When she arrived at the circus, she glanced around, hoping to avoid any unwanted attention. Though it was an overcast day, she wore her oversized sunglasses, feeling like a secret agent as she surreptitiously slipped into the circus tent.

The lights were still on and music was playing; Tracy watched as a pair of minders led two leashed tigers out of the tent, admiring the color and muscle of the giant cats. "I wonder if Mr. Sydney would look like that if he ate his vegetables," she joked to herself, giggling as she pictured her beloved cat with stripes on his back.

The lights went low, the music halted, and the stages cleared. Tracy noticed there was a large video screen that had been mounted on the far wall near the exit. The screen turned on, and a soft violin instrumental track began to play as images of Brett flashed across the screen.

Tracy choked up as a photo of Brett and Linda as a little girl showed; in the picture, Linda was laughing as Brett held her in place atop of an elephant, and Amy was clapping in the background. "They were happy once," Tracy thought to herself as a photo of Brett and Amy on their wedding day appeared. "They were a happy family..."

The next picture flashed, a shot of Brett and Amy striking a pose with two muscled circus performers. Tracy smiled, and then felt someone take the spot next to her on the bleachers. She turned and gasped. It was Tyler!

"Hey," he whispered, leaning in close to her. "I was hoping you would still come..."

She stared at him, her heart beating furiously. "I thought you were in the hospital," she whispered. "And then off to jail."

He winked. "You know I can get out of anything," he replied, his eyes sparkling with mischief. "Remember that time we broke into the ice cream shop after hours when we were sixteen? The manager showed up after we triggered the alarms, and I talked him out of calling our parents."

Tracy frowned. "Sneaking into an ice cream parlor is a little different than committing a misdemeanor as a grown man," she hissed. "Seriously, Tyler. What is wrong with you? This isn't funny."

He shook his head. "You've always been too uptight," he told her. "Relax. Amy paid my bail last night. I was released straight from the hospital. It's all legit, I promise."

She raised an eyebrow. "*Amy Goff* paid your bail? Why?"

Tyler shrugged. "She owns the circus now, Tracy," he explained matter-of-factly. "And we look out for our own around here."

Tracy narrowed her eyes. "What do you want?" she asked him. "Why are you bothering me? You already threatened my relationship and caused enough trouble in my life. What do you want from me?"

Tyler took a deep breath. "I never thought I would have a chance to say this to you," he began, staring down at his white converse shoes. "I always thought you would settle down fast; you're a gorgeous woman, Tracy, and you have a great heart. I didn't think you would still be single after these years."

"So?" she glared at him.

"So," he continued. "I think this is our second chance, Tracy. When we dated, we were young, selfish, and immature. We were kids! Now, we're both adults. I think it's time for us to have a real shot."

Tracy's jaw dropped. "Tyler," she protested. "You just got out of jail for assaulting two people. One of which is my serious boyfriend.

You work for a traveling circus. You have a drinking problem. What part of that screams *real shot* to you?"

Tyler studied her face. "I have plans," he told her. "Big plans. I have some money put away, and I'm ready to settle down, Tracy. I want to buy a house. I want a real job. I want to get sober. I want *you* by my side for it all. You're my dream girl, Tracy, and I won't let you go again."

Tracy rose from her seat on the bleachers and put her hands on her hips. "How can you say those things to me?" she cried. "You know I am in a relationship, and you should know me well enough to know I have the *integrity* to respect and honor the man I am dating. Tyler, I don't want to be with *you*. Listen to me."

Tyler stood up and faced her. "Integrity, huh? Then why are you hanging around the circus? I know you're here waiting for me. I bet that boyfriend of yours doesn't even know you're here."

Tracy glowered at him. "I'm not here for you," she declared. "I'm here for *her*."

She pointed to a photo of Brett and Linda that had appeared on the screen. "I'm here supporting Linda."

Tyler rolled his eyes. "Yeah, right," he laughed as he turned and walked away from her. "Cute excuse, Tracy."

She stared as Tyler walked down the bleachers and exited the circus tent. She was furious. Tyler was impulsive, conceited, and delusional; she had no interest in being with him, and if she never saw him again, it would be too soon.

Not wanting to cause a scene, she sat back down and finished watching the tribute video. When it was over, she applauded, and Linda appeared on the mainstage. The circus crew and performers entered the tent and clapped, and Linda gave a little bow.

Tracy made eye contact with her, and Linda dashed over to where she was sitting. "You came!" she cried, wrapping her arms around Tracy and giving her a huge hug. "What did you think?"

"I think you have a career in filmmaking," Tracy said. "Did you put that together all by yourself?"

Linda beamed. "I did," she told Tracy. "It wasn't easy, but looking through our old photos helped a lot. It made me feel closer to Dad."

"That's amazing," Tracy smiled. "What was your favorite part? Or the hardest part?"

Linda frowned. "Well, I had this vision of including a segment with the circus animals," she explained to Tracy. "I wanted the animals to be in the film; Dad loved them so much."

Tracy wrinkled her nose. "I don't think I saw that part," she told her, worrying it had been while she and Tyler were arguing.

"It wasn't in the film," she sighed. "I filmed the clip, but it's lost in my phone. I was trying to find it, but I ran out of time. I really want to see it, though. I just have so many photos and videos on my phone that I don't think I'll ever come across it again."

She pulled out the phone and waved it at Tracy. "I have ten thousand videos on this little thing," she told Tracy. "Isn't that crazy?"

Tracy stared at the phone. "Technology is crazy," she agreed. "Say, do you want a pair of fresh eyes to look for that video? I can scroll through your phone if you'd like."

Linda's face brightened. "That would be awesome," she grinned. "If we can find it, I want to re-edit the tribute video to include it. That would be such a cool way to start the real show."

"I'm on it," Tracy smiled as Linda punched in her password and handed her the phone.

Tracy glanced down at the photos. There were photos of Linda and Tiffany posing in the flower shop, both making duck lips at the camera. She saw pictures of Amy in the RV, looking grumpy as she lounged on the couch in a bathrobe. As she went further back, there were images of Linda doing cartwheels, Brett and Amy scowling at each other outside of the circus tent, and pictures of Linda manning the ticket booth with a silly look on her face.

"Did you find it?" Linda asked as she looked down at her thumbnail and began to pick at the polish. "It should be a little farther back."

Tracy flicked through the photos and then stopped. The color drained from her face, and she felt as though she were going to vomit.

"What?" Linda asked, looking up at Tracy's shocked expression. "What's wrong?"

Tracy held the phone in front of her, her eyes huge as she stared at the photo.

"Tracy? What's the matter? You look like you've seen a ghost," Linda noted, and Tracy stood up.

"I have to go," she told the teenager. "I have to go *now*."

20

Tracy scampered down the bleachers and darted out of the circus tent. She pumped her arms vigorously, trying to power walk as fast as she could. She had to get away from the circus as quickly as she could. Tracy reached into her pocket to dial Warren's number, and she cursed upon realizing her phone was dead.

"I should have used Linda's phone to call the police," she fretted as she strode past a pair of circus clowns.

"Tracy, where are you going in such a hurry?" Tyler's voice called out from across the fairgrounds. She groaned as he jogged over to join her. "What's wrong?"

"Leave me alone," she demanded, but he tugged on her coat sleeve to stop her. "Tyler! Leave me *alone*."

He tugged harder, and she quickly reached up to unzip her coat, slipping it off and leaving Tyler holding it in his hand. She shivered; it was a chilly day and her blazer was thin, and she took off in a sprint away from the circus.

She passed tents and RVs, and soon, the Goffs giant red RV came into view. She looked behind her; Tyler was not pursuing her, and she breathed a sigh of relief. Tracy slowed down, placing her hands on her knees and catching her breath.

"You okay?"

Her eyes huge with fear, she looked up to see Bruce Brown, the bartender, standing before her. She shook her head. "I'm not okay," she admitted as she stood back up. "What are you doing here, Bruce?"

"I was going to see the rehearsal," he told her. "I heard they put together a little tribute for my brother, and I thought it would be a nice gesture to make it over there."

She nodded. "I see. Do you have your phone with you by any chance?"

He stared at her. "What's the matter?"

"I know who killed your brother," she said breathlessly. "It took some time to figure out, but I know who it was."

Bruce's eyes widened. "Who did it?"

Her face was a ghostly shade of white as she murmured, "it was Tyler Foxely."

Bruce blinked. "Tyler Foxely? Are you sure?"

"Yes," she told him. "It was Tyler. I think he must have been in a drunken rage or something, like the night he fought you at the bar. He killed your brother, Bruce."

Bruce ran a hand through his silver hair. "And you know that for sure?"

She shifted. "I'm pretty sure," she sighed. "I need to talk to the police. They need to look through Linda's phone."

"Linda's phone?"

"Yes," she told him. "Brett gave Linda a cell phone, and she was always using it to take photos and videos. She would set it up for shots, leave it, and come back to collect the footage."

"And you saw footage that makes you think Tyler did it?"

"Yes!" she cried. "I saw a photo of Tyler and Brett fighting. I think that says it all. I need to go to the police and tell them to go through her phone! That will show them everything they need to see to arrest Tyler."

Bruce narrowed his eyes at her. "Are you on the way to the police station now?"

"Yes!" she exclaimed. "Unless I can use your cell phone to call them. My phone is dead."

Bruce shook his head. "I don't have a cell phone," he told her. "But I will gladly escort you to the police station. I wouldn't want you to go by yourself; it's getting dark, and that Tyler character is still running around out there."

Her face broke into a relieved smile. "Thank you so much," she said. "Let's go; it's only a fifteen-minute walk from here."

They set off, but as they neared the edge of the fairgrounds, Bruce jerked his head to the right. "Let's go this way," he suggested. "It's much faster."

She stared at the path going left. "Are you sure? This is the way I usually go."

He smiled, his eyes crinkling as he guided her to the right. "I've been coming this way longer than you've been alive, little lady," he laughed. "Trust me."

They walked a few more minutes. It was getting darker, and Tracy shuddered as a gust of cold air bit her cheeks. "I don't think we're going the right way," she insisted. "Town is the other way. We're going deeper into the woods, Bruce."

He turned to face her. "Yes, we are, aren't we?"

She turned around. "Come on. We'll just turn around and make our way back. We need to hurry, though; I think Tyler knows I am on to him, and I don't want him to make a break for it."

They stood in a clearing amidst a circle of evergreen trees. Tracy could faintly hear music and laughter from the circus, but she knew they were at least a twenty-five-minute walk away from Fern Grove. "Come on, Bruce."

He reached out and grabbed her wrist. "We aren't going to the police station," he stated.

She spun around and tugged at her wrist. "What are you doing?" she cried. "Let go of me!"

Bruce shook his head. "I can't, he sighed.

Tracy gasped. "Bruce, what is going on here? Let me go. We have to get to the station!"

Bruce furrowed his brow. "I can't let you march off to the police," he repeated. "I can't have them going through Linda's phone."

"And why not?" she demanded, giving her wrist another tug.

Bruce stared at her. "Because then they'll know that I was the one who killed my brother."

Tracy's mouth fell open. She tried to scream, but nothing came out. Bruce pulled her away and kept walking her deeper into the woods. "I didn't want to do this," he began. "But I'm going to have to get rid of you."

"Get rid of me?" she shrieked, the words finally rising in her chest. "Help! Help!"

Bruce took her by the shoulders and glared at her. "Shut up," he ordered, shaking her violently. "Don't make this harder than it has to be."

He turned her around and marched her farther into the forest, his calloused hands gripping her shoulders tightly. "Let go of me," she cried as she tried to slip out of his grip. "Please! Don't do this, Bruce. You're a good man."

He sighed. "I know I am," he grumbled. "But sometimes, good men have to do bad things."

The snow was getting deeper; it was over Tracy's knees, and the legs of her pants were crusted with the thick, white snow. "Please," she moaned. "Let me go."

Before he could reply, Tracy dropped to her knees. "What the--" Bruce stumbled, losing his grip on her shoulders and falling into the snow.

Tracy sprang up, moving her body as quickly as she could through the snow and back toward town. Her short legs were working harder than they ever had, and she could feel her muscles screaming as they lifted her up and through the rugged woods.

"Bruce killed his own brother," she screamed inside her head as she leaped through the snow. "Bruce murdered Brett."

She rounded a corner and glanced behind her; Bruce was running after her, but his pace was not quick. The snow was slowing him down, and she was gaining ground.

Tracy pumped her arms faster, trying to pick up her knees. She *had* to get out of the woods; if Bruce caught her, no one would ever find her or know what happened to her. She thought of Warren and Mr. Sydney and Aunt Rose and *In Season*. She *had* to make it out of the woods, and as she grunted through the snow, she was filled with adrenaline.

She was nearly back to the edge of the woods when she tripped over a log. She had not seen it in the darkness, and she fell to the ground with a hard thud. Tracy scrambled to get up, but before she knew it, Bruce was standing over her, a shiny revolver in his hand.

"I didn't want to do this," he told her as he pointed the gun at her forehead. "It was an accident. I didn't want to kill Brett. If I could do it over, I wouldn't."

"Then do it over!" she pleaded, closing her eyes and shaking in fear. "Choose to let me live. You don't have to kill again, Bruce."

He sighed. "You'll tell," he said simply. "And I'll be locked up forever."

She squirmed. It would take a miracle to get out of the woods alive, and Tracy knew she was running out of luck.

"I'm a good man," he repeated as he steadied his hand. "I didn't mean to kill Brett; we were fighting, as we always did when we ran into each other, and he fell. He hit his head on a rock, and I had to finish the job."

Tears streamed from Tracy's eyes. "I wish I could have let you blame that Tyler idiot," he continued. "The police surely could have made an arrest based on the photo you saw."

"Then why did you bring me here?" she cried.

"Because if there are photos and videos of the circus and the fairgrounds on that girl's phone, there are surely videos of the fight where Brett was killed," he told her. "And I can't risk getting caught. My brother ruined my family, and I won't let him ruin the rest of my life. Or you, for that matter!"

He lifted the gun, pointing it directly between Tracy's eyes. "I'm sorry," he apologized as he stared directly into her face. "I'm sorry."

Suddenly, the forest was filled with red and blue lights. Four police SUVs appeared, each outfitted with massive snow tires. Warren jumped out of the first vehicle and ran toward them, his gun drawn.

"Put your weapon down!" he screamed as Bruce dropped to his knees. "You are under arrest!"

21

"And after everything, *Tyler* saved me."

Tracy finished her story and looked down at her cup of coffee, breathing a sigh of relief. It was the day after Bruce had nearly killed her in the woods behind the circus, and after spending the night at the hospital, and then the police station, she was finally resting at home. Aunt Rose and Tiffany had come over to check on her, and they were all snuggled up in her living room, sitting under blankets and petting Mr. Sydney.

"Tyler?" Tiffany cried. "I thought you said *Warren* and the police showed up. You said they pulled up in their big SUVs and saved you, and Warren picked you up and kissed you on the lips."

"They did," she agreed. "He did. But Tyler was the one who called the police. He saw Bruce taking me off into the woods and thought it was weird. Thank goodness he was watching me and called for help, or I wouldn't be here right now. Bruce wanted me dead, and I am lucky to have made it out of those woods in one piece."

Aunt Rose blotted at her eyes with a handkerchief. "I can't believe this happened," she sighed. "And after everything, Tyler saved your life. That boy has a good heart, that's for sure."

"He did," she confirmed. "I'm not so sure about a good heart; Tyler has a lot of problems of his own to work out, and he left quite a bad impression in Warren's eyes. But now, thanks to this entire mess, he can save his own life. The police agreed not to charge him in assaulting Warren or Bruce if he went to rehab. Warren told me he left early this morning, and he'll be at an in-person center for at least a year."

"That's wonderful," Aunt Rose said. "He'll get the help he needs... the help he deserves. That poor boy never stood a chance with a family as damaged as his. He deserves to be happy and well."

Tiffany looked at Tracy. "So, what happened to Bruce? Did they take him off to jail?"

"He confessed," she breathed. "Which is a good thing, because Linda's phone didn't have *any* photos or videos of Brett and Bruce together. Can you believe that? He got spooked when I was talking about it, and he acted rashly. Thank goodness he confessed on his own accord, or there would be no real evidence besides my word against his."

The three ladies sat in silence for a moment. "Can you imagine hating your own brother so much that you would kill him?" Tiffany whispered. "My little brother always eats my cereal and borrows my guitar without asking, but I would never kill him. I might give him a hard time and steal his snacks when he goes to bed early, but murder? No way!"

Aunt Rose frowned. "It sounds like it wasn't planned," she suggested. "But rather, a tragic accident. I've known Bruce for years, and this honestly comes as such a shock. I can't believe he would do something like that to his own brother."

Tracy crossed her arms, grimacing as she felt the pain in her bones. She was still sore from the previous evening; she had been treated at the hospital for a broken rib and minor frostbite, and even shifting from side to side on her own couch was painful. "Tragic accident or not, he chose to drag me into the woods and try to kill me, Aunt Rose. I think Bruce's demons were certainly darker than Tyler's..."

Aunt Rose nodded. "I know. It's just terrible, honey. I am so sorry it all happened. You poor thing."

Tiffany studied Tracy's face. "Was Warren mad you went back to the circus? What did he have to say about all of this?"

Tracy laughed. "No," she assured her. "He was relieved I was *alive.* It's just so crazy, ladies. The whole time, I truly thought Amy Goff did it. She had such an attitude, and it seemed like she had some scheme going with the circus."

"Maybe she did, and maybe she does," Aunt Rose told her. "But at the end of the day, a bad attitude doesn't necessarily constitute a murderer."

"That's true," Tiffany giggled. "Or I would be a murderer every time I get grounded or have detention."

They sat in silence for a few moments, and then Tiffany's phone buzzed. "It's a message from Linda," she announced. "The police gave her her cell phone back. I've been waiting for her to text me all day."

"That's good," Tracy said. "How is she doing? Does she know about everything that happened?"

"She's fine," Tiffany smiled. "I think she's trying to focus on the show and she doesn't want to think about the murder. She wants to know if we're planning to attend the show tonight. She really wants us to be there, Tracy. She says it's important to her."

Her face paled. "I don't know if I can go back there," she murmured. "Everything just happened, and I think I would get too freaked out being back at the circus."

"I understand," Tiffany told her. "I wouldn't want to go anywhere either if someone had just tried to kill me in the woods. How about this, Tracy? Aunt Rose and I will go together, and we'll come back here tonight and tell you all about it. We'll take photos and videos and it'll be like you were there. Okay? What do you think?"

Tracy smiled softly. "It's a deal."

That night, her aunt and Tiffany returned to her apartment to check on her. They had smiles on their faces, and they surprised Tracy with a bag filled with containers of hot Chinese food.

"We thought a little pick me up would do you some good," Aunt Rose greeted her. "Tiffany, go set out the plates."

Tiffany scurried to the kitchen and returned with three giant plates and silverware. She tore open the white boxes and began shoveling food onto each plate. "We got one of everything," she grinned as Tracy watched her. "Orange chicken, lo mein, dumplings, hot and sour soup, kung pao chicken, dim sum... the works!"

Tracy grinned. "You know food is the way to my heart," she cooed as she sat down at the head of the table. "Thank you both so much."

Aunt Rose and Tiffany joined her, each opening a pair of chopsticks that had come with the meal.

"How was the show?" Tracy asked. "I hope you told Linda hello for me."

"We did!" Tiffany assured her. "They played the tribute video, and Linda even had a little part in the show tonight. She wore a sparkly red tutu and did a dance routine."

"It was lovely," Aunt Rose chimed in. "She did a dance number dedicated to her father, and everyone in the audience cried."

"We took her flowers, too," Tiffany grinned.

"Blood red roses?" Tracy teased, feeling better than she had all day.

"Absolutely not," Aunt Rose said primly.

"We took her a bouquet of poinsettias," Tiffany told her. "It was so pretty, and it matched her tutu perfectly. We took some photos together after the show. Want to see?"

Tracy nodded, and Tiffany pulled out her cell phone to show her. "This is Linda dancing," Tiffany narrated as she scrolled through the photos. "And here she is onstage with her mom after the show."

"Amy looks *happy*," Tracy commented. "I've never seen her look that way before."

Aunt Rose shrugged. "Maybe she found some closure in the killer finally being revealed?"

"Maybe," Tracy agreed.

Tiffany showed them another photo. "And here we are saying goodbye."

"Goodbye?"

She nodded. "The circus is moving on," she explained. "And Linda and her mom left town right after the show. They're done here, Tracy. They're finished with Fern Grove."

Tracy sat back on the emerald green couch and chewed on her lip. "Wow," she sighed as she thought of the events of the last week. "Tyler is gone, Brett is dead, Bruce is in jail, and Amy and Linda have left. What a week."

"I can't believe this all happened in Fern Grove!" Tiffany exclaimed. "It all sounds so crazy... like a movie! And it happened here, in our boring little town."

Tracy laughed. "I think I've realized Fern Grove isn't quite as boring as I thought it was when I was a teenager," she told them. "A lot can happen in a week, that's for sure."

Aunt Rose nodded. "Life moves fast," she stated as she wrapped her arms around her niece. "I think what happened shows us that tomorrow is *never* promised. You have to live your life well and live it happily every single day."

"Yes, you do," Tracy agreed. "Yes, you do..."

22

A week passed, and finally, Tracy felt as though things were back to normal. Her legs were less sore, she was sleeping better at night, and the circus had left Fern Grove without incident. The holidays were just around the corner, and she was looking forward to a happy, peaceful Christmas with her family and friends.

In Season was bustling with activity the week before Christmas. It was as though everyone in town had placed an order for the holidays, and though business was booming, Tracy, Tiffany, and Aunt Rose could hardly keep up with all the orders.

"It's like we're Santa's elves or something," Tiffany complained one afternoon as she cut red velvet ribbons to tie around sprigs of holly. "I don't ever remember the shop being this nuts!"

"This has been our best winter season yet," Aunt Rose said proudly. "Thanks to Tracy's marketing campaign. She's really elevated this flower shop, and I couldn't be prouder."

Tracy grinned. "It was a team effort," she insisted.

The phone rang, and Tiffany answered it. "It's for you," she mouthed to Tracy.

"Hello?"

"Hey, honey," Warren greeted her.

Warren. They had been inseparable since the incident in the woods. After Tracy was nearly killed by Bruce the couple had felt luckier and more in love than ever. Tracy blushed as she heard his deep voice over the phone, and she felt her lips turn upward into a smile. "Hi, baby."

"How's work?" he asked cheerfully. "Is your day going well?"

"We are so busy!" she told him as she watched Aunt Rose assemble a holiday arrangement in less than a minute. Her Aunt was so talented when it came to flower arrangements. "We've had over fifty orders today, and we are still trying to catch up from the orders that came in overnight."

"That's fantastic," he exclaimed. "You ladies are a flower powerhouse."

"Aunt Rose has the gift," she explained cheerily. "We just help out."

Warren laughed. "I have to make your day a little worse, then," he told her, putting on an apologetic voice.

"What's up, honey?"

"I need to place an order," Warren said. "I want to order something for the police chief as a holiday thank-you. Do you have a recommendation or something in mind?"

Tracy thought for a moment. "Do you want a bouquet or an arrangement?"

"Probably an arrangement," he answered. "A bouquet doesn't seem right for this. How about an arrangement of marigolds? Those are so pretty, and they'll brighten up the police station."

"That's a great idea," she praised him. "Except marigolds are out of season."

"Oops," he moaned.

"I'll help you out," she promised. "I'll put together something nice. What do you think?"

"I think that's great!" he told her. "I'll come by and pick it up around four. I don't have a lot of time; I have a meeting at four-thirty, so when I arrive, can you run it out to my car? Then I can sneak a little smooch with you, too."

"Absolutely," she grinned. "Not a problem."

They hung up the phone, and Tracy got to work creating an arrangement that would impress her boyfriend's boss. She selected a red basket and tied a gold ribbon around it, loving how festive the colors looked together. Tracy plucked several sprigs of holly from a bucket and scattered it about, making sure it was evenly placed. After carefully placing fresh red camellias in the basket, she added two small cinnamon sticks to make it fragrant.

"That's lovely," Aunt Rose complimented her handiwork. "Who is it for?"

"Warren's boss," she replied. "He'll be by in about twenty minutes to pick it up. I think it looks great!"

Aunt Rose agreed. "So, you'll see him in twenty minutes? Why don't you run back to the bathroom and freshen yourself up," she said. "You've been working all day, and you could use a touch of lipstick. I'll let you know when he's here."

"Okay," Tracy agreed, and she ran off to the bathroom with her purse in hand.

Warren called the shop at four. "He's outside!" Aunt Rose called to her, and Tracy emerged from the bathroom and looked a little more put together. "Your makeup looks nice."

Tracy had powdered her forehead and applied a thick layer of striking red lipstick to match the red turtleneck she was wearing. She had run a brush through her hair before tucking it up into a French twist.

"You look amazing," Tiffany commented as Tracy emerged from the bathroom. "And the flower arrangement you did is great, too."

"You two are being so nice to me today," Tracy noticed, smiling at both of them as she picked up the basket of flowers. "I'll run this out to Warren and come right back in. I know we have a lot to do tonight."

"Take your time," Aunt Rose winked at her. "Take your time."

Tracy walked outside, but she didn't see Warren's car. Snow began to fall as she looked around, and she shivered, wishing she had thought to pull on her winter coat. It was getting dark outside, and the evening air was bitterly cold.

"Tracy!"

She grinned as she heard Warren's voice. She followed the sound over to where he was standing, across the street from the flower shop at the public park. "Warren? What are you doing? Where is your car?"

"Come here!" he called out.

She stared at him as she crossed the street. Warren was standing at the base of the white gazebo in the middle of the park. He was dressed in a camel-colored coat, his hair slicked back, and he looked excited as she walked up to him. "Babe?"

Warren took a deep breath. Tracy heard Christmas music begin to play, and she turned around to see a jazz quartet set up behind the gazebo. "What's going on?"

Suddenly, the gazebo was filled with light; tiny, delicate strands of white holiday lights framing the structure turned on, and Tracy was filled with confusion. "Warren? What is all of this?"

Warren grinned, reaching over and removing the flower arrangement from her hands and setting it down beside her. He led her to the middle of the gazebo and took both of her hands in his.

"Tracy," he began, staring into her eyes. "The last few days have been filled with confusion, fear, worry, crime, and trouble," he began. "But I want you to know that no matter how dark the days are, I want to spend all of them with you by my side."

"Warren," she said softly, finally realizing what was going on in the gazebo. "Warren…"

He pressed a gloved finger to her lips. "Me first," he whispered, looking at her adoringly. "Tracy, you came into my life and changed it for the better. You have filled my world with joy and flowers and cats and jokes, and I am a better man for it."

She beamed. She had pictured this moment her entire life, and now Warren was standing in front of her, pouring out his heart.

"You are the love of my life," he continued. "You are the woman of my dreams, the person I want to spend every second with. I want to have a family with you, I want to see the world with you, and I want to make you the happiest woman in the world."

Tracy gasped as Warren got down on one knee and produced a tiny blue velvet box from the pocket of his coat. She heard the music swell, and her heart fluttered as strains of *Joy to the World* filled the park.

"Tracy," he murmured as he reached for her left hand. "Will you do me the honor of becoming my wife? Will you marry me?" He slipped a small, but beautiful emerald cut engagement ring on her hand.

Tracy's eyes filled with happy tears. "Yes," she cried as she pulled him to his feet and threw herself in his arms. "Yes! Yes! A million times, YES!"

Warren kissed her, pulling her face to his and holding her tightly. "We're getting married," he exclaimed as he gently pulled back, wiping red lipstick from his face.

"We're getting *married*!" Tracy shrieked, and she glanced over to see Tiffany and Aunt Rose running toward her with grins on their faces.

"You're getting married!" Aunt Rose cried as she embraced her niece and then reached to kiss Warren on the cheek.

"We knew the whole time!" Tiffany giggled, and she gave Warren a high five.

Tracy turned to look at her three favorite people in the world. She could hardly believe what had transpired over the last few days, but her Aunt's advice rang true. Tomorrow is never guaranteed, and as Tracy jumped and clapped with joy with her new fiance, her aunt, and the teenager she adored so much, she was determined to *never* take her happiness for granted.

"What do you think?" Tiffany squealed as she eyed the glittering emerald ring on Tracy's hand. "Are you surprised?"

"I think I am the luckiest woman in the world," Tracy grinned as she flashed the ring at the ladies, and then turned to hug her fiance. "The luckiest woman in the world."

The End

AFTERWORD

Thank you for reading these Holiday Christmas Cozies! I really hope you enjoyed reading it as much as I had writing it!

If you have a minute, please consider leaving a review on Amazon.

Many thanks in advance for your support!

ALSO BY AMBER CREWES

The Sandy Bay Cozy Mystery Series

Apple Pie and Trouble (Book 1

Brownies and Dark Shadows (Book 2)

Cookies and Buried Secrets (Book 3)

Donuts and Disaster (Book 4)

Éclairs and Lethal Layers (Book 5)

Finger Foods and Missing Legs (Book 6)

Gingerbread and Scary Endings (Book 7)

Hot Chocolate and Cold Bodies (Book 8)

Ice Cream and Guilty Pleasures (Book 9)

Jingle Bells and Deadly Smells (Book 10)

King Cake and Grave Mistakes (Book 11)

Lemon Tarts and Fiery Darts (Book 12)

Muffins and Coffins (Book 13)

Nuts and a Choking Corpse (Book 14)

Orange Mousse and a Fatal Truce (Book 15)

Peaches and Crime (Book 16)

Queen Tarts and a Christmas Nightmare (Book 17

Rhubarb Pie and Revenge (Book 18)

Slaughter of the Wedding Cake (Book 19)

Tiramisu and Terror (Book 20)

Urchins and Deadly Dishes (Book 21

Velvet Cake and Murder (Book 22)

Whoopie Pies and Deadly Lies (Book 23)

Xylose Treats and Killer Sweets (Book 24)

ALSO BY ABBY REEDE

The Fern Grove Cozy Mystery Series

Carnations and Deadly Fixations (Book 1)

One Daisy and Two Crazy Funerals (Book 2)

White Lily and a Fatal Chili (Book 3)

Mistletoe and Deadly Kisses (Book 4)

Freesia and Lethal Amnesia (Book 5)

Daffodils and Poisonous Pills (Book 6)

Red Roses and Bloody Noses (Book 7)

Missing Heather and Bad Weather (Book 8)

Marigold and a Nasty Chokehold (Book 9)

NEWSLETTER SIGNUP

Want **FREE** COPIES OF FUTURE **AMBER CREWES and ABBY REEDE** BOOKS, FIRST NOTIFICATION OF NEW RELEASES, CONTESTS AND GIVEAWAYS?

GO TO THE LINK BELOW TO SIGN UP TO THE NEWSLETTER!

www.AmberCrewes.com/cozylist